A BREED
OF HEROES

A BREED
OF HEROES
ALAN JUDD

**SIMON &
SCHUSTER**

London · New York · Sydney · Toronto · New Delhi

A CBS COMPANY

First published in hardback in Great Britain by Hodder & Stoughton, 1981
First published in paperback by Fontana, 1982
Published in paperback by Simon & Schuster UK Ltd, 2011
A CBS COMPANY

This paperback edition published 2018

1 3 5 7 9 10 8 6 4 2

Simon & Schuster UK Ltd
1st Floor
222 Gray's Inn Road
London WC1X 8HB

Simon & Schuster Australia, Sydney
Simon & Schuster India, New Delhi

www.simonandschuster.co.uk
www.simonandschuster.com.au
www.simonandschuster.co.in

A CIP catalogue record for this book
is available from the British Library

Paperback ISBN: 978-1-4711-7886-3
eBook ISBN: 978-1-4711-0104-5

Typeset in Sabon by M Rules
Printed and bound by CPI Group (UK) Ltd, Croydon, CR0 4YY

For My Family

How then can I live among this gentle
obsolescent breed of heroes, and not weep?

From 'Aristocrats', by Keith Douglas,
killed in action, Normandy, 9 June 1944.

Part One

To the Factory

1

'Northern Ireland is perfectly simple really,' said Edward Lumley, the company commander. 'There are no two ways about it.'

He gazed at the passing Midlands countryside, then at the faces of his three platoon commanders and then at the dirty railway carriage floor. The frown which had creased his forehead suddenly cleared.

'All you have to do,' he continued, 'is to thump 'em when they step out of line, and the rest of the time leave 'em alone. That's all they want, really, you know, just to be left alone. There's no doubt about it.'

He sat back and folded his arms. He was a balding, genial man with a round, foolish, good-natured face. After some years as a major he was still a company commander. The fact that he had not made staff college did not bother him, though it bothered his wife. He looked now for responses from his three young platoon commanders.

Charles Thoroughgood glanced up from his book in

3

acknowledgment. The other two, Tim Bryant and John Wheel, nodded their consent. Tim added that there was no doubt at all. They were both a couple of years younger than Charles, products of Sandhurst, keen, clear-eyed and subservient. Charles had also been to Sandhurst but before that to Oxford. He wondered sometimes whether he might have been happier in the Army if he had not been to Oxford. He was tall, red-haired and freckled. There was a threatened ungainliness in his body that was never fully realised because his movements were gentle and slow, but there was something untidy and sprawling about the way his limbs were put together. He had never noticed this before joining the Army but it had proved an important factor in his relationship with the NCO instructors at Sandhurst, who had reminded him of it daily. He crossed his legs carefully now, trying not to dislodge Edward's kit from the seat opposite. The floor beneath his legs was covered by his own.

'I didn't go much on old What's-it's lectures about the origins of the Northern Irish problem,' said Edward. 'You know who I mean, that poof – Philip Thingie, the education officer. Philip Lamb. All that stuff about the eleventh century: can't see what that matters to anyone now. And then when he went on about the modern period I thought he meant now, you know, or at least the twentieth century, not the seventeenth. Christ knows what the Ackies thought.'

Soldiers in No. 1 Army Assault Commando (Airborne) – No. 1 AAC(A) – were often known as 'Ackies'. Their reactions and opinions were frequently used as an acid test for any theory, policy, place or person. Tim, C company's second platoon commander, shifted in his seat. 'I'm not so sure. I thought it was quite interesting. I mean, at least it gave you an idea of the background and whatever.'

'A right bloody mess.'

'Exactly. I think the Ackies appreciated it, on the whole. At least they have an idea what they're getting into.'

Edward nudged Charles with his boot. 'What do you think, Professor? You can read and write better than Philip Lamb. Did he do a good job?'

'I thought he did. I knew more about Ireland after his lectures than I did before them. And I thought he put them over quite well considering his audience was six hundred tired soldiers crammed into a gym after an exercise.'

'I was bored rigid.'

'Perhaps that's because you were standing.'

'Point there, Charles. Not for nothing you went to Oxford.'

Charles's having been to Oxford was always a cause of comment. Opinions varied throughout the battalion. Most people thought it meant he was very clever, his brother officers were usually envious but would not admit it, the RSM, Mr Bone, was convinced he was a dangerous subversive, while the CO thought it was three years wasted out of a young man's life that would have been better spent commanding a platoon. After his initial surprise at being treated as though he had a criminal record Charles had tried to play down his past, but in an extrovert society where reticence was weakness this was a bad tactic. He had been tempted then to become aggressively academic but had sensed that this would be playing into the hands of his critics. Accordingly, he had become stubbornly matter-of-fact, an attitude that allowed as little scope for criticism as for his own self-expression.

Charles's first interview with the CO was not something he was ever likely to forget. Lieutenant-Colonel Ian Gowrie, MC, was a tall, energetic, black-haired man with earnest brown eyes and regular, good-looking features that were marred only by a too-tight compression of his lips, as though he were trying to express great determination. Charles had heard whilst at Sandhurst that Gowrie was a fanatic, an ogre almost, setting near-impossible standards for himself and others. His standards were apparently derived from a Boy's Own conception of life, according to which the good would win through in the end because of their faith, loyalty and perseverance. But there would be many setbacks on the way.

On joining the battalion Charles was shown in to the CO by the obliging and, he sensed, sympathetic adjutant, Colin Wood.

He marched in and saluted. The CO looked up from his desk. 'Go out and come in again,' he said.

Charles marched out. He felt it was best to march, being unsure whether it was regimental tradition that subalterns up for interview with the CO always had to enter twice or whether, as in one memorable incident at Sandhurst, his flies were undone. He turned about in the adjutant's office, knocked, was bidden to enter, marched in, halted and saluted again. If anything, this attempt was even more awkward than the first but the effort must have showed because the CO invited him to sit down. 'Welcome to the battalion,' he said.

'Thank you, sir.'

'Did you enjoy Oxford?'

'Yes, thank you. Very much.'

'Well, you can put away your James Bond books and *Playboys* and what-have-you now. You're back in the real world. Back among the men.'

Charles had never read any James Bond books and the majority of the *Playboys* he had ever seen were in the bedside drawer of the orderly officer's room in the Officers' Mess.

'You'll have to start work now,' continued the CO. 'Earning your living. Getting up early. How do you feel about that?'

'I did work at Oxford, sir. And we got up early at Sandhurst.'

'Don't try to argue with me, it won't work. Leadership,

that's what I'm concerned about. Are you a leader? Your Sandhurst report says you weren't as assertive as you might have been. Well, here you'll be in command of some of the best soldiers in the British Army. Commando soldiers. Airborne soldiers. Are you up to it? Are you man enough? That's what I want to know.'

'I hope so, sir.'

'So do I.'

The CO looked down and continued reading what Charles assumed was his Sandhurst report. He could see the MC ribbon on the CO's service dress – won, he had heard, in a particularly heroic and ill-judged operation in Aden. The CO looked up again. 'I see you're an atheist.'

'No, sir, an agnostic'

'It's the same difference.'

'With respect, sir, I don't think they are at all the same.'

'Don't argue. I won't tell you again. The point is, you're not a Christian.' He leaned forward and put his elbows on the desk. 'Now I'm the last person to dictate to someone what his religion should be, Charles. In fact, the Army doesn't allow me to do it and a jolly good thing too. None of us has any right to interfere with another person's private beliefs. But I just want to put two things to you. Two things.' He picked up an antique and highly-polished bayonet that served as a paper-knife and pointed it at Charles, the point quivering slightly.

'Firstly, your soldiers. If they don't have an ethic to combat communism they'll go under. I assure you communism, whatever else you may say about it, is a great rallying point. It's a strong, forceful belief that gives ordinary soldiers something to cling to when they need it, quite apart from the fact that they are indoctrinated in a way that we've never even dreamed of in this Army. Thank God. Now, how do you suppose you can prevent your soldiers from being corrupted by this evil – because that's what it is, you know – if all you've got to offer them is a wishy-washy, nought-point-one per cent proof agnosticism? Eh? How d'you propose to do it?'

Charles could not take his eyes off the bayonet. 'Well, sir, I don't see that my belief –'

'And the second point, the second point is yourself. How would you – I hope you never have to, but the day may come – how would you bury one of your friends who had had his face blown away, without God's help? Could you do it?'

'I hope I could.'

The CO slammed the bayonet on to the desk. 'You could not. Without belief you could not do it. Could you stand at your friend's graveside, with your soldiers around you, and lower your friend minus face into his grave and conduct a burial service – without a faith to fall back on? Do you seriously think you could do that and look your soldiers in the eye again? Do you?'

'As far as I can tell –'

'As far as I can tell you don't know what you're talking about. You would crack up, I can assure you. The Russian soldier has his faith and, fortunately, all the soldiers in this battalion have theirs. They're all good Christians. Think about it, Charles. I don't want to interfere with your beliefs, I just want you to think about it. It's all very well being long-haired, left-wing and atheistic, but when it comes to the crunch up at the sharp end it's not enough. It won't do. Now, anything you want to ask me?'

'No, sir.'

'Settled in the Mess all right?'

'Yes, sir.'

'Good. Well, if you have any problems you know you can come and see me at any time. This door is always open. Or the padre. Go and talk it over with him. You'll find he's very sympathetic and down to earth, a good man. Used to be a private soldier in the Regiment in National Service days.'

Charles stood up to go.

'One other thing.'

'Sir?'

'Hair.'

Charles repeated the word to himself. His hair had been cut the day before and washed that morning. Nevertheless, it seemed likely that the CO had in mind that it needed one or both again. He gave the response that seemed least likely to displease the CO. 'Yes, sir.'

'Today.'

'Yes, sir.'

It was worse than anything Charles had expected. He could not conceive how he was going to survive the remaining two and a half or so years that were expected of him. He would need a faith of some sort for that. He heard again the voice of his tutor, Manningtree, with its lisp and affected weariness: 'The only excuse I can think of for your joining the Army is that you are experimenting with yourself in a particularly unnecessary, unpleasant and narcissistic way. I hope you fail.' Manningtree was in no sense a military man and neither, Charles had to admit to himself, was he. He had known that all along, of course, but to have admitted to Manningtree that he might have been even slightly right about him would have offended Charles's particular brand of undergraduate honour. To have been 'got right' by the remote and listless Manningtree was almost a condemnation, and not to be borne. As he left the CO's office Charles reflected that Manningtree was probably at that moment supine in his leather armchair listening to somebody's predictable essay and sipping sherry that was almost as dry as his own comments. The faltering student did not know his luck.

Sometime later Charles had related to the padre what the

CO had said to him. The padre was a short, square Yorkshire-man who smoked a stubby pipe and was universally popular, having boxed for the Army. 'Silly bugger,' he had said.

Charles was jolted out of his musings by a particularly vicious bit of continuous welded rail. He realised that the noise of the train and Edward's voice had merged into an indistinguishable background, each as unvarying as the other. He tried to pay attention. 'We shouldn't be in Ireland at all, of course,' Edward was saying. 'It's all political, not our job. Let the bloody politicians fight it out if they must fight over it. I'd rather have a good clean battle any day. I don't like all this now-you-shoot-them-now-you-don't stuff. Bad for the Ackies.' Everyone knew that Edward had never been in a battle, but no one doubted his sincerity.

John, the third platoon commander, was a serious-minded young man. 'You can't avoid the political dimension when armies are involved in anything,' he said. 'Especially internal security situations. An army is then one among a number of political factors instead of being the decisive one, as in a war. In a place like Northern Ireland everything is political and everything has to be taken account of.'

Edward unfolded and then re-folded his arms, his chubby face perplexed. 'I daresay you're right. All you young chaps are so damn clever these days. Too much education, if you ask me.

I hope you know what to do with it when we get there.' The train jolted and lurched suddenly, throwing the four men against each other. Edward's kit fell off the seat and got mixed up with Charles's. Edward trod on Tim's beret, leaving a dirty bootmark on the clean black. 'When do we get there?' he asked.

'0700,' said John, who always knew times.

'Christ. It's not that far, is it? Have we got to put up with this all night?'

'That's to Belfast. We'll be in Liverpool in a couple of hours.'

'Thank God for that. I was going to say, all night's a bit long, even for British Snail.'

The door of their compartment was opened abruptly by the Intelligence Section colour sergeant, a well-known criminal named Fox. He grinned at Edward. 'O Group, sir. Orders Group. CO's carriage. Ten minutes ago.'

Edward's mouth dropped open. 'What for? What's he want to hold an O Group now for?'

'Search me, sir. Probably going to brief you on what to do if the boat's torpedoed. Russian subs in the Irish Sea. Could be nasty.' Colour Sergeant Fox slid the door to with a crash.

Edward started up and nearly fell in the swaying carriage. Mention of the CO never failed to arouse a degree of panic in him. 'O Groups even on the bloody train – would you believe it? God only knows what it's going to be like when we get there. Where's my file? Has anyone seen my clip file?' He cast about desperately, his face red, as it always was in a crisis. Crises arose frequently in Edward's life. His file was found for him. 'Gas mask,' he said. 'Respirator, I mean. Must take it with me. You know what the CO's like. He'll probably let off the CS canister to test us.'

'You're not serious,' said Charles.

''Course I'm serious. Standing Operational Procedures, paragraph 4b – "In vehicles respirators are to be available at all times." A train is a vehicle.' He found his respirator. 'I'd advise you all to find yours.'

'But we're not going to the O Group. And we're still in England.'

'For Christ's sake, Thoroughgood, stop being irrelevant. Just find your respirator and have it available.' Edward straightened his beret in the mirror and clambered over their kit to the door. 'Which way's the CO's carriage?' he asked.

'Left,' said Tim.

'Was it left?' asked John, when Edward had gone.

'Haven't a clue.'

The three of them rummaged slowly through their kit for their respirators. Charles couldn't find his. He had never learned to travel lightly and seemed to have as much kit as the other two together. He gave up and tried to read. The night before he had said goodbye to Janet, his girlfriend, and

14

memories of the uncomfortable evening kept coming back in snippets. There had been nothing positively unpleasant. It was just that he could not think of it without a sense of hopelessness, in much the same way as he felt about the ensuing four months in Northern Ireland. This was due not to any pessimistic appreciation of the situation there, nor to any dislike for the place, which he had never seen, any more than the previous night's hopelessness had been anything specifically to do with Janet. It was a more general malaise in which he was the only common factor, though he was inclined to blame the CO.

'Don't get killed, please,' Janet had said. They were in a restaurant in Fulham, and she had said it whilst sipping her mock-turtle soup, peering earnestly at him over the spoon.

'No, of course not,' he said, feeling absurdly British.

She lowered her spoon. 'Really, Charles, I'm very worried.'

'So am I.'

'It's worse in a way, staying behind.'

'I'm sure it isn't.'

'Don't be so selfish.' She looked down, apparently occupied in making patterns in the soup. With her forehead bent towards him and her gaze averted she always seemed at her most vulnerable, and Charles felt inclined to be tender. But it was a distant sort of tenderness and it could not survive in conversation. She looked up again. 'I still don't understand why you joined the Army.'

This had been a bone of contention for some months now. He suspected that what exasperated her most was not the weakness of any explanations he might have given but the fact that he had never really given any. He didn't know why for certain, though he was dimly aware of various promptings – a feeling he ought to do something different, uncharacteristic, a desire to shock his friends, a not-to-be-acknowledged desire to please his father, an insufficiency of cowboys and Indians during childhood, a surfeit of his subject, history, and the simple feeling that he ought to do something. Janet had become an enthusiastic social worker for Wandsworth Council. He knew that his obvious lack of concern for the difference between her profession – caring – and his – killing – annoyed her. She thought that he thought lightly of hers.

'You will write, won't you?' she said.

'Yes.'

'It must be awful, all that killing and suffering. I couldn't bear it. I'd have to do something.'

'It's the living conditions that worry me.'

'I know. All those dreadful slums.'

'Ours, I mean. There's no possibility of privacy. We have to sleep in school boiler rooms, factories, police stations and warehouses.'

'But you get paid extra for it, don't you? Hard lying money

or something. And lots of people have done it before, so it won't seem so bad.'

'It will.'

'It's your own fault for joining.'

'I know.'

'Well, don't be unreasonable on our last night.'

They went back to her flat, and thence to bed. Their love-making lacked both affection and passion. The thought that this was probably their last time for four months added nothing to the occasion. Charles had wondered whether he would be subjected to an oblique and tentative interrogation of his feelings for her afterwards, but she fell asleep immediately. He left in darkness early the following morning. If nothing else, the hour and the cold precluded any attempt at an emotional farewell, and they parted silently with a tasteless kiss. He wondered vaguely whether she would sleep with anyone else whilst he was away. There was very little chance that he would.

The journey back to Aldershot on the early train was one of the most depressing experiences he knew. The bleak suburbs slid past like a bad dream repeated. They seemed to emphasise the unreality of his life in the Army, which he had at first mistaken for an unpleasant form of reality. But the Yorkshire exercise had convinced him that his world was not a real one. Seven days and seven nights on the moors, digging trenches, then living in them, then filling them in, then digging more and living in them, and so on. Seven days and nights of rain, during which they had the first recorded case of trench-foot in the British Army for years. This was a condition, well known during the First World War, in which a kind of crust formed on the foot after it had been deprived of air and immersed in soggy socks and boots for days and nights on end. In very bad cases toes were lost. The envied victim, a private in A company, was sent to hospital. The CO urged everyone to think how much worse it would have been on the Somme.

During the first few hours of the exercise, kit became waterlogged and never thereafter had the chance to dry. The imaginary but ubiquitous enemy – to Charles, an obvious personification of the CO's paranoia – was more troublesome than a real one could ever be. After the first two days everyone was too depressed and wet to speak except to pass on orders and their subsequent amendments and contradictions. During the middle of one day – recognisably so because of a barely-perceptible lightening at the base of the clouds – Charles and his platoon came to a stone bridge over a swollen stream. The downpour continued. They were about to cross the bridge when Charles was aware of a surging in the water and the CO and his wireless operator emerged from beneath the bridge. They had been standing up to the tops of their thighs in the stream.

'You have been mortared,' the CO said to Charles. 'Your platoon is decimated and you are dead.'

For one wild moment Charles thought he might be sent home in disgrace.

'What do you intend to do about it?' continued the CO.

The rain hissed in the stream. The CO and his wireless operator were still standing in it. Charles's platoon gazed at them without curiosity. 'We had to make a detour via the bridge, sir,' said Charles, 'because there's a cross-country motor-cycle event upstream.'

'You could have forded it. Why didn't you do that?'

'We were told that the stream was the Rhine, sir.'

'Who told you that?'

'With respect, sir, you did.'

The CO waded ashore and scrambled up the bank, followed, at the second or third attempt, by his heavily-burdened wireless operator. The rain ran in streaks through the mud on his face and tiny droplets clung to his heavy eyebrows. His dark eyes looked for a few moments as though he were considering whether to have Charles shot or drowned. He then looked at the stream, as though he had decided the business was not worth a bullet, and then as far up the hill as the clouds permitted. 'You should have used your initiative. Anyway, how did you know this bridge was still standing?'

'Well, sir, I could see it.'

'Not this bridge, nincompoop, not this physical bridge. The one over the Rhine that you were attempting to cross. How did you know that was still standing, eh?'

'I suppose I didn't, sir.'

'I suppose you didn't too. Any more than you knew it was covered by heavy mortars, which you should've. D'you understand me?'

'Yes, sir.'

'Good.' The rain streamed down their faces. 'Now, what's all this about a motor-cycling event?'

'They're holding one upstream, sir, in the area that we were supposed to occupy.'

'But this is a military training area. It's MOD land. Didn't you throw them off?'

'No, sir.'

'Did you try?'

'No, sir.'

'You're as wet as the bloody weather, Thoroughgood. Show me.'

They set off back the way they had come. Charles's platoon was depressed beyond speech or gesture and squelched mindlessly behind the CO. The CO marched briskly, however. He seemed to be a man who enjoyed a challenge. He no doubt saw rain as a challenge, and the more it rained the more it challenged, so the more he marched. They reached the scene of the outrage, which consisted of a huddle of wet spectators watching men obliterated by mud drive noisy motor-bikes up and down hills, and fall off on corners. The CO approached the young man who was easily the tallest, rightly assuming him to be the leader.

'This is a military training area,' said the CO.

The young man had a pleasant, intelligent face. 'Good day, Colonel.'

'There is a military exercise in progress. If you don't get your people and your machines out of here within the next few minutes there is a very good chance that you will be mortared. My men are about to cross the Rhine.'

'That would be unfortunate, since I have a letter here from the Army Department giving us permission to use this area today.' He produced a soggy envelope.

'Civil servants interfering again. It's bloody silly.'

'I quite agree, Colonel. Where is your Rhine?'

The CO jabbed his thumb towards the stream. 'Down there.'

'Yes, of course. I see it now.'

They hung around. The CO clearly wanted to continue the conversation. Four motor-cyclists collided in a great shower of mud and then, moving like moon-men, slowly disentangled themselves and their machines. The soldiers gazed impassively at the spectacle. It was doubtful whether even a real mortar bombardment would have stirred them to interest. However, the CO could not leave without a parting shot.

'You must have a pretty spare job anyway if you can spend your afternoons watching this sort of rubbish,' he said.

The tall young man inclined his head politely. 'Actually, Colonel, the same as yours. Nicholas Stringer, Coldstream Guards.'

Though forced to acknowledge that there were elites other than No. 1 AAC(A), the CO always denied them real status. He referred to them all as 'self-appointed'. This was particularly true of the Guards, and of all the Guards regiments the Coldstreams – whom he always called 'magpies' because of their black and white colours – were the worst, in his view. He looked at the Guards officer with an expression of baffled anger, until a retort came to mind. 'Whose side were you on in the Civil War?' he snapped, then turned and squelched away. The Guards officer watched him go, his own face registering polite incomprehension.

Charles squelched after him, similarly puzzled. He had a vague idea that the Coldstreams had been on Cromwell's side. Whichever it was, No. 1 AAC(A) had no battle honours from that war, not having been raised until a century after and then not in the present form. Nevertheless, the CO's discomfiture was something he was able to savour for the rest of the exercise as a slight antidote to his own.

*

This time it was the sound of the sliding door of the compartment being slammed back that jerked Charles from his reflections. It was Edward returning from the O Group, red and flustered. He stumbled bad-temperedly over legs and kit. He had been berated because of C company's alleged scruffiness. His career was again in jeopardy. He seemed unaware of any other business discussed at the O Group. 'Lost your respirator?' he said to Charles. 'Your own fault for leaving it lying around for someone to walk off with. Care of kit, first rule of survival in the Army. You'd better nick one from somewhere before the CO finds out. Go and inspect your platoon.'

Charles's platoon was in the last but one carriage. It took about ten minutes of squeezing and shoving in the crowded corridor to reach them. When he found them the floor was littered with beer-cans and cigarette-ends, the air thick with smoke, laughter and obscenities. His soldiers sprawled in their seats, unbuttoned, feet up on the tables, happy. He knew there was no reason to inspect them, and nothing to inspect them for. It was simply that Edward felt someone ought to be doing something. He counted them and stayed chatting for a few minutes. Their company was frequently more congenial than that to be had in the Officers' Mess. Sergeant Wheeler, his platoon sergeant, was, as usual, nowhere to be found. Charles never ceased to be amazed by the ability of soldiers to transform an environment. Within minutes they could make anywhere look as though it had never been anything but a transit camp, handling thousands of troops every week. Perhaps one day he would take them for tea in Fortnum and Mason's.

For the rest of the journey Charles was able to read. Edward was gloomily silent, and Tim and John kept him company. None of them had books. The only interruption was when the company colour sergeant brought round cold tea and stale sandwiches, which were welcome none the less.

2

It was dark when they pulled into the station at Liverpool, and raining. They were to get the night ferry to Belfast. Charles struggled into his webbing and lugged his kit on to the platform. It took him two journeys. The noise and confusion combined with the darkness and rain to make the station seem like some vast purgatorial clearing house. Soldiers and their kit filled the platforms. Rumour flourished. It was said that the coaches that were to take them to the boat had not arrived, that they had arrived but had left, that there was a nonsense over the stations, that the ferry had left, that they would have to march to the docks. Charles's platoon was just outside the station, where there was no shelter from the rain. For once Sergeant Wheeler was where he should be. He was the playboy of the Sergeants' Mess, a good-looking, good-natured athlete, successful with women but too easy-going with soldiers.

'What's happening, sir?' he asked.

'I don't know.'

'How long are we going to be here?'

'I don't know.'

'How far is it to the boat?'

'I don't know.'

Sergeant Wheeler moved his dripping, handsome face a little closer. 'Sir.'

'What?'

'Any chance of us getting out of the rain?'

Charles was not sure whether 'us' was himself and Sergeant Wheeler or the entire platoon. He suspected the former. 'No,' he said. 'Look after my kit, will you? I'm going to find the lavatory.'

'Bog's closed, sir. For alterations.'

'Well, there must be one somewhere.' Charles trudged off and found that the main lavatory was indeed closed. After a search he found a tin shed marked 'Staff Only'. The rain drummed heavily on the corrugated iron roof. When he had finished he decided to wait there a while. Every scrap of privacy had to be savoured. He leant against the wall and filled and lit his pipe, gazing out at the rain and the teeming station. He was disturbed by a discreet cough and looked round to see the second-in-command, Anthony Hamilton-Smith, sitting fully clothed in a lavatory cubicle. The 2IC was reading the *Daily Telegraph*. 'Hallo, Charles,' he said, amicably.

'Hallo, Anthony.' All the other subalterns called the 2IC 'sir', as they were supposed to do, but for some reason unknown even to himself Charles never had. 'Anything happening out there?'

'Chaos. They can't find the coaches. The CO's going berserk and tearing strips off some poor RCT man.'

'Wheel-men, you see. They're all the same. Donkey-wallopers. Can't get you anywhere.' Someone had called Major Anthony Hamilton-Smith the last of the great amateurs, and it had not been meant unkindly. Aged about forty and probably passed-over for promotion – a fact that did not seem to worry him – he was still slim, fair-haired and fine-featured, with an elegant moustache. He never hurried, never worried and had never been known to be angry. Nor had he ever been known to work. No one knew what he did all day, but it was generally agreed that his presence lent to the battalion a certain tone, which was otherwise entirely lacking. He had an estate somewhere and bred race horses. No one knew how he got on with the CO, who seemed unaware of him most of the time, except as an afterthought. It was rumoured that during the Yorkshire exercise he had somehow contrived to avoid spending a single night in the open. 'Thought I'd pop in here out of the way,' he said.

'Nowhere else to go,' observed Charles.

'One more officer flapping his wings and squawking wouldn't help anyone very much.'

'Wouldn't help at all.'

'Might even be a hindrance.'

'Almost certainly.' There was a companionable silence for a few moments.

'What's that you're smoking?'

'Foster's number two.'

'Very agreeable.' The 2IC indicated his paper. 'Things seem to be hotting up out there again.'

'Belfast?'

'And Derry. Looks like we'll have to do a bit of head-bashing. Ever been there?'

'No.'

'I have. Years ago, mind you. Family has a few acres over the border. Beautiful country. Charming people. Very polite. Might pop over and visit it.'

'Will we get much leave?'

'Shouldn't think so for a moment. We'll be lucky to get any – certainly as far as you're concerned. Might be able to fix something, though.'

'Wouldn't that be rather dangerous?'

'Could be, I daresay. Could be. Still, may as well get what pleasure one can out of life. We're a long time dead.' He took up his paper again. 'Be a sport and give us a yell if anything happens suddenly, won't you? Wouldn't like to be left behind.'

When Charles had arrived back at his platoon he found that the coaches had arrived and that all the other companies were preparing to board them. He had already begun to struggle with his kit when Sergeant Wheeler said, 'Shouldn't bother with that for a while if I was you, sir.'

'Why not?'

'We ain't going yet.'

'But the coaches are here.'

'For the other companies.'

'What about ours?'

Sergeant Wheeler was quiet and prim. The burden of bad news sat well upon him. 'The commanding officer, sir, has inspected the train and found it to be dirty. He has suggested that C company clean it up. We're to follow on when we've finished.' He leant forward confidentially. 'That is, the whole train, sir. Not just our bit. The whole lot.'

Charles lowered his kit to the ground. 'Where's Major Lumley?'

'Most probably underneath it by now.'

C company eventually boarded the ferry ten minutes before it sailed. Their weapons and kit were locked in cages below deck and Charles set off to find his cabin with a lighter heart than at any time during the day. This took some doing and he seemed to walk miles in the corridors before finding it. He was to share with the new doctor who had joined the battalion the day before and whom he had not yet met – a mysterious Captain Sandy. The battalion apparently had a long history of mad doctors, the last of whom had been sent to prison for diamond smuggling. There were medical horror stories about his predecessors which made him seem normal. Charles opened the cabin door with difficulty, and discovered that Captain Sandy's kitbag was propped up against it. The cabin was very narrow and was made of stainless steel. There were two bunks, the lower of which was occupied by Captain Sandy. Sleeping, he looked more dead than mad. His pale cheeks drooped and his mouth hung open. There were bags under his eyes.

Charles heaved his kitbag on to the top bunk, at the same time knocking undone his webbing belt to which were attached his ammunition pouches, shoulder straps and water bottle. The whole lot fell to the floor, striking the doctor on the way. At first there was no reaction but after a few moments the doctor's eyelids fluttered open.

'Charles Thoroughgood. I'm sorry to wake you like that.'

The eyelids closed.

Charles undressed and went down the corridor to a shower he had noticed. It was hot and ample, an unexpected luxury. When he returned the doctor was sitting on the edge of his bunk, staring at the wall. Charles introduced himself again.

'Henry Sandy,' whispered the doctor, and they shook hands gently.

'Are you all right?'

'Yes.' He continued staring at the wall. 'Still a bit thick. Bad night.' His voice was hoarse. 'Were you there?'

'No.'

'D'you know who was?'

''Fraid not.'

'I wish I could remember where it was. It's very worrying. I've been thinking about it all day.' He eased himself off the bunk and began rummaging through his kit.

There wasn't room for them both to stand and so Charles climbed on to his bunk and dried himself vigorously. The effect of the shower and the sight of a man in a worse state than himself combined to heighten his sense of well-being. 'Dinner's in a quarter of an hour,' he announced.

'Dinner?' echoed Henry Sandy faintly. An even greater weariness came over his face. He nodded slowly and a certain resolution showed through. 'All right.' He went off and had a shower, and afterwards felt robust enough to have a cigarette. They went along to dinner together.

Perhaps because they were all dressed alike, Army officers seemed to outnumber civilians at the bar. In view of what he had described as the 'operational situation' the CO had decreed that they should all wear heavy duty pullovers, denim trousers, anklets and boots for dinner. At the far end of the bar the company commanders and a few hangers-on were grouped around the CO, who was addressing them forcefully while continually smoothing back his black hair with one hand.

'People say he's mad,' said Henry.

'I think he might be.'

'I thought the people who said that were mad, so Christ knows what he's like. Thank you, yes, a glass of white wine. It's usually the best thing for my condition.'

Charles had a gin and tonic – one of the few Army habits he had acquired easily – and they went and sat in a corner. Henry lit another cigarette, not very steadily. 'It's not so much last night,' he explained, 'as the trauma of the last eight weeks. I've just finished my parachute course which terrified me and I never want to parachute again. They said I was the worst one in living memory. Apparently I land spread-eagled like a crab, though I don't know because I always shut my eyes. And before that was BSTC.'

Charles had no difficulty in sympathising. BSTC – Battle Selection Training Course – was the four-week selection course for the Assault Commandos with a failure rate of four-fifths. The first ten minutes of the first day were spent seal-crawling and bunny-jumping across the huge gym in Tidworth, after which they were given three minutes to go out and be sick. From then on it had got steadily worse.

Looking back, Charles did not know how he had survived it. He had somehow muddled through by emptying himself of all thought or feeling for a month and never looking any further ahead than the next NAAFI break, when there was one. Officers in the Depot Mess who were doing BSTC were always conspicuous by the difficulty they had in getting up and down stairs, by their silence during meals, their occasionally alarming injuries and their practice of going to bed at about eight-thirty. Henry still had that mindless, gentle look that everyone acquired after the first week or so.

'It was the worst thing I've ever done,' he said. 'Even worse than the parachuting and the sea-landing from submarines. I still dream I'm on it. I think I only got through because they needed another doctor so urgently. They said they were being kind to me and I think they probably were. I collapsed in tears pulling the Land-Rover up that mountain in Wales and three of the NCOs kicked me to my feet, four times. I suppose it was kind of them, really. They could have failed me. Also, I was knocked out in the boxing.'

'So was I.' Charles was glad to find someone who appeared to have suffered like himself. He wasn't sure whether everyone else was bone-hard or whether it was simply not done to mention such things.

The two men became aware that the loud talk from the

CO's end of the bar was fading, and whilst they were still looking about it died altogether. This sudden loss caused other, lesser, conversations to falter and fade. The bar was silent. Soldiers and civilians alike looked awkwardly at each other; it was as though someone had died. The CO's face wore a look of frozen disgust. For a moment Charles thought that the gaze was directed at him and then that it was directed at the doctor who at the very least must have exposed himself or been horribly sick. But the doctor had done neither of these things and looked as uncomfortably puzzled as everyone else. The only sound was the hum of the ship's engines.

'Get out,' said the CO, his voice low and taut with anger. 'Get out and get dressed.'

Charles looked over his shoulder expecting to see a naked officer but saw only John, his fellow subaltern, blushing violently. 'I'm sorry, sir,' said John, in a voice that was higher than usual. 'I thought it was shirt-sleeve order.'

'Get out!' The CO's voice made everyone stiffen and visibly startled the civilians. John left hurriedly, the CO turned back to the bar and conversation was hesitantly resumed.

'What had he done?' asked Henry.

'He wasn't wearing his pullover.'

'Jesus Christ!' Henry's response was loud enough to bring all conversation to another temporary stop. He and Charles buried their faces in their drinks.

When they went in to dinner, Charles caught Edward Lumley's eye. Edward was clearly despairing. Once again, C company had publicly sinned; once again, his career was in jeopardy. He went through several crises a day. Charles grinned cheerfully at him.

At dinner they shared a table with a married couple from Belfast. The couple ran a business concerned with central heating systems and the husband had served with one of the airborne divisions during the war. He was plump, jolly and balding; his wife was also plump but had dark hair and dark eyes that stared with disconcerting directness at whoever she was talking to. It was difficult to tell whether she was unaware of it or was trying rather unsubtly to be noticed. They were both very friendly and talked about Northern Ireland for most of the time that they were all waiting to be served.

'Where exactly are you going?' asked the man.

'Killagh for three weeks, then on to West Belfast,' said Charles.

'That's a very bad area, one of the worst, as you'll no doubt know already.'

'Don't judge us all by what you meet there,' added his wife, with a smile that made her eyes glisten.

The husband leaned forward across the table. 'You could end the troubles tomorrow if you wanted. All you have to do is shoot two thousand Catholics. I think two thousand would be enough, don't you, dear?'

'That would be about right, I think, yes.'

They were joined by Anthony Hamilton-Smith, the only man on the ship to be wearing a dinner-jacket. 'Almost missed dinner. Nodded off on me bunk, would you believe? Old habits are hard to break, even at sea on the way to the Emerald Isle. Wine for all, I take it?' Regimental histories were one of Anthony's interests and when he discovered the husband's military past there was much rejoicing and more wine. After dinner he and the husband moved off to the bar and the wife excused herself, saying she was sure the men would prefer to talk men's things. Henry took himself off and Charles went for a walk on deck.

It was cold, wet and bracing. The ship heaved and rolled as she ploughed into the night, though not enough to cause discomfort. There were a few other strollers and Charles stood behind one for some minutes in the drift of his cigar smoke, which mingled with the tang of the sea. He returned to his cabin and, on opening the door, saw Henry on his bunk with the businessman's wife. He closed the door and went for another walk on the deck. This time he stood in the bows and felt the spray on his face and hair. When he returned to the cabin again he knocked and Henry, now alone, opened the door.

Henry's pale face was slightly less pale and he grinned boyishly. 'Sorry to have kept you out, Charles.'

'You didn't.'

'I meant to. I was in such a hurry I forgot to lock the door.' He sat down on his bunk and giggled. 'I saw it was there, you see, for either of us. But you didn't seem interested. Were you?'

'No. Yes. I don't know. I might have been.' Charles paused. 'No, I wasn't.'

'That's good. I was a bit worried in case you thought I'd cut you out. Which is what I did, of course.' He rocked backwards and forwards, giggling helplessly. 'I don't often do things like that, really I don't. Just – just whenever I get the chance. I needed something, you see, to wake me up. I feel much better now. I'm sure it's physiologically and psychologically beneficial. I haven't offended you, have I?'

''Course you haven't.' Charles thought he must sound pompous and strained. 'In fact, I rather envy you.'

'You did fancy her, then?'

'No.'

'It must be an ego thing.'

'I think it probably is.'

'It's partly that with me. I'm always afraid of not doing

37

things that afterwards I might wish I had done, so I do all sorts of crazy things that afterwards I wish I hadn't.'

'D'you feel like that about this one?'

'Oh no, not at all, it's made me feel much better. Though I didn't think I was going to get an erection first of all.' He lit a cigarette and lay back on his bunk. 'It's funny, you know, but they all seem to like uniforms. This is the second one that's made me do it in my shirt hairy. Do you find that?'

Charles recalled Janet's hysterical dislike of anything rough, hairy or military. She had a particular aversion to his hairy Army shirts, worn in cold weather and referred to, in typical Army fashion, as 'shirts hairy'. 'Not recently. I heard of someone who used to do it wearing his webbing belt, water bottles and ammunition pouches.'

'I've tried that. It's all right so long as you remember to empty your water bottles. Otherwise you get a bruised arse.'

Charles undressed and climbed on to his bunk. The search for sex was the preoccupation of many in the Army, more so than the preparation for war. Since joining, Charles had found that he was either in a mood of frantic sexual desire, in which anything female was acceptable, or he felt curiously asexual and remote. This latter mood corresponded to a feeling of remoteness from the Army in general, whereas the former he thought of as a simpler and more aggressive form of escapism made stronger and cruder by the rough and ready nature of male companionship. Being in the Army was so enveloping an experience that it did not occur to him that anything could happen independently of it. If he had developed appendicitis he might have been inclined to think it the result of too much weapons training.

It was some time before he fell asleep. The events of the evening, the noises and motion of the boat, thoughts of what lay ahead all jostled for priority in his consciousness. Then, just as drowsiness crept over him, Henry Sandy began snoring and making odd masticating noises, as though he were chewing in his sleep. These continued, on and off, for most of the night. Eventually, Charles's haphazard thoughts clustered loosely around the prospect of violence. The idea of suffering or committing an act of violence did not bother him at all, though he knew that for many people outside the Army – Janet especially – this was of crucial concern. Or, at least, they thought of themselves as concerned. He suspected that most of them, just like most people within the Army, would react to the fact of violence much as they reacted to the other inescapable facts of life – they would simply do what they thought had to be done. That, of course, was a thought that had its own particular horror, but it was not something that would concern many people.

Even before joining the Army he had doubted his own capacity for decisive action, and now that the time for action approached – or so he thought – he doubted it more. He feared that when the time came he would hesitate. He wondered now, as the boat took the swell of the Irish Sea, whether his real reason for joining was not, after all, an attempt to resolve this doubt about himself. Perhaps he was doing no more than experiment with himself in much the same way as Henry did through sex; only more subtly than Henry, less honestly and no doubt less enjoyably.

3

They were awoken early as the ship approached Belfast Lough. After a hurried breakfast there was the usual confusion in drawing weapons and kit and finding men. Eventually Charles stood on the crowded deck with his platoon complete except for Sergeant Wheeler. Charles made the mistake of asking his enemy, the RSM, if he had seen Wheeler.

'He's with you, sir.'

'He isn't.'

The RSM had a stupid, brutal face but was nevertheless capable of sarcasm. He looked pained. 'Is he not, sir? I thought he was.'

'Well, he isn't.'

'But he ought to be.'

'I know that, Mr Bone. That's why I'm asking you.'

'Bless me, sir, where d'you think he can have got to?' The RSM obviously hated subalterns more than he hated anyone, and he hated Charles more than he hated any of them. Added to the normal dislike that men with many years of service frequently have for newcomers was a special dislike for Charles because he had been to university. His manner was as sarcastically paternal as he could make it. 'Well, never you mind, sir, you just hang on here and I'll go and see if I can find him for you.'

If people annoyed Charles it was always by what they did accidentally or unselfconsciously. Deliberate attempts to annoy him or slight him left him quite unmoved. This morning, in particular, there was Belfast to consider. The water was calm, and in Harland and Wolff's shipyard the two huge cranes, Samson and Goliath, towered magnificently. The harsh, disjointed cries of gulls were thrown backwards and forwards across the harbour. The air was clear but there was already a dirty haze forming above the thousands of small rooftops of the city. Beyond them the hill called the Black Mountain lived up to its name. Charles's platoon was quiet for once. He imagined that each man was striving, like him, to see something in Belfast that differed from any other industrial British city before breakfast. They could see nothing startling, and it made their own presence seem incongruous. On the quayside was their transport – lines of lorries, as might be expected – but the sense of incongruity was heightened by the detachment of Ferret scout cars that were guarding them, their Brownings pointed at the main road. There were also soldiers from the

Wessex Scouts, the regiment that No. 1 AAC(A) was relieving, waiting in armoured Land-Rovers and Pigs – ancient one-ton armoured cars which no one had seen before and which had appeared out of storage especially for Northern Ireland. They had long snouts and carried nine or ten men, lumbering along with a distinctive whine. There was little or no movement by the escorts but a good deal of wireless activity. People walked past them to work without a glance. The whole thing looked absurdly tactical.

Sergeant Wheeler appeared suddenly. 'Sorry about the delay, sir, I got collared by the RSM. He didn't like the way I done me kit so I had to do it again. I did tell him I was supposed to be here but you know what he is, sir, not a man of reason.'

Sergeant Wheeler was a very plausible liar, but so was the RSM. Charles could not be bothered at that moment to try to sort it out. He was reminded of the problem of his own kit. Getting it all from the ship to the lorry without humiliation or undue delay would be a serious challenge. Then there was the problem of his respirator; everyone else had theirs, he noticed, but fortunately the CO was neither to be heard nor seen.

In the event he was able to make the necessary two journeys with his kit, and they boarded the lorries after a surprisingly short period of the usual hanging around. They set off with an impressive revving of engines, with the escorting vehicles from the Wessex Scouts and the military police interspersed between them. The soldiers stood in the backs of their Land-Rovers, one facing forward and the other backwards, their rifles at the ready. The Pigs rumbled along with their rear doors open and the Ferrets followed up behind. Protruding from the turret of one was the pink face of a young cavalry officer. He wore his beret and, round his neck, a dashing red and white spotted cravat that added a touch of quite startling colour to the scene. He had, though, taken the precaution of fastening the see-through and sometimes bullet-proof macralon screen around the top of his turret. Charles had heard of a corporal who had been looking out of the top of a Ferret in a similar fashion, though without the screen, and had lost an eye to an arrow fired from a crossbow.

The first streets they passed through were narrow and quiet, ordinary enough, but after a short while they became dirtier, and the walls, roads and pavements sported slogans, in some parts anti-British and in others anti-Catholic. Painted on the side of one house was a larger-than-life-size picture of King William on a white horse. Burnt-out wrecks of cars and other bits of twisted metal littered the gutters; many of the houses were empty and boarded up, many others had their windows broken; some walls were blackened by fire, and here and there a house was missing, leaving a gap as in a row of teeth. The convoy moved fast and the few people they saw did not bother to turn their heads. Soon they were in a more prosperous shopping area that looked normal except for one stretch of about a hundred yards in which not one shop window remained. Everything was boarded up, and one soldier, a native of Belfast, pointed to a mound of rubble, glass and metal girders that he said had been a car showroom.

Soon they were on the motorway, past the Milltown cemetery and out into the open country. This was rolling and lushly green but not very wooded. The farms were stone-built and looked bleak. Killagh before the bombings was a pleasant and not particularly interesting town, a mixture of eighteenth-century grey stone, nineteenth-century red brick and twentieth-century prefabricated blocks. There was a park and a rugby pitch. The barracks were on a hill, just beneath a new housing estate which sprawled almost to the summit. Built in the eighteenth century, they were enclosed by a high stone wall and had housed at various times redcoats, rebels and policemen. They now housed the Wessex Scouts. The entrance was through huge old wooden doors. It would have been homely and rather quaint as in any small English garrison town but for the coiled barbed wire along the top of the wall, a sandbagged position just inside the gates and an ominous-looking watchtower in the centre.

Ever since leaving the ship the soldiers had been waiting for something to happen. Despite the uneventful journey and their arrival in an apparently peaceful country town, their hopeful aggression was still aroused and it needed a focus. The Wessex Scouts provided it. As Charles's lorry rumbled through the cobbled entrance a sentry let go of one of the doors and it swung against the side of the lorry with a crash. There was no damage but the incident was sufficient.

'Wessex are shit,' someone shouted. This set the tone for the next twenty-four hours and became a catch-phrase for the next few weeks. The Ackies not unnaturally regarded themselves as an élite, and so were in constant need of an enemy. Anything wrong with the barracks, anything wrong with the town and any conceivable misfortune during the remaining twenty-four hours of the luckless Wessex's tenure was laid at their door. Fortunately, there were only two platoons of Wessex left – too few to be regarded as a challenge, and so there were no NAAFI punch-ups. Disdain was not confined to the soldiers. At his first O Group the CO referred to 'the appalling state in which these barracks have been left by the last unit, which I shall not name'. Only Anthony Hamilton-Smith had a good word for them. A fine old county regiment, he said, ruined by amalgamations forced upon them by grey civil servants and thoughtless governments. It was mixing good wine with bad, and the whole thing was very sad.

The barracks were very cramped. The quartermaster and his Q staff had arrived some days before in order to take over and allocate accommodation, and to cream off the best for themselves. Charles, after the usual confusion of wrong directions and missing kit, found himself sharing an underground cell with four others – Henry Sandy, Philip Lamb, the education officer, Tim Bryant and a newly-arrived subaltern from Sandhurst called Nicholas Chatsworth, known to everyone by his surname only. There was no furniture and no door, but eventually camp-beds appeared. The tunnel on which the cell opened led from the guardroom to A company's accommodation, and so it was never quiet. It was the oldest part of the barracks, a warren of tunnels, passages, cells and dead-ends. Everywhere was damp, cold and crowded. Charles would have found it more interesting if he had not had to live in it. As it was, potential architectural and historical curiosities were mere inconveniences, things to be cursed and moaned about.

The Officers' Mess was an incongruous 1930s-style house on a slight rise just inside the gates. The dining and living rooms formed the public rooms, while the bedrooms housed the CO, Anthony Hamilton-Smith and, in one, five company commanders. The quartermaster was rumoured to have another bungalow entirely to himself in another part of the barracks. He was a large, gruff, bristling man with a handlebar moustache and a sour dislike for mankind in general, subalterns in particular. No one had the temerity to tax him with the rumour, while the CO never heard rumours from below. No one aired them in his presence because if he did not like them he was inclined to treat the speaker as personally responsible for fabricating stories, while if he did like them he took them up as established fact and was all the more annoyed with the speaker if they proved to be untrue.

Charles went to the Mess for coffee. It was very crowded and he was about to go away when a platoon commander from the Wessex Scouts introduced himself. 'I'm supposed to show you people round,' he explained, 'but no one seems to want to know. You wouldn't fancy a trip round the battlements, I suppose?'

Charles did fancy it. His guide was in civilian clothes and looked happy. They made their way back to the old part of the barracks. 'I'm glad to be getting out,' the man said. 'Four months is a long time to spend kicking your heels in a backwater like this. Pleasant enough place, though. You're off to Belfast in three weeks, aren't you? Don't envy you that. Bound to be bloody. Mucker of mine from Sandhurst was killed there, less than twenty-four hours after arriving. But this place is all right. Not a bad social life. Plenty of birds to keep the soldiers happy. One or two for the officers too, if you've got a car.'

'Car?'

'Yes. Didn't you bring one?'

'No.'

'None of you?'

'No.'

'Oh dear. You can't have much fun without one, I'm afraid. We all brought ours. Still, it is only four months.' They climbed a winding stone staircase that led to the battlements, from where they had a good view of the town and the surrounding countryside. 'Not bad, is it? In fact, it's a damn fine view on a clear day. We used to come up here sunbathing when the weather was warm. Don't imagine you'll do much of that, though. That estate up the hill is where all the girls come from. They hang around the gates day and night, just asking for it. The lads see they get it too. That rugby pitch is the local club. We played them a couple of times. Good crowd. Fantastic drinkers. Some of our lads played for them too.'

They walked along the battlements and up into the watch-tower. It contained one bored soldier who was fiddling aimlessly with the rear sight on his rifle when they arrived. 'Nothing doing?' the Wessex officer asked the soldier.

'Sweet Fanny Adams, sir,' the soldier said.

The Wessex officer turned to Charles. 'There never is, you see. We have to man this day and night which is a bloody nuisance because there's no point. Unless you're expecting an airborne landing or something.'

'Have you had much trouble?'

'None at all.'

There was some shouting below them which sounded refreshingly distant. It seemed that a morning walk along the battlements might be no bad thing during the coming weeks.

'Even if there were any trouble,' continued the Wessex officer, 'you wouldn't see much from up here. You'd need to be on the ground.'

The shouting became louder. A small group of figures, which included the CO and the RSM, was looking up at them. The CO was shouting something with his hands cupped round his mouth and several people started running towards the entrance to the battlements. Charles looked up to see if there was imminent disaster overhead but the sky was clear.

'What do they want?' asked the Wessex officer.

'No idea.'

'It is something to do with us, I suppose?'

'Looks like it.'

The RSM was bawling as well. Charles distinguished a familiar phrase. 'They're shouting "hard targets",' he said.

'What do they mean?'

'They mean we should either get under cover or somehow make it difficult for the person who's about to shoot at us to do so without being shot.'

'No one's about to shoot at us, are they?'

'The CO might if we don't go down.'

They headed for the winding stairs. The Wessex officer looked concerned. 'Your CO's a bit intense, isn't he?'

'He is a little.'

'Frankly, I don't like him very much.'

'Me neither.'

They met a sweating regimental policeman on the stairs, who told them breathlessly that the CO wanted to see them both immediately. They thanked him. The CO looked furious when they reached him. The RSM at his side was full of pomp and portent. The CO glared at Charles. 'Do you want to die?'

'No, sir.'

The CO glared at the Wessex officer. 'Do you want to die?'

'No, sir.'

'Then what the hell were you both doing standing up there like that?'

The veins in the CO's temple were swollen. Charles was aware that they were being discreetly watched and gloated over by half the battalion from behind doors, windows and corners. He had long since learned the lesson of discretion. 'We were inspecting the defences, sir.'

'Who the hell told you to do that?'

'My CO asked me to show your officers round, sir,' said the Wessex officer.

The CO obviously suppressed the urge to regimental insult. 'Do you realise, both of you, that you were risking your lives up there? And not only your lives but the lives of those who would have had to go up and get your bodies? You're professional soldiers, or supposed to be, and you bloody well should have realised. Especially you, Thoroughgood. It would take only a very mediocre sniper indeed to pick you off from that housing estate over there. Did you think of that?'

Charles said nothing, but the Wessex officer came from another regiment. 'With respect, sir, there have never been any snipers here. We used to go up there all the time –'

'That does not matter.'

'– and the people in the estate have been very friendly –'

'Thoroughgood,' said the CO very slowly, 'take him away before I screw him into the ground.'

Charles led the now speechless Wessex officer away, watched enviously by the RSM. He heard later that it was the RSM who had drawn the CO's attention to what had, until that morning, been a normal practice. This did not alter his feelings towards Mr Bone. It was exactly what he would have expected of him. Mr Bone loved his job and worshipped the CO like a dog, adopting even his mannerisms. He was feared by the soldiers but did not have their respect.

Not surprisingly, the 'hard targets' episode was only a taste of what was to come. Security was tightened up all round. Edward Lumley felt that the watchtower incident had brought further disgrace upon C company. He shouted at

Charles, calling him a reckless young fool. During the next two days the CO's frenzied approach to security was carried several stages further than even the CO had intended. The sandbagged position by the gate was reinforced and another added on the roof opposite. The barbed wire was reinforced, the armoury strengthened and the guard doubled. The bored soldier in the watchtower was sent a companion and a general purpose machine-gun. There were practice alarms at all hours. However, what caused greatest consternation throughout the battalion was the order forbidding walking-out. This coincided with instructions that sentries who allowed themselves to be talked to by girls should be charged. Three days later the walking-out order was relaxed to allow officers and soldiers to walk out in groups of four for not more than two hours, in daylight, wearing civilian clothes and signing in and out at the guardroom. The CO saw girls as the greatest threat. 'The last thing I want is to have one of my soldiers shot in the back by some bloody gunman while he's walking his girl home. Assassination, they call it. I call it murder and I won't have it.'

On the second day the secretary of the local rugby club tried to arrange a fixture but was turned away at the gate. Amongst those who had arrived with the QM's advance party and had experienced the more benign regime of the Wessex there was noticeable nostalgia.

Edward called a company O Group during the evening of the first day. Company HQ was somewhere in the warren of tunnels and passages. When Charles got there Edward was again red-faced and panic-stricken. The other platoon commanders and the company sergeant major were expressionless. The company was to carry out an operation, Edward said. That night. He thought it was partly as punishment for the incredible risks taken by Charles that day on the battlements. He wanted no more such heroics. The CO was still furious. It was also, of course, a compliment to the company to be given the first operation to be carried out by the battalion since embarking upon active service in Northern Ireland. It was all highly secret. One platoon was to do a number of Vehicle Check Points (VCPs) before last light. It was not yet known where. It would be Charles's job and he would be told later. They would then lay an ambush near one of the customs posts on the border, moving into position under cover of darkness and withdrawing before dawn. There were to be absolutely no cock-ups. Even though the battalion was in the area for only three weeks it was vital to get a grip and show the local villains that they weren't dealing with a lot of idle bloody Wessex Scouts any more.

Everyone knew that Edward's briefings were almost word for word what the CO had said in his briefing. Details trickled through during the next two hours. They were to do six

VCPs before last light. A VCP consisted of five or six men with portable barriers and road-blocking equipment, sometimes including a tyre-puncturing chain. They were to search cars and their occupants and to change location frequently. Helicopters would carry them from one site to another. Charles's job was to be ferried from site to site, checking. The drill had been rehearsed many times and the need for politeness had been impressed upon everyone. The helicopters would pick them up from the hill above the barracks. The only difference between this and training was that their magazines would be filled with live ammunition this time. They would then have their evening meal in the field, do an approach march to the ambush position, lie there until 0430 hours and then withdraw. There was already a cold wind.

Charles went back to the cell to collect his kit. Philip Lamb, the education officer, was lying on his bed reading and started guiltily when Charles entered. He was a small neat man with a trim moustache. Though conscientious, he had nothing to do and felt unwanted, as indeed he was on the whole. He spent most of the next three weeks hiding in the cell and playing with his pistol, a thing that intrigued and baffled him.

'Have you got to go out on this operation?' he asked.

Charles nodded.

'All night?'

'All night.'

'When?'

'Now.'

'With tents and sleeping-bags?'

'No. With nothing.'

'You'll freeze to death. Customs post, I suppose?'

'Yes. It's supposed to be very secret. How did you know?'

'Apparently every new unit that comes here does it. It's well known for miles around. People even turn up to watch, I'm told.'

However, everything went well in that nothing went wrong. The series of VCPs was executed without trouble or result. The evening meal in the field, near a river, would actually have been pleasant but for the fresh wind and the prospect of the night ahead. They made the approach march to the customs post across several miles of fields and through two streams. Not trusting Sergeant Wheeler, Charles navigated them and to his relief got it right. It was quite dark and already cold. It was obvious to everyone that the post, a small and practically featureless modern building, did not need a platoon of thirty men to ambush it. A section of eight or nine under the command of a corporal would have been sufficient. They spent the night on their bellies in the grass and withdrew through the wet fields at four-thirty in the morning. Their transport – lorries this time – had got lost and did not arrive for another three-quarters of an hour.

Afterwards, Edward congratulated Charles. The CO was delighted with the way things were going. 'He's thinking of letting us do all the night ambushes while the other companies do all the boring daytime stuff. You've done us proud, Charles. Thanks a lot, old son.'

That day there were various barrack duties, briefings and working parties. Charles slept for a couple of hours in the afternoon. Dinner in the Mess that night was more boisterous than usual. The CO was in a good mood, but in this as much as in a bad his presence unconsciously intimidated and directed the conversation. Edward was a little drunk and, riding on the crest of the CO's good opinion, recounted anecdotes about various regimental characters.

'What about Chunky Jones with that fan in Aden? Sir, d'you remember Chunky Jones in Aden? Built like a gorilla with a solid bone head and no neck. Great man. Anyway, not a word of a lie – I'm not kidding, it's all gospel – in the middle of dinner one night he stood up on the table and – you know those fans we had out there, those big ones hanging from the ceiling – well, he stood on the table and he stopped it with his head. Clunk, just like that. With his head!' Several roared with laughter and Edward became even more excited. 'And then, sir, and then about five minutes later someone bet him he wouldn't do it again. Well, you know Chunky, he'll do anything twice. Anyway, he gets up on the table to do it again' – Edward climbed halfway up on to the table – 'like this, see, only this time you know what those bastards had done? They'd increased the speed of the fan. You know, they'd switched it on to fast. The bastards! So when Chunky stood up and put his head in the way of it there was this sort of dull clunk, really wooden sound it was, and he keeled off the table on to his back on the floor with this red line right across his forehead and his face covered in blood!' The small dining room shook with the guffaws and the CO thumped his fist on the table. Edward was ecstatic. 'There was blood everywhere, I've never seen so much! And d'you know what they did then? – whisky – they poured a whole bottle of whisky over him. Can you imagine? A whole bottle!'

Henry Sandy leaned across to Charles during the hubbub. 'It won't be long before it becomes a regimental custom, compulsory for all newcomers, whisky to be paid for by the subalterns.'

Dinner continued unabated. Eventually, when one or two people were well into their second course, the CO's voice was raised in anger and all conversation stopped.

'Get that out!' he said, emphasising each word for all it was worth.

Everyone looked for the offending person, but there was no blushing subaltern or grief-stricken company commander to be seen. No one moved, except Anthony Hamilton-Smith who continued to eat whilst gazing with mild curiosity at the CO.

The CO banged his fist on the table. 'Corporal James!'

The cook hurried in from the kitchen, his mouth hanging open and his flabby cheeks vibrating. 'Sir.'

The CO pointed to the dish of gravy on the table. 'Get that noxious liquid out of here.'

Corporal James picked up the dish. 'Something wrong with it, sir?'

'Everything's wrong with it. It's gravy.'

'Sir. Did you want something else, sir?'

'The point, Corporal James, is that it is gravy and I will not tolerate gravy in my Mess. I don't care what else you give us but I never want to see that revolting brown liquid in here again. Got that?'

'Sir.'

'Thank you, Corporal James.' Corporal James waddled out with the gravy. The CO poured himself some more wine and one or two people tried timidly to get the conversation going again.

Anthony Hamilton-Smith helped himself to some potatoes. 'D'you not like gravy, Colonel?' he asked.

'I detest it, Anthony. Ghastly stuff. Can't stand the sight of it.'

'Oh dear, I didn't know that,' Anthony popped a large potato into his mouth.

After dinner the Mess split into its customary two camps. One consisted of the CO, Anthony Hamilton-Smith, the company commanders and those captains who felt it was time they were company commanders. The other comprised everyone else and included the adjutant, an unusually popular man with more than his share of that weary resignation that is habitual with some officers. The padre, who was no respecter of persons, moved freely and apparently unselfconsciously from one to the other. Philip Lamb hovered uneasily in between.

Night ambushes on lonely customs posts and isolated crossroads were a major feature of the battalion's brief stay in Killagh. There were no results, although a sheep was shot, but the CO and the Intelligence officer, Nigel Beale, remained enthusiastic to the end. Nigel was a squat, broad-shouldered, newly-promoted captain who took his intelligence work very seriously. He was of an earnest disposition, a keen soldier who talked about the Need for Greater Professionalism. He sometimes engaged Charles in inconclusive conversations about the growth of subversive tendencies in the universities, the BBC and the press, and his manner suggested that he held Charles partly responsible. His definition of 'subversive' embraced the civilian population, the Royal Air Force and even certain regiments and corps of the Army, including Philip Lamb's. A regular feature of his daily briefings – from which he tried without success to exclude Philip Lamb – was his insistence that those ambushing roads near the border should look out for flat-bedded lorries without lights. This soon became a joke throughout the battalion and one night no less than thirty-six such sightings were reported. Nigel was hurt and the CO furious. Walking-out was suspended for three days and no one ever again reported seeing a flat-bedded lorry. Nigel also had to pass on the daily intelligence summaries from Headquarters. This was another duty he took more seriously than his audience, except for the CO. Most of the topics he mentioned had been reported on and speculated about by the television news the day before. He was frequently mortified by this, regarding it almost as a breach of the need-to-know principle. This was the doctrine that secret information should be known only by those that, for the purposes of their jobs, needed to know it. It was applied by Nigel and the CO with great determination but little consistency, with the result that most people knew most things but weren't sure what was secret and what wasn't.

After a spate of particularly serious mid-week riots in Belfast Nigel told them that an intelligence source graded A1 had prophesied further trouble at the weekend.

'D'you know who said that?' asked Henry Sandy after the briefing.

'No, I don't,' said Nigel, 'and I wouldn't tell you if I did.'

'Well, I know and I can tell you. It was Jimmy Murphy, who commands the Third Battalion of the IRA in Belfast and is now resident in Dublin. He said it on *Twenty-Four Hours* last night.'

'You shouldn't have said that,' Philip Lamb said afterwards. 'It was cruel. It hurt him.'

'Hurt him? It hurts me to think that we'll have to rely on him for knowing what's going on round the next street corner when we get to Belfast.'

Nigel Beale soon became a joke throughout the battalion, the more so because his intense earnestness seemed unaffected by reversals. The result was that his wrongs were recalled with relish while his rights, of which there were at least an equal number, went unrecorded.

One afternoon Charles went out for tea in the town with Henry Sandy, Philip Lamb and Chatsworth. The four of them, all young and variously disaffected, had instinctively formed a group apart from all the others. Though three were graduates, what brought them all together was not a shared education but a communal sense of discontent, albeit for differing reasons. Henry Sandy felt himself more suited to being a perpetual medical student than an Army officer, and did not like the CO. Philip Lamb had the sense of military inferiority common to many members of his corps and wanted very much to be needed and accepted, but felt neither. Charles, on the other hand, feared to be needed and accepted – dimly divining that that was a two-way process that would involve him in needing and accepting the Army – but was at the same time uncomfortable as an outsider. Basically, he wished people well but wished not to be too involved. Chatsworth, though, was perhaps more different than anyone. He had been posted to C company in place of John Wheel who had suddenly been moved to one of the other battalions without any reason being given. Chatsworth was tall, fair and gangling. He walked with his shoulders hunched, his hands clasped behind his back and his head nodding from side to side. He was nearly always grinning and was thought to be mad. On his first day he had mistaken Edward Lumley for the paymaster and they had had a long and confused discussion about allowances before Edward realised. On his second night he had ambushed and attempted to arrest an RUC patrol. He seemed unabashed by whatever happened.

'I like the Army,' he said, laughing after his scolding for the second incident. 'I want to be a general. Napoleon commanded an army at twenty-six, which gives me just over three years. But I don't think I like it here. I don't like some of the people and some of them certainly don't like me, particularly the CO now. But the main thing is there's no killing. It's boring. I hope it'll change for the worse when we get to Belfast.'

They found a tea-shop near the town centre. It was run by an old lady and two young waitresses. It smelt of polish and home-made cakes. It seemed the sort of place where there was small chance of meeting off-duty soldiers. Charles found it a great pleasure to wear civilian clothes again. He had that morning received an hysterical and loving letter from Janet who had seen television film of the riots in Belfast and had positively identified him as a wounded officer being helped away. They ordered tea, toast and cakes.

'I do enjoy tea,' said Philip Lamb. 'It's so civilised, so nice. Except in the Mess where it's like rugger and they all form a scrum round the toaster. I don't like rugger.' They all nodded seriously. 'I used to enjoy breakfast too but that's all become rather tense now. I sat down this morning and my pistol fell out of my pocket on to the floor with a great crash. Everyone stopped eating and the CO just stared. The only thing that saved me was that the same thing's happened to him twice.'

'What gets me,' said Henry, 'is the way we attached officers have to carry our bloody pistols night and day while the regimental officers who have rifles can put them in the armoury when they don't want to go out to play. I mean, we have to take ours to bed, to bath and to bog, with ammunition and a fifty quid fine if you lose any of it. Not that I'd know how to use the damn thing anyway.'

'In the last resort,' said Philip, 'they're for using on ourselves,

I suspect. I'm sure I'm the only target I could hit anyway. Although I must admit that just holding it and looking at it gives one a pleasant feeling of lethality.'

Henry snorted. 'The only lethal thing you could do with one of those is throw it at someone.'

'Not true,' said Chatsworth. 'The nine-millimetre Browning is a lethal weapon, used properly. It's more accurate than most of its users. But I agree about the pleasant feeling of lethality. I carry one all the time.'

'You don't,' said Henry.

Chatsworth laughed and slapped his thigh. 'Why does no one around here ever believe anything I say?'

'We usually hope you're kidding.'

Chatsworth opened his jacket enough to reveal a shoulder-holster. 'It's not the Army's, it's my own. Legally, more or less. Though we're not supposed to bring private firearms out here, are we?'

'Why do you carry it?'

'Well, you never know.'

'Never know what?'

'What might happen. I always used to carry one in Panama.'

'In where?'

'The CO does too. You look at him next time he's in civvies going to some dinner that he's refused on our behalf. You can see he's wearing a shoulder-holster.'

'I thought everyone in that Mess was mad,' said Henry. 'You're the maddest.'

'I hope you're right. I might make general yet. You see, none of the others know they're mad but I know I am so I can make use of it.'

'Just keep on the way you're going.'

The waitress was a plump, homely, blushing girl with dark curls and rosy cheeks. 'I haven't touched a woman for nearly two weeks,' Henry confided to her, seriously.

Chatsworth grinned at her. 'I like women. I like you. Do you like me?'

Henry continued to gaze earnestly at her. 'For two weeks all I've seen of women is photographs.'

The girl dumped the tea-pot in front of Henry, almost in his lap. 'Keep looking,' she said. 'You might have more luck with photographs.'

Chatsworth stood up. 'May I follow you into the kitchen?'

Trying not to smile the girl ran back into the kitchen as fast as her tray would allow. Chatsworth followed her and came out after a couple of minutes, still grinning. They paid and left and walked back up the hill to the barracks.

'What did you do in there?' asked Philip.

'Nothing. Just got her name and address, that's all. And telephone number.'

'But you won't be allowed out to see her.'

'I shall break out. I gave her the CO's name as mine. She thinks I'm a colonel.'

'You are mad.'

'I feel randy.'

'Since our interests seem to be similar,' said Henry, 'would you like to come to one of the medical centre porn shows?'

'Do you have any porn?'

'Quite a lot. One of the orderlies gets it. It's really hard stuff. I think you'd like it.'

Chatsworth nodded seriously. 'I would, yes. When shall I come down?'

'Any time. Just say you're reporting sick and ask for me.'

'How very appropriate,' said Philip.

Charles's platoon was doing the town patrol that night but instead of being able to sleep in the cell of the local police station from midnight on as usual, he was kept up until four in the morning by an explosion at the brewery. It was a small incendiary bomb and there was little damage because it had been badly placed on a window-sill. Charles's soldiers put out the small fire before the fire brigade arrived but there was then a lot of hanging around whilst the bomb disposal man, known as an ATO (Ammunition Technical Officer) searched the area for more bombs. The brewery manager appeared and gave Charles a couple of bottles of whisky for his soldiers. Unfortunately, the CO also appeared and redirected the bottles to the Officers' and Sergeants' Messes. The CO was greatly pleased by the event and said it was proof that the battalion's high level of activity had forced the enemy to waste his resources on soft targets.

The battalion's level of activity was very high. The frenetic tempo of operations at first bewildered the local people, then impressed them and finally, when no results were forthcoming, evoked their ridicule. Everyone was very tired by the end of the first week and so much more so by the end of the second that the lack of results was not even slightly depressing. No one bothered to enquire.

That morning Charles was telephoned at six and told to report with his platoon to the barracks an hour before time. They got there to find that three companies were to carry out an area search of some flat land about ten miles away. They were to leave at once. Edward was panicking. Charles pointed out that his men had had no breakfast and, for the most part, no sleep.

Edward put both hands on top of his black beret, forcing it down almost to the bridge of his nose. 'Charles, for Christ's sake, don't stand there arguing. Now means now. Just get your platoon in the lorries and get them out of here before the CO sees you haven't gone yet. Everyone else has.'

Charles got his platoon into the waiting lorries, which were smoking and coughing in the clear morning air. They got mixed up with some of A company and had to debus and then embus again. By this time Edward was frantic. Soldiers were milling around everywhere. 'Charles, just get in the nearest bloody lorry and go!' he shouted. 'Take everyone with you.'

Charles felt like shouting back but didn't. 'Nobody's told us where we're going,' he said. 'The driver doesn't know.'

'Don't be so pathetic. Find Sergeant Wheeler. I gave him the grid reference. You can map-read your way. I'll follow in my Land-Rover and hoot if you go wrong. Now clear off, for God's sake.'

Everyone scrambled aboard something and at last the lorries coughed and spluttered out of the gates. Charles was in the cab of the leading one. After a while he asked the driver if Edward's Land-Rover was following.

'No, sir,' said the driver with complete confidence and without looking in the mirror.

'How do you know?'

The driver grinned. 'His driver's in the back with us. That's what comes of all the hurry.'

The search lasted all day and covered several grid squares on the one-inch map. The land was very flat with many ditches and marshes and few trees. The weather was crisp and clear and it was a pleasant day's walk for those who had slept. No one really knew what they were looking for nor where to look. At about mid-morning they came across some tinkers with their horses and caravans. They were small, sullen, frightened-looking people from across the border who resisted any attempt to get to know them by speaking only Gaelic, and little enough of that.

There was a lunchtime rendezvous with one of the lorries, from which they were served pints of hot Army tea and sandwiches. Charles said to Nigel Beale, 'Why didn't you tell us last night that we were going to do this?'

'Need to know.' Nigel munched briskly. 'The only ones who knew were those without whom it couldn't be done.'

'What about those who are doing it?'

'No need to know.'

'Do you really expect to find anything?'

'Not necessarily.'

'What are we looking for?'

'Arms and explosives.'

'Yes, but any particular sort?'

'Need to know.'

During the afternoon the CO hovered overhead in a helicopter, causing everyone to poke more purposefully into the ditches and derelict barns. By last light the only thing found was a rusty shotgun in one of the latter.

When Charles got back, feeling very flat and tired, he had to see that his platoon cleaned their kit and their weapons properly as Sergeant Wheeler had once again disappeared. It turned out that he had been delayed returning from the search area as the provisions lorry, in which he should not have been, had become stuck in a bog and had to be towed out. By the time Charles got back to his own quarters all the baths were occupied and by the time he got into one the hot water was cold. However, the cold bath refreshed him sufficiently to turn his flatness into decisiveness for a while and, knowing he would soon be too tired again to bother, he sat down and quickly wrote a letter to the Retirements Board. He said that he was considering resigning, giving no reasons, and asked under what conditions his resignation might be accepted. He had been thinking about doing this for some time but had hesitated to take such a decisive and eventually public step. He knew that his resignation would have to be submitted through the CO, but he did not yet want the CO to know that he wished to leave. He would feel more sure of his ground when he knew whether or not it was possible to leave. He told no one what he was doing.

That done, he went over to the Mess but it was too early for dinner and, as chance would have it, he found himself alone with the CO, who was warming his backside against the fire. 'Have a whisky,' said the CO. It was not an invitation that could be refused. The CO looked tired and drawn and Charles, feeling guilty for what he had just done, as though he had betrayed the CO in some personal way, made a show of enthusiasm. 'Pity about today,' continued the CO. 'Would have done the battalion a power of good to have found something. Good for morale. Nothing worse than trudging round fields all day and not finding anything. I know, I've done it myself. And of course if one person finds something it makes everyone else look that much harder. Still, there you are, can't be helped. Stuff had probably been moved before we got there.'

'What was it, sir?'

'Four hundred pounds of home-made explosives in animal feed sacks. I think we were fairly thorough, don't you? Don't think we could've missed it.'

'I think we were as thorough as possible under the circumstances.'

'Yes, that's what I thought. You can't really tell when you're hovering up in the air like a bloody kestrel. Easy to get the wrong impression.'

Charles sat next to Chatsworth during dinner and heard how his contribution to the search had been to shoot a rat in a ditch with his rifle. This probably accounted for the shot that had been reported by the RUC. Whilst looking for what was left of the rat – he wanted to see what the bullet had done – Chatsworth had sunk up to his knees in slime and, judging by the stench of his trousers, socks and boots afterwards, had concluded that the ditch was formed by the overflow from a cesspit. He had attempted to exchange trousers, socks and boots for new pairs by claiming that there were no cleaning facilities that could cope with the contamination, but had been rudely rebuffed by the misanthropic quartermaster.

'They're all the same, QMs,' Chatsworth complained in a low, bitter voice. 'They all see their job as to prevent you from getting kit rather than to provide you with it. You'd think they had to pay for the stuff themselves. I reckon if our QM ever had to issue the whole battalion with new boots he'd go into a decline and not eat for a week. Except that, knowing him, he'd eat even more and dock it from our rations. I'll get the stuff clean eventually but it means our room's going to stink for a bit.'

'Can't you keep it outside?' asked Charles.

'Not without someone pinching it.'

'Who'd want it in that state?'

'The QM for one. He'd take anything if he could get it without exchanging. People would pinch it out of spite.'

'And what about the bullet?'

'What bullet?'

'The one you shot the rat with. You'll have to account for it. You'll be one round short.'

'That'll be all right. We're bound to get through a few dozen rounds in Belfast. At least, I hope we are. I hope it's not going to be as dull as this place. Anyway, I've got some of my own from home. I always carry a few with me.'

After dinner the Mess cleared unusually rapidly. Tramping

around all day seemed to have tired people. Charles had reached that stage of sleeplessness when he was prepared to delay going to bed, the better to savour the prospect of sleeping soundly no matter what noise was made by A company going up and down the tunnel outside their room, and no matter what stench Chatsworth had introduced within it. He lingered over a whisky.

Chatsworth sat back in his armchair and languidly crossed his legs, as though he were about to conduct a tutorial. 'I don't suppose you've ever killed anyone?' he asked offhandedly.

'No, I haven't.'

'Do you want to?'

'Not particularly, though I don't object to the idea. It depends on who and why.' It struck Charles that the conversation was beginning to sound very like conversations with Henry Sandy about sex. His replies were disturbingly similar. At the back of his mind there was a suspicion that he might quite like to kill someone just to see what it felt like, though it would never do to admit that to Chatsworth. 'Why, have you killed anyone?' he asked.

Chatsworth looked shifty. 'Well, not really. Sort of but not properly.'

'D'you mean they recovered?'

'No, no. No question of that. It's just that it wasn't deliberate.'

Chatsworth looked embarrassed, as though he regretted having raised the subject. However, discomfiture of Chatsworth was too rare an experience for Charles to be able to resist exploring it. 'Come on, what do you mean? What happened? Was it today?'

'No, no. No. It was – you won't tell anyone, will you? I won't like it to get out, you see. It was an old woman in Bogota. I ran her over at night. Pure accident. Didn't matter very much because they just leave the bodies on the streets out there. I don't know who she was. But as I didn't mean it I can't really claim it as a kill.'

'Perhaps you'll be able to make up for it here,' said Charles.

Chatsworth raised his glass. 'Let's hope so.'

Charles had meant it as a joke but seeing Chatsworth take his remark seriously caused him to doubt his own intentions. It was quite likely that someone was going to kill or be killed during the next few months.

Before he left the Mess that night Charles received a telephone call from Janet. She had got the number from military enquiries. In a conversation made awkward by enforced normality, she said that she was going to a wedding in Dublin the following month and suggested he came down for the night. He explained that he wasn't allowed south of the border and asked whether she could get up to Belfast – where he would be by then – for the night. She thought it might be possible. It then occurred to him that he didn't know whether he would be allowed to take a night off. She asked whether he was sure he wanted to see her. He said he was. She said that she didn't want to be in the way. He tried to reassure her, but was rather reticent because he was acutely aware of Chatsworth listening to every word. In the end they agreed that he should ring her nearer the time. She asked, with a slightly nervous jokiness, whether he had killed anyone yet. She daily expected to hear that he had slaughtered dozens, and added that she presumed that that was what he was there for. They bade each other a formal goodbye.

'Is she very attractive?' asked Chatsworth, immediately Charles had replaced the receiver.

'Yes, she is, quite.'

'I wouldn't mind meeting her when she comes over. You know, if you're on duty or anything.'

'That's very kind of you.'

Chatsworth nodded his acknowledgment. 'Let me know when she's coming.'

During the final week in Killagh, just before the relieving unit arrived, there was an event which made national and international headlines. Charles was involved by default of Chatsworth, a part of whose platoon had crossed the border by mistake and had been arrested by the Irish Army. The meanderings of the border were such as to make accidental crossings all too easy, but fortunately encounters with the Irish Army were usually amicable. Names and details of the soldiers and their weapons were taken, and they were then escorted back to Northern Ireland. Because Chatsworth was involved, however, there was the suspicion that the crossing might have been less accidental than most. Edward was upset because the CO was angry.

The result was that Charles's platoon had to patrol the key points, such as electrical installations, gas and water works. They divided the work between sections and Charles was in the leading Land-Rover of two on the way to inspect an electricity transformer when they heard an explosion. Though loud, it was difficult to tell from which direction it came but it felt large. They all seemed to feel it in the pits of their stomachs a split second before they heard it. They turned off the lane and drove up the rough track that led to the transformer. At the top of a short hill they rounded a corner and saw that something had happened to the track about halfway between them and the transformer. There was a large crater, the grass around was smoking and was littered with bits of yellow material. Charles stopped his Land-Rover and sat for a few moments looking. It was soon clear that the yellow bits had been an Electricity Board van. There were other, darker bits scattered about.

Charles ordered his men out of their vehicles and sent them all, except his own radio operator, to take up tactical positions on the crest of the hill. He warned them to watch for booby-traps. He feared an ambush and so dreaded having to account to the CO for dead men that he found himself shouting 'Hard targets!' as they doubled across the fields. He called up the rest of his platoon over the radio and then went forward to look at the mess. The crater was several feet deep, the engine of the van was about fifty yards up the track and one of the seats was smoking in the grass. A part of a body, wearing a jacket, lay nearby. When he reported to battalion headquarters he was told to do nothing but to wait for the CO and Henry Sandy. Edward was apparently still involved with Chatsworth and his troubles. It crossed Charles's mind that Chatsworth would be very jealous of his having witnessed the carnage.

When the CO arrived he made no comment on the scene, and his face was expressionless. 'Keep half your men as they are,' he said, 'and get the other half to help the medics with the bodies. You supervise them. They need an officer at a time like this.' He pointed to the plastic bags which the medical order-lies were unfolding and laying on the grass. 'Put the bits on the death sheets there. You don't know how many bodies there are, do you?'

'At least two, I think.'

The CO nodded, his lips pressed tightly together. He looked at the pieces of bodies on the grass, and then hard at Charles as though to see what he was thinking. 'Don't touch any bit of the vehicle until ATO's been and had a look at it,' he said. 'It's all good evidence for him. And keep a grip on your men. They're very young. This might upset some of them. It's their first time.'

They gathered the charred and reddened bits, enough to indicate three bodies but not enough to complete them, and put them in the back of Henry's ambulance Land-Rover. Charles's soldiers were pale and serious.

The device turned out to have been a mine activated by a trip-wire across the track. It had been intended for the Army's daily visit to the transformer but had instead caught three maintenance engineers. There was considerable press interest and Philip Lamb, to his delight, was made PRO. The CO was interviewed on television and described the incident as 'an appalling and mindless act of bestiality'. Nigel Beale thought that the brewery explosion had been a trial run for the real thing in order to test reactions, and Chatsworth felt slighted because nobody would describe the scene to him in the detail he wanted. Charles was a little surprised at himself for feeling nothing at all. When it came to it, there seemed to be nothing to feel or say.

4

I t was cold when they left Killagh and there was snow on the ground. This made night ambushes seem a bitter cruelty, though the days were bright, sunny and exhilarating. They were relieved by a regiment of gunners, a polite and rather formal people who often wore civilian clothes and soon slowed down the pace of operations to what seemed to them acceptable. There was talk of a fixture with the rugby club.

Cursed though he was, and absurd though he seemed, the CO's tactics of day and night patrolling on foot combined with ambushes and hides were ideally suited to the kind of warfare that was to develop in the border area, though it had not then. In the briefing for Belfast he stressed that they would maintain the same level of activity there but would have to discipline themselves to the notion of 'minimum force'. The eyes of the world – the press – would be upon them, and any force used – and they would have to use a good deal of it – would not only have to be the minimum necessary but would have to be seen to be so. Every rubber bullet fired had to be accounted for and treated with the same seriousness as the firing of a real one, to which it was the only alternative. They would not use gas for riot control since it was not sufficiently specific, affecting villains and innocents alike. He would have no cowboys blasting off at every lout on a street corner; on the other hand he was not prepared to stand back and see his soldiers murdered on British streets, no matter what the politicians might think. If the IRA, or any other bunch of thugs that tried to call themselves an army, gave him trouble he would hit them; if they gave more trouble he would hit them hard; if they continued to give trouble he would kill them. Otherwise, he would leave them alone and he expected every soldier in the battalion to do likewise.

The part of Belfast they were going to was one of the most notorious in the city. It was in the south-west and had a population that was eighty per cent Catholic and twenty per cent Protestant. The Catholics lived in IRA-dominated ghettos and the Protestants in a tight little enclave in one corner of the battalion area. The two communities were divided by the Peace Line – a tortuous, tangled line of wire, corrugated iron, concrete and sentry-boxes that had to be manned day and night. During the 1969 riots the Protestants had burned down a score of Catholic houses. There had been attempts by the residents to build new ones, mostly without planning permission and sometimes without planning. The Catholic part of the area had been prominent during the recent riots. According to Nigel there were two IRA 'battalions' in the area and both had been ordered to step up their activities during the next few weeks. This could provoke a Protestant reaction. The CO, however, took it as a compliment to the battalion to be given such a welcome by the enemy and he was sure that the harder it was the more his soldiers would like it.

Battalion HQ was to be in a police station, while the companies occupied schools, factories, houses and a disused bus garage. C company was the largest and had what the CO considered the most interesting area. It included a part of the Peace Line, a few Prot streets and a large Catholic estate of ill-repute where several soldiers had already died that year. Company HQ was a bottling factory. Charles did not need to see it to know that it was a move for the worse. The barracks in Killagh were almost academic cloisters by comparison. The Factory was a nineteenth-century building of six storeys set in the midst of a maze of narrow, mean streets and enclosed by a high wall. The iron gate was kept closed and there were two knife-rests in the street outside, which forced traffic to weave past slowly, at walking-pace. Inside and outside the wall the ground was littered with glass and rubble. The outgoing unit's Land-Rovers were battered, dented and holed.

Charles was greeted on arrival by the CSM, a popular,

gravel-voiced Liverpudlian whose face was almost as battered as the Land-Rovers. ''Tain't much, sir, but it's 'ome. Only four more months. Won't be so bad when we've cleaned it up a bit. Soon as this bloody lot clear off we can get started. Live like pigs, don't they? Must've caught it from the people round 'ere, by what I've seen of 'em.' He laid his hand confidentially on Charles's arm and indicated the broken bricks, bits of piping, paving stone and glass that lay scattered about the parked vehicles. 'See all this shit, sir? D'you know 'ow it got here? Kids threw it, little kids last night. 'Undreds of 'em in the street outside, lobbing it over the wall. I come down with the advance party, see, just in time to cop the lot of it. Like a bleedin' avalanche, it was. And the same thing happens every time one of their Land-Rovers pokes its nose out the gate, which is why they're all in shit order. So I says to the guard commander, like, well, what you going to do about it, ain't you going to stop 'em? Oh no, 'e says, it 'appens every night, it's nothing serious, we just let 'em get on with it. Containment, he called it. Containment, I ask you! Standing there letting a mob of kids chuck bricks at you. I says to 'im, I says, well, this is the last night they do it, you can tell 'em that from me, 'cos when we take over tomorrow night containment stops and ear-boxing starts. I'll give 'em bloody containment.'

Charles struggled with his unnecessary quantity of kit up the stone stairs into the Factory. There was a continuous sound of activated machinery, punctuated every few seconds by a crash that shook the building.

'The bottling,' said the CSM. 'That's what that is. They still use the first two floors, you see. Six in the morning till ten at night. They're all Prot workers but we still 'ave to escort 'em in and out in case of bombs and we have to do bomb searches when they're not 'ere. We live on the other four floors. The machinery's been ripped out but there ain't no separate rooms, not properly speaking, just a lot of cardboard partitions with a corridor down the middle. It's a bit noisy 'cos the cardboard's a bit thin and don't reach the ceiling anywhere. An' it's crowded. You an' the other officers, 'cept Major Lumley, sleep on the third floor in a kind of cubicle next to the ops room, so you're nice and handy like if anything 'appens. But it's even noisier for you.'

The Factory soon became known as the worst of the company locations. Defaulters were sometimes threatened with transfer to C company, as though to some particularly gruesome region of hell. It was never silent. Apart from the crash and thump of the machinery below there were televisions, a juke box in the NAAFI partition, countless transistor radios and all the zoo noises that soldiers make. From their partition next to the ops room Charles, Chatsworth and Tim were able to listen to radio talk and mush for twenty-four hours a day. The partition was furnished with three sleeping-bags, three lockers and one table. There was just room to move between them. Chatsworth and Tim had already claimed the two sleeping-bags farthest from the door, which was a piece of sacking nailed to the woodwork. Chatsworth's kit was strewn all over his sleeping-bag, but he was nowhere to be seen. Tim was lying down writing a letter, his kit neatly stowed away. Charles had often wondered whether Tim was oblivious to his surroundings or simply contented with anything. He wasn't sure which was worse.

'Edward wants to see you,' said Tim without looking up from his letter. 'Turn right and keep on till you reach the end of the corridor.'

Edward had a partition to himself. There was ample room for his camp-bed and locker. He was gazing dolefully at a street map of Belfast. 'Hallo, old son, come in and spread yourself about a bit. Better sit on the bed, there's no room to stand.' Charles sat rather uncomfortably next to him. Their shoulders touched. Edward looked pensive. 'Ever thought about leaving the Army, Charles?'

'Yes.' Charles wondered what was coming next. 'Quite often, actually. Particularly recently.'

'So have I, old son, so have I. Give anything to be out of here at the moment, quite honestly. Don't tell anyone, though. Trouble is, who'd want to employ a bugger like me? All very well being Commando trained and Airborne and being clued up on your infantry tactics and all that, but it's not much use in ICI, is it? The fact that I'm red-hot with a Carl Gustav rocket launcher won't cut much ice there, will it? Or I used to be, at least. Probably can't even do that now.'

Edward was one of those people who were at their most likeable when not trying to assert themselves. He was at heart a simple, nice man, not particularly suited to any job. Charles felt they had something in common in the latter respect, though possibly not in the former. 'You could claim you've had management experience,' he said. The concept of 'manage-ment' always made him feel uneasy. 'Good at dealing with people and that sort of thing.'

Edward looked reproachfully at him. 'D'you really think they'd swallow that?'

'Not really, no.'

'Nor do I. What would you do if you left – be an academic or something?'

'Maybe, if I could. Or journalism, or something like that. Something where other people do it and I talk about it.'

'Wise man. So long as you tell 'em what they're doing is a load of cobblers you'll never be out of a job. Let me know if you ever want an assistant, someone to add insult to injury, you know.' Edward seemed suddenly to recollect that he was the company commander. He stubbed his finger on the map. 'You've seen this, haven't you?'

'No.'

'You should have. It's the map of our area. You're supposed to have one.'

It was a large-scale street map shaded green and orange to indicate Catholic and Protestant areas, and unshaded to indicate mixed business areas. Charles looked more closely at it, as though to establish by inspection whether or not he had one. 'I thought perhaps I should have one.'

'See the sergeant major.' Edward held up a list of names and addresses. 'But you haven't seen this yet, have you?'

'Yes.'

Edward looked puzzled. 'Where?'

'On Chatsworth's bed.'

'How the hell did he get one? It's supposed to be secret. Company commanders only.'

'Perhaps it was another list.'

Edward seemed relieved. 'Yes, perhaps it was.' He stared gloomily at the list. 'This is what's so bloody depressing, you see. Not only do we have a larger area than anyone else but we've got a list of gunmen and villains twice as long as your arm. I mean look at it. You haven't seen this, remember. It's secret.'

'In that case, how are we supposed to identify them?'

'Dunno. Good point, though. I'll ask the CO.' He folded the list. 'God, I hate challenges. Why couldn't this area be given to A company? They're always so bloody keen. Anyway, must fight back, I suppose, which is where you fit in. I'm making you sort of acting, unofficial, unpaid second-in-command. Only you mustn't tell anyone. What it means is that I want you to send in the weekly Intelligence and Community Relations reports and deal with all the odds and sods and also with any PR that comes along – God forbid – that isn't being done by that queer, what's-his-name, up in battalion HQ?'

'Philip Lamb.'

'Lamb, that's it. Queer as a coot, if you ask me. So if you can deal with all that, plus anything else that crops up – you know, complaints and things – it'll leave me free to concentrate on – er – all the other stuff, tactics and whatever.' Charles nodded and Edward suddenly became brisk and cheerful. 'Good. Right. That's settled, then. S'pose you haven't been in the ops room yet, have you? Well, when you do you'll see a wallful of obscene photographs – mug-shots of the villains in the area whom we're supposed to look out for. Everyone's supposed to memorise them.'

'Right.' It was a word that Charles had discovered to be almost indispensable in the Army, so powerfully suggestive of grasp and prompt action that its user frequently escaped further enquiry. When he got back to his partition Tim had gone but Chatsworth was there, sitting on his sleeping-bag with his rifle stripped for cleaning. 'Have you got a secret list of IRA suspects?' Charles asked.

Chatsworth paused in the cleaning, the piston in his hand. He looked shifty. 'Not necessarily. Why?'

'I just told Edward you had.'

'Thanks a bunch.'

'I didn't realise you weren't s'posed to, so I then told him it was probably another list and he seemed only too happy to believe it.'

'Tell him it's my kit list if he asks.'

'Where did you get it?'

'I stole it from Nigel Beale. It seemed only fair. He always goes around as though we're more of an enemy than the IRA. It's an accountable document so I hope he'll get into trouble. There is another one in the ops room but it's an amended version and I'd rather know everyone who's likely to shoot at me rather than just some of them. Wouldn't you?'

'I'm not sure.'

'You can borrow it if you like, though.'

'Thanks.'

Chatsworth returned to his cleaning with loving care. 'How are you off for ammunition?'

Charles was puzzled. 'All right. I mean, I've got the regulation number of rounds, unless I've lost some since this morning. Why?'

'Nothing. Let me know if you need any extra, that's all.'

The company area divided naturally into Catholic and

Protestant ghettos. The Protestant area was very small, a few streets of back-to-back terraced houses. Their front doorsteps were scrubbed white every day, the kerbstones were painted red, white and blue and models of the disbanded B Specials stood in nearly every curtained window. It was a tight, defiant little area, surrounded by what it saw as the enemy. The streets were mean and clean. It was more British than the Britons, though a government that had disbanded the beloved B Specials – their own reserve police force with whom they felt safe – would never again be trusted. The Catholic area fell into two parts – the old part near the Factory and a new estate some way from it. The streets and houses of the old part were identical to those of the Protestant area, from which they were divided by the Peace Line. They were respectable, though not as stridently clean as the Protestant. Adjacent to the Peace Line there was even one street that was still mixed – Protestant on one side and Catholic on the other, but no one except patrolling soldiers ever crossed the road. In the middle, and not very far from the Factory, was a monastery. It was the only other large building and was rumoured to serve as an arsenal for the local IRA, though it had never been searched because of the popular feeling that would have been aroused. Nevertheless, the Army had access to an observation post on the top of it from which they could survey the Peace Line area. Nigel Beale said that this part of the Catholic community housed the important leaders of the IRA gangs that flourished in the modern estate.

This had been built after the war as a mixed community, billed then as 'homes fit for heroes'. It was a series of concentric streets built around a concrete circle of shops, known as the Bull Ring. Gradually, the community had become less mixed as more Catholics had moved in and the Protestants had moved out. One night in 1969 most of those that remained, concentrated in a small area near the primary school, had been moved out by Protestant leaders, who said they could no longer protect them. The few who had lingered on had soon been persecuted into leaving. Now the school had to be protected night and day by the Army because it included a community hall that had been built by a Protestant, and the IRA had sworn to destroy it. The estate was a violent, rat-infested slum. Long stretches of paving stones had been torn up for use in riots, and manhole covers and drains had been put to similar use. No street-lamps worked, no rent or bills were paid, hardly a house had all its windows complete, and the burnt-out wrecks of cars and barricades littered the streets. There had been frequent riots in the past few weeks and the previous unit had patrolled the area only in Pigs, and then not often. The RUC had not been into the estate unescorted since the troubles had begun.

About forty children gathered outside the Factory gate that evening for the usual stoning. Charles was in the yard when the first bricks flew over. One hit a Land-Rover bonnet and skidded off on to the wall by which he was standing. He buttoned up his flak jacket and moved away with what he hoped was officer-like composure, one hand behind his back. The children jumped up and down outside the gate, yelling and hurling as much as they could. For a while broken house-bricks rained into the yard and Charles was forced to abandon some of his officer-like composure and shelter behind a Pig. He was wondering about getting into it when he saw the CSM and a snatch squad of six men creep unobtrusively to the gate, open it suddenly and charge out. The bricks stopped and there was a lot of screaming and shouting. Children fled in all directions. In less than a minute the CSM and his snatch squad reappeared with seven of the largest children and dragged them quickly into the Factory. They were aged about twelve to fourteen and their struggles weakened as they got farther from the street. It crossed Charles's mind that they might be put into bottles on the conveyor-belt – or whatever it was that made the noise – and sent on their way. He unbuttoned his flak jacket and then followed them in.

Five minutes later he went to the ops room and found Edward, panic-stricken, shouting on the radio to battalion HQ. 'Alpha Zero, this is Alpha Three. I say again we are being attacked. We are under siege. Over.'

Back over the radio mush came Anthony Hamilton-Smith's

measured tones. 'Zero roger, could you tell us a little more? Over.'

'Alpha Three, wait out.' Edward turned to Charles. 'Give me details quickly. How many of them? What's happening? What weapons have they got?'

'Well, there were about forty and the sergeant major counter-attacked, capturing seven. They were armed with bricks.'

'Bricks?'

'And they were aged nought to fourteen.'

'Children!' Edward passed his hand slowly over his eyes. 'Hallo, Alpha Zero. This is Alpha Three. Reference my last – er – The attack has been repulsed and we no longer require assistance. Over.'

Anthony Hamilton-Smith was not a man to give way to strong feelings, nor did he try to impress upon others his state of mind, but on this occasion even his voice sounded faintly puzzled. 'Zero congratulations – very quick work. What about casualties and prisoners? Over.'

'Alpha Three, no casualties, but seven prisoners. Over.'

'Alpha Zero – very impressive – three and a half brace – send them to my location. Over.'

'Alpha Three – er – we'd rather thought of letting them go. Over.'

'Alpha Zero – I don't understand – why did you take them? Over.'

Edward pulled a face. 'Alpha Three – they'll be with you in figures one-five minutes. Over.'

'Alpha Zero – thank you. Out.'

Edward turned beseechingly to Charles. 'What's the CO going to say when I send him seven kids? He'll go spare. You know what he's like, he'll be expecting ringleaders at least. Where are they now?'

'In the showers being tortured.'

'Tortured!'

'I was joking. The sergeant major's put them in there because it's the only empty room.'

'Don't joke, Charles, it's bad taste. Take me to them, would you?'

Edward put on his beret and Charles went with him to the shower-room – so called because of three rusty and feeble sprinklers that projected from one wall. The seven victims were now standing more or less at attention, eyed almost affectionately by the CSM. Their bravado was gone and they looked very young and very frightened. Edward strode in purposefully. 'Well done, Sergeant Major.'

The CSM grinned. 'Sorry there wasn't more of 'em, sir, but there will be if they try it again tomorrow. I was just telling 'em about the water-torture but I 'adn't made up me mind who was goin' to be first.'

'Don't joke, please, Sergeant Major, I'm in no mood for it.

They're to go down to battalion HQ immediately. Send them in one of the duty platoon's Pigs.'

Contrary to expectations, the CO was delighted by the capture. He felt it had got the battalion off on the right foot and would set the tone for future operations. Anyone who made trouble would be sat on: that was the policy. The sooner it was understood around the neighbourhood, the better. All arrested people were to be sent to battalion HQ, where the RUC or, if necessary, the RMP, would deal with them. This included children. Although stoning was too common an occurrence to merit a summons, the children would be held there until their parents came to collect them. That would be an inconvenience that might lead to greater parental control. Furthermore, it had come to his notice that there were rumours of 'no go' areas in the city – no doubt press exaggerations – but they had to be taken seriously. He wanted to make it crystal clear that there would be no 'no go' areas in his parish. His soldiers would not even understand the meaning of the term, let alone acknowledge the thing if they saw it.

There were foot and vehicle patrols throughout the area, day and night. In the worst part of C company's area – the modern estate – the soldiers patrolled at night with blackened faces through the gardens and alleyways, avoiding the streets as much as possible. Meeting the soldiers unexpectedly outside their back doors brought forth some good and holy Catholic oaths from the wives of the estate. It made it difficult for them to signal the approach of patrols by banging dustbins, which was the way the Army was normally heralded. It also made the soldiers a more difficult target for snipers. It was the CO's idea, and although the Republican press criticised it as being both unreasonably military and deliberately sinister it soon reduced the random violence in the area. Unknown civilian cars were no longer stoned on sight, and even the Army Land-Rovers attracted only the occasional brick from over the rooftops.

The CO had promised that he would visit every company location every night, and this he did. He clearly thought that his appearance was good for morale, as well as contributing to military effectiveness. In fact, his visits were looked forward to with all the enthusiasm normally reserved for headmasters, and their effect was to deny any hope of autonomy to any commander with whom he came into contact. Edward, in particular, was hardly the man to stand up to the CO, but fortunately his company ran itself without either his assistance, or knowledge; and the CO, once he had issued his general directives, was often unaware of how they were interpreted in practice.

However, no one in the company could keep from Edward the knowledge that ultimately he would be held responsible for everything that happened. He lived in a fever of anxiety which he passed on to his subordinates in a stream of contradictory and mistaken instructions. What saved him from having to live with the results of his decisions was his failure to notice that they were generally ignored. The process by which this happened was a kind of unspoken conspiracy, tacitly acknowledged throughout the company, which actually did more for company morale than anything else.

Unfortunately, though, the CO's concern for his soldiers did not stop at tactics and morale: he also regarded himself as the guardian of the battalion's moral well-being, with the padre as an uneasy second-in-command. It was an incident in C company that caused him to launch a moral crusade within a few days of their arrival.

Charles was with Chatsworth in the ops room. They were each trying to drink an acrid liquid that the Army called coffee. Apart from its bitter taste at the time, it left the drinker feeling for an hour or so afterwards that he had consumed bile. All that could be said in its favour was that it was wet and warm and, sadly, this was sometimes reason enough for drinking it. Chatsworth poured his into the paper sack marked 'Confidential Waste'. 'There's going to be some more gate-thrusting tonight,' he remarked quietly.

'What's that?'

'Haven't you heard about it? It's having it off, you know, through the main gate. The sentries do it.'

'Through the gate?'

'Through the bars.'

'Who with?'

'The local birds, of course. Who d'you think?'

'But they all look about fourteen.'

'Nice, isn't it? Though I'm told there are older ones if you prefer them, unless they've been spoilt by having it off in bed.'

Girls turned out to be a problem throughout the battalion's tour. From the CO's point of view they were a menace to his young soldiers, whom he liked to regard as virgin. From the soldiers' point of view they were a forbidden paradise which it was almost impossible to enter but which was sufficiently close to make trying worthwhile. There was also a security risk: three Scottish soldiers had once been murdered after being lured away by girls, and even now the fat, prematurely old women of the new estate occasionally jeered 'Scots porridge' at passing soldiers. There seemed to be a great many young girls in the area, many of whom were prepared to risk tarring and feathering, or worse, to secure a soldier-lover who would marry them and take them away. As it turned out, few achieved marriage. Not many were even touched by No. 1 AAC(A), since during their tour the soldiers had no social life and no time off in which to have it. No one set foot inside a pub, no one went to dances, no one went shopping.

'I haven't done it myself,' continued Chatsworth. 'I don't

know what it is, but one feels somewhat inhibited in front of one's own soldiers. I'm not even sure how they do it, which is why I'd like to watch. They must be contortionists, though I s'pose love always finds a way. D'you fancy watching tonight? We could hide in one of the Pigs.'

As it happened, Charles was on duty in the ops room that night and Chatsworth had to take out a patrol. However, when the CO made his nightly appearance in the ops room, accompanied by the signals officer, the RSM, his driver and two bodyguards, it was clear that something was wrong. His lips were pressed firmly together, his expression was set hard and he stared bullishly at Charles. 'Where's Edward?' he asked.

Charles went to Edward's partition and awoke the dozing man. 'I was dreaming,' said Edward. 'I wish you hadn't.'

'The CO wants you. He looks angry.'

'Oh God.'

They returned to the ops room, Edward still blinking.

'D'you know what your soldiers have been doing?' said the CO. 'They've been screwing girls through the main gate.'

Edward's eyes opened wide. 'Good Lord, sir. Really? How?'

The CO exploded. 'How? How d'you think? What a bloody stupid question, Edward. What are you going to do about it, eh? What are you going to do?'

Edward reddened. 'I'll punish them, sir, punish them right away.'

'What with?'

Edward gazed helplessly at Charles, who looked away. Castration was the only answer that came readily to mind.

The CSM came to Edward's rescue. 'I suggest Section 69, sir,' he whispered.

'69? What do you mean, Sergeant Major? You're not trying to be funny, are you?'

'Conduct likely to be to the prejudice of military discipline. We might also throw in not being at a place at which it was their duty to be.'

The CO was slightly mollified, though clearly far from satisfied. It turned out there was only one offender, who had apparently been caught in the act, and he was marched into the ops room with unnecessary violence by the RSM and marched out again to be charged in the company office by the CSM. The CO stared disapprovingly at him but everyone else gazed with frank curiosity.

The CO took Edward aside. 'I've been worried for some time about moral standards in the battalion, Edward, and what I've seen tonight has absolutely sickened me. It was a disgrace. I never thought to see the day when Assault Commandos would behave like that. I know they're young men and have to be allowed a little licence now and again – let off steam and that sort of thing – but to do that in public, in uniform and on duty is going about a hundred miles too far. And as for those girls, I really don't know what to say. What sort of future do they have, eh? What chance of living a life that's even halfway decent if this is what they're like now? Where do they go from here? They're not even out of school, I bet you a pound to a penny. My heart bleeds for them, you know, it really bleeds.' The CO's dark eyes shone with sincerity. Edward stood before him like a schoolboy in trouble, nodding and staring at the table. The CO put his hand on Edward's shoulder. 'Not that I'm blaming you entirely, Edward, but I can't help thinking that they take their example from the top, so look to it. I shall send the padre round to talk to the company tomorrow.'

While dealing with the offender Edward wore his beret and assumed an expression of grave indignation. Afterwards he said to Charles: 'The CO wanted him to go up on battalion orders and be formally charged but I said I'd clobber him here. I fined him twenty quid for the company fund. You don't think that was too much, do you?'

'I don't know. Is there a precedent?'

'No. The sergeant major couldn't remember one so there can't be. Apparently they get one leg through.'

'What?'

'The gate, you know. They get one leg through and sort of twist their hip through the bars. I felt I should've been paying him twenty quid prize money instead of fining him. I s'pose he could've been shot, though. The CO's ordered us to put barbed wire on the gate now. Speak to the sergeant major about it when you see him.'

The battalion area was quiet for the first fortnight. Wherever the Assault Commandos went their reputation for aggression preceded them, and the CO's somewhat brisk policy did what little was needed to confirm it. Regular stoning soon stopped and the children were reduced to sporadic hit-and-run sorties, usually after dark. What might have become a serious spate of petrol bombing was nipped in the bud when Tim's platoon sergeant, with two men, caught three of the bombers. Mobile, as opposed to foot, patrols were the usual targets for such attacks and the sergeant, anticipating trouble at one particular corner, sent both his vehicles ahead whilst doubling round the back of the houses on foot. The bombers threw their bombs whilst the vehicles were still out of range and were caught as they ran away. They were teenagers and there was little fight in them. Belfast being a small city, and being divided into smaller tribal areas, even insignificant arrests like these had a quietening effect on the area in which they occurred.

Mobile patrols normally consisted of two Land-Rovers or one Pig. Charles disliked them because he felt more vulnerable in a vehicle than on foot, but of the two he felt safer in a Pig, and therefore nearly always found himself in a Land-Rover. One evening he was on a mobile patrol in the new estate when his corporal in the second Land-Rover recognised a car they had been told to look out for. It was parked in a cul-de-sac on the other side of a main road that formed the boundary of the estate. There had been a shooting earlier a few streets beyond that, outside the battalion area, in which a policeman had been wounded in the foot. This was thought to have been the get-away car. They cruised past the cul-de-sac at their usual patrolling speed, slightly faster than walking pace, and radioed back. After a pause they were told to stay with the vehicle as it was wanted for fingerprinting but not to go near in case it was booby-trapped. ATO was called and they were to guard it until he came. At the same time they were to look out for snipers in the area.

The car was a newish Cortina, evidently stolen for the job. Charles had the Land-Rovers parked across the road before and behind it and then dispersed his seven soldiers into the doorways and alleyways of the cul-de-sac. Though separated only by the main road, the people there were quite different to those in the estate. Their houses were well kept and they were friendly. Within ten minutes two had brought out trays of tea for the soldiers.

The first sign of trouble was when four women crossed the road and stood at the bottom of the cul-de-sac singing Republican songs. They were short, hard-faced, fat and ugly, either middle-aged or coarsened before their time, a kind that flourished on the estate. After a while they sat on the kerb, passing a bottle between them and still singing in unnervingly discordant unison. They could just be made out by the orange light of a distant and solitary street-light on the main road, but it was not possible to make out the words of their songs. Soon Charles realised that others were joining them – squat, waddling shapes – and the volume of singing swelled. The songs were now recognisably anti-Brit, as was to be expected, and aggressively obscene, as might have been predicted. Charles, more intent upon observing the situation than in calculating what it might mean, reflected that the image of their kind knitting at the foot of the guillotine was too passive to do them justice.

His attention was focused more sharply upon possible consequences when the original four women left the others – and their bottle – to begin a slow perambulation around the cul-de-sac. They walked arm-in-arm, still singing, peering into the doorways and alleyways. Even so, it was not until they were halfway round that Charles realised they were reconnoitring the number and positions of his soldiers. He wondered what he could do about it. Presumably, they had every right to walk the streets counting soldiers and singing; at least, he was not sure that he had any right to stop them. Nor did he know what they intended to do when they had counted. The people in the cul-de-sac had retreated behind locked doors and put out their lights when the singing first started. The tea-trays were not returned to their owners for fear of identifying them. Their recce completed, the four women joined the by now even larger group at the bottom. The singing stopped.

Of Charles's seven men, five had rifles, one (his radio operator) a pistol and one a pistol and a rubber-bullet gun. This latter was a converted signals pistol which made a very loud bang and could do a lot of damage at close range if fired directly at someone, which was forbidden. The projectile was meant to be bounced off the ground. Charles had a rifle. The simplest way to protect the three vehicles would have been to form a line across the cul-de-sac, but that would have made an easy target for a gunman and he could imagine only too vividly the subsequent enquiry into how he came to lose a soldier. It did not occur to him that it could have been him that was shot. He therefore kept five of his men dispersed among the alleyways with orders to look out for snipers and placed himself, his wireless operator, and Corporal Stagg, who had the rubber-bullet gun, between the vehicles and the crowd.

This had grown swiftly so that it was now forty or fifty strong and included a number of young children. There were no men. He reported the situation over the radio and was told by Edward that an escort vehicle had gone to meet ATO and that both would be with him as soon as possible. For a few minutes more nothing much happened; the crowd talked amongst themselves, shouted the odd slogan or obscenity and in general seemed quite good humoured. Then a black taxi, one of the many old London cabs that had found their way to Belfast, drew up on the main road behind the crowd and four men got out. The taxi drove away and the crowd immediately became more vociferous. It surged slowly forward towards the vehicles with the harridans shouting at the front and holding their children before them. The four men stayed at the back, urging the others on.

As he watched the crowd advance several scenes from his Oxford life flashed through Charles's mind, vivid and uncontrollable, and for a few seconds the scenes seemed to get between him and what was happening, as though the two worlds were jostling for reality. The present world won when he realised that the front women were within three feet of him, jumping up and down like wizened and frantic baboons. Though the noise was overwhelming he shouted that there was a bomb in the car. To his surprise, the crowd fell back and there was relative quiet; but still the feeling of unreality. He looked at Corporal Stagg's white and nervous young face and then glanced behind him at the other soldiers crouching with their rifles in the alleys. He felt that all eyes were upon him. He grabbed the headphones from the wireless operator and called for immediate assistance but before he could get a response the crowd began to rumble forward again, only quieter this time and more sinister. They didn't seem to believe, any more than he did, that the car was booby-trapped.

Charles was aware that Corporal Stagg at his elbow had raised and cocked the rubber-bullet gun, but he did not give the order to fire. No one in the battalion had yet had to fire a rubber bullet; they were accountable; there had to be definite provocation, an aggressive act. The crowd pressed closer, murmuring, the children held in front and no one so much as raising a hand or even shouting any more.

Charles realised that he was separated from his wireless operator by the Cortina. The operator was shouting that the CO was on the air and wanted a detailed sit-rep. 'Just tell them to get here!' shouted Charles. He turned round and bellowed for the other soldiers to join him. Corporal Stagg was still by his side. The front women were now within reach again, and Charles stepped forward and pushed one firmly back. Again, to his surprise, they fell back quickly. The rest of the soldiers arrived and they were able to clear a two-yard space between the crowd and the vehicles, but it was clear that it would not last for long. The crowd had increased again, and the same four men were busy at the back. What most inhibited him now about firing a rubber bullet was that it would be at point-blank range. It would frighten or anger the crowd. If the latter they could well charge before the gun could be reloaded, and the only way to stop them then would be to shoot them with real guns. As the crowd now completely surrounded the soldiers and the vehicles, shooting them would be the only way to protect their own lives and weapons. Technically, according to the Yellow Card they all carried, Charles would be justified in opening fire, but he could imagine the resultant publicity if unarmed women and children were shot dead in the street by 'heavily armed' Commandos. There would be an enquiry, if not a court case. Half hoping that they would do something to provoke retaliation, and half frightened that they might, Charles walked slowly up and down between the crowd and the vehicles, his knees trembling and with a great emptiness in his stomach. His soldiers were watching him, and so was the mob. He walked with his hands behind his back, trying to look as though he were deep in thought and entirely at peace. For some minutes nothing happened.

Then, with a kind of slow rush, a few of the crowd pushed past and got to the Cortina. The women started to rub it with their headscarves and cardigan sleeves – to remove fingerprints, Charles realised suddenly. He and Corporal Stagg managed to push them back but one of them threw a burning newspaper through the open window on to the back seat. Charles got inside the car and threw the newspaper out, but whilst he was doing so they surged forward again and pushed the car several feet back down the road into an invalid carriage. They were shouting and excited. Needlessly jamming on the handbrake, Charles tried to get out but found several of the women were pushing on the door. Seriously alarmed, and for the first time angry, he shoved the door open with his feet and jumped out, shouting, 'Prepare to fire!' Corporal Stagg, after hitting one of the women on the shoulder with the barrel of his gun, aimed it straight into the face of her neighbour, who screamed and ducked back. The women who had been struggling with the other soldiers also fell back for a moment. Both sides waited, neither sure what to do next. It was clear that the crowd still felt sure that the initiative was with them.

Charles felt his heart pounding. He looked at the excited faces in front of him, ugly with hatred, and still only a couple of yards away. Neither he nor his soldiers would have any choice but to shoot if they were rushed: if they had time for that. He pulled and cocked his pistol. If they were rushed after firing the rubber bullet he would do less damage shooting them with that than if he ordered the soldiers to use their rifles, which would go through three or four at that range. He would aim for the legs. As vividly as he saw the mob before him, he heard again some remark made in Killagh to the effect that a bullet from the nine-millimetre Browning would simply bounce off their bra straps. At such close range, though, it would be another matter. He imagined the carnage with disturbing clarity.

Charles was spared the decision by the arrival of the CO with his two long-wheel-base Land-Rovers and his oversize escort. He was not at first aware that help had arrived, only of a sudden commotion and sounds of pain and distress from the back of the crowd. Then he saw the CO's tall figure, his face set hard and his beret firmly down on his forehead. The CO, accompanied by the RSM and his escort, walked as though there was no one between himself and Charles, and very soon there wasn't. The escort drove a wedge two yards wide while the snatch squad, whose sole job was to make arrests, remained by the CO's Land-Rover, fingering their batons. One of the women who swore was grabbed by the RSM and marched briskly back to the vehicle. A shrill chorus of protest by the rest of her tribe was drowned by the CO's shouting through a loud-hailer: 'Right, you've had your fun, now you're going home. Anyone still in this street thirty seconds from now will be arrested and charged with riotous assembly. Good night!'

The snatch squad began to move with slow purpose into the mob, which drained away into the night quickly and quietly. Soon there was only Army left in the street. The adrenalin coursing through Charles's body did not drain away so rapidly. He was too relieved to feel elated. He told the CO what had happened with what sounded even to himself like schoolboy-ish urgency. He had never thought he would be glad to see the CO.

Having heard him out, the CO stared disconcertingly at him for several seconds before saying, 'I shall fine you twenty pounds, Charles. The alternative is to send you home in disgrace, but you're young, inexperienced and this is your first mistake. And your last. Two reasons: A, bad reporting – you gave us no idea of the gravity of the situation and your voice procedure was appalling; B, you jeopardised the lives of your soldiers and MOD property – not to mention your own life, which I shan't – by not taking a firm line before the situation got a chance to develop. You should've got a grip early on. You should've fired a rubber bullet the moment they started to come at you, after warning them, of course, but even without if you thought it was necessary. You need not have feared the consequences. I would have backed you up to the hilt. Minimum force is all very well as a political policy but in tactical situations I will not have the lives of my soldiers needlessly put at risk. A rubber bullet would have been minimum force but you used less than that. In fact you didn't use any force at all. In future, act firmly in the early stages and nip it in the bud. Got that? Good. Time you got rid of this airy-fairy university stuff and realised you're commanding the best soldiers in the British Army.' He looked at the Cortina, which was resting against the crumpled invalid carriage. 'Well, there can't be a bomb in it, anyway. How did that happen?'

'The mob pushed it there, sir.'

'Where were you?'

'I was inside it trying to stop it catching alight.'

'They should never have got that close. Go and find the owner of the invalid carriage, explain how it happened and write me a full report. Someone's bound to claim that you did it.'

Charles and his crew drove back to the Factory in the companionable silence of shared fear. The only remark came from the driver, who said, 'I was a bit worried there, sir.'

'It was a bit nasty, wasn't it?'

Back at the Factory Chatsworth confessed his jealousy. 'It was quite funny, though. You made the most awful cock-up on the radio. You sounded so vague and academic that everyone sort of lost interest, till your wireless operator came on. He sounded panic-stricken. Not very coherent. Rather let you down. Pity you didn't shoot any of them. I'd like to see what an SLR would do to a face at close range. And if you could've screwed one of the women at the same time the fine would probably have been forty quid. Would've made a great headline – "Assault Commando officer rapes and kills women. Many dead." Daresay they'd be queuing at the gates.'

Tim remarked that the whole thing sounded rather unprofessional but Edward said, 'Twenty quid, what a coincidence. Funny the way the CO's mind works. If you'd knocked off one of the women he'd probably have made it forty. Nasty situation, though. Nasty women, too. Rather you than me, old son.'

Charles's meeting with Janet took place only three days after the incident with the mob. The arrangements were made – mostly at the top of his voice – over the coin-box telephone installed in the part of the Factory used as the soldiers' canteen. As he had expected, he was not allowed to have a night off – Edward was not prepared even to put that to the CO – but he was permitted to take two hours off in order to have tea in the centre of Belfast. Because of the way the battalion worked, and expected to work, this did not seem to him ungenerous. He had to wear civilian clothes and to carry a Browning in a shoulder-holster. Janet spent the night of the wedding in Dublin and was given a lift to Belfast the following day by some people who lived in nearby Holywood.

They met outside a cinema showing a war film, one of the most popular forms of escapism in Belfast. They kissed briefly and self-consciously. Janet seemed prettier and more elegant than he remembered, an impression perhaps strengthened by contrast with the natives of Belfast who were, on the whole, squat and ill-favoured. She was tall and slim, with curly hair that was darker than it had been. She still had about her the brittle sheen of London social life, but there was a new promptness and decisiveness, an obvious confidence, that made him wonder whether she had a new man, or whether it was simply that life was treating her well. It was not a question that he cared to go into then. It was better left until after Ireland, if there was to be such a time.

'What's that?' she said after she had pressed against him. 'You're not carrying a gun, are you?'

'Yes, I have to. Only a pistol.'

'Oh my God, Charles, whatever's happening to you? Only a pistol, for God's sake. What a thing to say.'

He did not want to stand in the street talking about it. He felt conspicuous and awkward in civilian clothes in any case and felt as though the Browning might make him walk lopsided or with one shoulder held higher than the other. They went to the nearest café where a very young waitress served them tea at a dirty table, slopping it into their saucers. Charles would have preferred to go to the Europa Hotel but was unsure of his ability to explain away the Browning to the searchers at the entrance without drawing attention to himself. Janet talked about the Dublin wedding, which had been a very social affair. The people who had given her a lift had lent her their car for the afternoon and were to give her a lift to the airport that night if Charles could not.

'I've only got two hours,' he said. 'One and three-quarters now.'

'That's ridiculous. Why can't they let you have longer?'

'Because they won't.'

'But why not?'

'They just won't. I was lucky to get this. We don't have time off. Everyone else is working. We're supposed to be fighting a war.'

'It's your own stupid fault for joining.'

The conversation was becoming familiar, and he had neither the desire nor the time to rework old ground. He wanted to go to bed with her and had hoped she might have somewhere to stay where they could have done it. 'I could've booked a room in an hotel but I didn't know how long I was going to have, nor how long you were going to have,' he said.

She shrugged. 'Well, it wouldn't be worth it for two hours, would it?'

He smiled. 'I don't know.'

'Unless you just want a quick screw and then back to barracks. That's what soldiers do when they're fighting a war, isn't it?'

'It wasn't just that.' He had to acknowledge, but had not time to ponder upon, the eternal duplicity of the male. He asked her about her work among the deprived families of Wandsworth, questioning her in a detail that extended far beyond his real interest. She spoke enthusiastically about it and soon became more relaxed and friendly.

115

'It's such a pity you've only got two hours,' she said, taking his hand upon the table. 'I do miss you.'

'I miss you,' he said, and again postponed thought.

They walked around the centre of Belfast, holding hands and dawdling in the drizzle. He felt less conspicuous as part of a couple. 'It all looks so ordinary,' she said. 'Just as though it's had a few fires, that's all. It's difficult to believe what you hear about it.'

He found that introducing the city to a newcomer was a wholly unexpected pleasure. 'The difficulty is that the extraordinary happens in the context of the ordinary. If it were a foreign city with foreign road signs and everything it would all be much easier to cope with and probably less of a strain. But the fact that it's so ordinarily and shabbily British makes it that much more difficult and sinister. And the people who live in it love it. It's got real heart for them. If they leave it they nearly aways come back.'

'I can understand all that, but I can't believe it's really necessary for you to walk around with a gun under your jacket like some sort of amateur James Bond.'

'But that's just what I'm saying. It's because it seems ordinary that you don't believe it's necessary. You need to see the other side of the city before you can understand that.'

'Are you sure you're not deluding yourselves and creating the very thing you claim to be opposing?'

'As sure as I can be.' He looked at her calmly confident gaze as they passed through the crowds, and despaired of being able to convey the horrible unease which the apparent ordinariness of it all gave him. The week before, a policeman in plain clothes had been shot dead in his car in the Crumlin Road as he waited at the traffic lights. His fiancée was seriously injured. Charles despaired, too, of ever being able adequately to describe to her what had happened in the cul-de-sac the other evening. 'We live in different worlds,' he added uselessly.

She took her hand away from his. 'You didn't have to choose this one.'

Her car was in one of the city centre car parks and he accepted her offer of a lift back to the Factory because time was pressing. He didn't want her to drive into any of the dangerous areas but since she had said she would anyway – to see how people lived – he thought it better to let her drop him off and then drive back than to go wandering off alone in some such place as the new estate where strange cars driven by unknown English women were likely to attract hostile attention.

They took the borrowed Mini along the Falls Road and he pointed out well-known trouble spots. Signs of recent rioting were gratifyingly visible. She was impressed, though still would not admit the need for him to carry a pistol. 'I mean, it's like carrying a pistol in Dublin,' she said. 'It would be absurd.'

'Dublin is not like Belfast.'

'You've never been there.'

'That makes no difference.'

'Of course it does.'

He pointed to a corner shop. 'A man was murdered in there four weeks ago.'

'What happened?'

'Some Protestant extremists walked in and shot him.'

'What did you do about it?'

'We weren't here then.'

They were waiting to turn right into one of the narrow streets that led eventually to the Factory, but their way was blocked by a group of women standing talking in the entrance to the street. Charles was so struck by their likeness to the harridans in the cul-de-sac that for some moments he relived his experiences of that evening, caught and frozen in a flash-back. He did not notice Janet's growing impatience until she hooted indignantly. The women turned and looked down on them. A couple began swearing at them and very quickly several more people, including two men, came out of the corner shop to see what the trouble was. The next few seconds were a maze of vivid impressions for Charles in which the past was indistinguishable from the present. The ugly, hateful, contorted faces, the raised voices and harsh accents, the suddenness of it all and the ten-fold leap in tension brought him as near to blind panic as he had ever been. He did not know what was happening nor even whether he was doing anything about it. He sat in a kind of heavy, cold numbness, unable to respond. He was distantly aware of Janet shouting something through her open window and then the car jerked forward, the women parted and the narrow street was clear before them.

Janet accelerated angrily. 'Really,' she said, sounding, Charles thought afterwards, very like her mother, 'anyone would think they owned the road, carrying on like that. Who on earth do they think they are? Stupid old bags. And one of them was holding a baby, did you see? She called me an English bitch. I told her she wasn't fit to be a mother, standing in the middle of the road like that with a baby in her arms. If it hadn't been for the baby I'd have run her over, the old cow. That's just what she reminded me of, you know, a great, bellowing, stupid, ugly old cow.'

Charles said nothing at first. Very slowly, so that she would not notice, he took his hand away from the butt of his pistol, which he had grasped under his jacket. He did not remember gripping it. His mouth was dry, his throat tight and the palm of his hand tingling hot. He swallowed with some difficulty. 'They are pretty awful, some of these people,' he said.

'I'm afraid my giving them a piece of my mind won't have done much good for neighbourhood community relations. But, there you are, if they behave like that they must expect it. I've never seen anything quite like it. Serves them right if they're unhappy.' She changed gear and turned corners with unnecessary speed as he directed her towards the Factory. She pulled up abruptly outside the main gates, watched by the sentries. 'God, what an awful place. D'you really have to live in there? I don't know how you stand it.'

They kissed goodbye, a little awkwardly. 'Write soon,' she said.

'I will.'

'You're all hot. Are you all right?'

'Yes. It's just coming back, you know.'

'Are you sure, Charles? You're sweating. You haven't got 'flu or something, have you?'

'Perhaps that's it. I'll let you know.'

'I hope you're all right. Look after yourself.'

'And you.'

'Bye.'

'Bye.' He got out and she drove off with a wave, obviously buoyed up by her confrontation with the women. He walked slowly in through the gate.

'Some 'ave all the luck, sir,' said one of the sentries, with a grin.

Seconds after he had reported back into the ops room Chatsworth pounced upon him. 'Did you screw her?' he asked.

'No.'

'Why not?'

'There was nowhere to do it.' It was a truthful response, but truthful in a trivial way. It was untruthful in that it allowed Chatsworth to assume that Charles shared his view of the relationship. Perhaps he did, ultimately, but the truth at that time was that he did not know how he viewed it.

'Very unenterprising of you,' said Chatsworth, disappointed. 'There must be an empty sangar somewhere on the Peace Line. You'd have been all right as long as there wasn't a riot.'

Charles was on duty until four the following morning, but when he finally crawled into his bed he was still preoccupied with his reaction to the women in the street that afternoon. Janet had reacted decisively and effectively. What she had done could even be called healthy and normal. He felt that his own reaction had been more than simple indecision. It had amounted to a paralysis of the conscious powers. Perhaps there was some excuse after the events in the cul-de-sac the other evening, or perhaps less because he should have learnt. He imagined that Janet would have coped with the cul-de-sac better than he had. She would certainly have fired the rubber-bullet gun, for all her stated dislike of violence. He, on the other hand, could well have shot someone dead that afternoon, acting unconsciously and unnecessarily out of fear. Fear, after all, was what it seemed to come down to.

5

Life in the Factory was monotonous but, paradoxically, the time seemed to pass quickly. Charles often had the feeling that there was much he should remember, perhaps even record in a diary, yet successive days and nights were so much alike that he could not sort one from the other. Features of military life that seemed at first to be undyingly memorable soon became so obvious and mundane that they were no longer noticed and were soon forgotten. Overall, it was the drudgery and the pettiness that were ingrained most deeply into his soul. Incidental details, such as what should be worn with what and when, had an importance which sometimes overshadowed even operational matters. At their worst these could give to Army life a horror unimagined by mere civilians, as Charles now realised. It was no one's fault that the horror was so little known. The experience could not be conveyed to those who had not had it. It was like fear and suffering, an experience so particular to each man as to be ultimately untranslatable, except in general terms. Radio-watching during the long hours of the night, patrolling the dirty, unhappy and unfriendly streets, returning to a grim and noisy home where there was no possibility of privacy, eating, living and working with the same people amidst the sounds and smells of a hundred and twenty men cramped into poor conditions all contributed to a life which seemed literally to be monotone. The streets were no relief from the Factory nor the Factory from the streets, but it was necessary to keep changing one for the other in order to make both more bearable.

Yet the time passed quickly, perhaps because it was broken up. Even though the same activities were repeated day and night their order varied and the time of doing them varied. The working day, or night, was about seventeen hours, seven days a week; sleep was irregular and frequently disturbed; anyone who had a few minutes with nothing to do simply closed his eyes and usually experienced a rapid succession of very vivid dreams from which he could nevertheless emerge immediately because he never fully ceased to hear what was going on around him. Duties and watches were simply got through; no one thought further ahead than the end of the next one; tomorrow was irrelevant to today and yet it all would end sometime, and so the present was made endurable.

Henry Sandy came one day with a complicated form. He

was supposed to compile a medical report on the working and living conditions of the soldiers. At a time when everyone looked pale and tired, he looked still worse.

'You look like death warmed up,' said Edward.

Henry proffered cigarettes to the smokers. 'Shagged out,' he explained. Henry and his medical team lived at the military hospital, where there was an abundance of nurses. The kindest interpretation of their behaviour, which he himself provided, was that his and his team's debaucheries were a vicarious acting-out of the frustrated desires of the rest of the battalion.

'Wouldn't be so bad if you didn't make it sound as though you didn't enjoy it,' said Chatsworth. 'You make it sound like a duty.'

'That's what it's becoming,' said Henry. 'I'm not sure I do enjoy it. I don't think I do really. I think I do it just to see if I'm right in thinking I'm not going to enjoy it. And I am.'

'Why keep on doing it?'

'In case I'm wrong, I s'pose. You never know your luck.' He grinned and then giggled. 'That's not really why. I don't know why. I just do it whenever I can. Perhaps I'm too emotionally immature to say no, though Christ knows there's little enough emotion involved.'

'Well, I lack emotional maturity as well,' said Chatsworth. 'And I also lack the opportunity to be immature. What about

124

me and Charles coming out one evening if we could fiddle it? Reporting sick or something.'

'Great. Whenever you like. I can easily lay on a couple of nurses. I'm not sure that Charles really wants to, though.'

''Course he does. He's just so emotionally mature that he's frightened to admit it.'

Henry spent about an hour going over the Factory, ticking boxes on his form. When he returned to the ops room he said: 'It's unfit for human habitation. Too little light, poor ventilation, inadequate washing and toilet facilities, too much noise, too many people and the cookhouse is illegal.'

'Could've told you that on the phone,' said Edward. 'Fit for soldiers, not fit for civil servants. God, imagine if they tried to send some of those fat bums in the MOD somewhere like this. Wish they would. Send a few of them out here for a week and they might spend a bit more money on the poor bloody Ackies who do their fighting for them.' Edward, mug of tea in hand, overflowed with righteous indignation. 'So what's the good of your form, Henry? What's going to happen, eh? What are they going to do about it? Sod-all, I bet.'

Henry shrugged. 'They might close the cookhouse.'

Henry then had to inspect the sentry positions along the Peace Line, and so Charles took him round with a section that was doing a routine foot patrol. Most of the positions were incorporated into barriers that cut across streets, through which only pedestrians were allowed. Thus many streets were cut in half, Protestants on one side, Catholics on the other. The houses nearest the Peace Line, where they still stood, were usually unoccupied. They were blackened and scarred by riots and pockmarked by bullets. Flush against the wire defences at one point on the Catholic side, a row of new houses had been built to replace the dozen or so that had been burnt in that area during the early riots. They stretched right across a broad street with their blank rear walls facing the Protestants. Children played against the barriers for most of the day, whether there was school or not.

'Glasgow's the only other place I know that could end up like this,' said Henry. 'Peace on condition that you annihilate the other side. Unless we get race war in our other cities.'

'Depressing prospect.'

'The future always is. In our time, anyway. In the last century people looked forward to this one as a time when everything would be better. I suppose many things are. But we're not so optimistic about the next century, are we? If anything, we think of it as a time of diminishing humanity.'

They strolled along the pavement with the escorting section spread out in tactical formation on either side of the road. Henry seemed completely relaxed but for Charles the demands of the present easily outweighed those of the future. He was constantly looking for sniping positions in windows, alleyways and blocked-up doorways. 'Perhaps we'll be as wrong about the next century as others were about ours,' he said. He had noticed in himself before that states of nervous watchfulness encouraged opinions that were more reassuring than realistic. It was as though he was thereby staking a claim in a future he was not sure of reaching.

Henry, though, was apparently oblivious to his surroundings. 'I don't believe you're that much of an optimist, Charles. Beneath that cool exterior a cold heart freezes. Things generally get worse, don't you agree?'

'It depends upon the things, which means I don't agree. Some things get worse, some get better, some don't change. Generalisations are difficult, if you'll forgive that one.'

'They're also the only things worth saying. You could record your sordid particulars for the rest of your life but it's all pointless if you're not prepared to generalise on the basis of it.'

Charles smiled. 'Some philosophers argue that the general comes first and that we fit the particulars into it.'

'Some philosophers are arse over tit,' said Henry. 'I was being serious.'

'What makes you think I wasn't?'

'You? You never are, you bugger. You're always on the fence. Serve you right if you get piles.'

Henry found that all the sentry positions lacked everything

except ventilation. 'Makes me appreciate living in the hospital,' he said as they clambered down from one sandbagged, corrugated tower. 'It has its problems, of course – too many women – but it is comfortable. It's a funny thing about the women. I'm becoming utterly depraved and heartless. I just keep on doing it with as many as possible to see how long it's going to last. There must come a time when I shall reach the bottom and be able to sink no lower, but each time I think I've got there I find I can wriggle down a bit further. D'you know what I did the other evening?' – he giggled – 'but I won't tell you, I'm still ashamed about it. I'd like to find out if Chatsworth's ever done it, though. But the trouble is, after a while, you get so that you can't think about anything else. It infects every part of your life. Don't you find that?'

'It's the other way round with me. If I'm starved of women I'm more inclined to dwell on them.'

'If I'm starved of them I just sort of forget. I become asexual until I'm with one again, and then I just want to jump on her, stoat-like, without a word, anonymously.'

They were on the Protestant side now, where the kerbstones were painted red, white and blue and the slogans were painted neatly on the roads and walls. Union Jacks hung from some of the windows, and were occasionally strung across the street from house to house. Two very small boys with very dirty faces ran up, proffering ragged bits of tartan. 'Have ye killed any

Fenians, mister?' asked one. 'We'll help ye kill 'em. We'll help ye kill the Fenians.'

They refused the tartan, meant as a symbol of identification, and Charles watched to see that the patrolling section did the same. The soldiers were strung out along both sides of the road at five-yard intervals. It was a sunny, breezy, cheerful day but there was no grass or any other greenery to be seen. At one house they were offered tea, a regular stop in that street, and they drank it on the pavement, joking with the women and playing with the children. Henry and Charles stood a little way off. For some reason it would have seemed unofficer-like to accept tea.

'The trouble with being an officer,' said Charles, 'is that it's not possible to be anything else. Everything you do is determined by what other people expect of you. You just can't help it. You can't even look like anything else.'

'Unlike your soldiers, you don't need food and drink and you have no sexual desire.'

'Nor emotion, fear or envy.'

'You are indifferent to heat and cold and to any other form of physical discomfort.'

'Wherever you are is always the best of all possible worlds.'

The tea finished, they went on their way. Without wishing to identify with the Loyalist cause, they could not but feel safer in Loyalist areas. Except in times of very bad sectarian strife they were unlikely to be shot at, whereas in Republican areas they were quite likely to be. Although they were genuinely unbiased towards one side or the other, they were less relaxed, hence more tense and watchful, in Republican areas. It was more difficult for them to be friendly even if the people had been so inclined, which they were not. The Loyalist areas were more reassuring because of their insistence upon identification with the rest of Britain, but it was a fierce and un-British insistence which made it difficult to ignore the differences. Charles felt generally comfortable but essentially fraudulent in such places.

They crossed the Peace Line and approached the monastery that dominated the Republican area, on top of which there was an Army observation post. There were the same kind of houses and the same small streets here, but the flags hanging from the windows were Republican and the slogans, instead of being anti-Catholic, were anti-Army, anti-RUC and anti-Brit. They were not anti-Protestant, as the Protestant slogans were anti-Catholic, but the Republican flags were symbols of defiance. There were fewer people in these streets, no offers of tea, no well-scrubbed doorsteps. Instead, there was an atmosphere of silent and sullen hostility. The people were quiet on the whole but they had close, hard faces and they seemed to be able to make the very brickwork seem alien. At least in the new estate the hostility was open and vociferous, but here it was suppressed and bitter. The people lived in fear of their Protestant neighbours on the other side of the wire and they relied upon the Army for protection, for which they hated the Army.

'I had a row with the CO this morning,' said Henry. 'About VD. He's got very worried about it all of a sudden. P'raps there was an article in the *Telegraph*. He said he'll bust any soldier who gets it and I said that if any soldier comes to me with it the fact shall go no further.'

'I wonder he didn't bust you.'

'He can't. Deadlock. Many more words but he can't do anything. He's absolutely furious. I have to tell him how many are ill, who they are and what diseases there are but not who has what. He has no right to know that. It's one of the few limitations of his power – in practice, anyway – and I told him so. He was speechless. He left the room and bawled out Philip Lamb because he didn't like his haircut. Said it made him look like Rudolph Valentino and told him to get it changed.'

'I should think Philip was rather flattered.'

'Either that or he'd be hurt because he thinks he's dated.'

'But how many have got VD?'

'None that I know of. That's the curious thing. They haven't had a chance, poor sods.'

'Perhaps the CO's got it.'

'Not possible. Officers don't get it.'

They were in the shadow now of the monastery. The largest building in the area, larger even than the Factory, it was a massive, solid self-assertion in the midst of the mean streets. The monks, apart from one or two who sulked, maintained the appearance of a calm and reasoned neutrality which most people took at face value but which the CO instantly mistrusted. Naturally, they looked after only those of their own faith, but it was unreasonable to criticise them for not doing more since it was only their own that came to them. To reach the observation post in the monastery it was necessary to climb an exposed spiral staircase on the outside of the building, on which a sniper had killed a soldier the previous year, and then climb through a trapdoor into what looked like a disused cell. From here they went along a wide wooden corridor and then up another spiral staircase to the top of the tower. Though they rarely saw the monks, they were often warned to be quiet and not to spend any longer than they needed in the building. The observation post was valuable. From it they could see about half of Belfast when the haze permitted, and they had a detailed view of the Peace Line and its environs. Like the monastery, the houses were nineteenth-century, humped back-to-back, with little slate roofs, tiny backyards and common alleyways which looked homely and quaint viewed from the monastery during the day but which were dirty and sinister at night. During the night the sentries operated powerful searchlights which illuminated vulnerable sections of the Peace Line and also the houses of local IRA leaders. This latter was the CO's idea: at least one light was constantly on the home of one man who was well known as an organiser of bombings and shootings but against whom it had proved impossible to get a conviction. His house was bathed in harsh light throughout the night, ensuring that no one could enter or leave without being identified. It must have seemed to the occupants as though they were in the curtained centre of a circular stage, surrounded by brilliant spotlights and a silent audience. The CO was gleeful about the idea, claiming that he was dutybound to harass the man and his family as much as possible as long as they continued threatening to kill any who might be disposed to witness against them. He was also in the habit of knocking on the man's door and chatting to him about nothing in particular – 'Just to let him know we're sitting on him. Doesn't do any harm to remind him now and again.' Despite all this, or perhaps because of it, the man and his family seemed to live a life of irreproachable ordinariness. One or two of them would even pass the time of day with soldiers if they felt in a good enough mood, or if the sun was shining.

'This is the only OP that's warm, dry and comfortable,' said Henry. 'And lonely.'

''Tis all right, sir,' said one of the two soldiers manning it, a burly Mancunian. 'Leastways, you get a bit of peace an' quiet up here.'

'McCart didn't go out to collect his brew money this morning,' said the other soldier, referring to the local leader. 'You know, his dole money. It's his day, Thursdays, signs on regular as clockwork. Must be ill or something. Or maybe they send it to him now so he don't have to get out of bed unnecessarily, like.'

As they were walking back down the stairs, Henry said suddenly, 'D'you not like sex, Charles?'

Charles was a little taken aback, never having asked himself the question before. 'Er – yes. I mean, it depends who with, doesn't it?'

Henry nodded. 'You don't, then. Or at least we're not talking about quite the same thing.'

Charles tried to ask the question of himself, with regard to Janet. It seemed for some reason to be inapplicable. So much depended upon so much else. He couldn't even say whether he would have enjoyed sex with her more if he had liked her more, or less. 'What are you talking about?'

'The idea of it, which is what you like about it even when you're not doing it, in my sense. It doesn't depend so much upon who you're doing it with because you're trying not to let the personality enter into it. The more anonymous the better.

You're trying to reduce the other person and yourself to objects, not even feeling objects but objects who are attracted basically by an idea of their own objectivity. It's a death-wish really, I think. Pornography is basically that. You should talk to Chatsworth about it.' Henry spoke as though he were giving confidential medical advice, and was referring to a well-known specialist.

'Chatsworth? Why? Is that what he thinks?'

'No, but he would if he thought at all.'

'Why are you asking me?' Charles lowered his voice because they were walking along the corridor now.

'It just struck me,' whispered Henry. 'You don't talk much about it. I think you probably have a much healthier attitude but there might be scope for a little sickness. I haven't given up hope.'

'Thanks.'

'Keep me informed. Frustration might corrupt you. It probably won't, though, that's the trouble.'

One of Charles's duties, delegated by Edward, was to write the weekly Intelligence and Community Relations reports for the C company area. The former was comprised mainly of observations provided by the soldiers and a few generalisations of his own, which were either suggestively vague or unashamedly obvious. The soldiers on their patrols would talk to anyone who would talk to them, thus giving a fair indication of the mood of the area, and they would also record minor incidents. Charles would then compile a report out of McCart's not having been seen on Monday or Tuesday and of a neighbour's remark that he was resting after the weekend troubles, listing the number of stonings and arrests and adding his own comment on the mood of the area. He found it difficult to write without any clear idea of his audience and so tailored what he produced for Nigel Beale, who strove to see significance in everything. In one report he facetiously noted an increase in the number of children's bicycles in the area, which Nigel immediately related to the use of bicycles as bombs in Vietnam, where their frames were filled with explosive. He heard later from Nigel that this part of the report had been included in the Brigade Intelligence report and that the enforced searching of bicycles was under consideration. Nigel was disappointed, and Charles relieved, when Brigade decided to await further evidence. None was forthcoming.

Similarly, Charles's weekly Community Relations reports consisted in a little mild fantasising about the 'CR climate in the area' and deliberately lengthy accounts of minor good deeds done by soldiers on their rounds. There was relatively little CR work done by any part of the battalion, partly because Anthony Hamilton-Smith was supposed to be coordinating it but mainly because most attempts by the Army to establish friendly contacts in such a strongly Republican area were doomed to failure. Even those willing to risk it in the early days of the troubles had soon been intimidated out of it, and there never had been many. A number of schemes had been tried along the lines of the 'hearts and minds' operations which had worked well in other parts of the world, such as the building of community centres and the provision of sports equipment, but it was soon found that although the money for the projects was accepted with alacrity the work on them proceeded rather more slowly. The only completed community centre had been burned down within a week because it had received Army assistance. One of the very few successful projects was the boxing club started for the youth of the area by the C company sergeant major. Two nights a week some of the children who had previously thrown bricks into the Factory yard came into an old machine room and happily thumped each other under the sergeant major's watchful eye. Within a few weeks they were taking their hands out of their pockets and greeting him as 'Sergeant Major' when they met him in the street.

One Sunday afternoon there was what was called a 'confrontation' on the Peace Line. It began with a Republican parade that passed close to one of the main barriers, a large metal and concrete structure which completely blocked what had been a main road. The parade was a procession of several hundred people led by the Seamus Murray Memorial Band, a smart affair of pipes and drums with young men and young women, as well as girls and boys, dressed in green and white costumes. The music was lively, simple and militant, and the stretch of the road by the Peace Line was lined three deep with spectators. It was an annual event, not sponsored by the IRA, but in a land where bands and parades were so loved they were also symbols of defiance or reminders of victory. Although before the recent troubles there had been some interchange of instruments, and even players, between the two communities, this was now impossible. The band was viewed by both sides as a Republican gesture.

Tim's platoon was manning the barrier and patrolling the immediate area in case of trouble. Chatsworth's was doing guard duties and resting whilst Charles's was on standby in the Factory at two minutes' notice to move. Charles had persuaded Edward to allow him to go to the barrier with his wireless operator, partly because he was curious and partly because he preferred getting out of the Factory into even the meanest of streets for even the shortest of periods to staying in. In order to do this he had had to work carefully upon Edward for most of the morning since Edward's usual reaction to any suggestion was 'no', unless he thought that the CO might think otherwise. Charles felt it was no small triumph to have got Edward to agree that he should be on the spot in case his platoon were called out so as already to have a firm tactical grasp of the situation.

It was a sunny afternoon and the sense of carnival, with the band's gay colours and lively tunes, was a welcome change in the drab surroundings. For a time everyone watching – the Protestants on the far side of the Peace Line, the soldiers manning it and the Catholic crowd whose band it was – was caught up in the atmosphere and made a part of it. Differences were not forgotten but for a short time did not matter. The large crowd following the band was organised in the traditional Republican way, with men and youths at the front and women and children at the back. The latter straggled along in happy confusion but the men and youths attempted to march in the normal IRA fashion of files of four stamping their feet, so that the background to the band music was the sinister clump of boots. They carried no weapons and wore neither berets nor combat jackets. Their faces were serious and meant to be expressionless but the effort of concentration produced a pained look on some. The clumping was at its most eerily effective when the band was silent.

Charles and his wireless operator stayed close to the barrier but were in a good position to see the parade. The attitude of the watching crowd with regard to the soldiers was probably intended to be one of contemptuous indifference, as one might regard an uninvited guest whose presence one disapproved of but with whom it was useless to argue because he had no conception of good manners, except that the Irish were unpractised at appearing indifferent and the effort plainly showed. Charles asked four people who Seamus Murray was and why he was remembered, but got no answer from the first three. The fourth replied curtly that Seamus had been murdered by the British in 1942. Charles, who still lacked cynicism, retreated in discreet and apologetic silence, only to discover much later that Seamus had been hanged for the murder of two policemen.

The trouble started when the main body of the procession had already passed the barrier. The first Charles knew of it was when a lot of bricks and stones dropped out of the sky. Within seconds the spectators near him had scattered and reformed, armed themselves with rubble and were hurling it mightily back over the barrier. Charles ran over to the barrier and saw a mob of youths on the Protestant side about twenty yards along the street throwing everything that came to hand. Most of Tim's platoon had been concentrated on the parade side of the barrier and the Protestants had obviously concealed themselves and their ammunition behind the houses in their own territory. Both sides were shouting and screaming and both were increasing by the second. The television cameramen and press photographers who had been following the parade had run back with the Catholic reinforcements and were whirring and clicking enthusiastically, which inspired all the combatants to still greater efforts.

Tim was at the barrier looking pale and harassed. Quite a few bricks were falling short and bouncing and skidding off it. Charles looked at Tim and was reminded of himself when he had been guarding, or failing to guard, the getaway car. 'What are you going to do?' he shouted.

'I've sent a sit-rep,' shouted Tim.

'Can't you stop it?'

'How the hell can I?'

'Have you asked for reinforcements?' He did not hear Tim's reply because they were both ducking and weaving like hard-pressed boxers. Reminders of his night in the cul-de-sac were getting ever more vivid. He went to where his wireless operator was crouched by the sangar, called up his own platoon on the radio and, finding they had not been deployed, ordered them down. He then heard Edward on the air frantically asking Tim for more details and not getting them.

Meanwhile the stoning had worsened. There were now about fifty youths on the Protestant side and at least twice that number on the Catholic. Tim's soldiers in between were facing both ways, taking cover by the barrier or to the flanks of it. There was no need to keep the mobs apart since their own efforts did that but neither was Tim making any attempt to quell the trouble. His NCOs were looking to him but he was huddled with his wireless operator and doing some sort of adjustments to his set. Charles felt he could not take charge of Tim's platoon and had no clear idea what he would tell them to do if he did, except to attack the rioters. As the bricks crashed and screeched off the corrugated iron sangar he wondered how soon they would become petrol bombs. Already for each side the cowering soldiers had become targets. The press kept to the fringes on both sides of the barrier, trying to photograph every brick and exposing themselves to more risks than the soldiers.

Charles did not often feel strong emotion at the sight of Sergeant Wheeler but his appearance and that of the platoon on the Protestant side of the barrier in Land-Rovers and Pigs came as a profound relief. Sergeant Wheeler, wearing his helmet and carrying a baton, ran over to where Charles was sheltering. 'Which side d'you want us to take, sir – both of 'em?'

Charles looked across at Tim to see whether he was doing anything and this time caught his eye. Tim's momentary glance did not even show recognition let alone indicate any form of action. Suddenly one of the barrier sentries, who had done as he was told and remained in an exposed position facing the Protestants, keeled over clutching his face, blood streaming out between his fingers. His rifle clattered to the ground beside him. It turned out that the right side of his face had been opened up by a sharpened penny thrown by a boy of about twelve. 'Get the Prots,' Charles told Wheeler. 'Drive them back. Arrest as many as you can.'

The platoon was already organised into snatch squads. With the example of the wounded soldier still on the ground behind them they debussed and attacked the mob from three directions. The action was pursued with what, in military terms, would have been described as vigour and purpose; according to the victims and some of the press it was pursued with a vicious and unmerited violence; according to other sections of the press it was firm, pre-emptive action. Whatever the opinion of it, the result most closely resembled dropping a ferret into a rabbit-pen. Most of the youths escaped but five were caught. A press photographer had his camera broken during the brawl which occurred when one of the arrested youths tried to escape by lashing out at the soldier who had arrested him. He had bloodied his captor's nose and had partially freed himself before his captor and another soldier laid into him with their truncheons, after which he was half-dragged and half-carried to the waiting Pig. The mob was dispersed as quickly as it had formed and very soon all that was left in the street were Charles's soldiers, a shoal of press and a great deal of rubble and broken glass.

On the other side of the barrier Tim's platoon sergeant had wisely refrained from action and was allowing the procession's own stewards to persuade the crowd to disperse peacefully. Tim seemed to have recovered his power to act and was moving about amongst his own men. He seemed deliberately to avoid Charles for some minutes but then approached him and said brusquely, 'Isn't it time you cleared your men out? It's my patch, you know.'

'They're going soon,' said Charles. 'To take the prisoners back. It might be an idea if some of them hang around in case there's more trouble.'

'I can look after that, thanks.' Tim's manner was that of an offended minor official. He turned away as soon as he had spoken. He was still very pale.

There were now only soldiers, the inevitable bystanders and a few disconsolate press, most of whom had been unable to get near enough to the trouble when it was at its most picturesque. The procession had moved on and the streets were blessedly quiet. Then there was the familiar whine of Land-Rovers driven at high speed. Edward's was the first in view, closely followed by one from battalion headquarters containing, it turned out, Philip Lamb. They stopped abruptly, a door was flung open and Edward ran, bent double, across the littered street to where Charles was standing by the barrier. He was wearing his helmet and had his pistol in his hand. He looked neither to his right nor to his left. The soldiers, the bystanders and the press all stared. Edward pushed Charles back into a corner of the barrier. 'Hard targets!' he said urgently. Charles was too surprised to speak. Edward joined Charles in the corner. Their helmets touched. 'What's happening? Where are they all?'

Charles tried to ease himself out of the corner. 'Nothing's happening. It's all over. They've all gone.'

Edward turned with his back to the wall and allowed his gaze to traverse ninety degrees, which included his own Land-Rover and all of Charles's platoon and their vehicles. He pointed his pistol at everyone as he looked. 'Who are all these people?'

Charles looked to where Philip Lamb was talking to a group of pressmen. 'They're mostly press.' Seeing that Edward still stared suspiciously at them, pistol in hand, he added, 'I'd put it away, if I were you. It might inflame them. They could photograph you.'

Edward straightened and put the gun in its holster. 'It sounded like the biggest Peace Line flare-up ever. What happened?'

'The Prots started stoning the marchers and the marchers retaliated. We dispersed the Prots and arrested five.' Charles felt quite proud and was prepared to give a detailed account.

'Great stuff,' said Edward. 'Where's Tim?'

'The other side of the barrier, I think.'

Edward, now the confident and battle-hardened commander,

adjusted his holster and strode away, casting a proprietorial glance around the area. Charles noticed Chatsworth for the first time. He was standing a few yards away kicking disconsolately amongst the rubble. 'I always miss it,' he said petulantly. 'My platoon's always resting or on guard when there's trouble. I'm not even supposed to be down here myself except that Edward's flapping around at about forty thousand feet and hasn't noticed. Was anyone killed?'

''Fraid not.'

'So it wasn't much then?'

'Not by your standards.'

'Injuries?'

'One of Tim's platoon had his face opened up.'

'Weapons?'

'Only what you're kicking.'

'All pretty tame then. Wish I'd been here, all the same.'

It was Philip Lamb's job, as PRO, to deal with the press. It was something he took very seriously, not only because it gave him a role. He had been talking earnestly to a group of them for some minutes before hurrying over to Charles. 'Charles, can you give me a quick outline of what happened? They want to interview me for ITN.' He straightened his beret unnecessarily. 'I gave them an idea based on what I'd heard over the radio, only I didn't tell them that. I must say, it sounded pretty bad. I told them about a thousand.'

'A thousand what?'

'People. Rioters. You see, most of the press got here after the worst of it was over when there were just a few stone-throwing kids. They got some good film of the arrests, though. Good work on Tim's part. But how did it start? What was the worst like?'

'That was the worst.'

'Charles, don't be unhelpful. You know you only see a very small part of it when you're on the ground. And don't play things down. We must make the most of our successes. This is very good PR for the Army, not just the battalion, averting a major Peace Line clash.' He brushed the hair back from his ears, glanced in a Land-Rover wing-mirror and brushed some forward again. 'Don't get me wrong. I would let you speak to them since you were here, but the CO has said that I'm the only one who's allowed to be interviewed apart from him, and even then I've got to be there. Not that you watch much television, do you? How many arrests were there?'

'Five, but no deaths.'

'What?'

'No one was killed.'

'Oh, I see. Any injuries?'

'One of the Ackies had his face very badly cut.'

'Did they get a picture of it?'

'I've no idea. One of the photographers had his camera broken.'

'Who by? Not by us, I hope? Is he all right? Which one was it?' In looking anxiously about, Philip noticed Edward standing in the midst of a group of pressmen, talking authoritatively into several microphones. Two cameras were whirring. 'Oh my God!' he exclaimed. 'He's not supposed to do that. He'll probably say something awful.' He rushed over to the group.

The event was the main story on the television news that evening. It was said that what could have been one of the most serious outbreaks of intersectarian violence since the troubles had begun was narrowly averted by the personal intervention of Major Edward Lumley and by prompt action on the part of his company. There was film of Charles's platoon dispersing the 'hard core of upwards of a thousand rioters', followed by an interview with Edward in which he steadfastly refused to talk about his part in the affair but described how it had started, and reiterated the Army's firm determination to keep the Peace Line intact at all costs. For a few seconds Philip Lamb's excited face filled the screen, his lips moving without sound, and then there was a shot of Chatsworth kicking the rubble with a comment from the reporter about those for whom riots were all part of a day's work. Finally there was an interview with two local politicians, one Protestant and one

Catholic, in which the Army was criticised on the one hand for allowing the trouble to start and on the other for stopping it too brutally.

The CO was delighted, and on his rounds that evening said that the brigadier himself had telephoned his congratulations for the way the thing had been handled both from the tactical and from the public relations angles. 'The trouble with this damn war is it's a PR war,' the CO said. 'It's not a soldier's war at all, and like it or not that's the way we've got to play it. But if we can keep this up we'll be all right. Well done, Edward. You did a good job.'

Edward was buoyant and agreeable for the next few days. Nothing troubled him until Anthony Hamilton-Smith, after a briefing at battalion headquarters, casually mentioned an old plan of the area which had shown a river tunnel beneath the Factory. He couldn't remember where he had seen it but he had thought it interesting at the time. He liked old plans and maps and things. In fact, he knew someone who had served in Italy during the war and who had been issued, just prior to the invasion of that delightful country, with a copy of an old medieval map which had 'Here be Dragons' inscribed across the top. He thought the plan he had seen wasn't quite that ancient but was getting on a bit. Edward, who shared neither Anthony's interests nor his phlegmatic calm, immediately saw a danger of a huge landmine being laid beneath the Factory.

An exploration party, led by the colour sergeant, went through a trapdoor in the basement floor into a dirty little tunnel that had been pointed out by one of the Factory workers. They emerged with a bundle of old pornographic magazines and the news that the tunnel was blocked at both ends. It was about twenty yards long and there was no sign of a river. It served no obvious purpose. Nevertheless, Edward was unable to rid himself of his fear that explosives could be floated down the underground river, if it existed, and he instituted several more searches.

However, tunnels remained topical. Charles was lying on his sleeping-bag one night, having just come off radio watch, when he noticed Chatsworth eating a large slice of fruit-cake. Knowing that the composite rations on which they lived included no such delicacy, Charles asked where he had got it.

Chatsworth grinned. 'D'you want some?' He handed over a piece. 'I found it.'

'Where?'

'In a place I know.'

'Remarkable.'

'In the monastery, actually. To be specific, in the kitchens. I've been exploring on night patrol recently, a little freelancing. Don't go and blurt it out to Edward.'

'You'll be crucified if you're caught. British troops invade Holy Places –'

Chatsworth laughed and slapped his thigh. 'I know, it'd be great PR, wouldn't it? Valuable fruit-cake ravaged by British child-killers.'

'But they'd slay you, you do realise that?'

'That's mainly why I do it. I need the excitement, and there isn't enough going on at the moment. And I'm very careful – I only take a slice at a time. It's a huge cake. It's in the kitchens, which are quite easy to find. There are millions of cockroaches. If you shine a torch the floor is black with them. Also, I think they keep arms down there. There are miles of tunnels which I've been exploring and I've found these packing-cases where there weren't any before.'

'They're probably full of cassocks and candlesticks.'

'In which case you'd store them, wouldn't you? There's plenty of room. You wouldn't hide them in a grimy tunnel full of rats. They're very heavy and they come from America. If you don't believe me, come with me.'

'I'm not sure I want to participate in your fantasy world.'

'Bollocks, you're scared. And you're supposed to be the company Intelligence king. You might be missing the biggest arms find ever.'

'Or a court martial.'

'But that's what makes it interesting, isn't it? All generals have to take chances.'

'What's that got to do with it?'

'Everything, if you're going to be one, as I am. I'll put you in my memoirs if you come.'

Charles did not allow himself to be persuaded there and then, but knew he would agree. As usual with people with nice consciences, he needed a little time to introduce the appropriate excuses. Once properly prepared for digestion, however, there was usually no problem. Two nights later he went out on patrol with Chatsworth and one section of Chatsworth's platoon. They went to the OP on top of the monastery and then, taking only two of the soldiers – who were only too happy to do a little illegal exploration, as they bore no responsibility for the consequences – they descended into the bowels of the building. Chatsworth led them by a spiral stone staircase that opened off the landing and through a series of corridors and further stairs until they were in a brick-built tunnel with an uneven stone floor. It was almost completely dark but Chatsworth led the way with confidence. Eventually they stopped and stood for some minutes, listening, before he switched on his torch. The light revealed a stack of about twenty oblong wooden boxes.

'There are more now than there were,' whispered Chatsworth. 'It would make too much noise to open one, though. Could nick one.'

'They'd be bound to notice. And we'd look pretty stupid if they weren't weapons.'

'They are weapons.' Chatsworth ran his fingers over the nearest box. 'They're Armalites. I can tell by the boxes.'

'How?'

'I've got one.'

'Where is it?'

'At home. You don't think I'd be fool enough to bring it out here, do you?'

Charles had learned not to be surprised by anything Chatsworth said. It was not worth asking him how he came to have an Armalite. They counted the boxes, twenty-two in all, and then made their way back out of the cellar. Once in the street, Chatsworth said, 'I reckon there's more down there. I don't know where that tunnel ends and it's probably not the only one. D'you fancy going back down tomorrow night to do a proper exploration?'

'No.'

'Chicken.'

'Well, what could we do about it? We can't go to Edward or the CO and say we've been creeping around the monastery specifically against orders and we've found some suspicious-looking boxes that might contain arms.'

'They *are* arms.'

'And if they are we don't know who put them there. It could be that all the monks are in on it or it could be just two or three of them or none at all – there might be ways in to the tunnel from the outside and the monks might know nothing about them.'

'I'm going to do something even if you're not.'

'But what?'

'Bring some out.'

'You're mad.'

'If we were all as sane as you, Charles, we'd never do anything. A little madness makes the world go round.' Chatsworth laughed. They were walking slowly, side by side, along a poorly-lit street adjacent to the monastery. The little terraced houses were dark and curtained as though their eyes were tightly shut. There was a bang from somewhere behind, not very loud, and Chatsworth dropped forward on to his hands and knees. He stayed there, propped on all fours and looking straight ahead as though waiting for a child to sit astride his back and play a game of horses and riders. 'My God, I think I've been hit,' he said.

Charles's first reaction was disbelief. The stiff-upper-lip cliché made it appear that Chatsworth was clowning. But Chatsworth remained where he was and Charles realised that he had himself taken cover in the shadow of a house, unconsciously and immediately. The rest of the patrol was also under cover. Everyone was looking about him but no one knew where the shot had come from. Helped by the wireless operator, Charles dragged Chatsworth into the shadow.

'Christ Almighty, sir, there's a bloody great hole in your flak jacket!' said the wireless operator, delightedly.

Chatsworth groaned. Even in the poor light Charles could see that there was a gaping hole in the right shoulder of his flak jacket. 'Does it hurt?' he asked.

'No. Yes.' Chatsworth remained on all fours peering ahead with a preoccupied look. 'I'll be all right. You go on without me.'

'For Christ's sake! Can you sit up?'

Chatsworth sat up slowly.

'Does it hurt now?'

'No.' Chatsworth sounded surprised and mistrustful. 'Not yet, anyway.'

Charles looked again at the rest of the patrol. Nothing moved in the street or near it and the only sound was of traffic on the Falls Road a few streets away. It must have been a one-off sniper and the gunman would by now have made good his escape from wherever he had been. It was very peaceful in the street and the monastery looming above them was almost reassuring. Charles shouted to his men to remain under cover. He then tore Chatsworth's shell dressing from where it was taped on to his belt and began feeling his chest under his flak jacket. 'I can't feel any exit wound. Does it hurt to breathe?'

Chatsworth took several deep breaths, which seemed to take a long time. 'No.'

Charles then slid his hand under the back of Chatsworth's flak jacket, beneath the hole. 'I can't feel any blood. There's a lump, though. Tell me if it hurts when I press.' He pressed lightly and from Chatsworth's convulsion and muted cry he was able to form a judgment. 'That must be it. It hasn't gone into you. Just broken the skin, I think. Better not move it, though, till Henry Sandy's had a look at it.'

Chatsworth stood up slowly. 'He'll be too pissed to see it. Where d'you think it came from?'

'No idea. Could've been an alleyway back down by the crossroads or maybe from the monastery grounds. There's been no movement anywhere.'

Chatsworth was suddenly indignant. 'I haven't been shot by a bloody monk, have I?'

They radioed the news and then waited for another patrol to join them, after which they searched the area fruitlessly. Chatsworth walked back to the Factory, which was only a few streets away, apparently fit but a little pale. There was another search the following morning, this time to locate the fire position in the hope of finding the empty cartridge case, but nothing was found. The matter was reported in terms of an FUP that was NT after an NK gunman had fired one low-velocity .45 round – in other words, after the shooting by a not-known gunman there was a follow-up but there was no trace. The bullet was thought to have come from a revolver and had been battered almost spherical on its way through Chatsworth's flak jacket. It had broken the skin and caused slight bruising but had not penetrated fully. Informed opinion had it that it must have been a ricochet, but Chatsworth never accepted this, presumably feeling that it somehow lessened the seriousness of the event. Nevertheless, there was no doubt that his flak jacket had saved him from serious injury and he was more shaken than he cared to reveal. For several days he was quieter than usual but after that he recovered his assertiveness and became very proud of his wound. Henry Sandy was treating it and found that, instead of healing rapidly as it should have, it was getting worse from day to day. He threatened Chatsworth with lead poisoning and impotence and Chatsworth then confessed to daily acerbations of the wound in order to ensure a more dramatic scar than the faded boil mark he was likely to get. The wound then healed but Chatsworth kept his holed and slightly bloodstained shirt as a relic and refused to have his camouflage smock replaced. He repaired it himself with a conspicuous cross patch of tape on the tear but he did, nevertheless, exchange his flak jacket for an intact one.

There was a more immediate result of the incident. The CO came to the Factory that night to get a first-hand account from Chatsworth – who was able to tell him even less than anyone else since he had not even noticed the shot. None the less, the

CO listened gravely, smoothing his black hair with the palm of his hand, and then said: 'I've been expecting this for some time. You realise that. But I didn't expect it here. Deliberate, calculated murder – it would have been if it hadn't been for your flak jacket. You're a very lucky young man, you realise that. Strange that they should have used a revolver, if that's what it was. A high-velocity rifle would have been far more effective, as they must know only too well. Which leads me to believe that it might have been someone doing a bit of freelancing. Not a properly set-up job. It's a pound to a penny it was someone from the new estate rather than one of the boyos from here. They don't like shitting on their own doorsteps, these people.' He looked at the tired, respectful faces surrounding him in the ops room. 'But I'm glad it happened, very glad. There's a lesson here for all of us – hard targets. If I've said that once I've said it a thousand times. Have I not, Edward?'

Edward, who had been fiddling with a government issue biro, looked up earnestly. 'Yes, sir. More than once.'

'Hard targets, gentlemen. I cannot emphasise that enough, though God knows I've been saying it since before we arrived. And yet still – still – people – or, rather, officers – walk in pairs beneath street-lamps in terrorist areas and wonder why they get shot. Think yourselves lucky, all of you, even those who weren't there, because you could well have been. Any questions?'

The CO looked around, his jaw thrust forward as though that was where he wanted to take the questions when they came. But none came, his glance softened, he allowed his lips to relax into a wry little smile and his brown eyes twinkled. 'Good. Take it you all understand. Now for the good news. Within the last hour a car was stopped at a VCP in the City Centre. Five men in it, three of them armed, and all five live in the new estate. The brigadier wants us to search their houses in conjunction with the RUC, and we are at this very moment waiting for confirmation from Brigade. It'll stir up trouble, I daresay, but that's all right with me. Good. Now, three platoons from A and Support companies will RV here in fifteen minutes. Their job is to stand by in case of trouble. Edward, I want your platoons to do the actual search because they know the estate best. I shall lead the attack but I want you on hand to deal with any trouble the way you dealt with that Peace Line business – straight in and no nonsense. Don't give 'em a chance to get going. Okay?'

'Right, sir.' During the next half hour preparations were made and Edward bustled around busily, becoming the more irritable as his grasp of what was going on grew weaker. The CO was also busy being decisive but was obviously in high good humour. At one point he clapped his hand on Chatsworth's injured shoulder and said, 'Well done, my boy, well done. You've done the battalion a power of good. Keep it up.'

When the three standby platoons arrived there was more noise and confusion in the Factory than ever. The ops room became an extension of battalion headquarters, taking on its atmosphere of tension, panic, fear and frenetic activity. Very soon everyone seemed to have at least three things to do which depended upon their getting hold of someone else who either couldn't be found or also had three things to do. The CO gave orders in a loud voice and then demanded in an even louder voice to know what had happened about them. Edward flapped and squawked like a worried hen but no one paid him any more than the most formal attention. It was a place that Charles would normally have sought to avoid with all manner of ruses and stratagems, but on this occasion he hung around trying to have a word with Nigel Beale. He and Chatsworth had decided to pass on to Beale, in a suitably disguised form, the information about the boxes in the monastery. In remaining in the ops room at such a time they risked being given unnecessary tasks or being accused of being idle, which amounted to the same thing, but they had decided the matter was of sufficient importance to justify temporary discomfort. Chatsworth was despatched to do a weapon inspection before they had a chance to get to Beale, who was busy with the CO, but Charles persisted and eventually got him alone. He told him that a man had approached them on the street, some time before the shooting, and had told them that there were boxes with weapons in them hidden in a tunnel beneath the monastery. Such incidents were not uncommon: people sometimes approached patrolling soldiers at night and volunteered information of varying importance and reliability. Often they would just say that there was a weapon in number forty-six or that there was going to be trouble on Saturday, but they would never reveal their identities or how they came by the information. Nevertheless, the soldiers who patrolled regularly knew some of them by sight.

Nigel was intensely interested. 'He told this to you and Chatsworth? How reliable is it?'

'No idea. Never seen him before.'

'Sounds very plausible, though. Just the sort of place they would use if they could get access to it. Probably Armalites.'

'That's what we thought.'

Beale looked suspicious. 'What made you think that?'

'They said on television that Armalites were coming from America.'

Nigel drew closer. 'Keep this to yourself, Charles. Even if there's nothing in it we don't want it getting about. It would be a dangerous rumour to have around. I'll pass it on to the CO as soon as I can get a word in.' He made a crabbed little note on his mill-board and nodded conspiratorily to Charles.

The search teams moved out at 2245 hours. The search was

161

to go in at 2300. Charles had with him a corporal and three soldiers, as well as three RUC constables who were to do the actual searching. In charge of the RUC men was a Sergeant Mole, sent from the police station occupied by battalion HQ. He was a portly, silver-haired, easy-going man with a pleasantly soft accent instead of the usual Belfast one. 'Ever done a search before, sir?' he asked Charles.

'No, I haven't. I shall be looking to you for guidance, Sergeant Mole.' It had taken Charles some time to get used to the RUC's strict adherence to military command structures.

Sergeant Mole lit his pipe, his double chin bulging over his green collar. He looked reassuringly avuncular. 'Nothing to worry about, sir. I'll do the talking and you send your men clean through the house into every room straightaway in case there's anyone who wants to try any funny business. Tell them to get everyone in the house down into the front room. Then search the garden and any sheds. When we start to search we'll take a room each and have one of your men with each of us in case we find any villains hiding in the airing cupboard or in case anyone claims we planted a howitzer in there. Wouldn't be the first time, I'm afraid.'

They moved in convoy to the estate and then each search party, with its escort, drove quickly to its appointed address. The estate was unlit, as usual, although many of the houses still had their lights on. It was not a cold evening, and groups of people sat drinking on some of the doorsteps. Other groups were gathered on street corners. Derisive shouts followed the convoy as it moved in and there was a desultory banging of dustbins, but the operation was mounted too quickly for the warning to be effective.

The object of Charles's search was an end-of-terrace house with a rubbish-heap of a garden but no broken windows and a front door that still showed traces of paint. The escort party debussed and crouched by the tatty privet hedges in the street while a couple ran round to the back of the house to cut off any escape through the gardens. Sergeant Mole knocked on the door with Charles beside him and the rest of the party by the side wall out of sight. It was opened by a diminutive, middle-aged woman with grey hair, a bony, wrinkled face and glasses with very thick lenses. 'Mrs Ray?' asked Sergeant Mole. She stared at the uniformed men. Her lips moved once as though to speak but she said nothing. 'We've arrested your son Michael and I'm afraid we're going to have to search your house, Mrs Ray.' She still said nothing. Sergeant Mole stepped purposefully inside and she moved back hesitantly. 'I'm sorry, Mrs Ray, but we have to search the house.' She let go of the door handle and ran into the living room with one hand over her face. Charles stepped inside and beckoned the soldiers to follow. There was an unpleasant, airless smell, and the sounds of a television came from the living room. The corporal and one soldier ran straight

upstairs, their boots thumping heavily, and the two other soldiers went quickly through the downstairs rooms. Charles
followed Sergeant Mole into the living room. The woman
stood by the electric fire, still with one hand over her face, holding a girl of about twelve with the other. A short, fat man with
curly dark hair and wearing braces turned down the sound on
the television. 'Sorry to have to do this, Mr Ray,' said Sergeant
Mole, 'but your son was found driving a car in which there
were arms and wanted men. Could you tell me which is his
room?'

'Back room,' said the man, in a matter-of-fact way.

'He shares wid his brothers,' added the woman quickly.
'He's no harm, they're no harm, none of them.' She pulled the
girl closer to her. One of the soldiers came in with two boys,
one in his teens and the other about nine or ten. They were
tousled and frightened. The smaller one wore dirty underpants
and the elder held a pair of jeans around himself. The soldier
who shepherded them in looked embarrassed. 'Found them
upstairs, sir. No more.' He went back up the stairs.

Sergeant Mole then left the room and the woman put her
arm round the girl, as though to prevent her from being
touched by anyone. The little boy sat on the tatty sofa and the
elder one stood sullenly by the electric fire, his hands in the
pockets of his jeans. The man said something which Charles
had to ask him to repeat. He said it again but Charles's ear was

unaccustomed to the thick West Belfast accent. Finally, the man repeated the four words with sarcastic slowness. 'Is-he-all-right?'

Charles was concentrating so much on understanding that he had to think for a moment who was meant. 'Yes – yes, as far as I know,' he said. 'I think he's all right. There was no trouble, I believe.'

'Where is he?'

'He's in custody. I'm afraid I don't know where. I wasn't there.' There was a silence. Charles felt sorry for the people and wanted to say so, but he knew that anything he said or did would be filtered through the medium of his boots, beret, flak jacket and rifle. There was no escaping his role. 'I'll try to find out for you,' he said lamely in the end. Advertisements flickered soundlessly across the television screen. The man moved an ashtray from the arm of the sofa to the mantelpiece.

'I'll make tay,' muttered the woman. She took her hand from her face and walked with tightly-folded arms out of the room. The girl ran after her.

'I'll see if I can find out where your son is,' Charles said again, but the fat man turned his back and sat on the sofa without speaking. The two boys stared. Charles went upstairs and asked Sergeant Mole, who was turning out a cupboard in the front bedroom. 'This hasn't been turned out since the house was built,' he said with genuine disgust. 'You can smell it in the street, I reckon.' By the time Charles got back down the woman had made the tea and was standing sipping it, holding the cup in both hands. 'He's in Hastings Street police station,' he said.

The woman's eyes, enlarged by her spectacles, looked directly at him for the first time. 'He's never in no trouble,' she said. 'He ain't any of them. He don't have no trouble wid him.' Her lips trembled. 'God strike me dead if I lie.'

Charles was called out of the room by a voice from upstairs. As he left the room he caught his rifle butt on the door-jamb. He looked back to apologise but said nothing.

His corporal was at the top of the stairs. 'Found something, sir,' he said in a low voice. 'In the back room.' The room was very small and there was hardly room to move around the double bed. It was where the three boys slept, and was filthy. The room stank. One of the policemen held up the top end of the mattress. On an old brown blanket beneath was a rusty revolver with a broken handle. It seemed a pitiful gesture. Sergeant Mole picked it up in a piece of cloth. 'Old Webley,' he said. 'Very old. Loaded, too. Silly young fool. It'll have his paw-marks all over, I don't doubt. What a place to hide it, eh?'

Nothing more was found in the rest of the house. Sergeant Mole showed the revolver to the family in the living room. They gazed sullenly at it. The woman blinked tearfully. 'He's had no trouble before,' she said. 'He niver told us he had that.

It's no hisn, it can't be. Someone else has put it there.' She pressed a tightly-screwed handkerchief to her thin nose. 'It's never his, it can't be his. He never told us about it. Dear God, it can't be hisn. He would've said. He's not with them. He's not a part of it.'

Sergeant Mole wrapped the revolver preciously in a piece of cloth. The man stared at the threadbare carpet. No one looked up at them when they left.

Only one of the other houses searched yielded anything, in this case a worthwhile find. There was an old British Army .303 Lee-Enfield rifle, two hundred rounds of 7.62 ammunition, twenty pounds of home-made explosive and, under the floor of a shed, a home-made mortar. The CO was delighted and stayed in the area of the search longer than was necessary in the hope of provoking a riot which he could quell, but none came. It was likely that the trouble, if there were any, would be a planned demonstration some days later, although even this was not that likely since trouble usually followed fruitless rather than successful searches.

Back in the Factory the CO had drinks in the ops room and ordered everyone to join him. Drink and his own boisterous good humour accentuated all his normal characteristics, and he gave a lecture on the Lee-Enfield, using the captured one as a demonstration model. When he had finished, his eyes lighted upon Charles. 'Ah, Charles, I want to speak to you.' Still holding the rifle, he grabbed Charles by the arm and propelled him into a corner where he spoke in low, earnest, conspiratorial terms, apparently imagining that no one else was listening. 'You've done well, you've done bloody well, but it's not on, I'm afraid. Politicians won't allow it. Too much of a hot potato. Sorry to disappoint you.'

'Right, sir.' Charles was not certain that he knew what the CO was talking about, but it was a response that worked its usual magic.

'Good man. Knew you'd take it like that.' He squeezed Charles's arm hard, his dark eyes brimming with sincerity and alcohol. 'It's infuriating, I know. We know they're there but we can't touch them. Had it right from the top. They must have a source. Keep it under your hat. And to think they could be used on my soldiers, that's what makes me want to scream blue murder. I'd raze the place to the ground if I had my way. Rid these poor people of their priests, their politicians and their paramilitary thugs – and us, mind you, and us – and give them a chance to get on with their lives in peace. The day will come, I hope. For the time being no joy, though. But you did well, Charles. Let's have more of it.'

The CO grinned and punched Charles playfully in the stomach. His face was so close that Charles could see the back of his tongue. 'Good man. Have another drink. Don't argue. We'll knock this university stuff out of you yet.'

Charles made his escape unnoticed after the CO had finished with him. He lay down in his partition but could hear the drinking going on for another couple of hours. Months later it fell to the company officers to pay for the drinks.

Part Two

To Battalion Headquarters

6

The company's spirits remained relatively high for some days after the arms finds. The shooting of Chatsworth also contributed to good morale. Everyone was amused because it was Chatsworth, and the story was put about, to his annoyance, that he really had been shot by a monk. Soldiers made jests to him about what clerical gentlemen carried beneath their vestments, and how the real meaning of Holy Orders was 'Aim – steady – fire'. Spirits were lifted by the mere fact of a shooting, since something happening was always more exciting than nothing.

The worst times for everyone were periods of inactivity during which the boredom and the drudgery of military life wore on remorselessly. Like everyone else, Charles was short on sleep and temper and was, indeed, more tired than during active periods because then the excitement was stimulating and the tiredness healthy. Living conditions in the all-male military community were cheerless and sordid; patrolling, guarding, cleaning and watchkeeping formed a grinding and unending routine.

173

Underlying everything in his life was the feeling that no one in the world cared for him. He suspected that everyone felt this. It was evident in occasional surliness and in the deliberate, hearty display of lack of emotion. The positive side of this was that he found he worried less about his own concerns but at the same time he cared less for other people, and noticed them less.

Each man developed a front of unconcern, which in some was ingrained, to the extent that the more he hardened himself the more he relied upon the corporate identity to take the place of his own. This corporate identity could be seen and felt: each man borrowed from it and lent to it; it embraced all and excluded none, to such an extent that all seemed merely to be aspects of it. It was difficult to say how much these conditions contributed to the suicide of Lance-Corporal Winn but, whether or not they acknowledged it, everyone felt that the contribution must have been substantial.

Lance-Corporal Winn was a small, chunky soldier from Birmingham, a man of few words but reliable and conscientious. He appeared to have little or no ambition to distinguish himself but simply jogged along and 'kept his nose clean', as the Army would have it. Charles knew him by sight but had never spoken to him, except to give orders when mounting guard in Aldershot. In time he would probably have made sergeant. The day before his death he had been told by another soldier, who had had a letter from his own wife, that back in Aldershot his wife had been carrying on with someone from one of the other regiments there. He had not said much about this at the time. In fact, his informant had had the impression that he didn't much care. He had been on guard duty that night and had shot himself just after six, when he had come off duty. He had walked over to where the Pigs were parked in the Factory yard and had gone behind one of them. His relief, who had not spoken to him except to remark upon the cold, had assumed that he had gone to pee against the wall. When the shot came, he and one of the other guards had run to the Pig and found Winn on the ground behind it, but with the back half of his head splattered over the wall. He had apparently rested his rifle butt on the ground, bent over and put his mouth round the barrel.

Winn was in Tim's platoon and Tim had been roused immediately. Henry Sandy was sent for and the body taken away in his Land-Rover ambulance. The padre came and Tim was unnecessarily rude to him. Arrangements were made to inform Winn's widow through the Families officer in Aldershot. The CO appeared during the morning and talked to Edward, Tim and the soldier who had received the letter. The effect on the company – and, to a lesser extent, on the rest of the battalion – was to lower morale for a few days. Everyone was quieter and more serious, there was none of the normal banter and boisterousness amongst the soldiers nor any of the perennial grumbling that was so necessary to them. However, things were done quietly and conscientiously, and there was less fuss. But days pass in the Army as they do everywhere else and normality reasserts itself with the willing assistance of everyone, perhaps more quickly than in civilian life because of the consciousness of common purpose. Layer upon layer of daily and nightly routine soon smothered any exceptional event.

Charles was not sorry, though, when a telephone call summoned him with all his kit to battalion headquarters. There had been another shooting: Philip Lamb had inadvertently shot himself in the foot and Charles had to take his place as PRO. He was glad to leave the company and the Factory. The people and the place had become depressingly familiar, like a tedious argument for ever repeated and never resolved. There was a dreary intimacy about it all from which he was glad to free himself. The police station occupied by battalion HQ, though far from comfortable, could not fail to be an improvement upon the Factory, and dealing with the press would be a welcome change from the sordid concerns of his platoon, where kit inspections and deficiencies seemed to be the paramount concern in his life. Sergeant Wheeler was to look after the platoon until a new subaltern arrived from the Depot. Charles bade him goodbye in the Factory yard with what seemed even to himself an absurd formality considering he was moving half a mile or so.

''Spect we'll see you back with all them press poofters, sir,' Sergeant Wheeler said as they shook hands.

'No doubt, and I shall expect your help.'

'You'll be too good for us then, sir. You won't want to know us.'

'Goodbye, Sergeant Wheeler. Good luck.'

'Goodbye, sir, and you, sir.'

Despite the relief at leaving the Factory there were disadvantages about going to battalion HQ. It was renowned throughout the battalion as a place of madness and fear. In addition to the loathing which most soldiers have for the headquarters of higher formations, even their own, the personality of the CO pervaded the building and induced in all who entered it a sense of urgency bordering on panic and the feeling that heads were about to roll. As Charles's Land-Rover entered the gates into the yard around which the police station was built he already began to feel that there had, after all, been something homely and reassuring about company life. Battalion HQ contained much that was unknown and hence dangerous for second lieutenants. No move in the Army was entirely for the better.

'Going to be murder with the CO breathing down your neck all the time,' Edward had said. 'Rather you than me, old son. Still, it's more your sort of line, I suppose, all this press rubbish. You read books. Apparently, the new chap we're getting is very good. Bit of life and a drop of new blood won't do the company any harm. Drop in and see us sometime when you're swanning around. Don't forget to hand your kit in to the company stores. And your rifle.'

'No more action for you,' Chatsworth had said. 'You're being more or less pensioned off. There might be some women amongst these journalists, so bear me in mind. You know, the sort who have to do it to prove to themselves how liberated they are. With a chauvinistic Ackie shit like me they can feel they're even more liberated than they thought by embracing the opposition, so to speak. Poor fools. Bring 'em round for an interview.'

It turned out that Philip Lamb had shot his foot whilst entering B company's location with a TV team. While unloading his pistol for the sentry's inspection, as was compulsory when entering any defended area, he had carelessly cocked it with the full magazine still in and, pointing towards the ground, had squeezed the trigger to clear it. The TV team had filmed his subsequent writhings. It was the first negligent discharge in the battalion and the CO, who was furious, had fined him heavily. He had brought public disgrace to the regiment and the CO was determined not to have him back.

Charles reported to the adjutant, Colin Wood. Colin, who

had left the Army to go into business and had rejoined it after marrying, looked as weary and long-suffering as might be expected of anyone who worked closely with the CO. But he had a reputation for competence and sanity, and his face was kindly. Having been outside the Army, he did not regard all civilians as odd nor all subalterns as criminally irresponsible. 'Nice to have you with us, Charles,' he said, balancing on the rear legs of his chair and clasping his hands behind his head. 'We could do with a new face round here. You've got a pretty cushy job, but apart from that it's all bad news. You're sharing a bedroom with Tony Watch and an office with me. You're on the list for watchkeeping in the ops room, which means three eight-hour shifts a week – six till two, two till ten, ten till six. You also have to help me deal with complaints from the locals, of which there are many, and you have some sort of responsibility under Anthony Hamilton-Smith for community relations. Though I don't think there's too much of that going on. There's a telly in the Mess, which sometimes works, the food's awful and we're still not allowed gravy. You have to wear a pistol and carry ammunition at all times, including in the bath if you can find one, so better draw one from the armoury. We're not allowed out, of course, except on duty, and the press, I'm told, can be very difficult. If anyone in the battalion cocks it up the CO will hold you responsible. Apart from all that it's heaven.'

Colin's office was on the first floor of the building above the entrance, overlooking the street. The police station had been built during the late 1950s and, like many of Ulster's police stations, was halfway towards being a fortified barracks from its very inception. There were steel shutters on all the windows through which the defenders could fire, if necessary, by sliding little peep-holes to one side. The office floor, Charles was told, was eighteen inches of reinforced concrete and supposed to be blast-proof. Surprisingly, though, the entrance to the police reception area was unguarded – on orders from some civilian official, who was anxious that members of the public should not feel intimidated in coming to police stations. There was an Army guard inside, however. It did not take Charles long to settle in, if dumping his kit on a bed in the corner of a disused office could be called settling in. At least this time the bed was a real one, with blankets and sheets.

Charles was then sent down to the military hospital to be 'put in the picture' – a very common phrase – about his new duties by Philip Lamb. Philip was in a junior officers' ward for not too serious cases, a quiet and lightly populated place. His right foot was bandaged and supported. He was propped up on pillows, reading David Stirling's account of the formation of the Long Range Desert Patrol Group, later to become the Special Air Service. Philip was one of the few officers Charles had met who seemed to take a serious interest in war. His neat, precise face looked as worried and anxious as usual but he smiled when he saw Charles. 'I'm so glad it's you,' he said. 'Do sit down. The CO was going to appoint Chatsworth, of all people. Can you imagine? He'd kill somebody, he's so tactless. I sent a message to him through Colin saying that you were the only officer in the battalion who could read English, let alone write it. He must have listened to me for once. Because, of course, it is a job that requires a certain amount of judgment, as you'll have gathered, and you have to be able to see things from the point of view of a civilian. It's ridiculous to suppose that most of our comrades-in-arms could ever do that. You were the obvious choice. Of course, your problem's the other way round, if anything. You'll have no problem about not being too military but you mustn't let them forget that you are in the Army. Hope you don't mind being pushed into it like this?'

'It didn't take much pushing. I was only too pleased to get out of the Factory.'

'Of course, yes. Must've been rather grim there. I'm sorry to leave the job, to be honest. I didn't want to. I could've come back when I'm better but the CO didn't seem to want me. I think he's rather angry about what I did, though it could have happened to anyone, as far as I can see. Just one of those things.' He closed his book and changed his position carefully. 'There are a few perks to the job, you know, apart from meeting the journalists, who are very nice. You can occasionally put on civilian clothes and visit their offices, and you don't have to do watchkeeping.'

'I do.'

'Do you really?' Philip looked puzzled. 'I never did. Perhaps they didn't trust me. Anyway, you'll find all the necessary files in my office, as well as a kind of Who's Who of the press in Northern Ireland. The PR desk at HQ are also very helpful. That's another little swan you can arrange for yourself – visits to them. Not that they're a waste of time, far from it. But it's just very good to get out of battalion HQ now and again. Clears the cobwebs of the mind a little and even breathes hope of life into the soul. Perhaps that's going a bit far, but you know what I mean. It's good to get out.'

'Thanks. What about the press themselves?'

'Very charming on the whole. I think so, anyway. Of course, you have to protect them from the CO. He can be quite beastly and ruin in a minute all the good-will you've built up over a month. Actually, I think he's terrified of them, though there are a couple you have to be careful with, I must admit. There's one called Brian Beazely who's the most awful incompetent, drunken bore, to be avoided because he's a nuisance rather than malicious – has been known to misquote rather embarrassingly. And then no one ever believes your side of it. They all think you must have said whatever it was because it's there

in print. Such is the power of Master Caxton. And the other
one to watch for is Colm McColm of the *Gazette*, the *Southern
Irish Gazette*. He's very anti, and the trouble with him is he'll
quote you exactly, which is almost as bad. Very pro-IRA.
Probably in it, for all I know. He can hear a whisper from two
streets away, so watch him. Always asks awkward questions in
public.'

'Where do you meet them?'

'Oh, they'll come to you. You'll get to know them soon
enough.' He fidgeted a little with the bedclothes and Charles
was about to ask him about his foot, which he would have
done before had Philip not been so eager to talk about the job,
when he continued morosely: 'I suppose you'll have my pistol.
I'm sure there's something wrong with it, you know. I wish
they'd let me just have another look at it. I took it on the range
four times and it misfired on three. Then it fires when it
shouldn't. The armourer examined it and said it was just me
but I don't think he was interested, so do be careful, Charles.
As it was, I was rather lucky. Apparently, I'll be all right, but
I'll have to learn to walk again, they tell me. It was the first
time I'd ever hit anything with it.'

Charles tried to be cheerful. 'Perhaps you'll get compensation. Terrorists do, don't they? So there's no reason why you
shouldn't.'

'If I did it might go some way towards paying the fine, but

I don't suppose I shall. I mean, they look at it differently if you do it yourself. I've found my insurance doesn't cover it either. D'you know, the CO was going to charge me with self-inflicted injury, a court-martial offence, I think? I had to fill in no end of forms to prove it wasn't deliberate, though how they prove anything, I don't know.'

Philip was looking increasingly miserable. Charles made another effort. 'What are the other people in here like?'

'Oh, all right, I s'pose. Usual sorts, you know. Trouble is, they were all shot by someone else. It makes a difference. That I wasn't and that I am the education officer has become something of a joke. The whole hospital knows about it and all the visitors. Some of them even come to see me and laugh. I think it's all a little insensitive to be honest.'

Philip had been a joke in the battalion ever since joining it, and his manner of leaving delighted nearly everyone. However, he was soon forgotten about by all except Charles, who was really no more at home with a pistol than Philip had been and who feared daily to share his predecessor's fate. Though less cumbersome and heavy than the rifle he had been used to, the disadvantage of the Browning was that it had to be carried at all times, with two full magazines of ammunition, on pain of a heavy fine. It was so odd to be taking a pistol to the bath, or tucking it under the pillow, that it was not difficult to remember it on these occasions. The difficulty was to remember it at the meal-table or at the desk. When indoors Charles generally wore it tied around his waist or in his pocket and when out he wore it in its holster in the cross-draw position, mainly because it was more comfortable to sit in the Land-Rover with it that way round. Either way, it was a mental as well as a physical burden, and he felt some rare sympathy for the gun-toting boys who were supposed to be trying to kill him. At least he did not have to hide it as well as remember it.

The CO's briefing for his new job took place over dinner that night. The Mess was a small room adjacent to the ops room, from which the mush and crackle of the radios never ceased. Meals were eaten at a table behind a partition and were served from a hot-plate, as the cookhouse was at the far end of the building.

'Good to have you with us, Thoroughgood,' the CO said as they helped themselves to soup. 'Makes a change from the Factory, doesn't it?'

'Yes, sir.'

'If only the public knew what a pittance we pay our soldiers and what these blasted car-workers and miners and what have you get for kicking their heels and complaining because they have to work at all. Eh?'

'Yes, sir.'

They sat and the CO called for some wine 'Must have some

plonk to wash it down with. We take it in turns to buy every night. Your turn tomorrow, Charles.' He laughed and the others at the table laughed with him, except Colin Wood, who raised his eyebrows at Charles and shrugged discreetly. When he had finished laughing the CO continued. 'Reason I picked you for this job – which is a vitally important one and is becoming more so every day' – his stomach hardened and he held his chest for a moment's indigestion, before continuing to pour out the wine – 'God, it's an important job. This PR business is taking us all over, you know. We're fighting a politician's war now, not a soldier's war, as I keep saying till I'm blue in the face. Not even a decent shooting war, nothing to get stuck into. Aden and Borneo were different, of course, farther away, much easier. Government doesn't like shit on its own doorstep but that's its problem, not ours. We've got them over a barrel this time. They can't pull out of this one. But we must keep our noses clean, which is why I chose you, Charles. Bit of tact. The soft touch. Besides which, you're the only one of my subalterns whom I was sure could read and write. No names, no pack drill, but some of them graze their knuckles on the ground when they walk – not that they won't make good officers, mind, in time. First-rate some of them, what the regiment needs. And I imagine you must have met some of these journalist types at university, or something like them anyway. Same sort of animal. What's-his-name – old doings – Philip Lamb –

gave you a decent briefing, did he? Good. Well, you'll have your own vehicle, one of my escorts, so you can swan around and deal with these people when you're not out with me. Keep them off my back and off the backs of my soldiers, that's the main thing. No one in the battalion, including myself, will talk to any member of the press unless you are present. Got that? You will make sure that no one says anything bloody stupid and that nothing's wheedled out of them. You can't be too careful with some of these bloody journalists. You will also keep a sharp eye out for any of these directional microphones I keep hearing about and make sure no one says anything they shouldn't when they're around. And, of course, you'd better watch your own step when you're talking to these chaps. Remember that the American Army's effort in Vietnam was ruined because they had to cope with the press as well. Point is, Charles, if anything goes wrong I'll know who to blame. Okay? Good. You're responsible for community relations, under the 2IC. He'll brief you on that separately.' The CO raised his glass. 'Best of luck, and don't blow your foot off.'

Tony Watch, the signals officer with whom Charles shared his bedroom, was a brisk, chubby, cheerful man with a moustache. He seemed to be energetically efficient, enjoyed his signals and enjoyed his pipe, which he smoked nearly all the time. He was married but it was some weeks before Charles discovered that. Tony was not a man to talk about himself.

Indeed, he had little to say about most things, though he was prepared to comment briefly on anything. His views on most subjects boiled down to a simple choice of either/or; you could always have one thing or another but you could never have both, and you were darned lucky if you could even choose which; on the whole, you just had to like it and lump it, whatever it was.

Tony was already in bed when Charles decided to turn in. He was reading a car magazine and smoking his pipe. 'Hope you don't mind the pipe,' he said. 'Say if you do. Can't sleep without a pipe before bed. Can't open the windows because of these shutters. Though yours hasn't got one, has it? So you could. Might get shot, I s'pose.'

There was a window above each bed, and Tony's, as with every other window in the building, had a steel shutter over it which had to be shut whenever there was a light in the room. Charles's was the exception: no shutter and no sign of there ever having been one.

'Don't understand that,' said Tony, taking his pipe out of his mouth and craning his neck. 'Only thing you can do is stuff your kitbag in it. Not that that would stop a peashooter, but it'll make you feel better. You'll just have to be a bit careful how you get in and out of bed and not hang around with the light on.'

The bed was parallel with the wall, and the window was

about halfway along it. The room was so small that there was nowhere else to put the bed. That night, and for the rest of his time there, Charles entered his bed from the bottom, sliding on his belly like a snake. He left it each morning by lowering himself off the side.

Tony followed the first of these performances with interest. 'That's the stuff. Keep your arse down. You won't be spending much time there anyway, so it shouldn't be much of a problem. This is the first time I've been in bed before two since we got here. CO must be tired.'

Routine at battalion HQ turned out to be even more tiring than that in the companies. The hours were much the same but there was no patrolling to break the monotony. Because it was battalion HQ no one felt he could do anything safely, even though everyone would have benefited from more sleep, and so people sat at their desks or radios long after there was any need. The CO drove himself mercilessly and none of the officers felt justified in going to bed before he did. Just as he would probably not have noticed if they had, and would probably not have criticised them for doing so, so he did not notice that they were waiting upon him.

Sharing the adjutant's office gave Charles a different view of the workings of the battalion to that which he had seen so far. People in the companies tended to feel, consciously or not, that battalion HQ existed in order to support them. How well or badly they thought it did this varied from day to day, though at its best it was never regarded as being any better than it ought to be and usually it fell far short. The point was, they were in the front line, hence they were the centre of the world and everything else was eccentric. In battalion HQ, however, everyone was quite clear that this was where the war was really being waged, and that the companies were, at their best, merely an extension of battalion HQ's will and at other times selfish, myopic irritants who had to be coped with along with the lunacies of battalion HQ's other major problem. Brigade. At their worst the companies were thought to be a greater nuisance than the enemy, whoever he might be. Brigade was seen as a support organisation, usually inadequate and interfering, overstaffed and safe from all danger.

Fortunately, Colin Wood was an easy man to get on with. He had a quiet, wry humour and time for everyone. The only signs of the pressure he worked under – much of it caused by the administrative quirks of the CO – was that he smoked about sixty cigarettes a day and looked unnaturally pale. Charles, if he were free from his own work, would often help him out. After a while Colin became quite forthcoming about the CO, the company commanders, battalion rivalries and Brigade matters, but more often than not he had little time for small-talk. One evening the telephone they shared went out of order and Charles speculated that, with luck, it had succumbed to a telephonic disease that might spread to all the other phones in the building and give everyone a peaceful night. 'It might even drive the CO to drink and despair,' he said.

Colin shook his head. 'It might drive him to all sorts of places but not to drink. He never gets drunk. He gets merry, tipsy now and again, but he never has that much and he never gets really drunk. He likes the good cheer, but that's all.'

'I've never noticed,' said Charles. 'I mean, he often has a glass in his hand and you can see it in his eyes when he's had a few. I admit I've never seen him properly drunk.'

Colin leant back in his chair, balancing on the two rear legs with the back of his head against the wall. He lit a cigarette. 'His father was a doctor in Leeds, an alcoholic, and I think he gave the family a hard time. Eventually he left – ran off with another woman, I think – and died in Newcastle. The CO was brought up by his mother in much reduced circumstances and he was put through school by an uncle. He had a younger brother who died when he was very young – about four or five – and for some reason he always seemed to blame his father for that. After he'd joined the Army he paid back his uncle every penny of his education. He wanted to go to art school really but couldn't afford it, and his mother, who was a very strict Methodist, for some reason didn't approve anyway. She died last year.'

'How d'you know all this?' asked Charles.

'His wife told me. He never talks about it himself. You know one of their children is a spastic?'

Charles shook his head.

'Named Raymond after the brother who died. Children are the CO's soft spot. Any soldier who says his wife's having a baby can get all the leave he wants.'

'It's hard to imagine him at art school,' said Charles.

'I suppose it is now. You don't know what he was like then, of course. He has four pet hates now – adulterers, or anyone who's even reasonably promiscuous, drunkards, people who don't pay their debts and anyone who's unkind to children. He thinks journalists are the first three anyway so don't whatever you do introduce him to a child-beating one.'

'I'll look out for that,' said Charles.

In fact, his first substantial contact with the press was with the man called Beazely, against whom Philip Lamb had specifically warned him. Beazely rang, identified himself and invited Charles to dinner in his hotel that evening. Philip Lamb had not led him to expect such treatment as this, and he did not know whether he was allowed to accept. The adjutant referred him to the CO who agreed, saying, 'On condition you carry.'

'Sir?'

'Bertie.'

'Bertie, sir?'

'Bertie Browning, for God's sake. Where've you just come

from, Charles, the nursery? You're not at university now, you know. Carry your Browning nine-millimetre pistol. Wear a shoulder-holster. You've worn one before. I don't want my officers shot in the back over dinner.'

Beazely was in the Europa, the large modern hotel in the city centre. It paid no protection money to the IRA and so was elaborately fortified by wire, lights and security guards. It had been the target of several bombing attempts, one or two partially successful, but was still used by many of the press. Charles was dropped outside by Land-Rover, which made him feel unpleasantly conspicuous, and at first he could not see his way through the defences to the entrance. When with Janet he had not even attempted them. In fact, an uninformed observer would have been hard put to tell whether the wire and corrugated iron were meant to keep intruders out or guests in. However, this time Charles was elated to be in civilian clothes. He felt quite different – not normal, but at least he could begin to remember what it might be like to feel normal. Of course, the discomfort of his shoulder-holster would have prevented him from going too far in that direction. Instead of nestling snugly under his arm, as they appeared to do in all the films, the bulky Browning pressed heavily against his ribs and bulged awkwardly beneath his jacket. For all the defences around the hotel, the body search was cursory and he did not have to explain anything.

Beazely was bloated, bespectacled and friendly. He had a red face and a mop of brown hair which straggled over his ears and collar. A large signet ring was squeezed on to his podgy third finger and the half-smoked cigarette in his other hand looked just as permanent. His manner was both impersonal and intimate. His handshake was limp and wet. 'Glad to meet you, Charlie. What'll it be?'

'Lager, please.'

Beazely ordered two double whiskies. 'What's happened to the other bloke – Phil thingie?'

'He was shot.'

'Christ, that's going a bit far. Badly?'

'No, in the foot.' Charles had decided to spare the details partly for Philip's sake and partly out of latent regimental pride.

'He should've rung me. He promised he would if anything happened in your area. I could've done a piece on it. He could've been a hero. I hope you won't forget if you get mixed up in anything interesting. Cheers.'

'The incident was filmed. There was a camera crew there.'

'Was there? Can't compete with that. The old steam press has its limitations, you know. At least where that sort of thing is concerned. Same again?'

Beazely either ignored or genuinely did not hear Charles's

protest. 'We'll be seeing a lot of each other, Charlie, because I do a lot of Army stuff, you see. You scratch my back and I scratch yours. We can be very useful to each other. That's the way me and Phil worked it, anyway. Cheers.' Beazely swallowed with a practised gulp. Charles edged his barely-sipped first drink out of sight with his elbow and raised his second. Twenty minutes later there were four more lined up on the bar, filled to varying levels. Charles was vividly aware of details of his surroundings, such as the closeness of Beazely's sweating red face and the prodding of Beazely's fat forefinger, but felt pleasantly detached and remote.

Beazely was swaying backwards and forwards very slightly and talking all the time, his words accompanied by a liberal sprinkling of saliva. 'The root of the problem is sex, of course. That's the answer to the Irish question, only no one ever asked it properly. The men booze and so the women don't bother. The women are hags and so the men booze. It's the same throughout working-class Belfast, East or West, Loyalist or Republican. Beating each other up on a Friday night is about the closest they ever get to communicating, some of them. Nothing for them at home or in bed and so they go outside for their kicks, and there's your violent society. If the men knew how to make love and the women had enough self-respect to make themselves desirable it would be a different place, believe me. Balanced, fulfilled, sane, you know. As it is, the divisions in the society as a whole reflect the brutalities and animosities at home. You've only got to look at the kids. Old faces on young bodies. They scare me as much as anything.' The sweat on Beazely's face was mingling with tears. He put his hand on Charles's shoulder and drew closer still. Charles was distantly aware of laying his hand on Beazely's arm in comradely fashion. He was not aware of speaking.

'Be honest with you, Charlie, straight up. It bloody terrifies me. All of it. I'd rather go back to London and do accidents or gardening or any damn thing but they won't let me. Keep on about what a great job I'm doing. Great job, my arse. They can't get anyone else to do it, that's all. Won't ever let me write what I want, you know, what I've just been talking about. They want hard news all the time. There's enough hard news in the world without all this. Christ, I'd rather do the chess reports.'

He took off his glasses and, blinking, wiped his eyes upon his sleeve. 'Main reason I do a lot with the Army is because I'd rather talk to them than to the terrorists. Gives me the creeps just to go in the bad areas. All right for the likes of Jason Kyle and his rag, hobnobbing with the IRA all the time and proud of it. Me, I'm not proud of anything. Not ashamed either. What's more, I like the Army. Good blokes, know what I mean? Not always too bright, but you can trust 'em. Straight up, like yourself. No messing about. And they don't chuck bombs around. You and me will make a great team, Charlie, I can see it coming. Two more, please.'

Dinner passed. Charles was not sure how. He remembered going into the dining room and ordering. He knew he had eaten but could not recall whether it was a good meal or whether he just remembered someone – himself or Beazely – saying that it was. There had been an awful lot of talk, mostly, he thought, from Beazely. He clearly remembered leaving the hotel because Beazely had fallen in the reception area after shaking hands. He was glassy-eyed and feeling slightly sick when he returned to battalion HQ. There had been wine with the meal and something afterwards. Even on quiet nights no one in battalion HQ went to bed before two but, finding that neither his absence was commented upon nor his presence noticed, Charles crept away. He undressed slowly and made careful note of where he put everything. He did not put on the light. There was a moment of sheer panic, a draining, despairing, almost tearful moment, when he thought he had lost his pistol; but then he found it in the place in the bed where one would normally put a hot-water bottle. He passed an uncomfortable night.

Sitting at his desk in Colin Wood's office the next morning Charles feebly pretended to be busy. He copied Philip Lamb's list of names and telephone numbers from one book to another, then kept both. Philip had also established a card index and

Charles sorted it twice without altering it. He drank several cups of instant coffee, without tasting any of it, which was probably an advantage. Fortunately, the adjutant really was busy and had no time to notice anyone else. There were, however, two telephone calls for him. The first was from an unknown major at the PR desk at Headquarters, telling him that he should come up for a briefing, saying that they would all be delighted to see him and adding that, before they 'went firm' on anything, could he help out a TV team that afternoon. They wanted to do a feature on how soldiers spent their off-duty time. Charles asked the CO, who said, 'All right, so long as they don't take up more than half an hour of the Ackies' kipping time and so long as they don't interview anyone. I hold you responsible.' Charles then rang Edward, who said that the Factory was full enough already without half of Hollywood swarming all over it, but agreed to put a dozen soldiers at the film crew's disposal when Charles implied that the CO was keen on the idea.

The second call sounded at first like savage interference on a waterlogged line. After a while it became clear that a human being was responsible for the noise and a little while after that Charles distinguished the word Beazely. He greeted him with barely more enthusiasm than he felt. There was more crackling, during which he distinguished the word helicopter. A minute or so of questions and answers established that Beazely believed he had been promised a ride over Belfast in a helicopter. 'I'm afraid I haven't any helicopters,' said Charles.

'Not you, Charlie, the Army. They've got plenty. Use one of theirs.'

'I can't.'

'Why not?'

Charles snatched at the nearest reason. 'They don't do low-level flights over the city.'

'One went right past my window this morning. Woke me up.'

'They must have been looking for a car or something. They only do it then.' It did not sound very convincing. Weariness lessened Charles's scruples. 'Anyway, all the helicopters are on border patrol duty today.'

'What about the one outside my window?'

'Except for those with urgent operational tasks.'

There was a pause. He could imagine Beazely lighting a cigarette. 'Get me on one of those then. The border's better than nothing.'

'But there's nothing to see.'

'That's the point. There's a story in that.'

'Well, I can't do it. It's out of our area. Ring Headquarters. They'll fix it for you.'

'They won't. They know me. Come on, Charlie, you must

have something. I mean, a report on the incidence of flat feet would do. My news editor's going crazy. If I don't feed him something for tomorrow he'll kill me.'

Beazely sounded seriously distressed. One or two of Charles's stray scruples came wandering back. After all, he might have referred to the possibility of helicopter rides, in a general sort of way. 'How about a feature on soldiers' leisure activities?'

Beazely snorted, causing the telephone to crackle horribly. 'I did that last week. They didn't print it.'

'Well, do a follow-up. Jazz it up a bit. There might be a new angle.'

'What sort of new angle?'

'I don't know. You're the journalist. I'll take you to a terrible place where they live, if you like. Something worse than you've ever seen. Bring a camera.'

Beazely eventually agreed. He could think of nothing better to do, that was all. It was better to be doing something than sitting around in the hotel getting drunk and frightened.

When Charles arrived at the Factory that afternoon there was a large hire-car parked by the gates. Standing with their hands above their heads and their faces to the wall were three men. A rifle was trained on them from the sentry sangar opposite. Charles got out of his Land-Rover and approached the sangar with a growing unease.

'Can you identify these men, sir?' said the sentry's voice. From close to, his face was just visible.

'No, I can't,' said Charles. 'At least, not at the moment. Who do they say they are?'

'They said they're television blokes.'

'Well, that's who they are, then. They're expected. Did no one tell you?'

Even in the darkness of the sangar the sentry's expression could be seen to be disgruntled. 'No one told me, sir.'

'Did you ask for any identification – press cards or anything?'

'No, sir.'

Charles started to walk towards the men. 'You can lower your rifle now.' The sentry reluctantly withdrew the barrel. Charles introduced himself and apologised. They seemed to take it in good part and even smiled when he asked if they'd been there long. Long enough, it seemed, for their arms to ache. One man, large and bearded, soon produced a camera from his car and another, short and balding, produced recording equipment. The third man was beautiful. He was of medium height, slightly built, with wavy blond hair, strikingly blue eyes, a tanned complexion and a very friendly smile that displayed small even teeth. He wore an expensive light raincoat with wide lapels, belted tightly at the waist. He was the only one of the three unencumbered by equipment. He was

Jonathan Kingsley, a name well known from television documentaries. 'It's quite all right,' he said to Charles as they shook hands. 'You really must not worry.'

'Thought the car might have a bomb in it,' said the sentry as he opened the gates. 'Stop all cars. Major Lumley's orders.'

Jonathan Kingsley smiled disarmingly at him. 'A bomb? With us in it?'

'Edward Lumley is rather enthusiastic,' said Charles. 'He's the company commander.'

Jonathan Kingsley smiled again, looked straight into Charles's eyes, his head bent to one side. 'Sounds exciting. Hope we can meet him.'

Charles escorted them into the Factory and upstairs whilst they explained what they wanted to do. He had to leave them outside the ops room as the CO had said that no journalists were to be allowed in any ops room anywhere. He found Edward sitting on the map-table, eating an apple and discussing rugby with the CSM. His face fell when he saw Charles. 'Oh Christ, you here? You haven't brought them with you, have you?'

'They're just outside the door.'

'I don't have to meet them, do I?'

'It might look odd if you don't. You don't have to say anything, except hallo. They're not going to interview anyone.'

'Thank Christ for that.' Edward jumped off the table and

bounced his apple off the wall into the waste-paper bin. 'What do they want, then?'

'Just a couple of minutes' film, that's all. They've done the rest of the programme. This is just background for the commentary.'

When introduced to Jonathan Kingsley, Edward behaved like a bashful and tongue-tied schoolboy. He had to be prompted into revealing the whereabouts of the leisure activities they were to film.

'He's sweet,' said Jonathan Kingsley, whilst Edward was off finding his beret. 'I expected something far more butch from the AAC (A).'

As they were climbing the stairs to the next floor Edward tugged at Charles's elbow. 'What's his name again?'

'Jonathan Kingsley.'

'Christ, yes. Seen him on the box. You want to watch him.'

'Why?'

'Queer. You can tell by the way he shakes your hand. He squeezes it first then goes all limp, waiting for you to squeeze.'

'Is that what queers do?' asked Charles.

Edward frowned. 'What? No. How would I know? Thought you'd know all about it – Oxford and all that. It's just what I've heard, that's all.'

They found a dozen soldiers sitting in the canteen with their weapons, helmets, flak jackets and respirators. They stared sullenly at the new arrivals. Jonathan Kingsley turned to Charles. 'Surely this isn't how they spend their leisure time?'

Charles turned to Edward. 'Why are they in battle order?'

'They always parade with their kit and their weapons.'

'Parade?' The most delicate of frowns creased the smooth skin of Jonathan Kingsley's forehead. 'Have they paraded for us?'

Edward looked exasperated and his face puckered. Things always seemed to go wrong. 'Well, you wanted to film them, didn't you? Here they are.'

'We wanted to film them doing whatever they do when they're off duty. We didn't want them to do anything special for us.'

'They're usually asleep when they're off duty.'

'They sometimes play volleyball,' said Charles.

Jonathan Kingsley's frown faded. 'Oh, that would be lovely. Volleyball would be very nice.'

Edward turned to the soldiers. 'Take your kit off and go to bed. Pretend to be asleep. Stay there till you're called. Then get up and play volleyball.' The disgruntled soldiers filed out. 'Saves disturbing the ones who are really sleeping,' Edward added.

As they were preparing to film, Edward tugged again at Charles's sleeve. 'A word of advice, Charles.' Charles was unsure at first whether Edward wanted to give it or receive it.

'These press people, you must be firmer with them. No good being vague. They don't know their arses from their elbows most of the time. Must get a grip.'

The soldiers were duly filmed in feigned slumber in unfeignedly crowded conditions. While they changed for volleyball Edward excused himself, claiming he was busy. A desultory game was then filmed in the Factory yard, partly from the roof and partly from ground level. Jonathan Kingsley was pleased. It had the right flavour, he thought. The lacklustre nature of the game could be explained by the tiredness that came from the night vigils. Charles was summoned away at one point by a corporal who said that a man had presented himself at the gate, claiming to be a journalist there by invitation. When he went to the gate, Charles was told by the sentry that the man had been invited in by Edward some fifteen minutes before. Charles again climbed the stairs to the ops room, this time with a sense of foreboding. He was aware of the change in atmosphere in the ops room even before he entered. There was the same old radio mush and cackle but something livelier and jollier had been added. There was even laughter. The first thing he noticed was that everyone had a can of beer. Then he saw Edward sitting on the map-table, swinging his legs and talking to Beazely. Beazely was also sitting on the map-table, as tousled and red-faced as the night before, with his glasses askew. He threw

Charles a can of beer as he entered. 'Have some, Charlie. It's on the rag.'

Edward jumped off the table. 'Charles, old man, you should've said there was someone else coming. Poor bugger was nearly turned away at the gate, beer and all. Must say, he's a great improvement on that other bloody pansy.'

Beazely grinned, with just a trace of awkwardness. 'Thought the boys might like a drink, Charlie.'

'Don't worry about him being in the ops room,' Edward continued. 'He's too short-sighted to see anything. He said so.'

'True.' Beazely nodded impartially. 'This is a great place, Charlie. Terrific atmosphere, if only I can get it over. Troops living in worse conditions than IRA prisoners. It'll go down a treat back home. Something to kick the government with. Might even lead to improvements, you never know.'

'They can move the prisoners in here and us into the Maze any time they like,' said Edward. 'Nice cosy little cell would just do me.'

'Edward's been telling me about the screwing through the gate. Can I interview the man concerned?'

'No,' said Charles. 'The CO would go up the wall.'

'Oh, come on, it's great human interest stuff. Something for the technically-minded too, from what I saw of that gate.'

'It would compromise the girls. Soldier-lovers. We'd have tarrings and featherings. Bad for community relations.'

'Can I take a picture of Edward, then?'

'If you like, but what for? It's not quite the same thing, is it?'

'What d'you mean by that?' asked Edward.

'No particular reason,' said Beazely, fortunately preventing Charles from having to reply to Edward. 'Might want to use it some time, that's all. I'd clear it with you first, of course.'

'All right.'

Edward made a show of reluctance. 'Well, if the PR officer says so I suppose I'll have to. Queen and country and all that.' He straightened his jersey and put his beret back on. 'Bloody funny thing for a professional soldier to have to do, all the same. Shall I put my camouflage smock on? Looks a bit more warry.'

Charles was still uneasy at the thought of Edward and Beazely doing anything together. It seemed to be a recipe for trouble. 'Why not do it when there's more sun?' he said. 'The picture will come out better.'

'No time like the present,' said Edward briskly.

'You're still living in the age of box cameras,' said Beazely.

A few minutes later Jonathan Kingsley appeared at the door with his crew. 'Thank you, Charles, that was fine. I think it'll look good. The right ambience, you know?' His blue eyes flickered from Charles to Beazely, who was still sitting on the map-table.

'He's got special clearance from Headquarters,' said Charles. 'He's doing a feature.'

'Really? Dreadful man, isn't he? Charles, may I have your number? We'd like to use you again, if that's all right.'

Charles gave him the number. 'I'm sorry there was so little scope today. If I had more notice I could arrange something better.'

Jonathan Kingsley smiled directly into Charles's eyes and touched him lightly on the elbow. 'Don't worry. It was fine. Be seeing you again.'

The following day Beazely's paper carried a long article headed, 'Cool Major Who Lives With Bomb'. The centre-piece was a fuzzy photograph of Edward looking tough and determined, an effect heightened by the fact that his beret was crooked. The article described how Major Edward 'Buster' Lumley and the men of his company calmly lived above a huge landmine, which was concealed in a tunnel beneath the Factory. 'Top-grade Intelligence sources' had apparently described it as 'the largest IRA bomb ever – three tons or more of explosive'. Edward was the quiet, gentle, intelligent, perceptive, tough man who had been especially selected to take over one of the worst areas of Belfast. He had won not only the esteem of his own – also especially selected – men but also the confidence and friendship of the locals, who sensed in him an understanding, fair-minded, no-nonsense community leader. The article was attributed to Beazely.

Charles's day had started well, in that he had been able to have a bath. The fried breakfast was hot for once and the tinned tomatoes were quite soft. The discovery of this article spoiled everything.

'You've started with a bang,' observed Tony Watch. 'Surprised the PR people allowed it, let alone the CO.'

'They weren't asked,' said Charles. 'They don't know anything about it.'

'You took a chance, then.'

'I wasn't asked either.'

'This bloke Beazely did it off his own bat?' Tony whistled. 'Shit'll really hit the fan now. Better put your helmet on.'

When Charles reached his office the adjutant said, 'The CO wants you.'

'Reference the article?'

Colin nodded. 'Not pleased. Someone let you down?'

'Looks like it.'

The CO was the only person to have a room to himself, though Anthony Hamilton-Smith was rumoured to have one somewhere. When Charles entered the CO was sitting at his desk, writing. 'You've been a bloody stupid officer,' he said. He continued writing. Charles was trying to think of an appropriate reply when the CO stopped writing and looked up again. 'Just had breakfast, have you?'

'Yes, sir.'

'Think yourself lucky you're not on the boat home. If it weren't for me you would be. I had my breakfast hours ago.'

'Yes, sir.'

'Don't keep yes-sirring me, I'm telling you. Know where I've been since I had my breakfast?'

'No, sir.'

'I've been up at Headquarters, fighting for your life with the general. He wanted your guts on a plate. Know why?'

'The article, sir.'

''Course you do. Unbelievably crass though the whole thing is, I couldn't believe that you wouldn't realise it yourself when you saw the thing in print. That's how I saved you from being sacked, sent home in disgrace. I said you were new to the Army and to PR, that this was your first mistake and will definitely be your last. I stuck my neck out for you. Which is more than the Guards CO did for his PR officer. D'you know about that?'

'No, sir.'

'This man Beazely visited two units yesterday – us and the Guards. He obviously wrote his story out of what he gleaned from each. The Guards PR officer is on his way home at this instant. It's thanks to me that you're still here. What've you got to say for yourself?'

'As far as I'm aware, sir, I didn't –'

'I know, I know, Edward Lumley's almost as much to blame as you. But that's not the point. You're there to make sure he doesn't shoot his mouth off. And that includes your own. As it is, you broke every PR rule in the book. You talked in general terms about the situation here, you emphasised personalities, you spouted all this rubbish about special selection – which will be believed, you know, despite denials, and could do enormous political damage – and you made the most elementary and crass security blunders. The information about that tunnel came from a high-grade Intelligence source that is now prejudiced by your foolish disclosures. I can see you weren't responsible for the nonsense about the Guards battalion being equipped with special mining tools for digging us out of the debris, but that's about all. The general's furious, you know. He was told about all this by London at five o'clock this morning and he had me up there within an hour. You can thank God I'm a lenient man.'

Charles knew that none of the offending comments had come from him and he gave a truthful account of Beazely's visit, but it sounded unconvincing even to his own ears. He was sure that Edward had not mentioned the tunnel to Beazely but could not account for how Beazely had known about it, nor for all the stuff about special selection. He did not feel it would be politic to call to his aid the fact that Beazely's main interest had been in the screwing through the gate episode. Besides, he could not be certain that that might not appear in another edition. He was unable to offer the CO a more convincing explanation than that provided by the assumption of his guilt, and so was dismissed with further admonitions. 'Frankly, I would have expected more from a university man,' was the CO's final, and rather surprising word.

Charles rang Beazely's hotel several times that morning but was unable to get through to him. He left messages for Beazely to ring him, but nothing happened. Finally, late in the afternoon, he changed into civilian clothes and got the CO's escort vehicle to take him to the hotel, having told the CO that he had an appointment with Beazely. When he got there he found Beazely in the bar, talking to a loud and drunken group of men who could have been either local journalists or local politicians. Beazely left them and came over to Charles. 'Have a drink,' he said.

'No thanks.'

'I suppose you've come about my little piece this morning?'

'That's right.'

'Anything happen about it?'

'I was very nearly sacked.'

'Ah. I can explain, you know.'

'Good.'

'But please have a drink.'

They sat down. 'Wasn't my fault,' said Beazely. 'Wasn't yours, of course. Wasn't that other chap's either, that Guards bloke. Though I didn't go much on him, to be honest. Toffee-nosed, you know? Not like you.'

'He was sacked. He's on his way home.'

It was to Beazely's credit that he seemed somewhat shaken by this. 'Christ, they don't waste much time in the Army, do they? Any good me going to see them or writing to the general or anything?'

'The general will probably kill you.'

'See what you mean.' Beazely pushed his slipping spectacles back up on the bridge of his nose. 'It was all the news editor's fault really. Bit of a cock-up, to be honest, Charlie, from my point of view as well as yours. I mean, I'm not exactly persona grata with the Army now, am I? Not that I was before, I s'pose. I mean, they'll still see me. They can't not see me because of the rag I work for, can they?'

'Just tell me where you got the information about the tunnel.'

'The Officers' Mess bar at Headquarters. They were all talking about it. I went up there after I'd seen you and the Guards bloke to talk to the PR desk. Fat lot of use they were. You see, I'd already sent this photograph of Edward along with a little write-up about what a good bloke he is because I'd thought of doing a big feature on your lot one day – with you in it – and I wanted them to keep all these little titbits as background. Well, in the meantime London had got this agency report about tunnels, and they'd come up asking me if I knew anything about it, which I didn't until I went to the bar at Headquarters. Lot of loose talk there, Charlie. Always has been. A serious temptation to people like myself.'

'To which you yielded.'

'Yes and no. I reported what I'd heard, but I didn't realise London were going for it in such a big way. I especially didn't realise they'd link what I'd done about Edward with all the tunnel stuff. I mean, they were quite separate as far as I was concerned. That's news editors for you. No souls, no tact, no sense, no scruples. Didn't tell me what they were doing. First I knew of it was when I saw it this morning, just like you. Is your CO very angry?'

'Demented.'

'Oh Christ. I do all my work through the Army, as you know. If they make things difficult I'll be joining that Guards bloke. Might not be such a bad thing, in a way.' He mused for a few moments. 'Would a bottle of whisky help?'

'No, thanks.'

'Not for you, for your CO. I could send him one.'

'No.' It occurred to Charles that this might be the opportunity to get rid of Beazely once and for all. 'The CO has no tact and no scruples, just like your news editor. He'd probably kill you even quicker than the general. Best thing to do is lie low and wait for me to contact you.' Beazely's bloated face nodded mournfully. 'The only way you might be able to clear your name is if you're prepared to tell him what you've just told me – if he wants you to, that is.'

'Any time, Charlie. Just say.'

'I'll be in touch if he does. Remember – don't come near us until you hear from me that it's all right.'

When Charles told the CO what Beazely had said, the CO grunted and remarked: 'Just shows you can't trust these bloody pressmen. Always listening to other people's conversations. Watch your step in future.' Charles waited to hear that the Guards officer had been recalled, and his own name cleared. But he waited in vain. A few days later he asked the CO if the general was now aware of the source of the story, and added that Beazely was willing to testify to it. 'The matter's closed,' said the CO. 'No point in digging it up. You've learnt your lesson, I hope. Now shut up.'

7

Somewhat to his surprise, Charles found that he was writing two or three times a week to Janet. They were long outpourings, produced at speed and of a length and passion that he knew was not justified by the relationship. They were a self-indulgent rehearsal of all the things that preoccupied him, predominant among which was the question of how long he thought he could last in the Army. Sometimes he felt he could not last another day, at others that he could go on for ever. This latter mood was not the result of sudden enthusiasm so much as a growing inability to imagine himself doing anything else. Most of the people around him appeared to like what they were doing, and this imposed upon him a burden of silence, the only relief for which was letters to Janet. What made it worse was that he did not on the whole dislike the people he was with but did not know them well enough to discover whether the accumulation of sordid particulars and the inflexible but necessary attitudes of military life were as horrifying for them as for him. There were signs that the adjutant, in his weary cynicism, did not fully enjoy what he was doing; but never a word to say so. There were occasions when Anthony Hamilton-Smith showed a certain pained sensitivity. After spending nearly a whole day closeted with the quartermaster in an attempt to straighten out some arcane aspect of HQ company's ration issue – an affair which had also engrossed the CO, the adjutant, the RSM and the paymaster – Anthony had yawned behind the back of the disgruntled quartermaster and remarked in an undertone to Charles, 'That man, with all he stands for, shows us the essential horror of Army life. I sometimes wonder why I love it so dearly.'

All this, he realised, was a little unfair on Janet. Long though they were, his letters were not very explicit, and from her replies it was clear that either she saw what he was doing as something comparable with the battles of the Somme or she failed, not unreasonably, to see what he was complaining about. Since their meeting he felt more distant from her, and at the same time a desire to communicate with her more. Her letters were brisk, cheerful and hurried. She seemed to be enjoying herself in London. He telephoned her a few times, when the adjutant was out of the room, but found that that device did more to emphasise distance than to decrease it. After a while he confined his letters to accounts of the books he was reading and to descriptions of Belfast, making much of the dirt, and especially much of the fact that a jug of milk left by an open window would be speckled black in an hour.

His books were his real solace and fully justified his overweight kit. The more vividly colourful and imaginative they were and the more remote from his drab environment, the better. As a student he had always resisted Tolkien, as he had resisted most cults, but he felt free to read and enjoy him now. Even better was Mervyn Peake's grotesque and sinister fantasy. He started reading those Shakespeare plays he did not know but then found that he was largely ignorant of those few he thought he did know, and so went to those instead. His one disappointment was *Madame Bovary*; perhaps because style, like poetry, was what was lost in translation or perhaps because he read it only on duty in the deadest part of the night. So far as he could see, none of his brother officers read anything except newspapers.

Belfast was relatively peaceful during those few weeks. This was a time when a few shootings and a bomb or two comprised what the newspapers called 'a quiet night in Belfast'. To the CO it was 'this unbelievable lull'; he could not conceal his disappointment that nothing much was happening in the battalion area and frequently speculated aloud as to what 'they' were up to under cover of the lull. The sum of the CO's speculations was that whatever was going to happen was going to be worse than anything so far and woe betide those who were unprepared. Irritably, he toured the companies shouting 'Hard targets!' at all and sundry, and demanding to know of nervous officers what they would do if he were shot dead now, at this instant, talking to them in the false security of the company location.

Routine in battalion HQ was hardly enjoyable, but it was a framework upon which an existence could be based. The two essential elements were the eight-hour watchkeeping stints in the ops room, which occurred three times a week, and the daily O Groups at 1700 hours, known as 'prayers'. The CO insisted upon these whether there was need or no, convinced that they benefited the morale of the battalion. All the company commanders attended and all the officers in battalion HQ, plus the RSM who took notes of everything that was said, regardless of relevance. Edward, too, was a prolific scribe and Charles was able to confirm what he had long suspected – that Edward's company briefings contained practically none of his own words. Even certain mannerisms which Charles had thought were peculiar to Edward were now seen to originate from the CO.

Henry Sandy had also to attend, usually pale and tired after his nightly debauch. Even the paymaster was brought in from some mysterious and, everyone suspected, comfortable place known as 'the rear echelon', which he shared with the quartermaster. On one memorable occasion Henry Sandy had to be woken, publicly, by the RSM. What little charm the proceedings had was graciously given by Anthony Hamilton-Smith, who had frequent baths and seemed never to be depressed, tired or irritable like other people. He usually arrived at the meetings last, with the CO, and often had to slip out early for reasons which were never explained. He sometimes made a few light-hearted comments but rarely addressed himself seriously to the business of the day, so that his presence was a welcome balance to the CO's intense seriousness and the RSM's and Edward's furious scribblings.

The CO invariably sat at the front facing everyone else across a large desk, with a wall-map of the battalion area behind him. He had a long stick which was meant for pointing out things on the map but which he smashed against the map or down upon the desk in order to emphasise firmness of resolve, swiftness of action, or the importance of soldier-like behaviour. He usually began by expressing amazement that the lull had continued for another twenty-four hours, and then issued dire warnings for the next twenty-four. Mysterious A1 sources were said to have indicated that the time would be soon.

Nigel Beale would then have to stand and, with the aid of a much shorter stick, give the daily Intelligence summary. This comprised a description of what had happened in the past twenty-four hours, which everyone knew, and speculation as to what was in store for the next twenty-four, which no one believed. It frequently happened that Nigel had nothing to report and no reason to expect anything, but he was still expected to speak for ten minutes. Sometimes he announced that there would be searches, again on the basis of A1 information, but usually nothing was found. Had Nigel been less zealous and intense he might have had a more sympathetic audience; as it was, his awareness that he was preaching to the godless heathen made him more intense still. His one believer was the CO, and the CO would brook no criticism of Nigel's daily chore, no matter how kindly meant. Occasionally, though, the predictable pattern of the O Groups was shaken when the CO would suddenly formulate a new rule about dress or procedure and then castigate everyone present for not having adhered to it.

With regard to the watchkeeping periods, Charles found it strangely relaxing to know that whatever happened he would be keeping his watch at certain hours, riot or revolution notwithstanding. When it was quiet there was time for reading and letter-writing, and during the long watches of the night he would sometimes have conversations with the radio operator, which would later seem bizarre and implausible. Times such as these, when both fell silent, were the nearest that anyone ever got to privacy. It was the watchkeeper's job to respond to anything that came up on either of the radio nets –

the battalion and the brigade. Every message in or out had to be logged, and it was Charles's fear that he would have to deal simultaneously with one of Brigade's abstruse queries and some emergency, real or imagined, within the battalion area. His voice procedure had never been good, though it was usually adequate. Brigade were particularly hot on offenders, although the greatest offender was the Brigade commander himself. His voice procedure was a disconcerting mixture of ordinary conversation and incomprehensible telegraphese, which he would suddenly adopt for a few sentences when he remembered that he was on the air. He was the only man who ever came up without giving a call-sign, but this itself, combined with his drawling tones and extraordinary phraseology, made call-signs redundant. He was immediately recognisable to every listener. It was more of a problem to know when he had finished: he would sometimes say 'Out' crisply, sometimes not at all and at others would cut back in on other conversations.

Charles's time of greatest privacy and pleasure was after the 2200–0600 watch, which occurred once a week. After his relief had arrived he would go upstairs on to the flat roof of the police station. There was a sentry up there in a sangar but he could wander about freely without going near him. He did not worry about snipers since the IRA were not at their most active early in the morning. There was a view over a large part of West Belfast leading up to the Black Mountain, the only visible bit of greenery. The cold was enlivening and bracing and the air clear. Above all, though, the city looked clean and almost innocent in its freshness. Later, the industrial haze would settle and turn the sun, if it appeared, into something the colour of rancid butter and the rain into a dull, dirty smear on the windows. But at six in the morning the homely little rooftops and the quiet little streets looked pathetically human. It was possible then to feel some hope for the place. Then the traffic would begin and the people would appear, bringing with them the noise, dirt, slovenliness and ordinary harshness of everyday life. Children with hard, old faces would start their paper rounds, and Charles would go back down to breakfast.

Every night the CO visited the companies. His trip round usually started at about ten, but could be earlier if he were bored. It would last from two to six hours. Charles usually accompanied him in case, as the CO put it, he had to arrest any rascally journalists on the way. For Charles it was a good opportunity to get out of battalion HQ. Unfortunately, the RSM was of the same opinion, and he also regarded himself as being in charge of the CO's escort party. Frequently there was a silent and private feud between him and Charles to see who should sit in the front of the escort vehicle, the RSM regarding it as being beneath his dignity to give place to a mere second

223

lieutenant, while Charles was happy to give up the seat but not to have it taken from him.

It was well known that the CO was looking for trouble when he went out at night, and he would even poach on a neighbouring battalion's area if there was no life in his own. In the worst parts of his own area he would often leave the vehicles under guard and mount an extempore foot patrol under his own command, normally the job of a corporal. He would stop and search people who struck him as suspicious – nearly everyone did so strike him – and would mount sudden road blocks in the hope of catching stolen cars. Since most cars used in shootings and bombings were stolen, the search for such vehicles formed an important part of military life in Belfast, and everyone soon acquired something of the mentality of a traffic warden. There was an intense programme of VCPs and thousands of vehicles were stopped every week, occasionally with some result. Brigade were always worried about Ford Cortinas, which were said to be easy to steal and, certainly, were frequently used by terrorists. A representative for Ford, interviewed on the radio, denied that they were easier to steal than other comparable cars and suggested that their popularity was due to their reliability and speed. On some nights the CO would stop every Ford Cortina he saw. For about a fortnight Brigade issued numerous reports about blue Cortinas and the adjutant said that one of the RUC men had told him that if all the reports were true, every blue Cortina in Belfast had been stolen twice.

Anthony Hamilton-Smith sometimes did the rounds of the companies instead of the CO, with noticeably less drama. No one in battalion HQ knew how he passed his time, and no one thought it appropriate to ask. He was always fresh and immaculate, polite and charming whatever was happening. His persistent anachronisms earned him some good-natured ridicule, yet tinged with admiration. It was an army which admired bluff, which recognised its importance and which could forgive most sins provided they were done with a certain style. There were, of course, those – one or two of the more ambitious company commanders – whose sense of military virtue was outraged by Anthony's continuing lament over the demise of the horse in modern warfare. They regarded him as an ineffectual dilettante, but his own unfailing politeness and good humour prevented them from demonstrating their disapproval. There was, indeed, something in his playfully old-fashioned manner that indicated a mind at rest, but not asleep. The CO seemed only intermittently aware that he had a second-in-command and showed no curiosity as to what his second-in-command did with his time. His style of leadership rendered subordinate commanders unnecessary, and an amiable, unprotesting 2IC fitted perfectly. Anthony's responsibility for community relations remained almost entirely theoretical.

It would have been completely theoretical had he not had to chair a weekly meeting of the RUC community relations representative and the company representatives. Charles was made responsible for the minutes. The purpose of the meeting was to discuss and, where necessary, allocate funds for community relations projects. Such few projects as there were had been inherited from the previous unit, though B company's representative, a rather keen captain, wanted to build an adventure playground on some wasteland. The CO, though, was known not to favour community relations, and Anthony was not one to exert himself unnecessarily. The result was that the previous unit's projects dwindled and the adventure playground, though paid lip-service to by all, was talked about in such a way that everyone, except the keen captain, was able to feel reassured that it would still be under discussion when the battalion left Belfast. At best, community relations secured the friendship of the friendly, while the unfriendly remained unchanged. Anthony introduced each meeting, was not always able to stay to the end, but occasionally handed round some cigars.

One evening came the first serious riot in which the battalion was involved. There had been no indication of trouble at the five o'clock 'prayers' – indeed, Nigel Beale had forecast a quiet period during which the IRA were 'regrouping' – and there was no apparent reason for it, though it was later said to have been a test of the battalion's reaction. 'They wanted to know whether they were dealing with soft nuts or hard nuts,' the CO said afterwards. 'Well, now they know.'

It began during dinner, which was an event in itself that night. Most mealtimes were a forum for the CO to pronounce upon anything in the world, military or civil. Usually, he chose those aspects of the world that disagreed with him, and so there was never any shortage of subjects. His audience was mainly passive and respectful, which he interpreted as meaning agreement, though a few competed with each other in their efforts to heap fuel on the fire of his opinion. Anthony was the only one who would ever disagree, usually on some point of regimental history or etiquette or in some arcane area where he alone seemed to possess certain knowledge. In particular, he always seemed to know of some tribe somewhere whose habits contradicted any generalisation made about human behaviour. On matters of political or military moment, however, he remained silent.

On this occasion the CO was giving his opinion on an article by the *Sunday Truth*'s Hindsight team, which was about Army searches of Catholic houses. It said that nothing had been found in a large number of houses, that many families had been deeply upset and frightened, that several who were interviewed had alleged brutality and violence and that many felt the houses had been selected on a purely sectarian basis. There were accounts of two women receiving treatment for nervous afflictions and a few paragraphs about the effect upon children. The article ended by quoting a bland statement from Headquarters which denied sectarian discrimination and unprovoked violence and maintained that the Army had a duty to search houses if they believed there might be weapons hidden in them.

The CO dealt with the matter over his soup. 'Muck-raking, that's what it is. They're simply trying to stir things up. Some of these bloody journalists are no more than left-wing communist agitators.' He looked at Charles, whom he viewed as being in some way responsible for whatever appeared in the papers or on radio or television. If by nothing else, Charles was guilty by association. 'Isn't that true, Charles?'

'I've not met the Hindsight people, sir.'

'Don't be diplomatic with me. They're subversive. They're trying to destroy the fabric of our society. They're on the other side. No matter what we do they criticise it. And they're getting control of the media, which is why they're so dangerous. Not that all of them are downright evil, mind you' – the company waited in respectful silence whilst he sipped a spoonful of soup, some of which dribbled off the edge of the spoon and plopped back into the bowl – 'not all of them. Some of them are dupes. Well-meaning, academic, intellectual, left-wing dupes. The universities and the press are full of them. One thing they don't know is who's paying them, where the money's coming from. Whose dupes they are. That's why they're dangerous.'

There was a general nodding of heads. Charles concentrated on his soup, but the adjutant ventured calmly: 'All the same, there's probably a degree of truth in some of what they say. The Ackies can be rough if something's upset them and whatever reason we have for searching these people it must look to them as if we do it simply because they live where they do, especially when we don't find anything. I think a lot of these large-scale searches do more harm than good. We've been lucky with ours so far. They've been small-scale and we've usually found something. And I don't know that there's really any organised political conspiracy in the media.'

The CO banged his spoon down. 'There you are. Just what I've been saying.' There was an embarrassed silence for a few moments and then he laughed. 'They've even turned my own adjutant against me!' A ripple of relieved mirth ran round the table and the CO smiled indulgently at the adjutant. 'It's not an organised political conspiracy that I'm talking about, Colin, it's the coercion of opinion. They create a climate of acceptability in which everything is acceptable so long as you accept what they choose for you. It's a kind of political pornography they're trying to force down our throats. You'll just have to take my word for it, I'm afraid. When you get to my position and see some of the confidential documents that I see you'll know what I mean. You'll see these people in their true colours, which is more than they do themselves, I can assure you.'

The adjutant seemed content to have made his point. There was no arguing with the CO. Charles, whose turn it was to buy the wine that evening, occupied the ensuing pause by filling their glasses. The conversation then turned, as it frequently did, to the iniquities of the neighbouring unit, a regiment of gunners from Germany. The CO prefaced his remarks by saying that one shouldn't make disparaging remarks about other regiments, and that one should always bear in mind that these chaps were trained to fire missiles from thirty miles behind the lines; they were not the sort of chaps who could be expected to come to grips with the enemy. Anthony Hamilton-Smith thought they were all right at polishing their cannonballs and keeping their powder dry, but not very fleet of foot when it came to dodging round street corners. There then followed a catalogue of their misdeeds and inadequacies. Right or wrong, the CO was a prisoner of his own prejudices. There could be no serious opposition to anything he said, and so his own opinions were mirrored back to him, reinforcing the original, showing only himself, and himself as right. There was no chance of change or advance where there was no chance of contradiction, no limitation at all.

For some minutes all except the CO, who was talking, had been aware that the radio operator in the ops room next door was acknowledging more signals than usual. Tony Watch was the duty watchkeeper. After more radio chatter he hurried into the Mess and bent over the CO's shoulder, a little too confidentially. 'From Alpha One, sir, a crowd of youths in the Falls Road, stoning vehicles. Twenty so far and increasing.'

The CO swallowed his mouthful and gave himself a moment's indigestion. He put his hand on his chest until it had passed. 'The Falls is turning nasty, is it? We'll have our punch-up yet. Where on the Falls?'

'Junction with Leeson Street, sir. Border between us and the Gunners.'

'Right on the border?'

'Yes, sir.'

'Damn.' The CO put his hand to his chest again and there was another moment's silence. 'Inform Brigade and keep me posted, will you?'

Tony Watch returned to the ops room and could soon be heard calling up Brigade. 'Would be right on the border,' the CO continued. 'The Gunners'll probably have the most God-awful riot on their hands and not have a clue how to handle it, while we sit here and twiddle our thumbs and watch. Our boys could do with a riot, too. They're getting bored, idle and troublesome. Twice as many on Orders this week as when we arrived. Just shows you can't keep highly-trained infantrymen sitting around on their arses all day and all night.'

Charles resumed his argument with the piece of steak that was the officers' dinner that night – the soldiers, because there were more of them, had a choice. It seemed likely that dinner would be disturbed, and so Charles determined to eat as much as possible. The Falls Road and its neighbourhood was the traditional home of Belfast Republicanism, and although at one point it was no more than a few hundred yards from the Protestant Shankhill Road, the two were different worlds. Many of the inhabitants of each never had and never would venture on to the other. (Charles had heard that during a bombing raid in the Second World War some of the people on the Falls had lit bonfires to guide the German bombers, until they found that the bombers aimed for the fires.) Within a few minutes there were two RUC reports of large numbers of youths moving along the Falls. Someone said that an informer had informed to the effect that 'the word was out'.

There was a loud 'Roger. Wait out,' and Tony Watch strode purposefully back into the Mess. 'Alpha One report petrol bombing and heavy stoning, sir. They've deployed two platoons but they can't act effectively without going into the Gunners' patch.'

The CO grinned and drained his glass. 'Well, gentlemen, I

think we'd better get down there and sort it out. Call out the Rover Group.'

'It's been done, sir.'

Charles hastily swallowed his last mouthful and followed the CO out of the Mess. He found his flak jacket, combat jacket and webbing but could not remember where he had put his tin helmet. He eventually found it under his bed and hurried down into the enclosed yard where the Land-Rovers were already revving. There was a lot of movement and shouting. The CO was already in his Land-Rover and yelled to Charles to buck up. He then shouted at someone else and it was soon clear that he was shouting at everyone he saw. Charles scrambled into the back of the vehicle, helped roughly by the signals sergeant who always travelled with the CO. He accidentally kicked Nigel Beale, who was too busy with his folder to do more than glare angrily. The iron gates swung open and the Land-Rovers lurched noisily out, to the accompaniment of the signals sergeant's crisp 'Hallo Alpha Zero. This is Alpha Nine leaving your location now, over,' and battalion HQ's equally crisp, 'Alpha Zero, roger out.'

It was dusk and there was a lot of traffic. They went down the middle of the road as though there was none at all, before turning with an unnecessary squealing of tyres into the Falls. This was a broad (by Belfast standards), drab, winding road lined by small houses in bad repair and with many mean, narrow little roads opening off it. There was ominously little traffic here, and the CO pulled the heavy iron grille up over the windscreen. The escort vehicles behind them did the same. Charles touched his tin helmet on the floor with his foot, to make sure it was still there, and looked at everyone else's respirators, hoping fervently that there would be no need for them. His own was still missing, and he was far more concerned about the CO's reaction to this fact than he was about his own reaction to CS gas. Fortunately, it was a weapon the CO did not favour, being too indiscriminate, and so it was unlikely that they would use it.

Most other sounds were drowned by the high-pitched whine of the Land-Rover's differentials and tyres. They bumped uncomfortably along the road at an alarming speed. Two soldiers held macralon shields across the back, and through them Charles could just see the houses, which appeared to sway and jerk as much as the Land-Rover. He sat back against the side of the vehicle, only to find that the canvas was reinforced only by plywood and not by the macralon he had expected. Macralon was occasionally bullet-proof but the wood was not even properly brick-proof. He leant forward again, his stomach feeling light and empty. He drew some unjustifiable comfort from the presence of others and even some from the noise of the vehicle.

Very soon the ride became bumpier and Charles noticed a

lot of broken bricks and bits of metal scattered across the road behind them. The driver suddenly braked hard and Charles and Nigel Beale were flung to the floor. They sorted themselves out with some loss of temper but they were both so anxious to find out what was happening that they immediately forgot their disagreements. The Land-Rover was stopped and by peering between the bulky radios Charles could see through the front windscreen and grille. The street ahead was grey in the sinister twilight. It was littered with debris, and some hundred yards ahead was blocked by a large mob of youths. There was some shouting but only occasionally did a brick or bottle hurtle down and smash on the road, sending bits skidding across the surface. At this stage it still seemed gratuitous, even laconic. Some soldiers from the two A company platoons were crouched in doorways on both sides of the street and Ian Macdonald, their company commander, was talking to the CO through the Land-Rover window. His precise Scottish tones were calm and unhurried.

'They're just inside the Gunners' patch,' he said. 'What we can see is the back of them. Albert Street is the next on your right, and our boundary stops just this side of it.'

The CO was following with his finger on the map. 'What are the Gunners doing about it?'

'Nothing, so far as I can see. They're receiving a lot more stick than we are and they're just standing behind their shields and taking it. You can see them if you walk up closer to the mob.'

'Typical. No imagination, no flair. What do they intend to do – stand there all night, I suppose? Meanwhile, the mob is facing both ways.'

'What's more, the mob apparently have a petrol tanker,' continued Macdonald. 'I spoke to a Gunner officer earlier who'd come into our patch by mistake. He said they think it's round the corner at the bottom of Albert Street, out of sight. It was hijacked in North Belfast this afternoon.'

The muscles in one of the CO's cheeks twitched slightly as he compressed his lips hard. 'You're telling me that this mob has a petrol tanker hidden away, laden with fuel, that they've had it since this afternoon and this herd of Gunners are standing round like a lot of spare what's-its at a party doing sod-all about it?'

'That's what it looks like, sir.'

'And this lot of yobbos in front are creating a diversion while the real villains are down there syphoning off enough petrol to keep them in bombs till the unicorns return. You would not credit it. You would simply not credit it.' He looked down at his map. 'Where are your Pigs, Ian?'

'Round the corner, out of sight.'

'I don't anticipate much resistance from those louts. They'll simply fall back into Albert Street when we hit them and form a hard core round the tanker. Ian, one of your platoons is on foot and the other's in the Pigs, right? Keep the one on foot here for the time being to hold this stretch of the road. The one in Pigs should follow me at about thirty seconds' interval. I'm going to get Brigade's permission to trespass. I and my two escort vehicles will charge the mob and drive right through it. We'll then form a blockade across the road on the Gunners' side of the mob. Your platoon in Pigs will come thundering up behind them whilst they're chucking their all at us, will debus and make arrests. Prisoners to go back in the Pigs to battalion HQ. I think the mob will then scatter down the side streets, mainly into Albert Street, leaving us in control of the junction. We can see where we go from there.'

'Right, sir.'

Ian's grizzled head disappeared and the CO called up Brigade. He reported that he was under attack from petrol and nail bombs which were being thrown from the Gunners' area, and asked permission to enter and make arrests. He mentioned the tanker, for good measure. It was the Brigade commander who replied. As usual, his voice procedure was non-existent and his tone vague, even lethargic, but his message was clear. 'Thank you,' he drawled. 'I know about the tanker. I've known about it for some hours. I'm delighted that someone proposes to do something about it. Please go ahead. Let me know when you've done it.'

The CO grinned. 'That's a slap in the face for those bloody Gunners,' he said. 'Now let's sort out this mob.' He summoned Ian Macdonald again and issued final orders.

For once, Nigel Beale appeared to have a crisis of faith. He leaned across to Charles. 'Are we really going to charge them in the Land-Rovers?'

Charles nodded and Nigel leant back, looking thoughtful. Charles groped on the floor for his helmet, found it but then hesitated to put it on. No one else was wearing one. Even the men in the doorways were not wearing helmets. The black beret was a symbol that was not lightly discarded and Charles, against what he considered all reason, still hesitated to be the first man in the battalion that day to allow an operational situation precedence over regimental tradition.

His dilemma was resolved for him when the driver let out the clutch with a jolt and the Land-Rover jerked forward, shooting Charles's helmet out of his hands. With a whining and roaring of overstrained engines and gearboxes, and with the two escort vehicles on either side, they accelerated towards the mob. They bumped and crashed over the debris, flinging those in the back alternately on to their backsides, heads, backs and knees. The CO clung to his door, guffawed and shouted 'Geronimo!' at the top of his voice. A few bricks landed on the road on either side of them and then one crashed on to the bonnet and bounced on to the windscreen grille with a juddering thump. Seconds later the whole vehicle shook and jumped as they ran into a deluge of bricks and bits of metal. It was as though they were driving through a wall that was falling continuously upon them. Twenty yards ahead Charles could see the mob dancing like demented demons in the headlights, throwing everything they could find. They showed no sign of giving way and the driver involuntarily slowed a little. 'Step on it!' bellowed the CO, and the driver accelerated again.

For one moment it looked as though they were going to crush dozens of demons, but then the crowd suddenly scattered like minnows, leaving an empty road. 'Keep those shields up!' Nigel shouted at the two soldiers in the back, who had been thrown about so much that their shields had slipped out of place. The Land-Rovers had stopped a few yards past the junction. The only people in sight were some startled Gunners, crouched in doorways behind shields. Sensibly, they were wearing helmets. The CO whooped delightedly. 'Swing around and block the road,' he said. 'We'll show the buggers.' The three Land-Rovers lurched round, narrowly avoiding each other, and parked sideways across the road. Behind them, where the mob had been, the A company platoon went in fast and hard. Rioters were fleeing in any direction they could find, mostly into Albert Street. Several had been caught and were being dragged back to the waiting Pigs. Most became very docile once they had been caught and even appeared physically to shrink. On closer examination they appeared to be puny and dirty teenagers, disappointingly ordinary. Charles saw one offer violence to his captor, which was accepted and repaid in kind, with interest.

The CO was out of his vehicle and striding gleefully round the captured junction. When he saw Charles he beckoned him over. 'A company have arrested some of your pressmen somewhere back along the Falls. Go and sort it out. We don't want to ruffle their feathers unnecessarily. In fact, I shouldn't be telling you this. You should be telling me. Why didn't you know about it?'

'No one told me, sir.'

'That's no excuse. It's your job to find out. I'm not going to keep doing it for you. Get on and sort it out. Don't stand around here.'

It took some time to find the captured pressmen. None of the soldiers whom Charles asked knew anything about them. He eventually found them in the boarded-up entrance of a disused shop, where a stocky little corporal stood guard over them. They looked tired but patient. One had a camera. They identified themselves as belonging to a local Belfast newspaper, and were obviously familiar with the routine. It was not clear why they had been arrested, but Charles presumed it was for not being members of A company. 'It's all right, they really are press,' he said to the corporal.

'Been told not to let civilians loose on the streets, sir,' said the corporal.

'Except the press. They can. Any more you find bring them straight to me.'

The corporal reluctantly released his charges and went off to rejoin his platoon. The one without the camera looked towards Albert Street. 'Looks nasty,' he said. 'Especially with that tanker in there. It's going to be an all-nighter.'

'D'you think so?'

'No doubt about it.' He looked at Charles. 'You're new. First riot?'

'First big one.'

'You can tell after a while. You get a feeling for it. This one is bad. There'll be deaths, I don't doubt. I wish they'd have them earlier, I do. Get them over by midnight so we could all go home.' It was getting colder and he turned up the collar of his anorak. 'What's this about your CO personally leading the charge that broke up the riot at the junction? Is that true?'

Charles imagined the headlines, and the CO's reaction. 'No. There was a group of youths at the junction and when we approached they ran down into Albert Street. There was no riot.'

'Any arrests?'

'One or two.'

'Was your CO present?'

'Yes.'

'Did they know it was him?'

'He was in a vehicle.'

'So he didn't lead a charge?'

'No.'

'Bit odd, isn't it, the CO getting involved like that? Who controls things back in Headquarters?'

'He just happened to be passing.' Charles did not want to get further involved. He suggested they let him escort them up to near the junction where they could see what was going on.

'I could write it for you now,' said the reporter. 'When you've seen as many as we have you get to know the pattern.'

It was now quite dark, except for a lurid, flickering glow that came from the bottom of Albert Street. Charles was told that the CO and his Rover Group had moved on foot to a point a few yards down the street. As he approached he could see the crouched figures of soldiers on each corner and identified the nearest group as the CO's. They were not, after all, quite in the street. The CO was talking urgently to the RSM about a charge. Charles slipped past them and put his head round the corner, to see what was causing the glow. Less than fifty yards away there was a burning bus wedged broadside across the road. It had been put in position earlier and set alight only in the past few minutes. It burned fiercely, with flames leaping high into the night and dancing on the walls on either side of the street. Already the metal frame of the bus showed through and soon it was silhouetted starkly against the flames. It burned with a continuous crackling roar and it was impossible to see past it. For a few moments Charles stared at the myriad reflections of flame in the broken glass that lay scattered all over the road, until he sensed something pass very near his head. A brick smashed on to the road, closely followed by two more. Whether they were being thrown over the bus or from behind the adjacent walls, it was not possible to say. The way they crashed unseen out of the night seemed expressive of a blind, indiscriminate violence that had nothing to do with anybody. Charles withdrew his head and was then startled by being gripped firmly on the shoulder. For one moment he thought he was being arrested.

It was the CO, his teeth bared in what Charles decided was a grin. Charles could just see his eyes by the light of the fire. 'Glad to see my PRO up in the front line. That's where all good soldiers should be. Want to see some fun, eh?'

The grip tightened and the CO grinned more broadly. Charles could think of no reply that would be both honest and acceptable, but the CO did not need one. He shook Charles good-naturedly. ''Course you do. That's why you're out tonight. That's why we're all out, including the hooligans who set light to that bus. I'll tell you what we're going to do about that. It's protecting their tanker, isn't it? That's obvious. They've got it tucked away in a courtyard behind there and they want to keep us out till they've finished with it. They'll be syphoning off the petrol and then maybe wiring it up as a booby-trap. But they're not bloody going to. We're going to take it before they start throwing bombs and getting really nasty. And we're going to do it with a good old-fashioned cavalry charge on shanks's pony, straight at 'em between the bus and the walls. We'll jump right down their throats. You and me, Thoroughgood. Chance of a lifetime for you.' After another affectionate shake he released Charles and shouted across the road at the RSM, who had crossed to the other corner with his party by doubling back round over the Falls, out of sight and out of range of the bricks. The RSM shouted that he was ready and the CO turned to his own party, which now included Charles. 'Okay?' he asked. Then, with a boyish grin, 'Go!'

There was no time for Charles to consider running away, or not moving, which was his most natural inclination. It was clearly a lunatic escapade but he felt himself in the grip of a collective madness. The CO had already started to run and Charles could not afford to be seen by the others to hesitate. He sprinted along the rubble-strewn pavement towards the conflagration, keeping as close to the wall as possible. It was a hectic, unthinking dash, though at one point when he realised that he was ahead of the others he had the presence of mind to slow down. He kept stumbling on the rubble and several times lurched against the wall, once grazing his cheek. Very soon he was upon the burning bus and the heat hit his face like a prolonged slap. He had no idea what he would do when he got there. The flames had blackened the wall at each side and, though they were not constantly on it, they were continually licking it as though the fire at the centre of the bus were breathing rapidly. Charles hesitated and was pushed roughly aside by the CO who bellowed 'Charge!' and ran into the flames by the wall. He disappeared and Charles followed blindly. There was a moment of intense heat and then he was through. Facing him was a narrow crossroads and a lot of people, who began to run away as soon as they saw the CO. The CO, still yelling, ran after them. Charles followed and even heard himself yelling something incoherent. At the same time a small part of himself felt sufficiently detached to consider the spectacle of the rest of himself following an apparently demented, bellowing middle-aged man after a crowd of people along an Irish street. Fortunately, the CO stopped on the far side of the junction to grapple with a struggling youth, whom he held by the hair. After a couple of seconds he pushed him into Charles, shouting, 'Arrest him!' and ran on. Charles and the youth looked at each other, both panting, before the youth ran off.

For a while there was confusion, with people running in all directions across the junction. There was a lot of shouting. Two youths had been arrested by the RSM's group and were being frogmarched back towards the burning bus. Very soon there were more soldiers than civilians visible, and the mob retreated down the side roads, leaving the junction to the Army. It took Charles some minutes to realise that they were being stoned from somewhere in the darkness, and he ran, ducking, to a large gate in the wall where there were several other soldiers. Inside was a large yard and parked in it was the petrol tanker. Beside it were a lot of milk bottles, some empty and some half filled with petrol and with rags hanging out of them. The CO and his Rover Group were examining them.

'Caught 'em at it,' the CO was saying. 'They were still filling the things when I got here. Got away over the wall, the little buggers. At least they haven't made a bomb out of the lorry yet.'

The burning bus was perilously close and the heat could be felt in the yard, so it was decided that moving the bus was the first priority. Charles was trying to hear how this was to be done when he was accosted by the RSM, who was flustered and breathless. 'Journalists in the Falls. Will you get up and deal with them?'

His tone could hardly have been more urgent if he had been announcing the presence of Russian tanks, nor less respectful if he were talking to a newly-joined private. Charles looked at him before replying, as though to see if there was something he had misunderstood. 'Thank you, Mr Bone.'

'Can you get up there right away? They could be dangerous.'

'Don't worry about them, Mr Bone. They'll be all right.' The RSM looked at Charles as though he thought him mad, then turned away without a word. Charles delayed his departure from the yard for a while, and then sauntered out with careful nonchalance. He then ran across the junction towards the bus, which was no longer burning as fiercely. He had almost reached it when there was the sound of breaking glass behind him, followed by a sudden whoosh and a scorching heat up the side of his right leg. He crouched against the nearest wall, clutching his leg, which he found not to be burnt, and looked round to see a pool of fire flaring in the middle of the junction. The flames quickly died, revealing more broken glass, and he realised it had been a petrol bomb. A couple of yards from him a soldier pointed his rubber-bullet gun down one of the side streets and fired. For a moment the flash and the bang were even more alarming than the petrol bomb. Charles could not see what he had fired at, nor whether there was any result. 'Did you hit him?' he asked.

The soldier shook his head. 'Just making sure they keep their distance,' he said.

It was now possible to get between the bus and the wall without danger. On the other side the sense of urgency and danger diminished sharply. Two of A company's Land-Rovers were parked on the pavement and several soldiers stood leaning against them, talking and gazing reflectively at the almost-gutted bus. An armoured water-cannon – a great lumbering vehicle that Charles had heard about but not seen – began dowsing the flames. Up on the Falls there were more soldiers, including two of B company's platoons, but little activity. One of the A company Pigs had taken prisoners back to battalion HG and three more prisoners were being loaded into another one. Beside it, a fourth figure was spread-eagled against the wall and was being searched by two soldiers. Charles was about to pass by when he recognised the figure as Beazely's. For a brief moment he considered passing by none the less but something got the better of him. 'What have you done?' he asked.

Beazely turned his head cautiously, just enough to see over his shoulder. 'Thank Christ it's you. Tell them who I am.'

'Haven't you?'

'Yes, but I've lost my bloody card. My press card. My lifeline. I know I had it on me when I came out. They won't believe me.'

'We found him in the alley,' said one of the soldiers. 'It looked like he was hiding. He was behaving suspiciously. We thought he might be a petrol bomber.'

'I was hiding,' said Beazely, without a trace of petulance. 'I was hiding from the petrol bombs.'

'There weren't any up here.'

'Well, how was I to know that?'

'What made you think there were?'

'I heard an explosion.'

'Rubber-bullet gun.'

Charles was enjoying himself but felt he shouldn't be. Beazely was still spread-eagled against the wall, his head bowed. 'Is he all right then, sir?' asked one of the soldiers. 'Can we leave him with you?'

Charles continued to look thoughtfully at Beazely.

'We did search him, sir. He was clean.'

'All right. Leave him with me.' The two soldiers left. 'You can move now if you like,' added Charles, after a while.

Beazely straightened himself, though not without looking cautiously around, and rubbed his hands slowly. He looked towards Albert Street, from which bangs and shouts were becoming more frequent. 'I thought I'd had it when they got me. I thought that was it. Up against a wall and shot as a spy. What's going on down there?'

'Just a riot.'

'Oh Christ.' Beazely's fat red face wrinkled in distress and he took off his glasses and wiped them. 'What the hell am I doing here?' he murmured, sounding near to tears. 'What the hell is anyone doing here? Why don't they all go home so we could just do local boy stories and council meetings? What's all this fighting going to do for anyone?'

He replaced his glasses awkwardly and they both stared at a sudden increase of activity on the Falls. A huge digger, or lifter or crusher – it was not clear what it was – was making for the bus in Albert Street. It was a famous and much-loved vehicle known throughout the Army in West Belfast as Scoopy-do. It had vast wheels, jaws at each end and made an impressive noise. It was driven by a diminutive, pale-faced Sapper armed with a Sterling, looking for all the world like a chirpy sparrow on the back of a dinosaur. Charles and Beazely followed it to the top of Albert Street. The burning bus had been extinguished. Its charred and twisted skeleton smoked and hissed. The nearby walls were thoroughly blackened and the roads were very wet. With a great revving in its belly and a lowering of one set of jaws, Scoopy-do charged the bus. It hit it at one end and pushed it round in the street with a maddening screech and scream of protesting metal until there was a large enough gap for a waiting Pig to pass through. But the Pig continued to wait, respectfully it seemed, until Scoopy-do had disengaged from its victim and then itself proceeded through the gap. On the other side of the junction below the bus figures could be seen moving against the light of petrol bombs. A bevy of photographers, cameramen and reporters was following the

Pig and Scoopy-do down the street. 'I'd better go down there,' Charles said.

Beazely was aghast. 'What about me?'

'You can come if you like.'

Beazely's face was screwed up in anguish. 'I can't go down there. You know I can't.'

There were renewed bangs and shouting. 'Up to you,' said Charles with a nonchalance he was far from feeling. A prisoner, yelling and kicking, was dragged past the bus by two soldiers and bundled into the back of a Pig. The incident was avidly filmed by the waiting cameramen.

Beazely grabbed Charles's arm. 'Look, we'll do a deal. I'll wait here and you go there – which you've got to do anyway – only you can take my camera, take a few action snaps, and come back and tell me what happened. Firsthand account, you know. You'd do it much better than me anyway because you know what everything's called. And I'll pay. I'll pay well.'

Having Beazely out of the way was a chance not to be missed. Charles quickly overcame his instinct to refuse. 'Okay, but no photos. I can't do that. No money either. It's not allowed.'

'Why not?'

'Regulations.'

'No, all right, but why no photos? It's too easy. It's got a built-in flash, look. You just click it and bob's-your-uncle.'

251

'Not allowed. Regulations.' Military law was bound to be beyond the comprehension of a mere civilian, requiring, as it did, no obvious reason or justification. Beazely was in no state to argue. He slunk thankfully back round the corner and lit a cigarette. Charles headed down past the bus, surreptitiously fingering for the umpteenth time the butt of his pistol to check that he had remembered to load it. His boots crunched glass as he passed the blackened and water-soaked area of the bus. There were more soldiers at the junction than when he had left it but no journalists. A Pig stood in the middle of the crossroads pointing down a dark side street from which came noise and missiles enough to indicate a sizeable crowd. The Pig acted as a focus of attention, and stones, bricks, bits of drain and guttering rained steadily upon it. The soldiers were crouched at the sides of the roads, some carrying shields but none wearing helmets.

Charles discovered the entire press corps in the yard with the tanker. The CO and his party were still there, and all were watching Scoopy-do as it sniffed around the tanker. Its headlights were on, as were those of the tanker, and this made it look even more like some prehistoric creature sizing up its prey as it lurched from spot to spot. The tanker was still almost full and the brakes were seized on. Eventually, after an energetic altercation between the Sapper driver and some soldiers, a wire was connected to the front of the tanker and, with a great growling but no more apparent effort, Scoopy-do began dragging it out of the yard. Its jammed tyres left a lot of rubber on the ground. After considerable shunting and manoeuvring, including renewed altercations, it was got out of the yard and into Albert Street, up which it was dragged like a great yellow carcass towards the Falls. Photographers and cameramen followed it all the way, holding lights for filming as they ran along.

The CO was pleased. 'Press all right? Not giving you any trouble?'

'No, sir.' Charles was conscious of not having spoken to them yet but they seemed happily occupied.

'Good. Fascinating business, isn't it? Now back to the war, I suppose. Make sure all the press stay together if you can. Don't want them getting in the way of anything or getting hurt. Enough to worry about as it is. There's going to be a fair bit of stuff flying about down there before we sort this lot out.'

Charles caught up with the press and introduced himself. There were about twenty of them and he was surprised at how pleased they seemed to see him. He soon discovered, though, it was not his own charm or personality; after some minutes of questions about times, street-names, numbers, units and incidents he realised that he was their only source of even remotely reliable information. Nevertheless, it was a little perturbing to see his own hazy estimates noted so assiduously, and later to see them quoted as official calculation or even as commonly acknowledged fact. The journalists said they wanted to be nearer the scene of what they obviously thought was going to be a battle worth recording, and so Charles led them back down towards the Pig at the junction. He had no authority to direct or stop any journalist anywhere but he had been told several times by Philip Lamb that the more help he gave them as an organised group under his own direction the less likely they were to be a hindrance to others or a danger to themselves. 'It's the art of the possible,' Philip had said, with the grand manner of one who is asked to comment on a life's work. 'Grant as many of their desires as are compatible without crawling up the CO's backside. And keep him on your side at all costs. It doesn't matter what anyone else thinks.'

They were a varied lot. Most of the nationals were represented, there were three television teams, including one American, one man from the radio, two Frenchmen and a Swede who was gathering material for a magazine article on the evils of British oppression. Charles led them down one side of the street and had almost reached the Pig when there was a flash and a loud explosion very near him. He threw himself on to the ground behind the Pig. He was later told that he had acted with impressive speed. He lay for what seemed a long time with his arms round his head and his knees drawn up in to his chest. His shoulder was pressing against the wheel of the

Pig and so he knew his head must be beneath it and therefore reasonably well protected. There were a lot of flashes but no more bangs. He cringed, waiting for pain, his backside feeling very vulnerable. Something touched it and he shuddered, thinking of shrapnel. Again it was touched, this time more vigorously, and on the third occasion he felt what could only have been a kick. A voice was calling him 'sir'.

He moved one hand slightly and then opened his eyes, closing them immediately because of the dazzling brilliance in which he was bathed. For a moment he thought he must be in an operating theatre. He reopened them cautiously, squinting and still not moving. He then went through surprise, wilful disbelief and final realisation in an ascending scale of unpleasantness. He was surrounded, he found, not by debris and bodies, nor by surgeons, but by whirring cameras and their hand-held lights and popping flashbulbs. A soldier he vaguely recognised was bending over him speaking quietly.

'It's all right, sir, you can get up now, it's all over. You're all right. Come on, now, be a good sir.'

Charles crawled from beneath the Pig but remained in the very depths of humiliation. He stood, swathed in embarrassment. Fortunately, though, at the sight of him standing uninjured and with all limbs present the press lost interest. The lights and cameras stopped, and they moved as one body into the darkness of the side street on the other side of the Pig, from where there were sounds of renewed fighting. Charles looked at the soldier, whom he now recognised as Lance-Corporal Van Horne, the battalion photographer. 'What happened?' He had not wanted to ask the question but Van Horne was volunteering nothing.

'It was the RSM sir. He's a bit trigger-happy with his rubber-bullet gun. You were a bit close.' There was no trace of a smile. 'I must say, sir, you got down very quickly. Even the RSM was impressed.'

Charles looked around but there was no sign of the RSM, nor of any other likely witnesses. The story would be round the battalion in no time. Perhaps in the press, too, and on television.

'I don't think the journalists knew that's what it was,' said Van Horne. 'They thought you'd been shot at. That's what I told them.'

Charles glanced rather than spoke his thanks. Van Horne, he recalled, was unfailingly polite and unreadable. Of Dutch extraction, better educated than most soldiers, one of those voluntary misfits you sometimes come across in the AAC(A). There could be worse accomplices. Charles adjusted his belt and flak jacket and checked his pistol yet again. 'It's very kind of you to have helped,' he said finally.

'The CO sent me to find you, sir. I've been working in the Intelligence Section because Captain Beale didn't realise I was supposed to be with you. Neither did I, I'm afraid to say, sir, or I'd have been here before.'

'How long are you with me for?'

'Permanently, sir. I'm your assistant.' Van Horne smiled politely. Throughout their acquaintanceship Charles never knew him simply smile. If it was not a polite smile it was usually enigmatic, or ironic or, occasionally, triumphant. He rarely allowed himself the luxury of an uninhibited smile. He had even features and intelligent green eyes that gave away nothing. He also had an easy assumption of familiarity that almost, but never quite, went beyond the bounds. 'Our position is rather exposed, sir,' he said.

'What?' Charles dragged his thoughts away from contemplation of his recent buffoonery. 'Yes, of course. We'll join the others.' They made their way to the side street where the rioters now were, a seething mass somewhere further down in the darkness. Soldiers were crouched at the sides of the streets, while the press wandered nonchalantly about waiting for something to happen. 'Have you got a camera?' Charles asked Van Horne.

'Yes, sir. With a built-in flash.'

'Take some pictures if anything happens.' Charles thought he could ensure that at least one paper would not be carrying pictures of himself cowering. Beazely would be grateful for anything. He and Van Horne strolled amongst the press, he with his hands clasped behind his back in the usual manner of officers conscious of their position but not knowing what to do with it. The problem was that officers did not need hands and, pockets being forbidden, there was nowhere else they could go without looking untidy. To his relief, none of the press mentioned his recent humiliation. He decided it must have been a judgment for having relished Beazely's plight.

Once again, Van Horne was perturbingly perceptive. 'The press were very impressed by your evasive actions, sir. I was myself, if I may say so. In fact, you were so fast, sir, that it was some seconds before I realised what you were evading.'

8

During the next twenty minutes or so nothing dramatic happened but the trouble continued in a haphazard sort of way, sustained by its own momentum and by the fact that everyone involved was still there. It was expected that worse was to come but no one had any idea what it would be.

Presently two Ferret scout cars were ordered down because of the spotlights they carried. They came from a Brigade armoured unit, part of which had been made available to the CO, and arrived with a fiendish whine and a screech of brakes. They stopped a short way past the leading soldiers with their Brownings, which they were forbidden to use except on single shot, pointing at the mob. One of them switched on its lights and the street ahead was bathed in a hard glare. It was only seventy yards or so long and ended in a T junction formed by a row of squat houses and another, even narrower, street. A mob of not more than fifty people stood at the far end, doing nothing very much and obviously startled by the lights, against which many of them were shielding their eyes. The CO stood just behind the leading Ferret and spoke through his mega-phone. 'Go home. I am warning you to go home immediately. If you do not clear the area voluntarily it will be my duty to clear it. I shall say it once more – go home.'

The megaphone distorted his voice slightly but it was slow and loud and clear. There was a cluster of microphones around the CO as he spoke and he looked flustered. Charles and Van Horne moved them back a little. One journalist, a well-dressed young man with an Irish accent, pushed past Charles and asked the CO how he was going to clear the area. 'Wait and see,' snapped the CO. 'Speak to my PRO.'

Charles moved him away and answered, 'I'm waiting to see, too.'

'Is he going to shoot these people?' Charles could not see the man's face properly. His voice was hard and aggressive.

'It depends on what they do. You know the rules of the Yellow Card.'

The man pointed to the Brownings on the Ferrets. 'Is he going to use those things on them?'

'They're only allowed to fire single shots in this sort of area.'

'So he's not?'

'Not on automatic, no.' Charles felt less certain than he sounded. If the CO were again gripped by his Light Brigade fever it could well lead to the deployment of RAF Strike Command. Further conversation was prevented when the mob responded to the indignity of being lit up. A shower of petrol bombs arc-ed through the air and smashed on to the road, making a dozen instant fires. The flames spread in sheets around the point of impact and burnt fiercely for a few seconds, often an inch or so above the surface, depending on the vapour. One landed amongst the journalists, scattering them, and another slightly burned a soldier near Charles. A third crashed on to the front of the leading Ferret and the vehicle was instantly engulfed in flame as the petrol coursed over it. Charles could see the commander struggling in his hatch. He thought the vehicle would either blow up or the crew would be starved of oxygen by the flames. For a few seconds he had no idea what to do and stood watching with everyone else. Fortunately, a sergeant with more presence of mind ran forward, pulled an extinguisher off the back of the Ferret, and applied it to the flames, which quickly died. There was some shouting as the Ferret reversed sharply, its lights having gone out. The second one immediately put on its lights and moved forward to take its place. Though the crew was unharmed the incident dramatically heightened the tension. Everyone suddenly became more purposeful and businesslike, including those who, like Charles, had at that moment nothing in particular to do. It was as though all that had happened up till then had been part of a ritual, but now someone had broken the rules.

A couple more petrol bombs provoked a fusillade of rubber bullets in reply, though the range was too great for them to be very effective. Nevertheless, the noise was impressive and sent several bombers scurrying away behind corners. The mob had now thinned down to a hard core of probably no more than twenty or thirty at the very bottom of the street. The Ferret's lights were not powerful enough to show them clearly at that distance and they could only be glimpsed as vague forms against the houses as they ran from cover to cover, or stepped out momentarily from behind corners to hurl a fizzing petrol bomb. Then there were three very loud explosions which ripped viciously through the narrow street, leaving a deafening silence. Someone said they were nail bombs – six-inch nails embedded in lumps of gelignite with a hand-lit fuse. They fell well short of the nearest soldiers since the bombers did not venture into the light.

Charles and Van Horne crouched together in a conveniently large doorway, a couple of yards back from the leading soldiers who were on the opposite side of the road. Several of the more adventurous cameramen were also in the forefront of things, and Charles had to prevent them from using their flashes or lights because these illuminated the soldiers' positions. The CO had several times shouted warnings about the possibility of gunmen and the need to keep heads down. Filming had therefore to be done by the lights of the Ferret and the occasional flaring petrol bomb. The cameramen wandered about the street with impressive unconcern, always looking for the best angle. Charles would have been content to admire had he not every so often had to go and retrieve one who had wandered too far forward. Sometimes he left it to Van Horne, but he seemed equally unconcerned and Charles felt he had to do more than his share so that he would not appear to be as frightened as he felt. The cameramen were nervous but it was a different kind of nervousness. They flitted about like anxious birds, always wanting more light, more movement and more action, never satisfied. They were thin, sharp-faced, agile, worried-looking men, completely absorbed in their work. They rarely had time for a word with anyone. The soldiers, on the other hand, though also sharp in their movements, kept up an unceasing back-chatting humour which consisted largely of expletives. They were perky, bouncy and keen, but cautious.

The more bombing there was, the more elated Charles found he became. He also experienced a growing sense of unreality, almost of untouchability. The discomfort in his bent legs, the shapes of flame, the half-glimpsed outlines of the bombers and the sound of breaking glass were all-absorbing, while the fact that he could be engulfed by flame, torn by shrapnel or shattered by blast was something he could appreciate only as a possibility, like a statistic of road accidents. In the face of violence the idea of violence, sometimes so seemingly awful, lost all its potency; indeed, it hardly existed. It was replaced by details, many and incidental, haphazard and individual, a bomb bursting here, a soldier ducking there, a gun firing from somewhere. It was becoming as enjoyable as childhood games of cowboys and Indians.

Soon he noticed that several soldiers had taken up sniping positions under cover of doorways and corners. Their rifles were equipped with starlight scopes – night sights that gathered all available light and showed up targets as darker or lighter greens against green background. Occasionally the soldiers would take aim at figures Charles could not see, but without firing. The rubber-bullet guns, though, continued to belch forth, but with no visible result. Presumably they kept the bombers at a distance. There were no signs of the people who lived in the street. The doors of the houses were locked and the windows had no lights. It was likely that people were in, huddled fearfully on the floor. The snipers continued to raise, aim and lower in dumb rehearsal.

Charles received word that the CO wished to speak to him. Leaving Van Horne in the doorway, he stole back up the road and crossed it under cover of two Pigs which were now parked there. The CO had established his headquarters behind them and as Charles approached he could feel the barely-suppressed frenzy which gripped everyone near the CO when he was in action. Macdonald, the A company commander whose responsibilities had now been taken over by his own commanding officer, was shouting unnecessarily at one of his NCOs.

The CO beckoned impatiently to Charles the moment he saw him. 'Where've you been? I wanted you twenty minutes ago. I've had that blasted Irish reporter at me again. Sent him away with a flea in his ear this time so it'll be all over the headlines tomorrow, I don't doubt. Now listen' – he put his hand on Charles's shoulder and gripped tightly – 'if these bastards don't stop this soon I'm going to give the order to open fire. What's held me back so far is that there are people in those houses at the bottom of the street and I don't want half a dozen innocent corpses upon my hands. And if I don't stop it now it's going to go on all night until one of my soldiers gets his head or his foot blown off, and I certainly will not stand by and watch that happen. I will not have a bunch of thugs and murderers throwing bombs where and when they like on the Queen's highway.' Charles had learned to look at the CO's lips rather than his eyes, as this gave the impression he was looking at the latter. He did so now at the cost of receiving a fine spray of saliva in his face. 'What I want you to do,' continued the CO with great deliberation, 'is to keep these bloody cameramen out of the firing line. Not that I would break my heart if we shot a few, but they are in the way, d'you understand? And that's not what we're here for. So before I open fire I'm going to warn them, the – er – thugs, the bombers – I'm going to warn them to pack it in. I'm going to give them a chance. Which they don't deserve, I might add, and which is more than they would give to you or I. What I want you to do is to ensure that all the world's press get themselves out of the way and understand that I am warning these people and that I am ordering the snipers to aim low to avoid anyone who might be in those houses. Got that?'

'Yes, sir.'

'I want no bad publicity, no allegations. I shall hold you personally responsible. Go and fix it.'

With the help of Van Horne, Charles was able to round up all the press in sight and move them back up to near the Pigs. This was not easy since although some were only too ready to be organised at the mention of shooting, there were others who considered that their neutrality was being threatened. They saw themselves as having a special position in relation to any conflict and resented attempts to direct or control them. Van Horne suggested that it should be left for the bullets to decide. By exposing himself to what he considered dangerous risk, Charles was able to round up all the remaining obstinate cameramen save one. He had not seen this man but was told he had wedged himself between the leading Ferret and the wall of a house. He was a particularly adept and justly renowned BBC man. From his position he was able to use the lights of the

Ferret for filming and he could see all of what was being thrown, especially as much of it was aimed at the scout car. Charles was about to dash across the road to him when the CO's voice boomed over the megaphone: 'Stop bombing. If you do not stop bombing we shall open fire. I repeat: if you do not stop we shall open fire.' The response was a shower of nail bombs which seemed to shake the street, and then a lull.

Charles ran across the road behind the Ferret and worked his way forward along the wall. The part of the street that was shown in the glare of the lights seemed to be strewn with enough rubble to build a house. Out of the range of the lights it was just possible to see figures moving. The cameraman really was wedged between the Ferret and the wall. Charles had to move sideways to get up to him. If the Ferret were to move they would both be crushed. The crew probably did not know they were there. The CO repeated his announcement as Charles tugged at the man's jacket. The man looked round and Charles beckoned to him. To his relief, he started to edge his way back.

'What is it?'

'Shooting. They're going to open fire.' They had to raise their voices above the noise of the Ferret's engine. Once out from behind it they began to move back up the street, keeping close to the wall. On the other side of the street a sniper had moved forward to a new position. He crouched, nursing his rifle and gazing quietly before him. The cameraman stopped to film him but Charles pushed him on. There was a flash and a crashing explosion that, despite its loudness, seemed more of a crump than a bang. It left Charles's ears ringing. The cameraman had stopped but Charles pushed him on again. There was another flash and crump, followed this time by a fiendish whining sound. The whole street seemed to be ringing. As though from a great distance Charles heard the CO's megaphone repeating, 'Aim low. Aim low.' He clutched the cameraman by the jacket again and they both crouched where they were.

The marksman opposite went about his work with patience and concentration. He raised his rifle and aimed for what seemed a long time before the barrel jerked sharply upwards and there was a crack, a sharper and more incisive sound than the bangs made by the rubber-bullet guns. The marksman fired three times, the empty cases pinging on to the pavement after each shot. Other marksmen had also fired but there were less than ten shots in all. The bombing had stopped but the CO's voice was still saying, 'Aim low. Aim low.'

They waited for some time but nothing happened. The cameraman, indefatigable as ever, had tried to film the marksman but there was not enough light. Charles rested his hand on the butt of his pistol, which was still in its holster. All the tension had gone from the street. They could sense that the other end, dark and quiet, was deserted. Nothing moved in the floodlit middle but at the top both soldiers and press were impatient to be allowed forward, waiting for the CO to give the word. Charles reflected that the whole scene would have made more impact on film than in the flesh, as it now seemed mundane and even a little tedious – though that could have been a reaction to previous nervousness. Both he and his charge then moved carefully up to the top of the street. The CO and his group were still behind the Pigs. A company's commander held something in the palm of his hand which they were all looking at and which several of the press had photographed. When he saw Charles the CO took the object, a lump of metal, and showed it to him. 'See that? Know what it is?'

Charles looked at it, convinced that he ought to know but utterly at a loss. 'No, sir.'

'Well, you bloody well should do. It's the base plug from a number thirty-six hand-grenade, as any private soldier will tell you. It missed your head by about half an inch. These things can kill at great distances on concrete. Two of them were thrown at you when you were chasing some bloody fool press-man who should've known better round and round the Ferret. It's a miracle you're alive. It's a miracle no one else was injured. I can't understand why you aren't dead. Didn't you realise what was happening?'

Charles took the proffered lump of metal. It was heavier than it looked. 'I heard the bangs, sir,' he said lamely.

'You should be dead. You ought to be dead. Anyone else would be.' The CO sounded annoyed but as he turned away he gripped Charles's arm in a comradely fashion and said in an undertone, 'You did a brave thing, foolish or not. Well done. It won't be forgotten.'

Charles pocketed the little lump of metal. He was not sure what it was that he was supposed to have done but he rather hoped that it would be forgotten, in case he were called upon to do it again.

The reason for not advancing down the street immediately was apparently to give the bombers time to retreat. The CO did not want a shoot-out in front of the houses. It would also give time for the Knights of Malta, the voluntary ambulance service which assisted the IRA, to take the wounded away, if there were any, but that could not be helped. Eventually the CO allowed the Ferret to creep forward, which it did with its Browning swinging ominously from side to side. Its mobile spotlight flickered along the walls, reflected dazzlingly by those windows that were still whole. Parts of the walls and the road were blackened by flame and its wheels crushed the glass that lay everywhere with a continuous crackle. The CO and his party followed on foot behind it, Charles with them. He had been told to keep the press back, which task he had delegated to Van Horne while he went forward to check that the area was clear before they were allowed down. Soon the Ferret's lights lit up the end of the street. It was as littered as the rest but the row of houses across the bottom looked undamaged. The spotlight danced into the corners on either side but there was no movement. The Ferret suddenly accelerated and stopped as it reached the end, but all was deserted. The only sounds were the purring of the Ferret's engine and the gentle crushing of glass beneath the boots of those following it. The road forming the T of the junction dwindled into alleyways on each side and in both there was a number of unbroken bottles intended as petrol bombs. Charles noticed that the CO had drawn and cocked his pistol and so he drew his own, but did not trust himself to cock it. The chances of an accidental discharge were, he felt, greater now than the chances of being shot, and the results would be almost as unpleasant. For a few moments everyone paused and there was almost a sense of peace. It began to rain again.

'Someone died here,' said the CO, shining his torch into a puddle. 'We hit three for certain. This was probably the one who lost the top of his head.'

It was a large pool of blood, dark and still. It was three feet or more across. For a moment Charles could think of nothing but Lady Macbeth's, 'Yet who would have thought the old man to have had so much blood in him?' Then, following the light

271

of the CO's torch, he saw there were six pools in all as well as trails of blood leading into the alleyways. Soldiers were sent to search the alleyways but nothing was found.

More blood was splashed on the window-sill of one of the houses, and there was what looked like a bullet-hole in its front door. 'Exactly what I was worried about,' said the CO, pointing to the hole and turning to lecture his audience. 'This very thing. These poor people have their houses used as firing butts. God, I hope we haven't hit anyone. They do it deliberately, you know, these thugs, because they think we won't open fire. Not that it worries them if we do. They don't care if we kill fifty innocent people. In fact, they prefer it. It's good publicity for them. Words fail me, gentlemen.' He turned to the RSM. 'Knock them up, Mr Bone. It's the very least we can do.'

The RSM began a prolonged and loud knocking on the door, a task in which he clearly found fulfilment, and it was eventually opened by a hard-faced but frightened-looking woman of about thirty. She had mouse-brown hair, at which she kept tugging, and staring brown eyes which she at first shielded against the glare of the lights. The CO introduced himself with a formal and old-world courtesy, which obviously baffled her, and apologised for the disturbance. He even saluted and Charles thought for one brief moment that he was going to order everyone to salute. 'Is everyone in your house all right?' he asked. She nodded. 'No one is injured?'

'No.'

Her manner was sullen and resentful but the CO's courtesy, once decided upon, was invincible. 'The reason I ask, madam, is that a bullet probably fired by one of my soldiers, on my orders, looks as though it has gone through your door here. I was worried in case anyone had been injured and I may say I'm profoundly relieved to hear that no one has. The order to open fire is not one that comes lightly or easily in such a situation, believe me. I hope you understand that.' She tugged at her hair and said nothing. 'There is the question of compensation. If you will permit us to enter and trace the path of the bullet we will make a note of the damage and I personally will see that you are properly compensated.'

The mention of compensation cheered her up and during the search for the bullet's path she became almost loquacious on the matter of damage. The bullet had passed through the door and then through the living-room wall behind it and then into the kitchen wall, where it was embedded. The woman and her three young children had been hiding in an upstairs back bedroom. She was asked several times where her husband was but she just shook her head and said, 'Dunno.'

When the inspection was complete, the CO grabbed Charles by the shoulder again. 'This young officer is Charles Thoroughgood. He is my public relations officer and my community relations officer, which means he deals with complaints. If you make a list of damage similar to the one we have made and bring it with you to our headquarters, along with an estimate for repairs, Charles Thoroughgood will see that you get it. All right?' The woman nodded and glanced mistrustfully at Charles. 'His telephone number is – what's your telephone number?' Charles told her. 'You can ring or come and see him at any hour of the day or night and he will help you. That's what he's there for. He sits on the end of the telephone waiting to help people. Any time you want anything at all just ask for Lieutenant Thoroughgood.'

Three days earlier, at prayers, the CO had warned everyone against revealing their names, telephone numbers or any other details to people who might pass them on to the IRA. As they left the house he turned to Charles and said, 'My heart goes out to these poor people, you know. They've got no choice, you see. They live here and they can't afford to stand up against the thugs, especially if they've got children. It's more than their lives are worth. We should always bear that in mind when dealing with them.'

After Charles had reminded the CO of their existence, the press were allowed down to the bottom of the street. For two or three minutes they filmed and photographed the blood enthusiastically, illuminating it with flashbulbs and very bright hand-held lights. There was speculation about the number hit but all Charles was able to tell them was what the CO had told him. After he had done this he realised he had been standing in a puddle of blood that had started to go sticky, as he could feel it on the soles of his boots. There were more requests to interview the CO. Charles found him searching for more bullet-holes. 'They want to interview you, sir.'

'I've got better things to do. Keep them out of my hair. That's what you're supposed to be here for. Let them interview you.'

'They want you, sir, because it was you that gave the order to open fire.'

'What do they want, blood?' The CO seemed genuinely angry and then sighed. 'All right, I suppose I'd better. It's all part of the job these days. God, how I hate a press war. Bring 'em round.'

Charles feared that in his present state any remotely hostile questioning might produce an angry reaction from the CO. 'It would be better to do it back at battalion HQ, sir.'

'Why? Why not here? Scene of the action and all that stuff, that's what they like, isn't it?'

Charles thought quickly. 'It's much better back there for all their equipment – for the filming. They can set their lights and things up properly.'

'All right. You're the expert.'

Charles announced that there would be a press conference back at battalion HQ and most of the press headed gratefully off, though some left to meet deadlines for the early editions. Farther up the street Scoopy-do was at work again, dragging the carcass of the bus off to some wasteland on the other side of the Falls where the carcasses of all sorts of vehicles rotted after previous riots. The metal squealed as it scraped against tarmac and brick; otherwise, the city seemed dead. The CO and his Rover Group left with an unnecessary revving of engines but Charles, having arranged a lift with one of the other vehicles, lingered on for a few minutes. It was raining steadily now, big drops that splashed in the puddles, diluting and washing away the blood. A few soldiers were left to finish the search and the street glistened in the lights of the waiting Pig. The only sounds now were of occasional vehicles in the distance and the steady, soothing patter of the rain. After the excitement and noise the calm seemed correspondingly deeper. Everyone moved carefully and talked in undertones, as though in the presence of the dead. When someone kicked a brick which bounced with a clang off the side of the Pig the corporal in charge swore angrily at the offending soldier.

Charles and Van Horne walked slowly up the street together. Charles had forgotten Beazely and groped ineffectually for his pistol as the portly figure lurched from the darkness of an alley.

'All right, it's me, it's me,' said Beazely in a hoarse whisper.

Charles pretended to have been fastening the flap on his

holster and Van Horne, who had been rather quicker on the draw, replaced his pistol. 'I'd forgotten you,' said Charles.

'Thought you had. You've been a bloody long time down there. Is it all over?'

'Everyone's gone home.'

'Thank Christ for that.' Beazely's sheepskin jacket was wet and dirty, his face red and flustered as always but adorned by raindrops. He touched his glasses nervously. 'Sounded bloody awful down there. Hell of a noise. Must've been a real battle. You're all right, are you? Not blown up or anything?'

'No, we're all right. Why, were you worried you wouldn't get your story?' Charles regretted the remark as he said it.

Fortunately Beazely never took offence quickly. 'Well, I won't deny that crossed my mind,' he said. 'But, you know, when two blokes you know and like disappear off into the dark and there's a lot of banging and shooting and shouting it's natural to wonder if they're all right. Nice to have you back, that's all. Must've been a real battle.'

Charles found that he didn't want to talk about it now that the time had come. Anyway, there wasn't much to say. 'Not really. We shot two or three bombers and the others went home. There were no bodies and no prisoners. One soldier was slightly injured by burns and another by a brick.'

'What about details? I must have details. Eye-witness accounts, you know.'

'There's a press conference back at battalion headquarters. Come to that.'

'That's no good, you know it isn't, that's all the official stuff. I can't use that for my I-was-in-the-front-line-trapped-between-both-sides, can I? Come on, Charlie, give me the story. You said you would.'

'I'll give it to you there.'

Beazely grabbed Charles's arm imploringly. 'For Jesus Christ's sake, Charlie, look, I have a deadline to meet in twenty-five minutes for the early editions and if I don't meet it I'm finished – you know, cut throat finished. The press conference stuff is for the later editions. Everyone else has filed theirs and I still haven't even got mine and then I've got to find a phone that works in this God-awful place. Come on, Charlie, please, you said you would.'

Charles turned to Van Horne, who had maintained an air of polite disinterest. 'Did you notice anything suitable?'

'Blood all over the place,' Van Horne replied promptly. 'Lying in puddles in the road, spattered over the walls of the houses, brains in the gutter. Grenade-thrower's head taken off in the act of throwing. Mothers and children cowering in the houses, priests in attendance –'

'Priests?' asked Charles. Beazely was avidly noting everything Van Horne said.

'There must've been at least one, sir. There always is.'

Beazely shot him a quick glance of grateful appreciation. 'Vicious attack with nail bombs and grenades in narrow streets, designed to kill. Army opened fire only after repeated warnings. Minimum force but enough to be effective. Armoured car ablaze, crew saved by brave sergeant. Dramatic rescue of petrol tanker bomb horror that could've blasted entire neighbourhood. Army tempted to blow it up where it was and save themselves trouble –'

'Not that,' said Charles.

Beazely's pencil hovered. 'How about Army defuse massive tanker bomb and save families?'

'If you like.'

'You'll be rewarded handsomely for this, gentlemen,' added Beazely.

'No need,' said Charles.

'We've got photos too,' said Van Horne.

'Great. Thanks a lot. I should be able to do something with this.'

'How long will it take you to write it?' Charles asked, more because he felt a little guilty at having been so unhelpful than because he really wanted to know.

'Whatever time I've got. Ten minutes maybe, then I'll probably alter it as I ring it in. Less than that if I don't get to a phone quickly. Thanks for your help. Hope you have a quiet night, what's left of it.'

Beazely did not get to the conference because he was still telephoning his story. Given a few of the right phrases and a few facts, true or false, he seemed to be able to knock one into shape very quickly. There was no doubting his proficiency in this respect. The story, when Charles saw it the next day, was a convincing and exciting account of a riot and its aftermath which could be faulted only in its not resembling the riot he had attended. Though perhaps, on reflection, that would not have been regarded as a very serious fault.

The journalists were crowded into the Mess, with all the wires, lighting and cameras needed by the TV people. It was not difficult to sense a degree of impatience with all this on the part of the steam press, as they called themselves. These men needed only notebooks and access to a telephone to make their news. The cumbersome, time-consuming technical demands of their more glamorous TV counterparts were exasperating and the result, in their eyes, was not worth it. The radio reporters, able to offer the most immediate news of all, were only slightly encumbered by their equipment and had more in common with the steam press. A space was cleared at the far end of the Mess for a table and two chairs. Pleading that the CO would not answer questions he was not prepared for and was required by the Army to stick strictly to facts, Charles ascertained that they wanted comment on why the CO had decided to open fire, what effect he thought it had had, the dangers arising from the hijacking of the petrol tanker and whether or not the CO had himself led the charge on the bus.

The CO was upstairs in his room and Charles went up to brief him. Looking tired and drawn, he was sitting at his desk with an untouched glass of whisky before him. He heard Charles out and then passed his hand wearily across his eyes. 'Dammit, how I hate having to talk to these wretched people,' he said. 'It's not their fault, of course. They've got a job to do just as I have, but it's all this going back over it, having to say the right thing, resurrecting the whole terrible business. It's worse than actually doing it, you know. When I think of those poor, stupid, foolish, ignorant, tragically misguided young men whom we probably killed tonight it makes me want to weep, you know, it really does. They could've been my sons, or yours if you were older. They were somebody's. It certainly would have been at least one of my soldiers if we hadn't done what we did. Those are the people the press should be talking to, the bloody Provisional IRA, not me. They should be saying to them, "Look, for God's sake stop this bloody lunacy, this violence, because it'll get out of control and kill all of you and a great many more besides." Don't you think, eh?'

Charles nodded. When the CO needed someone to talk to he did not need them to say very many words, although he paid full attention to any they did say. At such times Charles felt close to him despite himself, and at the same time awkward, as though he were there under false pretences.

The CO held out his hand, as if to show something in his palm, and kept his dark eyes fixed upon Charles. 'If only these people could be made to see that if they consistently break the law, if they consistently use violence they will meet with violence, and if it comes to a showdown the side with superior force wins. And that's us, they must know that. And to keep up a war of attrition is simply to prolong the agony, their own as well as everyone else's, without getting anywhere because no British government, of any complexion, is going to pull out of Northern Ireland against the wishes of the majority of people as expressed in the ballot box. They must see that, they must. They can't surely be so stupid as not to, can they? And to go on as they are, where does it get them? How are they one jot the better? How is their cause advanced one inch further? If anything, it goes backwards. There's nothing to be gained by violence of this kind and everything to be lost, and they're losing it.' His tired face was now tense and his eyes hard with passion. He gripped his glass of whisky tightly and raised it but put it down again without tasting. 'Don't you think that's what the press should be doing, telling them that, eh? Trying to stop it instead of asking me damn fool questions about why I opened fire when there were grenades rattling around in the street?'

Charles nodded again but still said nothing. After gazing thoughtfully at his whisky for a few moments, the CO knocked it back in one and stood up, smoothing down his jersey and stamping his feet so that his anklets fitted snugly over the tops of his boots. He clapped Charles on the back and grinned. 'Hang it all, I nearly lost my PRO to those grenades, and then where would I be? The only one I've got. I hope they realise that.'

They went downstairs and made their way through the crush, the smoke, the wires and the hubbub to the table by the wall. The CO appeared calm, grave and self-possessed. As he took his seat the hubbub ceased. Charles sat next to him.

At first, all went well. The questions were much as antici-pated, with the rival TV interviewers irritating everyone by each asking the same questions and requiring the same answers to be delivered to them individually. They for their part were irritated by what they regarded as unnecessary and inarticulate interruptions from the steam press. The CO's replies were stiff and rather lengthy but the points were answered. He used a lot of phrases that were typical of him and of no one else that Charles had met, such as 'denying the Queen's highway', 'the Queen's writ will not be flouted', 'the un-Christian monsters who so tragically misguide these young men', 'the honour and integrity of the British Army', 'my soldiers will not stand by while the Queen is insulted' and 'the appalling dilemma confronting every commander which only God can resolve'.

Charles knew that such phrases and concepts were not only part of the CO's everyday conversation but were central to how he saw himself and the world, but he did not know how the press would react. He feared mockery or disdain but saw neither, only attentiveness. Whether they sympathised with the CO's all too obvious sincerity or whether such remarks made good press, he could only guess. Trouble came from the well-dressed, thin-faced young man who had earlier displayed his potential animosity. It turned out he was Colm McColm of the *Gazette*. He did not speak until the conference was about to finish and the TV people had begun to dismantle their equipment. When he spoke it was with a quietness born of confidence.

'Colonel, on your own admission you ordered the shooting of several people this evening, of whom at least one is probably dead.'

The room quietened and the TV men stopped their dismantling. The CO had his elbows on the table and his hands firmly clasped. 'I said that we opened fire and we think we hit at least three bombers.'

'Colonel, could you tell me what kind of weapon your men were using?'

'They were using the 7.62 millimetre self-loading rifle. It's the standard weapon in this and other NATO countries.'

'I see. Correct me if I'm wrong, but is it true to say that it is a high-velocity weapon that is lethal at ranges of well above five hundred yards?'

'It is, depending on the accuracy of the man using it.'

'What was the range at which your men opened fire this evening?'

'About sixty or seventy yards.'

'About sixty or seventy yards. And will a human body stop a 7.62 bullet at this range?'

'Not usually, no.'

'Not usually. So the bullet goes straight through. And what about the thing behind the body – a wall, for example. Will it go through that?'

'It depends on the wall.'

'Let us say, an ordinary terrace-house wall like those we all saw this evening. Would that stop the bullet?'

'Probably not.'

McColm was very relaxed, with one arm along the back of the seat next to his and a notebook balanced on his knee. The TV cameras were going again and the CO was staring at his questioner, his lined face held in a brittle composure. 'Are we to understand, then,' continued McColm, 'that you knowingly and deliberately opened fire with high-velocity weapons in a built-up area at human targets not more than seventy yards distant?'

Charles could see the veins on the CO's hands as he gripped tightly, as though in fervent prayer. He looked down at the table and then said in a quiet, taut voice, 'I ordered my soldiers to open fire at identifiable targets who were throwing lethal bombs and hand-grenades on one of Her Majesty's highways. I ordered them to aim low in order to avoid injury to anyone in the houses behind.'

'But you admit that you opened fire with high-velocity weapons at short ranges, Colonel, and you admit that the bullets could have gone through the walls of houses in which innocent people were living, but you don't admit to the terrible danger to anyone in that area nor to this obvious flouting of the Army's so-called minimum force policy. I ask you, Colonel, a 7.62 bullet at seventy yards, what does it do to a man? Takes his head off, I'm told. And perhaps the head of the man behind him. How can you justify such tactics? How can you sit there and justify them?'

The CO's tightly-compressed lips and his prolonged downward glance betrayed a rising tension which threatened his self-control. He still spoke very slowly, staring straight at the reporter. 'I took what action was necessary to prevent the murder of one of my soldiers. As well as to protect the lives and property of the surrounding population from destruction by the bombers. I ordered my soldiers to aim low in order to minimise the risk to the inhabitants of those houses. And I have since inspected the damage myself and arranged for compensation. There were no injuries.'

'And we have only your word for this?'

Something seemed to snap inside the CO and he got to his feet, his voice rising as he spoke. 'Young man, I don't know who you are or what paper you represent and I frankly don't care. But I'll tell you one thing. If you'd stood in my shoes on that street this evening for just two minutes – that's all, two minutes – you wouldn't come in here looking for a bloody autopsy. You have not the remotest idea what it means to take the kind of decision I had to take this evening, not the remotest. God forbid that I ever thought the day would come when I had to order a platoon in battle-order down a British street and tell them to open fire. But it has. And God knows it's not easy but as God is my witness it has to be done. So you're not going to find any bodies here. Go to Dublin and ask some of your friends down there. Go and ask them!'

The CO was pointing at McColm by the time he had finished, his teeth clenched, his face red and his finger shaking. The cameras were still going and a couple of microphones were discreetly held at table-level. McColm was still lounging in his chair but his face had paled and hardened with self-consciousness. Seeing that he was about to speak, Charles got to his feet. Everyone looked at him and for what seemed a long moment he could think of nothing to say. He thought of Manningtree, his tutor, who had a habit of ending more than usually boring tutorials somewhat abruptly. 'Gentlemen, we called this conference in order to discuss matters of fact, not the ethics of violence. If you have no more questions we shall consider it closed.'

To his great relief there was a general scraping and shuffling of chairs and a growing murmur. People started to move towards the door and the TV men again began packing up their equipment. McColm was one of the first out, saying nothing to anyone. As the London *Times* man – a kindly-looking, avuncular figure – left he raised his bushy eyebrows at the CO and Charles. 'Still get complaints if they issued you with peashooters,' he grunted.

When they had gone the CO sat down, resting his head in one hand. When he looked up at Charles his face was very weary and his eyes dull. 'Sorry, Charles, I blew my top,' he said quietly. 'Let you down. Let us all down. A CO should never do that in public.' He stood and stamped his feet, with an effort at cheerfulness. 'Glad you stopped it when you did. You were splendid. God only knows what I'd have said if I'd gone on. Has it done any harm, d'you think?'

Charles was embarrassed by the CO's humility, as though by his mere presence he was taking advantage of it. 'I don't think so, sir. There was nothing politically unwise. I don't see why it should.'

'Good. Well, we'll see. Bloody press. Get me a whisky, will you?' Charles went to the drinks tray, poured a large whisky and gave it to him. He took it rather gruffly. 'You know I don't drink alone. Get one yourself. Fine state of affairs when a CO has to order his own officers to drink with him.'

Later, Charles found Van Horne in his office. He had attended the conference, standing at the back, and had shown all the press out. The corners of his mouth showed the merest beginnings of a smile. 'That bloke dropped a right bollock in front of the CO, didn't he, sir?'

'Something like that.'

'If he hadn't been a civvy the CO would've had his guts for garters.'

'I thought for a moment he was going to, anyway.'

Beazely telephoned, asking what had happened at the conference. Charles resisted his first impulse and gave him a boring and doctored account, to make sure that at least one daily did not splash the CO's anger all over the front page. He then rang the PR desk at Headquarters to tell them what had happened but instead spent most of his time trying to convince them that the major they had sent to assist him at nine o'clock this evening, without telling anyone, had never arrived. With the facetiousness that sometimes comes with tiredness, Charles suggested that he might have found a better story on the way but the suggestion was taken literally and without humour. It was one of a number of options. Others were that he had either been killed or kidnapped. An enquiry was to be started. To those on the streets Headquarters was a remote world and what happened there was a matter of indifference or at best ridicule, unless it directly affected them. It was gone four in the morning and Charles felt no compunction about leaving them to it.

9

The post did not arrive in battalion HQ until late afternoon as it had to be collected from Headquarters by the diminutive post corporal and his escort of two Land-Rovers. It had been late the previous day and by the time it came Charles had no time to collect his because of the trouble. He got it before breakfast the following morning. Those mornings were the most leisurely part of the day because the rioters and terrorists had little enthusiasm for rising early. The CO had remarked several times that it would be the best time to carry out a shooting attack on the Army because people were least on their guard then. The mornings were also the time when it was possible to get within sight of that lost world in Army life, privacy. There were no rules about breakfast, and anyone could simply get up and eat roughly six hours after whatever time he had been lucky enough to get to bed, and at the appropriate time breakfast merged painlessly into lunch. There were no papers that morning, which was not unusual because they sometimes arrived late. It was something to be thankful for, in that the CO could not have seen them either. In the meantime, the reading of letters would provide an effective barrier against Nigel Beale, who was sometimes inclined to talk over breakfast.

However, Charles did not need the barrier that morning. In fact, he did not get a chance to use it. Nigel and Tony Watch were at breakfast when he arrived and, there being no papers, Nigel was particularly chirpy. He was claiming to have predicted the previous day's trouble.

'Well, I didn't hear you,' said Tony.

'Pay attention in the briefings.'

'I do. You never said there was going to be trouble yesterday.'

'Maybe I didn't say it was going to be yesterday in the briefing. You don't hear everything there, you know. There's a lot of need-to-know stuff that I brief the CO on personally.'

'How come he didn't know about it, then?'

'What makes you think he didn't?' Nigel shoved a forkful of egg, bacon, fried bread and tinned tomato into his mouth and munched aggressively. Charles was helping himself from the hot-plates when Anthony Hamilton-Smith arrived and did the same. Anthony never spoke to anyone at breakfast. He always read *The Times*, beginning with the back page, and when there was no paper he simply ate and stared as though there was no one else in the room. He gave the impression of a great solitude, as of one who had renounced the world, and if he were ever forced to acknowledge other people – such as by having to ask for the marmalade – he did so in a way that made them feel he had never seen them before and had no wish to again. He usually began to be more sociable within about an hour of breakfast, and by the time of his lunchtime gin and tonic he was spritely and cheerful. On this morning he and Charles executed a kind of ritual dance around the hot-plates, based on unspoken principles of fairness, temporal priority and the respect due to rank and age. Each came away with what he required and sat down with the other two without speaking. Unfortunately, the table was small.

'Anyway,' continued Tony Watch. 'What makes you think it was the Provisionals that organised it? How d'you know it wasn't the Stickies?'

'The who?' Nigel's mouth was still full and his cheeks bulged.

'The Stickies,' repeated Tony irritably.

Nigel swallowed. 'Who the hell are they when they're at home?'

'The Stickies? Don't you know who the Stickies are?' Tony's plump face showed a mixture of triumph and genuine surprise. 'The Stickies are the official IRA. I thought everyone knew that. It's common knowledge.'

'Not to me it isn't.'

'The CO knows.'

'I've never heard of it.'

'Well, don't look at me. You're supposed to be the Intelligence officer. Go and ask the first Ackie you meet. He'll tell you who the Stickies are.'

'Sounds bloody unlikely to me,' said Nigel. He looked disgruntled and uncertain.

Without a word to anyone, Anthony got up from the table, walked over to the hat rack, put on a black beret, taking care to adjust it neatly with the badge in line with the left eye and the brim an inch above the eyebrow, returned to the table, sat down and continued calmly with his breakfast. Nigel and Tony forgot their argument for a while and stared at him, but neither ventured to say anything. Charles was careful not to stare but could not help glancing several times, surreptitiously. Anthony ate solemnly and silently, as though wearing a beret was as much a part of the breakfast ritual as food. He supposed it was Anthony's way of indicating his disapproval of the conversation and admired him for it, though without following the logic of the act. He decided to postpone opening his letters until he had finished eating. He did not want Anthony to feel obliged to get up and put on his overcoat.

Nigel Beale was less sensitive, being one of those people who do not seek to enquire after the causes of odd behaviour in others. What interested him was the problem in hand. He put his knife and fork down and pushed his plate away. 'So why are they called Stickies?' he asked Tony. 'If they are, that is.'

'I don't know,' said Tony. 'Go and ask them. Or get Charles here to ask the press for you. They'll know.'

Anthony put his cup into his saucer with a noise as decisive as an auctioneer's hammer. 'Stickies,' he said with chilling precision, 'is the name by which the official IRA have been known since one Easter a few years ago when they departed from Republican tradition by sticking their Easter lilies to themselves rather than pinning them. As an Intelligence officer you should know the regimental history and traditions of your enemy.' He sipped his tea, almost demurely, and then looked again at Nigel. 'And as an officer you should also know that talking at breakfast is not a habit that is encouraged in the British Army, especially talking shop. It's unfortunate that it's allowed at all. In some regiments it is not, while in my father's regiment, the wearing of head-dress at a meal indicated that the wearer did not wish to be spoken to. Indeed, it was considered polite not to speak in his presence. That is a custom we would do well to adopt.' Anthony then got up and took his tea to an armchair, where he sat and sipped calmly, still wearing his beret.

Tony Watch raised his eyebrows and smiled at Charles. Nigel Beale looked as though he were about to reply, played for a few moments with his teaspoon, then got up and walked out without looking at anyone. Tony soon left and Charles went and sat with his coffee and letters in the armchair opposite Anthony. The silence continued for some moments until Anthony looked up. 'Charles.'

To his surprise, a slight smile played upon Anthony's features. 'Yes, Anthony?'

'I think I may have started a regimental tradition.'

'I hope you have, Anthony,' said Charles, sincerely.

Still smiling, Anthony took off his beret. His triumph seemed to have made him light-hearted and almost loquacious, for the time of day. 'Should shut young Beale up for a bit,' he said. 'I'm very pleased he left when he did, though. This beret ain't mine. Tight at the band. Must belong to some pin-head. Thought I was in danger of passing out and spoiling the effect. Mine's upstairs.'

Charles laughed. 'It did the job anyway.'

Anthony stood and stretched. 'Just goes to show,' he said, mysteriously. He put the beret back on its peg on his way out of the Mess. 'Have a good day, old boy.'

'And you, Anthony.' Charles turned at last to his letters. There was a postcard from Janet, posted in York, where she had been for the weekend. She did not say with whom. One of the other letters was from Regimental Headquarters asking for subscriptions and the other was from the Retirements Board saying that he could be released from the Army on repayment of one thousand pounds. The earliest date was the day after the battalion's return from Ireland, by which time he would have to have paid the money. He was not entitled to terminal leave nor to the normal gratuity. A copy of the letter was being sent to the CO.

Charles had had no idea that it could be so easy. Pessimism had set in after he had sent his letter and the recent busyness had pushed to the back of his mind all thoughts about resignation, but now the knowledge that he could be out of the Army in two months shook the sleep out of him and made even his present surroundings seem almost pleasant. He rose from the table and poured himself another coffee with the delight in detail of one who sees for the first time. His boots, his beret, his heavy wool jersey could all be viewed now with affection, rather than sickening familiarity, because he would be leaving them. It was clear that his main task now was to stay alive, complete and uninjured. He thought about this as though it were a holy vow and resolved to consider how best to eliminate those activities that offered the most danger.

There was, of course, a problem about the money. The very most he could raise by selling everything saleable, including the old Rover (if it still was saleable) and his mess kit and blues (if Regimental Headquarters still bought such things), was a little over five hundred pounds. He could think of no job he wanted and would be in no position to borrow from the bank. He thought briefly of Janet, who had money of her own, but felt this would be ignoble. He was then a little annoyed because he had considered himself above thinking such things were ignoble – it was the kind of reaction he associated more with the CO than with himself – but he then had to admit that the real reason was that he did not like to commit himself to her any more than he had.

These intriguing speculations were ended by the arrival of the CO. Charles nervously expected a reaction to the letter from the Retirements Board but the CO ate his breakfast quickly, saying nothing to anyone, called sharply for his vehicles and drove off to the Brigade O Group. When he had gone one of the mess orderlies brought in the newspapers, from the state of which it was clear that someone had read them hurriedly. It appeared that the CO had had them sent up to his room the moment they appeared. Charles was apprehensive but they turned out on the whole not to be as bad as he had feared. The riot and subsequent shootings were headlined throughout and there were lots of fuzzy, confusing pictures. There were a few quotations from the CO's outburst, which came over surprisingly well, and no one had taken up McColm's point about high-powered weapons except the *Irish Times* man. The *Gazette* carried essentially the same stories as the others but with the addition of extensive coverage of the views of local residents. It claimed that soldiers had broken into houses on the pretext of searching for wanted men but that their real purpose had been to vandalise. The damage in the house that the CO had inspected was accurately listed, although McColm had neglected to mention that the holes in the walls had been caused by a bullet and not by the soldiers. Inside there was a short feature entitled, 'The Man who lets God decide'. It said that the CO had been beside himself with rage at the press conference and asked whether such a man could be trusted to remain cool in more dangerous situations. It questioned the use of high-powered weapons in built-up areas and cited the CO as one who shifted the responsibility for such decisions to a suspiciously Unionist God, using the Queen of England as his authority. Surprisingly, none of the papers speculated about the cause of the riot, which remained unknown.

Charles read Beazely's paper last. He was reassured by the report on the front page and Beazely was on the way to having some of his lost credibility restored to him when Charles reached the centre-page spread. There was a large photograph of himself cowering beneath the Pig at the crossroads, captioned, 'Lieutenant Charles Thoroughgood, 41, takes no chances as grenades pepper the streets'. It was a press agency photograph and had beneath it an article by 'Our Special

Correspondent' in which Charles read some of his own and many of Van Horne's words, fortunately without their being attributed to either. Beazely had added the punctuation and a few imaginative flights of his own.

The only other surprise was a leader in a staunchly Unionist paper calling for more shooting, more units like AAC(A) and, strangely, for stricter enforcement of the law relating to road fund licences. It was the adjutant who later pointed out that cars in Republican areas were never taxed.

There was more trouble that afternoon up in the new estate. The fact that it began about an hour after lunch, as convenient a time as any, was due to the CO's having started it. That morning he had returned from his O Group later than usual, and had stomped straight up to his room, still without speaking to anyone. The adjutant was summoned a while later and Charles feared that it might have something to do with himself, especially as the adjutant was tight-lipped afterwards. Later, though, the ops officer and Nigel Beale were summoned and Charles began to relax. Over lunch there was a great deal of important secretiveness amongst those in the know, except for the adjutant who looked as disinterested and weary as usual by then. Anthony Hamilton-Smith was either oblivious to any secret or was particularly good at keeping it, whilst Tony Watch was aggressively but unsuccessfully curious. Nigel Beale exuded a passionate furtiveness and communicated with the ops officer in cryptic monosyllables. It was all spoilt by the CO who was brisk and talkative when he came to lunch and informed everyone that he had got clearance from Brigade to do a search of selected houses in the new estate before dusk. There was information – doubtful, according to Brigade, who couldn't see beyond the ends of their noses, but white-hot, according to the CO – that a large quantity of gelignite had been moved in to the area in preparation for a series of bombings. Swearing all present to eternal secrecy, he said that this was the result of a decision taken by the Provisional IRA leadership at a conference in a Dublin hotel to increase terrorism and to decrease rioting. Apparently they thought that terrorism was more likely to drive the British from Ulster and would convince the Ulster people that to live in an Ireland united by the Provisional IRA was what they really wanted. Eternal secrecy was vital in order that the Eire government should not be embarrassed by the suspicion that it harboured terrorists.

Elements from throughout the battalion were involved in the search and they entered the new estate in an impressive convoy, to the accompaniment of banging dustbins. There was also the usual shouting and jeering. It was some time since Charles had been into the estate and he would not have thought deterioration possible, but before his eyes the worst had clearly got worse. Unbroken windows and unsmashed paving stones were now so unusual that they caught the eye and prompted speculation. Garden fences had long been pulled down but a few tatty privet hedges remained. Many of the houses had tiles missing and cracks in their walls. Dirty, unhappy-looking children swarmed like flies and mangy dogs started up everywhere. Because of the very high unemployment a large number of men were at home and, it being afternoon, most of them were up.

Grilles were up on the Land-Rovers. The CO sat in the front with his map-case open. 'There is nothing that pleases me more,' he said, 'than to ride at the head of a convoy of military vehicles. If only we were going to war instead of searching these wretched people's homes. My God, we'd better find something, you know, or we'll look pretty stupid.'

'It's bound to stir them up if we don't,' said Nigel Beale.

'It'll stir them up if we do. Anything we do annoys them. If you were to walk round here tonight and give every man a pound he'd go and drink it and then throw the empty bottle at you. And if we didn't do anything they'd hoard enough explosive to blow themselves and the rest of Belfast sky-high. Maybe that's the answer, I don't know.'

Once well into the estate the convoy split up and different bits went to different houses. Charles went with the CO to one of the white-hot certainties, the home of a well-known

Republican family. The thought that because he was leaving the Army he would never come back to Belfast, made him pay more attention to what he saw. It might, after all, be the last search they would do. He hoped it would. He was too English not to feel apologetic about such an invasion of privacy. The house in this case was a tattered semi-detached with a larger than usual garden, which was no more than a patch of earth and scrub excreted upon by dogs and children. They surrounded the house and entered by the front door, which had had a hole kicked in the bottom and didn't close properly. There were at least a dozen occupants of all ages and both sexes. Some protested vigorously and loudly to the pale young soldiers who concentrated on their first duty of entering every room and counting the people, before trying to get them all into one room downstairs. Meanwhile, a shouting and chanting crowd had gathered outside but were kept at a distance by the escort. The accompanying RUC men were older and more accustomed to abuse, and they went about their work with none of the nervous hurry of the young soldiers. An indefinable stench, a combination of many smells, old and new, pervaded the house. On entering, the CO turned to Nigel Beale and said in an undertone, 'This is where the stuff is, you know. I'm sure of it. If it's anywhere in this estate, it's here.'

Soldiers with mine-detectors were ordered to search the

garden. After taking a couple of steps into the hall Charles had attempted to linger on the doorstep, but was summoned inside by the CO to deal with complaints. The house had been searched many times before and after their initial hostility most of the people settled into a sullen resentment. Their names were taken and it turned out that they were all family, or so they said. There was a likeness running through them all, but it was more a likeness of expression and manner than of anything physical. A plump, unhealthily pale and prematurely old man who sat quietly in the corner said, when his name was taken, 'Youse searched this house seventeen times since 1969 and never found nothing. When youse gonna stop?'

'When you tell us where the gear is,' said the soldier.

'There's no gear here. I don't know where no gear is.'

'Then we won't be long, will we?'

Charles knew better than to invite complaints, since everyone would have complained at the house being searched at all. However, he was picked upon by two teenage girls with lank dark hair and hard, expressionless faces. They had probably chosen him because he was the only one standing around doing nothing. 'Some of your soldiers have made a mess of our toilet,' one of them said.

'What have they done?'

'Come up and see.'

He followed them upstairs and they showed him into the

bathroom. There were smears and deposits around the toilet in such positions as to suggest wild, uncontrolled and aerobatic excretions. It was only his involuntary recoil on entering that saved him from the indignity of being locked in, as they tried to push him forward and close the door behind him. He pushed back and they ran downstairs, laughing loudly and humourlessly. He followed them, conscious of the stares of the soldiers who wondered what had happened. For some time he hung around awkwardly in the hall as searchers came and went. Then the obese lady of the house offered cups of tea to him and several others. It was a suspicious gesture but they felt obliged to accept it. The cups were presented to them on a tin tray with a packet of biscuits. As they raised their cups to their lips each one gave off a powerful smell of urine. Charles replaced his without a word, but he heard later from two soldiers who had eaten them that the biscuits were all right.

Charles then followed the CO out into the garden where a tunnel had been discovered, starting with a manhole cover near the wall of the house and ending in the bank of a ditch near the bottom of the garden. The man of the house said that it was the drains and that there was nothing in it except rats.

'We'll see for ourselves,' said the CO. He looked around. 'Who's going down? Any volunteers? Somebody small.' Charles drew himself up to his full height and could see others doing the same. 'Nigel, you're a little chap. You'll do.'

Nigel Beale never liked to be reminded of his height, but he always liked to feel useful. He was clearly torn now between pleasure and humiliation. The manhole cover was pushed to one side, showing the hole to be deep, dark and stinking. Nigel began taking off his webbing while everyone else looked on with relieved curiosity – except for the CO, who said, 'Come on, you're not doing a striptease. Get it off.'

Charles held Nigel's webbing and equipment, thereby, he hoped, giving the CO an impression of willing participation whilst making it slightly less likely that he would be the one sent to follow Nigel, if anyone was. It had begun to rain again. Nigel handed over his kit with an air of puzzled martyrdom and lowered himself gently into the hole. A renewed stench wafted up. 'Don't be too long down there,' said the CO. 'We've got a lot of work to do. And watch out for booby-traps.'

Nigel's anxious face popped up again. 'Anyone got a torch?' A torch was handed to him. 'It's very low, sir. I'll have to go on my belly to get along it.'

'Well, don't sit there talking about it. Do it.'

They saw Nigel huddle up at the bottom and then disappear head first in the direction of the ditch. There was a lot of grunting and squeezing as though he were being dragged by a rope. His lower legs and boots were still visible when there was a muffled shout and a young rat ran along his calf, jumped up out of the hole and made for the next-door garden. It was ineffectually chased by the RSM, who aimed several clumsy kicks at it and tried to hit it with his truncheon. When Nigel's boots had vanished the watchers went to the ditch to see him come out. All they saw was two more rats, one a very large one, before Nigel clambered from the manhole he had entered. He was red-faced and puffed and covered in sludge. 'Couldn't get right down, sir,' he said. 'It gets narrower as it goes on. Thought I'd got stuck, actually.'

'Did you find anything?'

'No, sir, it's clean.' Everyone laughed, except Nigel and the CO.

'Pity. Well done, anyway. At least you frightened the rats. Good effort.'

The CO went back into the house and Nigel began brushing himself down briskly, with little result. 'Bloody filthy down there, you know. Really gungy. There'd better be some hot water when we get back.'

Charles handed him his kit, his pistol and his beret at arm's length. 'D'you think you'll be able to clean yourself before you get back into the Land-Rover?'

Nigel pulled at some sludge that was clinging to his hair. 'Doubt it. Don't s'pose these bastards'll let me use their water, if they have any. They must've been chuffed to blazes when they saw me go down there. Anyway, if I have to put up with that I don't see why the rest of you buggers shouldn't put up with me in the Land-Rover.' He bent forward and shook himself, holding his collar back. 'At least we know there's nothing down there.'

'Yes.'

'Well, that's something, isn't it?'

'Did you think there would be?'

'You never know. It's as good a place as any. There still might be, of course, in the narrow bit. But the only way to search that is to tie a rope to one of their kids and use him as a pull-through.'

The search of the house was fruitless and they moved on to a local school, where the largest search operation was still going on. A disgruntled mob was gathered outside and there was sporadic stone-throwing which worsened while they waited for the search teams to finish. The mob grew larger and the stoning became suddenly and persistently worse, obviously a result of organisation. One soldier had his face opened up from the mouth to the ear and snatch squads were deployed. They caught two boys in their teens and brought them back behind the barricade of Pigs and Land-Rovers. One of them came from the group that had stoned the soldier and Charles saw a knee go into the boy's groin as he was pushed into the Pig. His head came forward on to a convenient elbow and he was bundled inside. Like most arrested rioters they did not seriously struggle once arrested. They seemed overawed by the very semblance of organisation. Henry and his ambulance Pig were called to treat the injured soldier.

One rubber bullet was fired and, although the stoning continued, the crowd was kept at too great a distance to be a serious menace. They turned then to building a barricade of cars across the road out, rocking them from side to side and then turning them over. Most were old wrecks anyway but one or two were probably stolen. By this time a number of the press had arrived and hovered uncertainly between the Army and the mob, before making hurriedly for the Army as the stone barrage worsened. Charles was always surprised at the speed with which a relatively minor disturbance could become a dangerous confrontation. It needed no more than a drop of bitterness, mixed with the odd injury or two, to turn the whole thing. Charles resumed one or two acquaintances of the previous night and learned from them that trouble was breaking out throughout Belfast. There were Republican demonstrations against the shootings and Loyalist demonstrations in support of them. Londonderry was quiet and somebody pointed out that the two cities were never aflame together. The arrival of the TV men seemed once again to constitute an important part of the ritual without which no riot seemed real. The press symbolised both crowd and referee at a football match but it was a match in which the referee's decisions were long delayed, and in which one side was able to conduct itself with regard to them alone while the other was hampered also by a set of rules known to all but applied to itself. Once the cameras were in place the game could begin in earnest.

However, it was not to be. The search teams in the school finished, with nothing found, and the CO decided to pull out. 'You can tell your press friends we're going home now,' he said to Charles. 'We're going to walk right through their barricades, and first thing tomorrow morning when there are no press around and all these buggers are in bed I'm going to get Scoopy-do down here and dump all these old cars slap bang across their front doors. If they want to build barricades in my patch they'd better understand they're going to get their own back. So you can tell the press it's all over bar the shouting for tonight, once we've pushed that lot to one side. These people aren't going to cause more trouble in case we search the whole area. I'm certain the bloody stuff's here somewhere though, absolutely certain. Still, it'll wait.'

The barricades, which were still being built, were to be taken simply by driving the Pigs through them. This pleased the press because it would be dramatic, pictorial and, above all, quick – there were other, potentially more interesting incidents in other parts of the city. The search teams were still clearing up and the Pigs were revving their engines in hungry anticipation when Van Horne told Charles that he was wanted.

'By whom?'

'Dunno, sir, but they've been calling for you for about five minutes now.'

'Where?'

'Out there.' Van Horne pointed down the street at the mob.

'*They* want me?'

'Yes, sir.'

'Well, I'm not going. How do they know me anyway?'

Van Horne smiled patiently. 'No sir, not them. The soldiers, sir. Our side. Down by the telephone box – look.'

Some thirty yards away between the Army and the mob there stood a telephone box. Some soldiers were crouched behind cars and low walls nearby. They were a snatch squad deployed to keep the mob back out of stone-throwing range. One of them was beckoning to Charles and pointing at the telephone box. 'What does he want?'

'Maybe someone's telephoning you, sir.'

There was no trace of a smile on Van Horne's face. 'You can come with me,' said Charles. There was no great danger in reaching the telephone box, as the occasional brick could be easily avoided, but it was against Charles's principle of minimum involvement. Running, with so little obvious need and in front of so many people, would have appeared unofficer-like, and so he was obliged to walk in the normal officer fashion, his hands behind his back. Van Horne mysteriously got there ahead of him and crouched on the pavement behind the box because something had provoked the mob suddenly to bombard it with stones. Charles joined him, having run the last few yards despite his feelings about appearance. One of the soldiers lying in a garden nearby said that there was a journalist in the telephone box who wanted to speak to him. Charles did not need to ask who it was. Propped up against the back of the box, he carefully poked his head round the side and then withdrew it sharply as a lump of iron whistled past. 'Beazely!' he shouted. There was a pause and then he heard Beazely's voice shouting something indecipherable. 'What are you doing in there?' Charles shouted again.

'I can't get out. Every time I open the door they stone me.' Beazely sounded frightened and distressed.

Charles leant back against the box, safe from the stones. The nearby soldiers laughed. 'Ring for the police!' Charles shouted.

'Bloody funny, ha ha. Now what about getting me out?'

'Make a dash for it and come round here.'

'I can't. There's some kids behind the houses just waiting. They'll get me.'

'Try it.' Charles poked his head carefully round the other side. Like all telephone boxes in the area, and like most throughout Belfast, this one lacked glass and a telephone. He could just see Beazely's baggy trousers and dirty sheepskin jacket. 'Come on, try it!'

312

Beazely began to edge open the door with his foot and immediately a shower of stones and debris came crashing down. Some very small children, less than twelve years old, were throwing them and laughing before running back behind a house. Beazely let the door close. Charles again withdrew his head as a stone made sparks on the road a few inches from his eyebrow.

'Want us to move up and take 'em out, sir?' called the soldier from the garden.

'No. The CO's going to move up on the barricades in a couple of minutes.' Beazely was shouting something again. 'Speak up!' shouted Charles.

'I said, is anyone coming to rescue me?'

'In a couple of minutes. We're just organising it. Hold your ground.'

'For Christ's sake.' Beazely sounded desperate.

There was a pause while nothing seemed to be happening anywhere. It was impossible not to relish Beazely's predicament. Charles raised his voice again. 'How old do you think I am?'

'What's that got to do with it?' The reply was muffled, as though Beazely had pulled his jacket over his head.

'You said I was forty-one in your paper.'

'I didn't.'

'You did.'

'Slip of the pen. Sub-editor. Jesus Christ, Charles, get me out of here, can't you? They're going to kill me soon.'

Charles could see that the Pigs were about to move. 'I'm just about to get it rolling.'

'Speed it up. Please. Before they get me. Look, we can do a deal. I've been thinking about it.'

'What kind of deal?'

Beazely's reply was drowned by the roar of the oncoming Pigs. Two abreast, they rumbled down the street and ploughed into the flimsy barricade with a great rending of metal. The mob fled like minnows before a perch. With their engines revving high so as to give an impression of much greater speed than they had attained, the Pigs nosed and shrugged the cars aside. The CO and his party walked down the road behind them, chatting amicably. A few more stones came from behind the houses but they were no more than a parting gesture. The trouble was over.

Charles walked round to the front of the telephone box and opened the door for Beazely. Seeing Charles he straightened himself, touched his glasses nervously and stepped out. 'I've never been so glad to see anyone in my life,' he said. 'I thought I'd had it in there. It would only take one of those lumps of metal on the head and that'd be it. Look at it all. Don't know where they find it all from.'

Charles looked at the debris around the telephone box. It

wouldn't have been difficult for Beazely to have been killed or seriously injured. 'Just as well we came when we did,' he said. He felt slightly guilty at having made fun of Beazely now. 'You sure you're all right?' he asked.

Beazely smiled a grateful smile. 'Shaken and stirred but still in me glass,' he said. He blew his nose and then looked at the bent cars askew across the pavements. 'I'd better take some piccies of this lot.'

'I'll do it for you if you lend me your camera,' offered Van Horne. 'That all right, sir?'

Charles nodded. Beazely was only too pleased. 'That was a great picture of Charles they used in this morning's. Blood and thunder. Fear and danger. You could see it all.' He gave his camera to Van Horne, who went off and happily clicked away. He pulled a crumpled packet of cigarettes from his pocket. 'I thought I'd had my lot then, I really did. Very impressive rescue operation you laid on there, Charles, very impressive.' Beazely was obviously beginning to feel he could cope again with the world. Charles decided he preferred him when he was frightened. He was more likeable and natural. 'Little bastards,' Beazely continued. 'They had me in there for about twenty minutes, you know. Every time I poked my nose out they chucked half a house at me. Killing themselves laughing too. I'd kill 'em, I tell you, kids or not, if I had your job. 'Course, it would've been different if I'd had a gun.' He pulled on his cigarette, his confidence returning with each puff. 'Listen, about this deal. What do you say to fifty-fifty?'

'Fifty what?'

'Don't be thick, it doesn't suit you. Fifty-fifty. We'll go halves. Half my salary while I'm out here for you and your oppo with the camera. I can live on expenses, see, no trouble. In return for which you and him do my reports. Nothing I wouldn't be reporting anyway, nothing confidential, just what everyone else is writing about except that you're there and they're there and I'm not. I can sit in my hotel snug as a bug. You know what all this aggro does to me. I just can't do it, I can't function. But you've got to be there anyway, haven't you? You've got no choice, so you might as well do my job at the same time and get paid for it. And you hear about things that happen in other areas so you can tell me about those. See, you're in the thick of it in a place like this. This is what you like, isn't it? What you join for. I don't, see. It's not what I joined for. And if you don't know something you can ring the PROs in other areas and get the story from them. See what I mean, Charlie?' He tapped on Charles's flak jacket with the two fingers that held his cigarette, his confidential saloon-bar manner now fully in order. 'You could do it, you know. That stuff you and Van what's-it told me last night, it was bloody good. Crisp, to the point, an eye for detail, I didn't have to add much to it. Superb. You could both be great journalists, you know. In fact, this could be good practice. And it don't matter if it's not always like that. So long as I can get the bones of it I can hack the meat about, see. I just stay in the hotel and you ring in when you've got something. Fifty-fifty. What d'you reckon? Couldn't be fairer.'

Charles strove to see a flaw in the idea. He needed the money to leave the Army and it sounded so simple. It was not, after all, giving Beazely any more than he would have got anyway, nor more than any other journalist would have got. Also, where something like this was concerned, he felt he could trust Beazely. He sounded as though he knew what he was talking about. Certainly, there was no other way of getting out of the Army soon. But for the present the very novelty and simplicity of the idea baffled him.

'Come on, you idle bugger, it's easy. Just give me two or three stories a week, that's all. For Christ's sakes, your own PR desk at HQ could give you that. Then you just phone 'em through to me. No one will know. I did it with a Yank when they sent me to Vietnam and it worked like a bomb till he got zapped. And with one of the delegates at the Labour Party Conference till the drink got him. You can't lose, Charlie. Hundred a week minimum, no tax, guaranteed, plus bonuses of course. How you split it with your oppo is your business but I'd suggest fifty-fifty. Keeps people happy. Anything else and they either think they're hard done by or they think you must be getting a rake-off that they don't know about. How about it?'

Speedily, furtively, the deal was done. Van Horne was brought in, listened to the explanation and simply nodded at the end of it. Involving a soldier was the only aspect about which Charles felt uneasy, but Van Horne was no ordinary soldier and his immediate acceptance of the deal suggested that he would have thought any other course mere foolishness. Perhaps he, too, wanted to buy himself out of the Army.

'Great stuff.' Beazely pulled out another mangled cigarette. 'I'll do this afternoon's story as I happened to be here. I wouldn't have hung around of course if I hadn't wanted to talk to you. You can start tomorrow.'

All the other journalists had gone off to the Ardoyne where there was more trouble, according to Van Horne. Most of the Land-Rovers and Pigs were pulling out.

Beazely put his cigarette back into his pocket. 'I'm not staying here without the Army. No disrespect to you two, but I have faith only in numbers in these situations. I'll go back to the hotel. Can you fill me in on the Ardoyne business? Before ten if you can. Basic facts plus a few details. Children and injured soldiers, that sort of thing. Make them up if you like.' He buttoned up his coat as he left, as though to keep out the danger.

It turned out that the CO had got Brigade to send Scoopy-do

that night rather than the following morning. There were no journalists around, no rioters and just a few soldiers. Scoopy-do lumbered down the road like a hungry beast let out for feeding and paused in front of the CO, who stood with his hands on his hips looking very pleased with himself. It was a different Scoopy from the night before and a different Sapper. The CO explained that he wanted the cars dumped in people's gardens as close as possible to the front doors. 'If these people are prepared to steal them, make barricades out of them and then no doubt burn them, they can bloody well have them in their living rooms.'

Everyone, including the startled residents, watched Scoopy-do go about its business. It would move itself alongside its victim, so that it was in a killing position, and then raise one huge paw and with ponderous but unerring accuracy smash it on the head. It would then back off a few yards, as though to survey its crushed victim for signs of life, before raising its gaping bucket-jaws, lowering them gently on to the victim and fastening with an appetising crunch. Next it would pick up the car by the neck, like a dog with a rat, exposing the wheels like legs, and would trundle off to someone's front garden and lower it carefully on to its side across the front door. The occupants were confined, for once, to hurling abuse from the upstairs window.

'The only drawback,' said the CO, 'is that we don't know

for certain that it was people from these houses that actually caused the trouble. It could have been people from the next street. But they all hate us anyway and this might persuade them to try to restrain their friends next time. Though I doubt it.'

'We will not tell Beazely about this,' said Charles to Van Horne.

'There'll be complaints. He'll get to hear of it.'

'But not from us. Not this.'

They pulled out when the cars were positioned to the CO's liking, leaving the onlookers scratching their heads and swearing. The rain was falling more steadily now and dusk was approaching. It was one of those afternoons that are never really light and that slip with relief into night. They had reached the outer ring of the estate when there was a loud explosion from somewhere back within it and a small plume of dark smoke rose rapidly behind them. The CO was as aware as everyone else that this could be a come-on, a bait to lure them back into an ambush, but he was never a man to wait and see. 'Turn about!' he shouted. His Land-Rover and its two escorts lurched round and headed back down different roads towards the Bull Ring. They had not gone far when they saw that the smoke, which was all but finished, seemed to have come from a scrubby bit of no-man's land at the side of a house. Several women and a couple of men were looking at something on the ground, and more were joining them every moment. As usual after an explosion, other sounds seemed cowed into silence. When they got out of the Land-Rovers the engines on tick-over were the only noticeable noise. Several of the escort party ran doubled up across the road and took up fire positions facing the surrounding houses. The CO's party, with the CO inevitably to the fore, ran over to the sullen little group. As they reached them the group turned and tried to stop them seeing what it was they were surrounding. For a moment the resistance was real enough but the RSM and Nigel Beale put their heads down as though in a rugby maul and the people were pushed aside. Even then, though, they did not go away but still kept shoving and pulling resentfully. A fat woman grabbed hold of Charles's sleeve above the elbow with both hands and for a few moments he struggled with her in silence before elbowing her in the belly and winding her. Throughout all the tussling no one spoke and no one shouted. It was conducted in an eerie, bitter silence and seemed all the worse for it. When they finally broke through they saw that the object of the crowd's attention was a small, dark-haired boy of about eight or nine. He was lying on the ground in a curiously twisted attitude. His head was resting on his right shoulder, his eyes were closed and his face was calm as though in peaceful sleep. His right arm was stretched out beside him with the palm upturned. His left arm appeared to go straight down the side of his body but it was difficult to see where it ended because from the elbow all the way down to his knee was blood and mangled red flesh. No hand or fingers were visible. The right side of his body looked complete and normal.

It was Nigel Beale who acted most promptly. He got down on his knees beside the boy and pulled the shell dressing from his belt, tearing it open with both hands. No one from the crowd tried to help. Charles got down beside Nigel and pulled off his own shell dressing. The boy was still breathing but there was a lot of blood on the ground and it was still oozing out of his body from the great wound down one side. Charles pressed his shell dressing on the reddest and most exposed bit he could see and stuck it down. He did not like to press too hard. He felt very calm but noticed with a rather remote curiosity that his hands were bloody and shaking. He heard the CO's wireless operator calling for Starlight – Henry Sandy – and being told that he was on his way. The crowd had grown considerably and there was now a lot of shouting. A space had been cleared round the boy but not without some scuffling. The CO was calling for his parents and eventually a fat, dark and dirty little man stepped forward. He demanded to know what the CO was doing with the boy.

'We're taking him to hospital, what do you think?' snapped the CO.

'You're not takin' him nowhere, you're not takin' him from me.' The little man stared in wide-eyed appeal at the crowd. 'Holy Mother, they're taking me dying child!' There was uproar at this and renewed struggling. Henry Sandy and his team arrived in the ambulance Pig and forced their way through the crowd with a stretcher. Henry looked very quickly at the boy, feeling the wound, eyes and heart. It was the first time Charles had seen him without any facetiousness. He spoke and moved simply and directly, treating all alike. 'Help me get him on the stretcher,' he said.

Charles helped with the feet. The boy was very light. Then the stretcher-bearers lifted him and made back towards the Pig. The crowd had gathered round that now and tried to stop the boy being loaded into it. They fought and shouted as though to stop him being dragged off to prison. A couple of them had chalked slogans about the Queen, including the abbreviation 'FTQ' – the Republican answer to the Protestant 'FTP' – on the side of the Pig. For one moment they succeeded in bringing the stretcher party to a standstill and it looked as though they were going to snatch the boy back. Charles grappled with a yelling woman who had grabbed hold of the stretcher. He pulled her off it but she then turned her attentions to him, pulling his hair and hitting. She fought with a ferocity which for a moment shocked him but even so he could not bring himself to hit her with his fist. He kept trying to catch her arms and, due to some deeply-instilled sense of military propriety, let go of her with one hand in order to catch his beret and prevent it falling to the ground. Then the awareness of lost dignity took over and, still holding and being held by her, he kicked her hard on the shins, twice. She let go with a howling scream and was immediately surrounded by sympathetic companions.

By this time the Pig was moving off with the boy and his father, whom the CO had allowed on board. Even so, a couple of other men tried to climb on to it before being roughly repelled. Charles saw one of the CO's bodyguards lay his baton across the front of one man's face with a calculated precision that a few months, or even weeks, before would have seemed shocking. The man dropped to his knees and bent right over, clutching his face. Van Horne appeared at Charles's side, unruffled and apparently untouched by the struggle. 'I can't help noticing you have a way with women, sir.'

Once the Pig was gone they pulled out. Charles got back into the CO's Land-Rover with Nigel Beale, who had a bloody nose. They were still surrounded by clamouring people claiming to represent citizens' action committees and various residents' associations. The word 'kidnap' was being thrown around a lot. 'Accelerate forward and don't stop or swerve for anyone,' the CO told his driver. 'If we run over one or two of the bastards so much the better.' However, the protesters showed a nimble concern for their own safety and the Land-Rovers left the estate without further incident. It was said that the boy had been injured by a pipe bomb; he had been playing with some other boys and had picked up a piece of pipe about a foot long which had exploded as he threw it.

The CO spoke to no one on the way back except to order the driver to stop off at C company's headquarters in the Factory. Edward and the others were all there. An unease had developed between Charles and them since he had gone to battalion HQ, almost as though he had changed sides. Their greetings now were rather formal, except for the company sergeant major who was as friendly and jokey as ever. But the CO did not want to listen to anyone else's words. He wanted to unburden himself. 'Those bloody people down there are not people,' he announced to everyone in the ops room. 'No animal would do what they did. Animals look after their own. These people are not fit to have children. They're not fit to be people. First of all they make a lethal gelignite bomb, then they leave it lying around where kids can find it. Then when some poor little sod loses his hand and half his arm as well as very nearly his leg they just stand around like a lot of stuffed dummies and stare at him. That's what they were doing when we arrived, wasn't it, eh? Just standing and staring watching him bleed to death on the pavement. And not one of them lifted a finger, not one little finger. I didn't see them do anything. Did you? Eh?

Did anyone see them do anything?' He looked at everyone in turn. People nodded or lowered their eyes as though they themselves were guilty. The CO so often launched into tirades that Charles had not realised at first how moved and upset he was now. His teeth were clenched and his eyes hard. 'And as though that's not enough, watching him die, they actually tried to stop us helping, didn't they? Tried quite hard too. If they'd tried a little harder I'd have happily left one or two more in the gutter for good. What kind of people are they, for God's sake? Psychopaths? Ghouls? And they won't thank us, you know. It won't do us any good. I know we're not in a place where we can do any good. I know that. But I don't care what they think of me, or what they think of my men, or what they think about anything. I am going to make them behave like human beings even if they are ghouls. From now on it's war as far as I'm concerned.' His cheeks were taut with emotion and he stared at everyone for a few moments as though they were all his enemies. Then he suddenly relaxed and rubbed the back of his neck with one hand. 'All right, let's be off,' he said quietly.

Out in the yard they were getting back into the vehicles when the CO paused with his hand on the iron grille over the windscreen. He turned to Charles and said, 'You're leaving us, are you?'

Caught off guard, it was a moment before Charles could reply. 'Yes, sir.'

The CO looked at him and then got into the vehicle without saying anything. Charles climbed in the back, sandwiched between the signals sergeant and Van Horne. He felt as though he had been caught out at something and was angry with himself for feeling like that. After all, he knew he needed no convincing that he would be glad to leave the Army.

On the way back the CO said to Nigel Beale that if the boy's father turned out to have a sense of gratitude after all he might be prepared to talk about the local Provisional IRA men. It was a very long shot, but worth trying.

10

The deal with Beazely worked well. There were a few teething troubles, due mainly to busy telephones and inflexible deadlines, but after a while a system of information-gathering and transmission was established that worked at least as well as those of the Army and the press. This was a source of pride for Charles and Van Horne, though it should not have been because their system was no more than a combination of the resources of the other two. Beazely was given no more than he could have got for himself, and did not ask for more, while they accepted without question whatever price he paid. The extra five hundred pounds that Charles needed to get himself out of the Army did not include living expenses for any time thereafter. It did not even include his post-resignation train fare from Aldershot to London, though as he was entitled to a number of concessionary leave warrants a year he might not have to pay that anyway. In which case, he reasoned, he might just as well go from Aldershot to Edinburgh, a city he had long wanted to see. He did not think very much about what he might do after leaving the Army, but carefully nursed an inner conviction that he would not know until he had left. This was, perhaps, yet another symptom of his growing tendency not to think about whatever might be problematic or unpleasant.

Sharing the money with Van Horne was the worst aspect of the deal with Beazely – not the fact of sharing but the physical act of counting and handing over the cash. Handling the money was necessarily conspiratorial and Charles felt shabby and corrupt at such moments. Neither of his associates showed anything but a matter-of-fact, businesslike approach to the transactions, handing over and pocketing the notes as though they had not the slightest interest in them. There was the further problem of what to do with the cash. Charles never went near a bank and he did not care to entrust it to the paymaster, since that would be official. When his wallet would hold no more he took to stuffing it into a sock in the bottom of his kitbag. One night he dreamt of being raided by the Inland Revenue whilst the CO argued passionately on his behalf, believing him to be innocent.

However, there was no trouble with the arrangement itself. The advantage, so far as Charles was concerned, was that he knew what the Army did and did not want publicised and, through Beazely, what alternatives might appeal to the editorial mind. Events in the battalion area were usually witnessed by either himself and Van Horne or by people they both knew; details of those outside could be got from the PR desk or from other PROs. Van Horne was invaluable. Not only was he sensible and discreet but he had a genius for sniffing out stories around the battalion during inactive periods which resulted in so much favourable publicity – often of the much-desired 'human interest' sort – that the battalion came to be used as a show-piece by the PR desk. The CO, despite his aversion for journalism, was delighted.

'A small war is the best recruiting sergeant,' he said, after reading an article on the rigour of Assault Commando training, 'but this is the next thing to it. It's not all accurate, though. It's up to you to make sure they get that sort of thing right, Charles.'

During busy periods, when Charles could not get to a phone, Van Horne relayed the information. He also took photographs and was said by Beazely to have an 'eye'. Charles concentrated on building up a good relationship with the regular journalists, who were on the whole competent and agreeable. Though careful not to poach their stories or angles, he was able to judge from them how to select his own. Their questions displayed the direction of their interests. It was a matter of pride to himself and Van Horne that they fabricated nothing, though it would have been easy to do so. The trouble was, they would both get so involved in their stories that they were hurt and irritated by editorial and Beazely-inspired cuts.

'I keep on telling you,' Beazely would say, 'that sub-editors have no souls. They care only for column inches and circulation figures, not for truth, realism, intelligence and virtue, like you and I. You are casting pearls before swine. Take it from one who knows. I'd be a wealthy man if I'd had a penny for each word I've had to keep back from these barbarians.' He was, in fact, a good teacher. He insisted on reports being short and to the point and usually would alter them only if they were not or as a result of fresh information gleaned from other items of furniture at the bar of his hotel. Sometimes, though, he would cut a passage because his sub-editor would recognise it as not his own. Such passages were invariably Charles's little essays into social comment. One such began, 'The children of West Belfast are familiar with colour TVs but cannot name the colours.' A paragraph of political assessment started, 'It must be clear to any but the most partisan observer of the Northern Ireland scene that the events of last weekend marked a worsening of the perceived situation for all those involved.' While there was his exposition of military tactics which needed a footnote to the effect that, '39 Airportable Brigade differs from most infantry brigades not only in its role and deployment but also in its provision of equipment and its numbers.'

Beazely would put a line through these forays without removing the cigarette from his mouth, like Wilfrid Owen when writing to the next-of-kin of his dead soldiers. 'When the Kingdom of the Word takes its rightful place,' he would say, 'and the Killers of the Word are burned by flaming adjectives and tied to the stake by unending sentences, then, Charlie, you shall take your rightful place and these fine phrases of yours will be remembered annually. Instead of fighting we'll all talk, talk, talk. It will be beautiful. But until then keep to the point and save the rest for your prayers.'

Charles once asked him if he had been to university. 'Yes,' Beazely replied, with a confident nod. 'Very much so. Several times, different places, you know. Nowhere very long. You?'

'Yes. Only one, though.'

'That's odd. Van Horne said you hadn't. Said you went straight to Sandhurst from school.'

'He's wrong. I don't know why he said that.' He had never discussed his past with Van Horne.

'Just guessing, I s'pose.'

It was not easy to get the Army to overcome its deep-seated mistrust of the press, but Charles and Van Horne soon found that an air of reluctance and apology, suggestive of irresistible pressure from authority, was the best way of getting things done – better, certainly, than argument. It was best to preface requests for film-crew visits or yet more local-boy stories with the phrase, 'The CO was wondering whether ...'

Very occasionally the CO did wonder, and then surprisingly. He had grown quieter and more moody and seemed to spend much of his time scheming how to discredit the Provisional IRA. He turned to Charles one day and said, 'That boy who lost his hand last week, the one whose life we saved. What are you doing about him?'

'Sir?'

'Don't answer questions with questions. Tell me what you're doing.'

'Nothing, sir.'

'Well, you should be. It's your job, not mine, to think of these things. It's good publicity for us; we saved his life. Bad publicity for them because they left the bomb lying around. What about getting some of your press friends to do a photograph and a story?'

It was, perhaps, one of Charles's faults as a PRO that he had still not fully grasped the way that news is made rather than happens. The idea had occurred to him, vaguely, but some shreds of an outmoded notion of fair play still clung to him and it seemed unfair to take advantage of the boy's condition. Also, he had recently discovered in himself a reluctance to deal with press matters that would not result in profit. He could see no way of working Beazely into this one and his policy in such cases was to keep what the Army loved to call a 'low profile'. He sought to narrow his life so that all unnecessary initiatives and responses were cut out. 'Might he not be a bit of a mess, sir?' he asked.

'The messier the better. They made him like it, not us. Go and fix it. It's unpleasant, I know, but we're at war. Or some of us are.'

The issue presented no problems for Van Horne, who would happily have publicised piles of intestines. They contacted one of the tabloid newspapers which usually had good photographs and which, like the other papers of its kind, excelled in the simple and effective presentation of human interest stories. They arranged to meet a reporter and photographer at the Royal Victoria Hospital.

'You should give the lad a present,' said the CO. 'Go and buy something out of the community relations fund. How do we stand with that?'

'It's unused, sir.'

'Good. Waste of public money otherwise.'

The expedition to buy a present was a major undertaking. It involved changing into civilian clothes and going into the centre of Belfast where a similarly-dressed soldier had been murdered the week before. Being quite unused to mixing with normal people going about their normal business of shopping, Charles could not rid himself of the notion that he was the centre of attention and that every coat concealed an Armalite. He spent a nervous twenty minutes in a bookshop, imagining bombs as well as bullets and paying more attention to cover positions, escape-routes, probable direction of blast and of flying glass than to what he was supposed to be buying. The fact that the main shopping centre was ringed by barriers through which no cars could pass and at which everyone was supposed to be searched did not reassure him. Two girls in front of him had not had their handbags searched and for his part the bulky shoulder-holster containing his Browning had not been discovered. If it had he would have had to produce his ID card, thereby identifying himself as a soldier to everyone around him. He again wore it at the CO's insistence and felt lopsided and misshapen rather than deadly and confident. He eventually slunk out of the shop with an illustrated sporting encyclopaedia of a kind he remembered having as a child.

When he and Van Horne met the reporter and photographer they were questioned about the incident in detail. On hearing that Charles had put a shell dressing on the boy, the reporter said, 'That's great. We'll have one of you sitting next to him on the bed – the soldier who saved his life. What's your name and rank?' Charles told him and he then said, 'Sorry, no good. It's no good with an officer. Doesn't work. Not the same impact. What about a soldier?'

Charles, relieved, did not hesitate to volunteer Van Horne. 'He's a lance-corporal.'

'A private would be better.'

'I could take my stripe off,' said Van Horne.

There stirred within Charles a faint but developing instinct for where the Army line would lie in such matters. 'No, he can't do that.'

'Why not?'

'Queen's Regs. Regulations.'

'All right. Did he put his shell dressing on the boy too?'

'No.'

'Was he there, in the vicinity?'

'Yes.'

'That'll do, then.'

An officious, plump little nurse took them through a children's ward, where Charles felt gigantic and self-conscious, and into a small room opening off it. There was a bed with what appeared to be a mound of bandages in it. The nurse bent over the bed and said in a sing-song voice, 'Hallo, Terry, how are we then, eh? Here's some gentlemen come to see you. And they've bought you a lovely present.' The mound moved and they could see a hole in the bandages enough to show most of the boy's face. His eyes moved and registered the visitors.

'Is that him?' asked Charles.

'Who else d'you think?' said the nurse sharply. She did not seem to like the Army.

'But his head was all right. Why is it bandaged up?'

'His head was most certainly not all right. There were bits of metal in it, especially the back. Now do what you want to do and be quick about it. I don't want to disturb him for long.' She bent over the boy again. 'Lots and lots of nasty cuts soon be better, better, better, eh, Terry? Nasty men go away soon and we'll be better, won't we? Ever so better.'

The photographer looked on gloomily. 'Can't do anything with this. Whatever angle I do it's going to look a bit sick, isn't it? I mean, handing a book to a lump of bandage.'

Van Horne looked on impassively. 'Where's his hand?' he asked the nurse.

She sssh'd him and whispered, 'He's lost it. He doesn't really know yet.'

'But where is it?'

'What do you mean, where is it? It's gone.'

'You haven't got it?'

'Certainly not.'

Van Horne lost interest.

'Is he going to be all right?' asked Charles.

'Yes. Anything else?'

They said goodbye awkwardly and left the uncomprehending child. The reporter said he might do a little piece on it anyway, just a paragraph. Charles realised he still had the book and so Van Horne was sent back with it. When they got back the CO's reaction was as surprising as had been his original suggestion. 'Good. I don't really like publicity for the sake of it. It would have been distasteful even if the poor little blighter hadn't had a mark on him. And our soldiers don't like being photographed like that, you know. It's not what they joined for. Very sensible of you to call it off. Well done.'

A few days later they conducted another search in the new estate, this time of a Gaelic football ground. The search went in at about eleven in the morning without previous notice as the CO and Nigel Beale had applied the need-to-know principle so rigidly that many of those who needed to know in order to take part were away doing other things. Several vehicles were away being serviced or repaired and others were out on patrol. Charles was told by Van Horne about the search at six minutes to eleven and was just able to scramble aboard the last Land-Rover as it was leaving. He left Van Horne behind to deal with any telephone enquiries.

It was a fine sunny morning with a fresh breeze. The green turf of the field was refreshing after the dirty bricks and concrete which was all they had seen for weeks on end. There were three platoons plus search teams, about a hundred men all told, and no trouble was expected as no houses were to be searched. The platoons dug into the grass banks surrounding the pitch, directed by NCOs trained in searching, but there was to be no excavation of the pitch on orders from Brigade, who did not want to inflame local feeling. There had already been complaints that the Army was seeking to intimidate and terrorise the Catholic population. The sun, the grass and the fact that many of the men were stripped to the waist gave to the sports-ground a holiday atmosphere that enlivened everyone. Even the sporadic stones lobbed over the banks by children from the surrounding streets did not detract from the previous euphoria.

Charles strode about the field with the CO and his gang, all in the hands-behind-the-backs position. The CO talked good humouredly about tanks. Because of the banks around the field the roofs of the houses could not be seen and it was possible for a while to imagine that they were in England. Charles kept an eye on the entrance to see if any journalists turned up. He more than half expected Van Horne to appear, having found some quite unanswerable reason for deserting his post. He was aware of Van Horne as an interesting man about whom he had no more curiosity than was strictly necessary for them to perform their tasks together. Had Van Horne not been a soldier, or had they not been involved in their scheme with Beazely, he might have tried to get to know him better. He sensed, and sensed that Van Horne sensed, that they had something in common but he was suspicious of what it might be and felt it was better left unexplored. It was perhaps a common assumption of being an outsider, with possibly an added, secret something that was best summed up by the word 'uncare'.

Whatever it was, it was better not to admit it. Sometimes he could fancy Van Horne as a kind of Mephistopheles or perhaps a Mosca, though he could never even at his most fanciful see himself as Faust or Volpone. Yet at the same time Van Horne was like many other soldiers in that he shirked irksome duties whenever he could, lied glibly and was reluctant to accept any responsibility unless he had someone over him who was more responsible.

But for a long time that morning no one came and Charles was able to enjoy the field and the sun. He was warmed, too, by the thought of his approaching freedom. It was something he could allow himself to think about more and more as the money paid by Beazely mounted up. He was still not sure what he would do next, but there was a pleasant sense of possibility about the future, which remained intact so long as nothing too explicit was demanded of it.

The first find was made within twenty minutes on the outer slope of the first bank. It consisted of an old Lee-Enfield .303 rifle, a newish Russian twelve-bore shotgun and two rusty Webley .38 revolvers, all carefully wrapped in polythene. 'This is excellent,' said the CO, 'we're on to them now. This entire stadium is an arsenal. I only wish we could plough up that damn pitch. It's probably a magazine. Everybody look for discolourations in the turf. Charles, fetch the press.'

'They're on their way, sir,' Charles lied, hopefully.

'Well done. Good timing. Make sure they see all this.'

Shortly afterwards a soldier on the north-east corner of the bank noticed a strip of old polythene protruding from the earth. He dug carefully round it and found that there was a dustbin in a large polythene bag. He took the lid off the bin and found it was filled with decaying, unstable gelignite. The search team commander estimated that there was between fifty and seventy pounds of explosive. It was so unstable that a child jumping on the ground nearby could have detonated it. It was too dangerous to move and the bomb disposal team was called to burn it off.

The effect of the find was to invigorate the searchers. Only the CO looked troubled. 'You see what these people are,' he said. 'No concern for their own. Burying it here where people stand to watch football and where children play all day. It could've killed dozens. It ought to be on film so that the world can see what bloody lunatics these people are. Charles, where are those pressmen? They're swarming over you like flies when you don't want them and nowhere to be found when you do.'

'They're on their way, sir. Just coming.'

'You said that twenty minutes ago. Where are they?'

'I'll go and get them, sir.' Charles strode purposefully back towards the entrance. There was nothing whatever that he could do but the CO liked to see action in response to his demands. He had expected that the press would have arrived by now since the jungle telegraph was so efficient that they often arrived almost simultaneously with the search parties. On occasions like this the CO expected his PRO to be able to summon up squads of press as he himself would summon up a fresh platoon. This, however, was not the time when Charles had to disabuse him of this error, for as he neared the gate he saw an ITV television crew arguing with the guard over the question of admittance. He saw that they were allowed in and behind them another crew from Spain. Several other journalists arrived and so he was soon able to lead a flock across to the two finds. A knowledgeable colour sergeant was recorded giving an enthusiastic description of the state of decay, composition and probable damage that could be caused by the explosive.

After this they dispersed over the ground. The TV teams filmed their interviewers giving accounts and asking questions of which they had already filmed the answers. Another journalist arrived, a woman in her late twenties. She had dark hair straddled over her shoulders, a suede jacket with matching suede boots that just failed to conceal the size of her calves, a bag slung over one shoulder and a king-sized cigarette in one hand. She was quite short and had a wide gash of a mouth which widened with easy confidence as she introduced herself as Moira Conn, one of the *Sunday Truth*'s Hindsight team. 'Some guy called John at your headquarters told me your name and said I'd find you down here. He said he worked with you.'

'Ah yes, Van Horne, Lance-Corporal Van Horne.'

'Pretty smooth guy. Are all your soldiers like that?'

'No.'

'Pity. I usually find I prefer soldiers to officers, though. They're somehow more real. I mean, the officers are always a bit inauthentic. They're trying to be something they're not but the soldiers just are. They just stand there and they are. You can feel it. Whereas the officers are always chasing some ideal of themselves that doesn't exist and they end up not being any-thing at all.'

It was clear that this was not one for the CO. The Sergeants' Mess, perhaps, but more likely the Junior Ranks club. She had obviously been to an English public school and was trying to lose it by lengthening some of her vowels and flattening them all to a mid-Atlantic monotone. 'Would you like to see some explosives?' asked Charles.

'You found some? That's great. I didn't think you would. I've never seen explosives before. How're the locals reacting?'

'They're not yet.'

'Why not?'

'It's a bit early in the day.' They climbed on to the bank and walked along it. The digging soldiers eyed her as they passed.

She lit another cigarette and offered one to Charles. 'Not when in uniform, I s'pose? That's what gets me about you officers. You're so bloody hidebound and self-conscious.'

'I don't smoke.'

'Not you in particular but the officer class in general. All stiff upper lip and understatement. They look as if they never shit, some of them.'

'But some do, from a great height.'

'You don't rile easily, do you? I think I'm going to like you. How come you're in the Army?' Her mouth widened into a slow, confident smile.

'I just joined.'

'But why?'

Charles still felt cheerful because of the greenness of the grass. He looked her in the eye. 'I wanted to kill people.'

She blew out a lot of smoke. 'Holy shit, that's bad. That's mean. At least you're honest, though.'

'Yes.'

'The name O'Hare mean anything to you?' She had kept the smile going.

'No.' It did, though. O'Hare had been a soldier in the battalion two years previously and was now reputed to be a leading Provisional IRA gunman in the Ardoyne area. The CO had told them about this at a briefing which he had labelled 'Top Secret', but he made such promiscuous use of this category that it was not always easy to know what was secret and what was not. However, Charles felt fairly certain that this, for some reason, was. 'It's Irish, isn't it?'

'Yes.' She nodded. 'You see, there's an IRA marksman of that name who used to be in your regiment. At least, we're pretty certain he did. We know he left the Army and why he left and what he's done since. Only we're not positive that that's his real name and we're not one hundred per cent sure it was your regiment. Obviously it's a good story if it was. We just need confirmation, that's all. Passive confirmation.'

'First I've heard of it.'

'He's deeply involved, this guy. He's into everything they're doing. We've got the story all ready. We just need the confirmation.'

'Never heard of him.'

'Can't you find out?'

'No one would tell me even if they knew. Ask the IRA.'

'They don't name their people on operational duty in the North.' She stopped walking and turned to face him, lowering her voice. Charles felt she was becoming more attractive. 'Look, just the name, that's all. You don't even have to say it. Just nod if it's him. I mean, no one will know it's you because if you can confirm it I can check back through other sources and make it look as though it came from them. In fact, it will have. It's just that it will have come from you first, that's all. No one will ever know, I promise you, Charles.' She was not smiling now, but was looking at him sincerely.

Charles put his hand on his heart. 'Believe me, if I knew you could tempt me.'

'Will you keep your ears open for me? Some of your friends must know.'

They neared the dustbin of explosives and Charles persuaded her to put out her cigarette. The knowledgeable colour sergeant repeated his exposition. She tried to touch the weeping gelignite and was prevented. They moved on to where the weapons were exhibited and she lit up again. 'I don't know much about weapons. It's something I ought to learn, though on Hindsight of course we do more in-depth investigation of the people behind the action. Still, weapons are good local colour.'

'Aren't they quite important for your investigation?'

'Quite. Quite. Great word, that. Very British. No – but the really important thing for me is not the technology of urban guerrilla warfare so much as the thought behind the bullets, you know. I'm more interested in why they're doing what they're doing than in how. But I ought to know all the same.'

She took herself very seriously. Charles could think of nothing to say but found that nodding was all that was expected of him. They came to where the weapons were displayed on a polythene sheet on the grass. She exhaled two parallel jets of smoke through her nostrils. 'That's not much.'

'Well, it's a pretty representative sample of the technology of urban guerrilla warfare.'

'Is that a machine-gun?'

'No, it's a rifle.'

'You haven't got a machine-gun?'

'Sorry.'

'The IRA do have them, you know. M60s they're called. I've seen one. One of their Northern commanders showed me.' She pushed back the hair which had fallen across her eyes. The bright sun illuminated the pallor of her skin. Charles no longer fancied her, though he kept trying. Her wide mouth was appealing but her eyes were small, hard brown stones set in puffed white flesh. Still, it was a long time since he had been near a woman. 'You should be talking to these people,' she continued. 'You should be trying to understand the people you're fighting. They're interesting guys. That's why the press is so important to you. We can look at things objectively without taking sides, whereas you're involved and you're bound to be biased. It's like this man was telling me, the whole weight of the broadcasting media is on your side by nature so we have to make a conscious effort to present their point of view. Which is quite legitimate, you know. I regard the IRA as expressing a point of view with as much right to be considered as anything you say. You see, we're the guardians of democracy. Army officers seem to think that democracy is an upper middle-class thing that no one else should be allowed to join unless they've been to the right school or regiment or whatever. Our job is to protect the majority from exploiting minorities like yours. If you see what I mean. Being exploited by, that is.'

It was not what she said that bothered Charles but what to do with her. The nearest soldiers were leaning on the spades and listening. Judging by their expressions they were about to break out into the vociferous ribaldry at which they so excelled. If they did he would have to discipline them, a task which never came easily to him. Moira Conn would like neither the ribaldry, which she would take to be an attempt to reduce her to a sex-object, nor his defence of her, which she would take to be an attempt to patronise. 'Would you like to see the rest of the site?' he asked.

'In the short term any tactics are justifiable in an urban guerrilla war so long as they help to bring about an equal and classless society in the long term.'

However, further conversation was averted by the arrival of some stones. One landed near enough to make her jump. 'What was that?'

'A stone thrown by some children behind the houses. Here come some more.' They were thrown by half a dozen children who ran out from behind a house. No one was hit and the soldiers carried on working, as though the stones were no more than rain.

'Do they often do this?' asked Moira.

'Only when they can see us.'

'They must hate you.'

'They enjoy it.'

Some more stones whistled over and thudded into the turf a few feet away. A corporal and two men went down the bank and across the fence to drive the children back out of range. A tiny, grubby, blond child of about two feet six had wandered forward almost to the bank. As the soldiers walked past him he looked up at them seriously, his soiled mouth working a few times before the word would come out. 'B-b-bastards,' he said.

'Perhaps we'd better get down out of the way,' said Charles, as a few more stones came from another direction.

Moira hitched her bag further on to her shoulder. 'I'm not scared. You needn't worry about me.'

Charles thought of pleading that it was he that was scared, but instead said, 'It's only that if you're seen and recognised with us they might not trust you and might think you're not being objective. There's bound to be someone taking note of who's here, and we're very exposed on the bank. It's happened

before that journalists seen with us are never spoken to again.'
They moved back on to the pitch where a snatch squad was
being organised by a wizened and popular colour sergeant. He
swore at one of his squad, a negro, and then the whole squad
laughed at his surprise at seeing Moira behind him. He asked
to be excused for his French.

'Is there much of that sort of thing?' Moira asked as they
moved away.

'There's quite a bit of swearing, yes.'

'No, not that. The way he picked on that black guy. Racial
prejudice.'

'No, there isn't any.'

'But did you hear what he said to him? He called him an
idle black bastard.'

'That's because there isn't any racial prejudice.'

'Personally I can't stand men who feel they have to apologise
for swearing in front of a woman. It's so bloody patronising,
you know. It pisses me off.'

Unfortunately, they bumped into the CO near the grand-
stand. He had been standing amongst the seats, surveying the
ground, and came down the stairs three at a time and leapt the
fence as Charles and Moira walked past. He was making for
his Land-Rover by the entrance and was in high good humour.
'Charles – everything all right? Good. Womanising, eh? Why
don't you introduce me to this charming young lady?' Charles

introduced them and they shook hands. 'I can't say I like your paper, Miss Conn, but I trust that when you write about what you've seen today you'll redress the balance a bit. Have you shown her the weeping jelly?'

'Yes, sir.'

'There you are, then. That shows you the sort of people we're up against.'

Moira Conn dropped her cigarette on to the ground and extinguished it. 'I know the sort of people you're up against – better than you do, I should think. I've spoken to their brigade commanders myself. And I don't think operations of the kind you've mounted here today prove anything or do any good to anyone. They just turn people against you.'

The CO shot a quick glance at Charles, as though he were at least partially responsible. 'If you'll take my advice, young lady, which I don't s'pose you will for a moment, you'll be very careful in the company you keep in future. You've been had, you've been done. These men are dangerous, clever, cruel and fanatical. They're just using you, that's all, and you don't even know it.'

Moira Conn grasped the strap of her bag firmly. 'On the contrary, Colonel, I get the impression they're not as fanatical and dangerous as many so-called real officers I've come across. But some of them are a bit more clever.'

Charles gazed in the direction of the north bank, hoping for an explosion from that direction, but the CO remained calm. 'I'm not going to argue with you,' he said slowly, as though to a child. 'You know you're wrong, and if you don't you very soon will. I hope you're intelligent enough not to be deluded all your life. If security permitted I could prove to you the error of your ways, but it doesn't and so that's that. You've got my word for it. One thing I will say, though, is that you'll be doing all decent people a service if you stop crediting these mindless, bitter thugs and villains with the rank and status of an official army. That's exactly what they want, you see. It makes them feel good. They think they're getting somewhere then. In fact, they're no more brigade commanders and such like than you are, or Charles here. Just because some wretched plumber calls himself a brigadier and intimidates a few criminals and hare-brained youngsters you go ahead and call him a brigadier. You give him everything he's asking for – recognition, power, fame. As it is, they're simply imitating us, you see. There's nothing original about it. They're just corner boys. Rank structure, titles, so-called military courts and all that – that – that balls, if you'll excuse my French, Miss Conn. I feel very strongly about it. I hope I haven't taken up too much of your time. Good day to you.' He stood to attention and saluted her, then turned on his heel and walked away.

Moira Conn was pale and seething. 'Is he real? Is he really like that? Did you see what he did? He saluted.'

'You touched him on a tender spot.'

'He's one big bloody tender spot if you ask me. Jesus Christ, I didn't know such people existed. Where's he think he's at, you know? Give me the IRA any time.'

'He's very good-hearted.' Charles was not used to defending the CO and was having to feel his way.

'Crap. Are you telling me you're content to let your life be ruled by a man like that?'

'I'm leaving soon.'

'And he apologised for swearing. That's two this morning.'

'I'm very sorry about that.' They wandered without further speech back towards the entrance. Charles was wondering how to get rid of her when she saw Father Murphy, the local priest, arguing with the soldier on the gate.

'Is he the one who's been organising the local citizens' action committees?'

'Yes.'

'How does your colonel get on with him?'

'He doesn't.'

'I'm going to interview him.' She rummaged in her bag for pen and paper. 'Can you give me John's number?'

'Whose?'

'John Van-what's-its. That guy I told you about.'

'Van Horne. He doesn't have a number of his own.'

'Well, it must be possible to contact him if he helps with the press. Where does he hang out?'

'In my office, mainly.'

'So I can use your number?'

'I suppose so.'

'And you can take messages if he's not around?'

'I suppose I can, yes.'

'Great. Thanks. And thanks for showing me that stuff. It was very useful. Let me know if you hear anything about O'Hare. Bye.'

Charles saw no more of her. She rang Van Horne a couple of times but there was no question of his having an evening off to see her. No one had that much time off. Instead, he arranged to see her in London at the end of the tour. 'I've got her flat number in case you're ever interested, sir,' he said, with no trace of a smile.

This conversation had taken place in the office Charles shared with Colin Wood, Colin being out at the time. Charles took the opportunity to slip Van Horne his share of the latest payment from Beazely. As he was handing over the money Nigel Beale poked his head round the door. 'Where's Colin?' he asked.

'I don't know,' said Charles, feeling he must have started guiltily. He saw Nigel's eye alight upon the money. 'He may be upstairs with the CO.'

'Thanks.' Nigel went and Van Horne raised his eyebrows slightly as he put the money in his pocket before following Nigel out.

Later, in the Mess, Nigel said to Charles, 'You seem to be rolling in it. Why were you giving it all to Van Horne? You paying him yourself or something?'

Several others were present, though not the CO. 'Taxpayers' money,' said Charles promptly. 'Community relations fund. Let me know if you want a hand-out.'

'Great. What do I have to do?'

'Build a community hall, then wait for the Provisional IRA to burn it down and claim the insurance.' It came very pat off his tongue without the slightest hesitation. His sense of guilt had evaporated quickly under the threat of discovery. The twin evils of exposure and of being unable to save enough to leave the Army soon had made him hard and determined. He felt that he was fast losing all compunction about almost everything.

11

Nothing much happened during the next few weeks. The meals, the remarks, the routine, the pettiness of battalion headquarters continued without hope of alleviation until the tour ended. During the long watches of the night it was difficult to believe in any other existence. Quiet conversations in the early hours revealed surprising aspects of people, sensitivities and feelings deeply hidden during the day, but repetition soon robbed them of their impact. The only real privacy to be had was in bed, in the few delicious moments before sleep. Life seemed to revolve around the tribal map of Belfast, the humming radio and the cheerless obscenities of the soldiers. The battalion was becoming lethargic and restless. Every day the number of soldiers on CO's Orders seemed to grow.

The CO himself continued to become moodier and quieter. Although he never mentioned it, it was clear to those who studied him most closely – which were those whose lives were most subject to his whims – that the affair of the boy and the pipe bomb had made a deep impression on him. In conversation he referred to the IRA only as monsters or brutes. The nearest he came to acknowledging them as people was when he called them psychopaths or thugs.

'The CO's idea of people,' the adjutant said to Charles one day, 'is a moral one. He can't accept the idea of immoral people. For him it's a contradiction in terms.'

'He can't accept as a person anyone who differs from himself.'

'That's not fair. You're judging too harshly. He accepts idiots and geniuses and other regiments. It's just villains he can't accept.'

Between his moods the CO would have enthusiasms. Several days would be spent in cabals with Nigel Beale, then he would give up Intelligence and take to lecturing the O Groups on what was going on in other battalion areas. There was a noticeable switch from rioting to terrorism. Shootings, claymore mines and bombings became more common. Fire bombs in city centre shops were a great favourite. But nothing happened in their area. 'It's because we're sitting on them,' he said. 'It's because we harass them day and night. I want company commanders to do it even more often from now on. Knock on the doors of all known leaders – politely though. Just let them know you're around and watching them. Give them the impression you know everything about them, right down to what toothpaste they're using and how often. If they use it.'

On other occasions he would say that the quiet was simply the lull before the storm and would urge all ranks to keep on their toes, with their noses to the grindstone, the same to the coalface, their ears to the ground, their eyes peeled and their socks from slipping.

'Bloody funny position you'd end up in,' said Henry Sandy after one O Group, during which he'd been awake throughout. He normally fell asleep because of his nightly debaucheries at the hospital, and had to find out from other people afterwards whether anything had been said that applied to him. One day, though, he announced to Charles that he had become impotent, and he continued in that state for some weeks despite valiant efforts by a series of bewildered and disappointed ladies. He said he didn't mind so long as he didn't go on wanting to do it when he couldn't and after a while he stopped wanting to. Chatsworth would ring from the Factory every day to get an account of Henry's doings and was unashamedly cheered by his decline, which he saw as a judgment upon him for having indulged in a surfeit. But a more than usually tired-looking Henry announced one day that the judgment had been lifted. 'It was Olympian,' he said quietly and sincerely. 'An anaesthetist from Londonderry. I knew it when I saw her in the theatre. We were doing an appendix.

There weren't even any preliminaries. I just asked her up to my room and we undressed without speaking. We shagged each other silly all night. It was beautifully clean and anonymous. I think it would be wrong to see her again, though, except by accident. It would spoil it. I shall try someone else tonight.'

'Chatsworth will be sorry.'

'I'll tell him myself. Make him suffer.'

But for the CO the war continued. He was convinced that something was going to happen and was quick to punish slackness, especially what he thought were violations of the hard target principle. Within a period of three days he fined six soldiers twenty pounds each because he was able to see them as he approached their sentry positions. 'If I were a gunman I would have shot you,' he said. 'Regard yourself as dead. Take his name, Mr Bone.'

All times were busy for Nigel Beale, as he regarded all information as Intelligence. What he regarded as a major coup, and which sent him into a passion of intense secrecy for several days, occurred with the arrest of a squalid, middle-aged, incoherent man smelling of whisky, who had returned from the United States in order to avenge the murder of his brother, the victim of an IRA feud. He had in his jacket pocket a loaded Colt .45 and over two hundred and fifty Green Shield stamps. He kept saying that he was going to wipe out the Provisional leadership. 'Why did you arrest him?' Charles asked Nigel.

Nigel was immediately on guard. 'What makes you think we have?'

'I saw him, like everyone else. I spoke to him on the way in. He seemed keen to talk. He was drunk.'

'You're not supposed to know. Keep it quiet.'

'Why don't you let him go so that he could kill them? We could give him their addresses.'

'There's more to this than meets the eye.'

'What?'

'Need to know.'

But nothing happened. The man went to prison for possession of a firearm and was not heard of again. The leaders of the Provisionals continued to come and go as they pleased.

Meanwhile the deal with Beazely continued to work well. Charles and Van Horne regularly wrote his reports and he paid just as regularly. They did not even have to see him very often as most business was conducted over the phone. This suited Beazely particularly well as he became ever more reluctant to leave his hotel. 'They're going to get me,' he said in his cups one day. 'I know they are. I can feel it in my bones, or wherever you're supposed to feel these things. They're coming for me.'

'Why you? They don't even know you.'

'Why not? They don't need to. It happens to other people. A bloke walks to work and a tile falls off a roof and kills him. Why him? you say. Why not? I say. It has to be someone. And I'm in a city where people are actually trying to kill each other and succeeding too bloody well for my liking. Well, one fine day it's going to be me. I just have this feeling it's going to happen.'

'It needn't be you. It could be me or Van Horne.'

'It's a comforting thought, Charlie, and kind of you to say so, and if it had to be one or the other I'd be a little happier. But it's more likely to be as well as, you see. You and me and Van Horne, but most likely just me.'

Meanwhile, the money mounted up, and Charles, with three weeks left in Northern Ireland, was within one hundred and thirty of his five hundred pounds. He needed a couple of big stories to supplement the continuing trickle of small ones.

One evening he was writing the minutes of the latest community relations committee meeting, which had lasted twelve minutes and had been chaired as usual by Anthony Hamilton-Smith, who had had to leave early, when he was summoned downstairs to deal with a complaint. The complaints desk was on the ground floor of the police station, just off the entrance hall. It was a chore which he shared with the adjutant. Complaints were either vivid and obviously false, or exaggerated and based on an uncheckable truth, or true and checkable but impossible to do anything about. There had been two cases where soldiers had been reprimanded, once for damage to property and once for brutality, and the victims had been compensated; but the issues were rarely clear-cut, and the truth of the matter was invariably unclear. On this occasion the complainant was Mary Magdalene, a girl from the Falls area whose nickname, origin unknown, had been passed on by the previous unit. She was unusual in that she was young, attractive and a graduate of Queen's University. Her complaints were detailed, literate and always minor, but nevertheless demanding extensive and time-consuming investigation. Despite this Charles and Colin Wood competed for her, a battle which Colin was winning as he held the complaints file to which, with her, reference always had to be made. The affair of the V-sign and the invitation allegedly delivered to her by a soldier from the back of a Land-Rover had provoked a lengthy and dignified correspondence between her and Colin which was the outstanding feature of the file. It finally petered out because of an inability to agree whether the intention behind such gestures and invitations was to flatter and compliment or to shock, degrade and terrorise.

She was already seated at the desk when Charles got there. There was no need to go through the preliminaries with her and so he pushed an empty form across. Though it was one of the unwritten rules with her that neither side ever smiled or indicated friendship, it was clear that she enjoyed the process, and manners were kept at all times. 'Would you please get me a pen,' she said.

'Of course.' This was a new development. He had left his upstairs and looked about for one, noticing her long, carelessly crossed legs and trying not to stare at them.

'On second thoughts, I believe I'm permitted to dictate my complaint, am I not?'

'You are, yes, but I still need a pen.' In the end he borrowed one from the RUC man at the desk in the entrance hall. Mary Magdalene got a light for her cigarette from a grinning corporal of the regimental police. She uncrossed and recrossed her legs. She had Irish looks of the best sort – dark hair, blue eyes, pale complexion and a gentle directness of expression that, for dealings with the Army, hardened into a provocative determination. 'Are you ready?' she asked.

Charles held his pen poised. 'Carry on.' She set off at great speed and he had to ask her to slow down, which was one up to her. The complaint concerned the searching of a car in which she and her parents were travelling. They had signed the clearance certificate to say that nothing had been damaged but when they had asked the soldiers under what authority they were acting they had been foully abused. Worse, her father had been propped up against the car and searched, his feet kicked apart, and he had then been pushed roughly back into the car when he protested. She dictated fluently and several times spelt words aloud, unnecessarily. Charles was able to get even on this by asking her to repeat them. When every last detail had been completed to her satisfaction, and she had read it, she signed and Charles took the form back upstairs. A telephone call would confirm whether or not there had been a VCP at the time and place she had said.

The adjutant had turned his back on his overflowing in tray and was leaning against the window, smoking. He was gazing at the shattered lamp-post on the other side of the road, another victim of urban guerrilla warfare. About half a pound of gelignite had been strapped to it one night the previous week, for no apparent purpose. A few yards away stood the telephone junction box which controlled all the police station's telecommunications.

'Mary Magdalene,' said Charles. 'All legs this evening.'

'Bitch.'

'She claims that she and her mummy and daddy were abused at a VCP last night.'

Colin grinned. 'Ah. We've got her this time. I know about it. The soldiers concerned were bright enough to report it and C company rang through this morning. They must've known who she was. Their version is that the old man took a swing at one of them. I think it's probably true otherwise they'd have kept quiet about it.' He stubbed out his cigarette and picked up the rest of the packet. 'Give me the form and I'll go and suggest that her statement be broadened to include all the facts. She must've had enough of you, anyway. She'll be wanting the real thing now.'

He went out with the form and Charles sat down at his desk. It occurred to him that no one would notice if he fabricated the minutes of the community relations committee. He balanced on the rear two legs of his chair, resting the back of his head against the wall. Someone shouted something from the ground floor. He decided to do a trial run. He would invent a project which had come to nothing and see if it was commented on. If it were he could always say it was a hangover from the previous unit. He would start with a detailed description of what it was and then go on to show why it was impossible for it ever to have worked and record the committee's unanimous decision. He sat the chair down on four legs again and bent forward over his desk, his elbows resting upon it. His pen had almost completed the T of 'also' when a sheet of redness leapt up from the floor in front of his desk. Simultaneously, a tremendous shock whipped up through the seat of his chair and the soles of his feet, stinging his calves and thighs. He felt himself rising, along with his desk and chair, and suddenly was near the ceiling. He brought his hands up to protect his face and then toppled backwards and half right. He landed on his right side in a foetal position, his knees up to his chest and his head in his arms. He felt he was enveloped in a continuous roar as in a great sea. After he hit the ground there was the sound of things falling and smashing all around him.

He lay still for what seemed a very short time, but afterwards he worked out that it must have been several minutes. Perhaps his internal clock had stopped. He did not move at first, waiting to see if there was any pain. Then he could not move because of a great weight upon his thighs, which he realised was the desk. His first clear thought was that he might be paralysed. He feared that above all else. He wriggled his toes inside his boots and felt them move. He flexed his feet. Though pinned down by the desk, he could move his legs. His head was still in his hands, and the left side felt wet. Something trickled across his eyes. He moved his hand in front of his face and saw it wet with red and blue liquids. He stared uncomprehendingly for some time whilst more liquid ran across his eyes. He could not think what it might be. Then he struggled out from beneath the desk and stood, unsteadily at first as his feet slipped on the books, paper, glass, plaster and rubble that covered the floor. He could not see the other half of the room where the door was because of a dense and continuously revolving cloud of dust. His Browning was attached to his shoulder by his lanyard and dangled by his thigh. The CO had insisted that it should always be so attached. He had the notion that the bomb would be followed by an attack on the building and so he pulled a magazine from his pocket and loaded and cocked the pistol.

He then walked, still unsteadily, to the great jagged holes in the walls where the windows had been. There was debris all over the street, the shops opposite looked as though they had been shelled, with parts of their walls and roofs blown away, and there were upturned cars on the far pavement. A figure was running across the road towards him. Holding the Browning in both hands, elbows locked, eyes open, Charles moved down through the target to the centre of the body, where two or three inches out in any direction would still be a stopping hit. He looked straight at the man so as to line up the mid-line of his body. As he took up the first slight pressure on the trigger it was borne in upon him very slowly, from somewhere far back in his mind, that the man was wearing a uniform. He was a military policeman, a Redcap. Charles lowered the pistol and uncocked it with hands that did not shake. His legs and his stomach felt empty but he was calm. He put the pistol in his pocket with the magazine still in, just in case.

The dust in the room had thinned and he could see the telephone on the floor where Colin's desk had been. To his

surprise, it worked. He dialled 999 and was told by the operator that they already knew about the bomb. Of course they
knew. He must think more clearly. He next noticed a large
blue stain on the ceiling above where he had been sitting, with
bits of his inkwell embedded. The ink was dripping off the
ceiling on to his upturned desk. He put his hand to his face and
head and found that he was wet with ink and blood. The blood
came from a couple of tender places on the side of his neck and
on his left eyebrow. At his first attempt to leave the room he
was forced back by the dust which made him cough and stag-
ger clumsily. However, he got through the door at the second
attempt and found himself on the landing. Soldiers were running purposefully to and fro. No one seemed to notice him. He
went to lean on the stair rail but found that it swayed. The
stairs were littered with bits of wood, concrete, plaster and
glass. An upturned helmet rocked gently by itself in the exact
centre of the centre stair. There were a few small splashes of
blood.

He stood in the door of the ops room where everyone was
active and everything seemed to be working. Again, no one
noticed him. He made his way down the stairs, where a lot of
people were moving about. Two soldiers came running up the
stairs three at a time. One stopped. 'You all right, sir?'

'Yes, thank you.'

'Want me to get a medic for you?'

'No thanks, I'm all right.' His own repetition of the soldier's 'all right' echoed in his skull, along with the 'all rights' of a hundred other voices. He thought, with the clarity born of supreme detachment, of how this was an Army stock phrase, an all-purpose measure of spiritual welfare, military competence and personal affability. He seemed able to think only of irrelevancies.

The soldier was still staring at him. 'There's one in the cookhouse. I'd go along there if I was you.'

'Thank you.'

He lost his bearings for a moment at the bottom of the stairs because several walls had disappeared, there was daylight in unexpected places and the floor was covered by concrete rubble. Some soldiers were bending over something on the floor. They straightened and Charles saw that they were carrying a door, upon which was Colin. His head lolled oddly to one side. The empty feeling in Charles's stomach increased so much that he put his hand to it. As he watched the door go past he felt a deep and secret elation because he was alive and whole. They carried the adjutant out through a hole in the wall and put him on a stretcher in the back of an ambulance. Charles followed them out into the street. A group of squat women were standing on the corner jeering and laughing. There were several youths on the other side of the road. One shouted, 'Let's get their guns!' and started forward but was pushed roughly back by some soldiers from A company who had just arrived in their Pigs.

Charles was facing a TV camera and a reporter he knew. He was being asked what had happened. 'There has been an explosion,' he said. More people were asking him and he repeated it several times. He was asked how it happened and how many injuries there were. 'I don't know,' he said, again many times.

Then he was looking at the CO, whose face was drawn and grim. 'Charles, are you all right?'

'Yes, sir.'

'You're not.'

'No, sir.'

'Go to hospital and get cleaned up.'

There were more questions from the press. Then he was standing inside amongst the rubble, again facing the CO. 'I thought I told you to go to hospital.'

'Yes, sir.'

'Well, go on then.'

'Yes, sir.' He made his way to the cookhouse where he found Henry Sandy's medical sergeant, grinning. 'They told me you was dead, sir. I was all ready to go on telly meself. Sit down here and let's have a butchers. Blue blood, eh? Always knew you were different. Red stuff too. At least you're human. More blood than cuts, I reckon. You got some glass in there. Where does it hurt? Sorry. Where else? Won't even need stitching, this won't.'

A normally reluctant and surly cook produced gallons of tea in a very short time and with no visible equipment. As Charles drank his he began to feel a little more in touch with the world. The cut above his eye was throbbing. When he got outside a troop of Sappers had arrived with lorries to clear away the debris. One half of the ground floor of the building was completely wrecked and the upper two storeys remained only because the pre-stressed concrete structure was designed so that the pillars stood firm even if the walls blew out. The quarter-inch steel shutters on the windows on the ground floor had disappeared, as had those in Charles's and Colin's office, which had been directly above the blast. One pair of shutters had been blown across the road, through the front of the house opposite and into the kitchen at the back. There were press swarming everywhere and, after many enquiries, Charles was able to establish that about thirty people had been taken to hospital. A baby, the adjutant and one other not yet identified were seriously injured. The rest were civilians who had chanced to be in the area. It was believed that the bomb had been in a suitcase brought into the police station by a young man, who had run out. Someone had shouted, 'Bomb!' which was the shout Charles had heard.

He answered queries for about an hour, repeating himself

often. Later he saw himself on the television news saying, 'There has been an explosion,' with the devastated building in the background and blood down one side of his face. Then there was a close-up of his cuts, robbing them of their impressiveness, to the commentary, 'Officers refused to have their wounds treated until all the injured had been accounted for.'

Chatsworth and his platoon turned up to help clear the rubble. 'If it had gone off ten minutes later I'd have been here anyway,' he said.

'Then you might not have been here now.'

'True.' He enjoyed the scene but was obviously disappointed. 'I don't think much of your wounds. They won't last. Mine will last longer. Even though it's hidden by clothes most of the time it'll still be there. The one on your neck is quite near the jugular, though.'

'Did you hear about the adjutant?'

'He's bad, isn't he? That's a bit serious. Brings it home to you. All because they won't let us shoot the bastards unless they're doing something. I wish I'd seen it, all the same.'

Arc lights were set up as it became dark. It was impressive how quickly and easily the necessary equipment and personnel were mobilised. The artificial glare made the scene of toiling men look slightly unreal. Some of the local women protested about the noise. They stood on the spot where the complaints desk had been and shouted in their harsh Belfast accents about civil rights. The operations officer also had a complaint for Charles: 'Some bloody oppo of yours called Beedley or something keeps ringing up on the ops room phone to know what's happened. I keep telling him to come down and see for himself or piss off but he won't. Screw him or something, will you?'

It proved to be Van Horne's hour of triumph. Uninjured, apart from an already picturesque scar on the cheek that excited Chatsworth's envy, he composed and phoned through Beazely's copy whilst Charles dealt with the more adventurous press. Later Charles was called back up to his office by the CO, who was examining it. The room was a shambles. There were gaping holes where the windows had been, cracks in the other walls and everything movable was smashed or twisted. Even the floor was unevenly shaped, with a great cracked hump in the middle where Charles had seen the sheet of redness leap up. 'You ought to be dead,' said the CO. Charles remembered having been told this before and wondered whether, if he were to be killed, the CO would then say, 'It ought to have happened some time ago, of course. I've told him twice before.' The CO paused and then began again, as though the point needed emphasis. 'By all that's reasonable you ought to be dead. This floor is reinforced and blast-proof and it's still come through it. If it had been a normal floor you wouldn't be here. Nor if you'd been sitting in a different position. I can't understand why you weren't cut to pieces. How's your eye?'

'Fine, sir, thank you.'

'Well done. You did well to escape.'

When they got outside again there was alarm because a car had been spotted parked around the corner against another wall of the building. It was thought it might be another bomb. A warrant officer from the bomb disposal team was summoned and the street cleared. From the safety of the corner they watched him advance alone to the car and examine it. He got down on his knees and peered beneath the boot. Charles was indulging in the warm pleasure of relative safety when the CO, after peering impatiently round the corner, said, 'Go down and see if he wants a hand, Thoroughgood.'

Charles walked down the street as slowly as he dared. It was pointless to hazard two lives instead of one and he knew nothing about bomb disposal. It was probably even contrary to Army procedure but he did not have the nerve to disobey the CO. Even if he had, the habit of obedience would probably have sent him down there. He felt calmly fatalistic as he stood by the car. 'D'you want a hand?' he asked the warrant officer.

The man was half under the car. 'There's a wire here I can't identify.' He wriggled out. 'We'll go in from the top. You can hold those for me.' He handed Charles some tools, selected a strange-looking drill and cut a hole about four inches in diameter in the top of the boot. 'All clear,' he said after a minute or so.

Charles was very relieved, despite his calmly fatalistic feelings of a few minutes before. He offered the man a cup of tea, which was all he could think of to say. 'No time,' he said as he collected his tools. 'Got another one in the city centre. They're popping up like mushrooms tonight. This is my third. Mostly hoaxes.'

Much later Henry Sandy returned from the hospital. He looked very tired. 'Colin's dead,' he said.

Again, the secret thrill of being alive. It was a shameful thrill though his heart leapt within him to hear Henry's words. Yet it was still a shock to hear it said. He knew there was no reply, as Henry knew, but there was a desire to say something. 'Blast?'

'No. A severely fractured skull. The whole of the right side was smashed in. He must've hit something or something hit him. He never had a chance. His brains were coming out of his mouth in the ambulance. They did everything possible at the hospital. They had two surgeons working on him for an hour and a half.' He pulled slowly on his cigarette, talking quietly. His face was expressionless. 'And there's a baby with a part of his brain outside his skull. He'll live. They've saved him, as a vegetable. He was in one of the cars, apparently. And some bird who's lost both legs. She was in the building, I think.'

'Mary Magdalene.'

'What?'

'Local girl.'

'Ah.'

The Army had a way of dealing with death that took the edge off the acute sense of futility and helplessness that afflicts most people. Woven into its collective subconscious was an expectation of death and even a vague sense that it was apt. It was a part of the contract. Besides, the war had to go on and there were things to do – repairs, new defences, reports to write, kin to be informed, precautions to be taken. Two clerks packed Colin's kit that night. They stripped his bed, collected his clothes, gathered the family photographs, the cigarettes and personal oddments from his locker. His money was counted and recorded. Charles pointed to a family photograph that included Colin in uniform. 'I'd better have that for the press,' he said. The two clerks hesitated, sullenly. 'Otherwise they'll be bothering his wife and family for one. It's better if they get it from this end.' He signed for it and within an hour the only trace of the adjutant was a pile of kit stacked and labelled in a green metal cupboard in the orderly room, waiting to be shipped off. So long as the procedure was followed, the now-living and meaningful book which was so often abused, everything would be all right. Slow and unwieldy as it was in normal times, the Army was one great system designed for disaster and, so long as enough of it survived to work the system, that was when it worked best. It was believed in. Tony Watch took over as adjutant that night.

By four in the morning there seemed nothing left to do but go to bed. Charles was present when the CO gave an interview to a young radio reporter, one of the few journalists he liked. The man had flown over from London on the last plane on hearing of the bomb and was rewarded by a simple and touching piece for the seven o'clock news, with details of Colin Wood's death which were released only that morning, too late for the dailies. When the reporter had gone, the CO rubbed his eyes wearily. 'It's terrible, simply terrible,' he said slowly. 'One simply doesn't know what to say. I've known Colin since he was a young subaltern, and to see him killed like that – there simply aren't words. I don't know a better young officer, you know, I really don't. D'you know Diana his wife?'

'No, sir.'

'Lovely girl. God knows how she's going to take this. Two young children, you know. And for you, sharing his office like that. You must have got to know him. How terrible for you, how simply terrible. Of course, it could have been any of us, and we're extremely lucky it was only him. We could've lost half a dozen soldiers down there tonight. The press will no doubt say he was trying to save that poor girl, but I don't know, I just don't know. It's the sort of thing he would do, but one will never really know. I don't suppose the girl herself will know.' He stood and began walking round the room. 'And that wretched baby. What will become of it? These are things, you see, that are forgotten about, these trivial, incidental little details, the suffering of people who don't matter. These people will be forgotten while those who maimed them will go prattling on about the cause and all that other rubbish. We should remind people everyday about this sort of thing but it's no good, they don't listen. And even if they did they'd get used to it and stop noticing. It almost makes one despair of people entirely, doesn't it, Thoroughgood, eh?'

'It does, sir, yes.'

'I mean, they must be warped, they must be only half there, they can't have all the normal human responses. But I'll tell you one thing, within these four walls. I promise you, as God is my witness, if I get half a chance to bury some of these people before I go, I'll do it. I know it's not ethical, I know it's not moral, I know one shouldn't feel like this, but half a chance, that's all. Half.' He was pale with emotion and gripped the back of his chair so hard that his knuckles whitened. His eyes were hard on Charles and his teeth set firmly against each other.

He wanted a response but Charles sought a way out for

himself. 'Some of the press have been asking why it was so easy.'

'I'll tell you why. Because we weren't allowed to put a proper guard on the door because some misguided do-gooder in the powers-that-be decided it might inhibit people from coming to complain about us. That's why. If you think I'm crazy, take a look at them. It'll be different now, of course. It'll be sandbagged and bunkered and netted and God knows what else. We just had to wait for someone to be killed, that's all. Tell that to your press friends. Only you'd better make it a bit more diplomatic.'

Charles was about to go to bed, not because he felt tired but because he was afraid of feeling tired if he didn't, when Beazely rang. He was suddenly irritated. 'What do you want?'

'I just wanted to talk, that's all.' Beazely sounded hurt.

'What about?'

There was a long pause. 'I think I'm going to die.'

'So you are. So are the rest of us.'

'But I don't want to die.' He sounded tearfully drunk.

'Tough.'

'You don't understand. It's going to be soon. I thought you would understand, Charlie. You of all people. Can I talk to Van Horne?'

'He's not around.'

'What shall I do?'

'Go to bed.'

'I suppose you're right. What are you going to do?'

'Go to bed.'

'Good night then.'

'Good night.' He rang off, and Charles, instead of going to bed, went up on the roof where the night air was cool and clear and there were only the silent sentries to be seen. He felt anything but tired. He was sustained by a pure, selfish joy at being alive. He could not feel sorry for Colin. Things happened, they just happened. There was no more to be said. He could go through the motions but essentially he was untouched and he could not deceive himself. He recalled the CO's words, 'How terrible for you, how simply terrible,' as though they were said about someone else. They didn't fit him.

Part Three

The Factory Again

12

Charles slept little during the next few days. He did not need sleep. There seemed to be enough adrenalin coursing through his veins to keep him going almost indefinitely. He felt untouched by the normal adversities and perversities of life and took a positive pleasure in the ordinary. There was even joy in sipping Army tea. Behind his every thought and word, like some film in his mind, was the memory of the blast as it flashed through the floor. Whenever he looked at a building he had an involuntary picture of it exploding.

Two weeks previously the battalion had had to watch an IRA funeral on its way to the Milltown cemetery. They had had to stand at a discreet distance whilst the tricolour-draped coffin was marched past, escorted by self-conscious marching men in berets. D company, with Pigs and Ferrets, had waited behind the sliding doors of the bus garage opposite the cemetery with orders to intervene and make arrests if volleys were fired at the graveside. This was because the Loyalists would have been so angered by yet another demonstration of IRA violence that they would have reacted. They, with their industrial muscle, were the only force capable of bringing the province to real chaos. Even the CO had admitted that it would have been carnage at the funeral if D company had had to intervene. 'But now we will take a leaf out of their book,' he said. 'We'll have our own funeral, only we'll do it better. We'll give Colin a send-off the like of which they've never seen since the bloody place was converted to paganism.'

It was arranged that night. A gunner regiment which the CO had not offended lent one of their gun-carriages which it had brought with it to Ireland so that the Gunners would not forget how to clean them. It was polished throughout the night. Buglers were obtained and companies allotted their places along the route, which ran by design along the Falls and through the new estate. 'The cortège will be escorted by a Pig and two Ferrets,' ordered the CO. 'It will stop at battalion HQ for two minutes' silence and the Last Post. The coffin will be covered by the largest and brightest Union Jack in existence. All traffic will be stopped for half an hour from 0845, and I don't care if that causes a traffic jam all the way to Dublin. In fact I hope it does. The people who cheered at Colin's body that night are now going to have to stop for him and pay their respects. Drivers will switch off their engines and pedestrians will stand still with their mouths shut and their hands out of their pockets. Anyone who doesn't will be lifted and brought down here, and if we can't charge him he'll at least be held as long as possible and have to walk home in the rain. Any troublemaker will be sat on.'

In the event there was no trouble. The people were taken too much by surprise and, anyway, the CO had underestimated their real enjoyment of funerals, parades and processions. There was no trouble with Headquarters, either, who were told when it was too late for them to be obstructive. Nevertheless, such an event was unprecedented in the Republican areas of Belfast, and Headquarters were worried that it might be seen as provocation. 'That's exactly what it is,' the CO said to everyone around him, several times. 'And I told them that if anything raises its ugly head to cause trouble it will be firmly smashed, and in any case things don't raise their heads when they're being firmly sat on. Even Headquarters should know that.'

On the CO's orders, Charles told the press and, not on the CO's orders, arranged for Van Horne to take the necessary photographs for Beazely. It was an impressive spectacle and it achieved national coverage. One platoon from each company was drawn up in ranks outside battalion HQ. Though unrehearsed, the drill was adequate and the cortège gleamed in the cold morning sunlight. The only sound during the silence was the rapping of the rope against the flagpole in the breeze. From the roof of the building the Last Post was sounded and it echoed unchallenged across the streets of South-West Belfast. The television cameras whirred gently as the cortège creaked forward and Colin Wood began his journey to the airport. All along the route bystanders stared sullenly, though with more bewilderment than resentment. Snatch squads with batons surrounded those who tried to move away. People watched in silence from the windows. There were no repercussions, then or later. 'Good for the morale of the Ackies,' said the CO. 'Gives them a bit of self-respect.'

Later in the day they were visited by the general who, it was rumoured, privately congratulated the CO. Charles was among those introduced, with a description of what had happened to him during the explosion. The general gripped his hand firmly and said, 'Well done.'

Chatsworth was out with a foot patrol when the CO drove past with the general, and did not salute. He was operational and thought he was in a place where he was quite likely to be shot at and so thought there was no need. The CO disagreed, and so every day for the next week Chatsworth was drilled by Mr Bone, the RSM, for thirty minutes on the roof of battalion HQ. Mr Bone, though not his pupil, took to this task with a relish that was almost obscene and which took no regard of the prospect of being sniped at. Henry Sandy also got into trouble when some of his medical section, drunk, tried to break into a nurses' hostel at the hospital. They were turned away by a female warden but returned a while later with the most drunken of their number stripped naked and bound with masking tape as a peace offering for the warden to play with whilst they ravished her charges. The military police were called and there was a fight. Henry was found alone in his room, too drunk to be able to do anything, though later that same night he apparently assisted with an operation and passed out afterwards. The next day he was let off after being shouted at by the CO for ten to fifteen minutes. Drill seemed somehow inappropriate for a doctor, and there was in any case a suspicion that he did not really know how to do it.

During the days following the explosion a new coat of normality was painted upon life at battalion headquarters. It covered the cracks well enough and, in fact, the headquarters functioned more efficiently than before. There were, though, one or two little blisters, invisible air-bubbles that worked away secretly and then suddenly broke through, taking everyone by surprise. Most of these minor blemishes were due to changes in the CO's behaviour. Charles, had he had energy to spare from wondering whether he would survive the next few weeks and what he would do after that, would have concluded that nothing the CO might say or do would now seem odd. He would then have had to accept that he had been wrong. At first the CO went into a period of withdrawal, almost to the point where he stopped being CO. He spent a lot of time alone in his room but would occasionally sally forth at any hour of the day or night in full kit and demand to go on a tour of the area immediately. People were sometimes summoned to his room only to hear him reminiscing about his early days in the Army, and then be subjected to a lecture about their own future prospects. He never mentioned Colin to anyone. He became forgetful about little things, referring to conversations he had intended to have as though they were yesterday, having tea made for him in a hurry and then ignoring it. One memorable day he forgot to shave. No one dared say anything, though there was a story that he went upstairs so abruptly during dinner and reappeared clean-shaven because Anthony Hamilton-Smith had fondled his own moustache and asked the CO whether he preferred dung or fertilisers.

Anthony Hamilton-Smith became more in evidence during this period, not because he did any more than usual but because people turned to him in the absence of the CO. His advice and instructions were usually brief and sensible, given with a lightness of touch that could have been due either to an innate dislike of the dramatic or to a genuine unconcern. Responsibility did not so much sit easily upon him as sprawl playfully at his feet. Another effect of the CO's withdrawal was that the RSM began to play a greater part in everyone's lives. Mr Bone was not a man to be either brief or sensible, but the way he extended the area in which he was able to exercise his peculiar brand of bureaucratic stupidity and spite argued a cunning tenacity. Reflecting later upon Mr Bone's rise to power Charles was reminded of Yeats's lines, 'What rough beast, its hour come round at last, slouches towards Bethlehem to be born?' It was because Tony Watch, the signals officer who had taken Colin's place, was new to the job and had to rely heavily upon the RSM's advice that Mr Bone was able to triumph over Charles by having him evicted from battalion HQ.

He did this by securing for himself control over nearly all routine administrative matters and presenting it as helpfulness. The explosion had destroyed one corner of the building and had affected the rest in surprising ways. Of a pair of glass doors on a top-floor corridor one was torn off its hinges and the other untouched. In another corridor every door handle had been chopped off cleanly as though with a butcher's axe. All the nails in a wooden partition wall in the ops room had been driven through until they poked out the other side by nearly an inch. Some windows were smashed and some were whole. The room in which Charles and Tony Watch slept was above the damaged corner but did not appear to be harmed.

ALAN JUDD

By a reasoning that no one ever understood, if only because it was never explained, the Department of the Environment was responsible for the building in just the same way as they were for paper and clothing stores and government buildings in other parts of the United Kingdom. It was up to them to decide what should be done about the damaged building and to say which bits could continue in use. With the same sense of urgency as in the rest of the United Kingdom, they arrived from their office in East Belfast a week or so after the explosion. They were four stout, genial, self-important men in raincoats. Mr Bone took it upon himself to show them round and then took them to the Sergeants' Mess, after which they were seen no more. Charles ran into the flushed and cheerful-looking Mr Bone later. Mr Bone smiled, never a good sign. 'Very grateful if you could have your kit packed and stacked in the yard by 1700 hours, Mr Thoroughgood. There's a Land-Rover going over with the post then. You can get a lift with it.'

'What do you mean, Mr Bone?'

'What I say, Mr Thoroughgood. If you don't catch that one you won't get over in time for dinner and you're off ration strength here with effect from this morning.'

'Get over where? Where am I going?'

'Back to the Factory, sir. C company. Captain Watch not tell you?' Mr Bone's round eyes bulged with feigned surprise and concern. 'Very sorry, Mr Thoroughgood. Thought you knew by now. DOE survey. Your room's not safe. You and Captain Watch have got to move out. We've cleared a store-room for him but there's nowhere left for you, so you'll have to live in the Factory. They've got plenty of room there, as you know.'

The thought of going back to the Factory, combined with Mr Bone's offensive and unctuous satisfaction, was sufficient to pierce Charles's post-explosion euphoria. He argued, though he knew it was useless. Mr Bone would not have made such a move without preparation.

'DOE say-so I'm afraid, sir. I've got it here in black and white.' He tapped the file he was carrying. 'Room not safe for human habitation. Structural defects. All mumbo-jumbo to me, but to an educated man like yourself it might mean more. D'you want to see the report?'

'No thank you, Mr Bone. I'll see Captain Watch.'

'Good idea, Mr Thoroughgood. You'll find him in his office. Unfortunately he agrees with me that there's no other room available for you. I've searched high and low. 1700, don't forget.' He saluted smartly and turned away.

Had Colin still been alive Charles felt he could have got things changed even at that late date, but with Colin around Mr Bone could never have pulled off such a coup in the first place. To Tony Watch Charles's fate was an unimportant detail amidst the welter of administrative matters in which he now gloried. 'Don't worry, you'll still be able to deal with the press and whatever,' he said. 'You can meet them in the Factory, if you like, and anyway there are vehicles going backwards and forwards umpteen times a day. And you've got Van Horne here still. He can answer the phone and all that sort of thing. Only bloody problem is it leaves us one short on the watch-keeping list. Unless you come back for a night shift once or twice a week. Don't see why you shouldn't. You wouldn't need a bed. Trouble is, Edward Lumley will probably want you to do the same over there. We can sort that out later. Pity about our room, wasn't it? I was almost getting to like it. At least I've got one to myself now anyway. Cheers. Look in next time you're in.'

Before he left that afternoon Charles was summoned by the CO. He assumed it had something to do with his move. They talked for a while about press reactions to the explosion and then the CO said, 'When do you leave us?'

'1700, sir. With the post.'

'What?' The misunderstanding was cleared up. The CO had been referring to Charles's leaving the Army. He had not known about the move to the Factory and was not interested. 'As long as it doesn't prevent you from doing your job, which it shouldn't. You must have got the hang of it well enough by now.' Charles told him that he was due to leave the Army when the battalion returned to England. The CO nodded. 'The important thing in life is always to make a positive contribution. You have done that. I'm very grateful.' There was an embarrassing silence which the CO, who was staring out of the window, appeared not to notice. 'What are you going to do?'

'I don't yet know, sir.'

'Any ideas?'

'No, sir, not really. Unless I go back to university and do research.'

The CO appeared not to take this as a serious suggestion. 'You'll have to do something. You can't do nothing.' There was another pause. It was impossible to tell whether the interview was at an end or whether the CO was collecting his thoughts, or had perhaps forgotten that Charles was there. He looked tired, drawn and remote. 'I have to go to England myself for a few days,' he said eventually. 'Senior officers' seminar, of all the daft things to have to do when you're supposed to be operational. Daresay it's a concealed way of making me take a break which I haven't asked for. Also to talk about my next posting. I haven't got long left with the battalion, you know. God, they've gone quickly, these last two years.' He was silent again and Charles sensed that the interview was at last finished. He left feeling that he must have been summoned for an altogether different reason that had not been revealed, and that the failure was partially his.

He met Anthony Hamilton-Smith immediately afterwards. 'CO in, is he? Awake? Good. Didn't want to disturb his shut-eye. He's been sleeping a lot recently. Tired, I daresay. What did he want you for?'

'I don't know. Nothing in particular, I think.'

'Overdoing it, you see. Can't afford to let that happen. We must look after our CO. Perhaps I'll leave him be after all. He might want to drop off again. Very few things in life that can't wait till the morrow. You're changing accommodation, I hear? What d'you want to go there for? Dreadful place. Much better to stay here.'

This was an unexpected ally. 'I don't want to go at all but Mr Bone says there's no more room now that mine has been condemned.'

'Very likely.'

'But I don't believe him. I think he's lying.'

Anthony nodded. 'Almost certainly.'

'I'd much prefer not to go.'

Anthony looked sympathetic. 'Don't blame you, old boy.'

'Can't something be done about it?'

Anthony patted Charles on the arm. 'Awfully difficult just at the moment, Charles, with the CO here and not here, if you see what I mean. Best not to make a fuss about things. I should grin and bear it and don't forget your ear-plugs.'

When Charles arrived in the Factory that day with all his

kit he found that everything was different but that nothing was really changed. The ops room had been moved, there were more hardboard partitions, people slept on different areas of floor and there was a new subaltern in charge of Charles's old platoon. Called Stuart Moore, he was thin, pale and quiet and looked far too young. Everyone else was pale except Edward, whose face was as red, mobile, foolish and good-natured as ever. Tiredness in Edward showed itself in bags under his eyes and an irritable nervousness that caused him to repeat himself so often that those around him, dulled by their own tiredness and his repetitions, hardly reacted at all. This made him even more exasperated. However, his basic good nature showed through. 'Great to have you back, Charles, even if you're not going to do anything for us except a spot of watchkeeping. Want some coffee? Two coffees, Green. You're better off here, I tell you, than in that loony-bin you've just come from. Touch of reality will do you good. Is it true the CO won't speak to anyone? Bloody Godsend if it is. We haven't heard from him for ages. Has old Hamilton-Smith found himself a punkah-wallah yet? Jesus, what a case. Pity they didn't blow up the whole building whilst they were about it, eh? Green, where's that bloody coffee? People take sod-all notice of me these days. Might as well talk to yourself. D'you find that? Green – Where the hell is he? Corporal Lynch – go and find Private Green and shove something up his arse to get him moving, will you? He was here two seconds ago.'

'He's making your coffee, sir.'

'He can't be, the kettle's here. Unless he's looking for a bloody cow for the milk.'

'No more milk till tomorrow, sir.'

'Jesus Christ, what a dump this is. No milk. Have you ever heard anything like it? You were better off where you were, Thoroughgood. We've got no room here anyway. Moore's got your old space. You'll have to share with Chatsworth.'

'Share what?'

'His bed. Well, not literally. It's a bunk arrangement, sort of. He made it himself. Pity about Colin, wasn't it? Nice bloke like that. I can think of a few I'd put in his place. Nasty business, though.' Edward then went on for some minutes about someone who had been killed in Aden, while Charles hoped that there was a mistake about his having to share a bunk with Chatsworth, and concluded gloomily that there almost certainly wasn't. Edward was stopped by the appearance of another soldier. 'Green – where the hell have you been?'

Green was plump and pasty-faced. He looked as though nothing in the world could interest, surprise or amuse him. 'In the bog, sir,' he said tonelessly.

'What about our coffee?'

'What coffee, sir?'

The very lifelessness of Green's speech inhibited argument. Edward turned to Charles, his face wrinkled in exasperation. 'See what I mean, Charles? It's a bloody madhouse. Everyone walks around in a world of his own except me. No wonder I'm losing my fuzz.'

The noise in the Factory was undiminished. Charles had forgotten how much the building shook to the rhythm of the machines that made the bottles. He sought out the CSM and Sergeant Wheeler for company that evening. With them he found some of the down-to-earth sanity so often talked about by Edward but never by him attained.

'You must've dropped a right bollock to be back here with the riff-raff, sir,' the CSM said. Charles explained what had happened. The CSM laughed until his eyes watered. 'He may be solid bone, the RSM, but he's a cunning bastard, ain't he? Trouble is, the CO don't see him like that. The CO's blind to a lot of people, I reckon. He gets a fixed idea about them and then that's it like, he don't notice them no more. Same way that Sarn't Wheeler here don't know he's alive half the time. Just forgets to notice, like. Give hisself a real surprise one day, he will.'

Sergeant Wheeler squatted on an upturned ammunition box. He looked tired and did not smile. 'I'll notice I'm alive when I get home,' he said, without looking up.

'Yeah, but will anyone else? Don't know when he's well off,

do he, sir, with blokes like you and me around to cheer him up? Best time of your life, this is. Think about that.'

'If I did I'd bloody shoot meself.'

'No need to be generous, we ain't asking for no favours. Cheerful bugger you are. If you're going to do it take someone with you for company, starting with old Bone-head. Mr Thoroughgood here will put a good word in for you in the next world then, so you might get your heavenly stripes back despite having done yourself in. He might even stand you a pint of nectar when he gets there, eh sir?'

'How about a couple of pints now?' said Charles. 'In case I don't go to the same place.' The CSM was never a man to turn down an invitation and it soon turned out that Sergeant Wheeler's depression was not beyond the reach of even canned beer. By the time Charles had gathered his kit and turned with a heavy heart towards Chatsworth and his bunk he had at least accepted his new situation, though he knew it would not be a good one.

Chatsworth was unchanged. Indeed, it was difficult to imagine that he could be Chatsworth and different. It was clear that he had achieved an easy dominance over Moore, whose kit and sleeping space were squeezed into a narrow area just by the sacking that made do as a door so that people who entered when he was there had to step over his head. Tim now shared Edward's partition. Chatsworth's famous bunk was a curious and unstable-looking construction of odd bits of wood and canvas, except for the lower bunk that comprised a sheet of corrugated iron. His kit was piled on this and he slept on the canvas top bunk. He was appalled when Charles mentioned the matter of sharing. 'Who says you've got to?'

'Edward.'

'Bugger Edward. I made this thing myself. It's not the Army's, it's mine. The bottom bit is a rack for my kit, not a bunk. Who's he think he is, for Christ's sake?'

'Go and ask him if you want but that's what he said.' Chatsworth was one of the few people with whom Charles felt he could deal without compunction.

'There must be somewhere else. What about the roof? It's mild enough weather and there's plenty of room.'

'I'm not sleeping on the roof.'

'Why not? It's not bad. You're not afraid of heights, are you?'

'You go there if it's that good.'

Chatsworth took a kick at the absent Moore's kit. 'Or Moore's space. You could use it when he's not in it.'

'What about when he is?'

'He isn't very often. He's dopey, he's asleep on his feet half the time. He probably wouldn't notice.'

'And then there's all my kit, of course.'

'You've got kit?' Chatsworth's tone and expression were as near to moral outrage as was possible with him. He put on his belt angrily. 'Right. I'm going to see Edward. And don't you go sneaking on to the bunk when my back's turned.'

The struggle was brief and decisive. Edward's shouting could be heard above all the other noises of the Factory. Chatsworth returned less than two minutes after setting out, looking like a man most grievously put upon. 'When I run this army there won't be room for people like Edward. Dead wood. It's that that stops us from getting ahead. Mentally unstable too. Not fit to command, in my opinion. D'you know, in the Israeli Army everyone, no matter what rank, has to retire at forty? Good idea, I think. All this balls about having to provide a career till you're ninety-three – just pay them off, that's all. Anyway, they wouldn't all last that long.' He started moving his kit from the top of the corrugated iron sheet and stowing it on the floor underneath. 'Well, don't blame me if the whole thing breaks. It wasn't designed for brutes like you. And my kit's going underneath. There won't be room for yours. You'll have to find somewhere else.'

Chatsworth's resentment was the matter of a moment, like most upsets in military life. People endured trouble, misfortune, dressings-down and insults either because they were inevitable or because there was nothing personal in them. It was all a question of form. If you had transgressed you were shouted at or punished in the same way that anyone else would have been in your position, and it was then forgotten. The man who bawled you out one minute would share his water-bottle with you the next. Very soon Charles's moving into Chatsworth's bunk was just another fact of life, something to be coped with and thought about no more, rather than the gross violation of territorial integrity it had been at first.

Not that it was without problems. Charles had to pile so much stuff on the corrugated iron, including his sleeping-bag, to act as a mattress thick enough not to conform to the corrugations, that there was very little room between that and the top bunk. Once again, he found himself unable to sit up in bed and compelled to wriggle in and out on his elbows and knees. Every time he or Chatsworth entered or left the bunk, or even when Chatsworth turned over, the whole structure creaked and wobbled. Charles was in constant fear that the top would give way and Chatsworth would come crashing down on him, although most of the time their periods of sleep did not coincide and whoever was trying to sleep would be woken by the other returning. Even when they did coincide Charles's rest was often interrupted by Chatsworth's climbing in and out on unexplained personal missions throughout the night. Chatsworth denied a weak bladder or a history of sleep-walking. He even attempted to deny the mysterious missions but in the end conceded that he might very occasionally get up during the night in order to 'keep an eye on the place' for the benefit of everyone else. No more could ever be got out of him. Indeed, Charles gave up questioning him altogether after being awoken one night by a painful blow on the side of the head, caused by a Browning which had fallen from beneath Chatsworth's pillow when he turned over. Angry, and feeling a swelling already forming on his head, Charles had wriggled out and woken Chatsworth, only to see another Browning clatter to the floor when Chatsworth sat up. Chatsworth was unapologetic but did promise to put the Brownings 'with the others'.

Overall, though, Charles's new life was only moderately unendurable. He was better off than many people in that he was expected to be in two places – the Factory and the battalion HQ – and so had good reason for not being in either and was accountable to no one. It also meant that he was not really wanted in either place, except for watchkeeping, and so led a largely purposeless and peripatetic existence. There was just over a fortnight to go before the battalion was due to leave, and so the quiet week following his removal to the Factory was very welcome. With every day that passed he felt his chances of survival were better. He saw no journalists and even heard nothing from Beazely, though Van Horne claimed to have taken a call from an incoherent drunk that could have been him. The CO went back to England for five days,

Anthony Hamilton-Smith took command and a torpor fell upon Belfast that was every bit as persistent and universal as the rain.

Whether the events of the Sunday that ended the week could have occurred if the CO had been there was a matter for discussion by the more thoughtful for some days afterwards. There was no doubt that his presence would have made a difference, as it did to every occasion, but whether for good or ill it was impossible to say. The fact that all had turned out well could not in all fairness be attributed to Anthony's being in charge, though it was difficult to imagine them happening in the way they did without him. It would probably have been fairest to describe him as a necessary though not a sufficient condition.

It began at about two in the afternoon with an anonymous telephone call to the RUC which warned of a landmine in a tunnel beneath the Factory. To the RUC, who spent their lives dealing with such matters, this was a run-of-the-mill business that would have to be heeded but which was no cause for real alarm. There were many hoax calls every week and this smelt like one. Edward, however, had spent months worrying about just such a possibility and to him the call was confirmation of his worst fears. He had regarded the first search of tunnels beneath the Factory as almost criminally superficial and had at one time attempted to establish a permanent presence down there. He was thwarted only by not having enough soldiers to go round. With regard to Anthony and others in battalion HQ the warning was something to occupy them on a dreary Sunday, and it was very obviously just this for the local people, who turned out in force to watch the search teams arrive, and the ensuing confusion. Very likely the caller was among them, finding it a better way to pass the time than anything else within the scope of his imagination.

Edward immediately ordered the evacuation of the Factory. Without actually refusing to obey the order everyone within hearing pointed out to him that this would render the company non-operational and that once this were known they could expect similar calls every day. He compromised by insisting that only essential personnel should remain on duty in the Factory and that all others should assemble in the yard outside. The argument that they were no safer there than in the building as there was no knowing where unknown tunnels went – if anywhere – carried no weight with him. He also insisted that all vehicles be moved into surrounding streets and guarded. As the company was under strength it fell to Moore's platoon to do this, despite their having had no more than four hours of proper sleep in the last fifty, and they moved into the streets like youthful zombies. 'Perfect for snipers,' Chatsworth remarked quietly.

'Is it true the major's got sponge in his boots to absorb the blast?' asked the CSM. 'Looks more like hot nails from the way he's hopping about.'

Search teams arrived from Brigade to help with the known tunnels, and those in the company who had been down them before wearily prepared for another futile and grubby descent. Anthony and what was normally the CO's Rover Group arrived with good humour and a lot of unnecessary revving of engines. He jumped out of his Land-Rover. 'Glad of a chance to straighten the old pins after lunch,' he said to Edward. 'Does 'em no good to be folded under you all the time. When's lift-off, d'you think?'

Edward's puckered face looked hurt and serious. 'This is no time for flippancy if you don't mind my saying so, Anthony. It could be the real thing.'

'Shouldn't think so, old boy. It was the real thing up at our place last time and no one bothered telling us about it in advance, did they? Wouldn't have thought they would this time.'

'You never know. It might be a ploy to lure more troops into the area and get us all at one go.'

Anthony looked at the disconsolate and weary soldiers hanging around in the yard and lounging by their vehicles in the streets. 'In which case they reckoned without your precautions. Dispersal in the face of nuclear attack. Is that it, eh?

That's the stuff to give 'em.' Anthony laughed and strolled away to talk to some of the soldiers, his hands behind his back and his moustache bristling cheerfully.

Nigel Beale followed him like a neglected and irritable terrier. His sympathies were clearly with Edward. Since being shut up at breakfast his conversation when in Anthony's presence had been relatively muted, though he made it plain from his tone and attitude that he regarded Anthony as unforgivably flippant. 'You can't be too sure,' he said to Charles. 'Anything's possible in a case like this. We could be standing on a whole bed of gelignite.'

Charles, like most of the others, had been looking forward to a nap that afternoon. 'So why are we hanging around here?'

'Because there's nowhere else to go, is there? We can't just abandon the area to the enemy.'

'Exactly. So we might just as well go back inside and lie down.'

'If it goes off while we're inside, the building might come down on us.'

'So it will if we're outside. It's big enough.'

Nigel buttoned his flak jacket up to the neck. 'Strikes me you have a rather over-casual attitude, Thoroughgood. One has to be alert.'

'You intend to die with your boots on, I suppose?'

'Yes, frankly. Don't you?'

'I've never thought about it.'

'Well, there you are then. Time you did.'

Henry Sandy and his ambulance arrived, summoned unnecessarily. He was pasty-faced and bleary-eyed. 'Bloody well woke me up,' he said. 'Couldn't think where I was and I forgot my pistol. Thank God the CO's not here. I've stuffed my holster with shell dressings. Anthony won't notice. I need my afternoon kips to get me through the evening. Where's Chatsworth? He owes me money.'

'Haven't seen him. Try the ops room. He might be able to lend you a pistol. He seems to have three or four.'

'Sell me, more like. Where is the ops room in this place? I keep forgetting.' He wandered off towards the Factory, one boot undone and his holster bulging with shell dressings.

To everyone's surprise, the sun came out. The pale faces of the soldiers looked even paler in its light. It was a gentle, warm sun and it was oddly moving to see so many very tired, very young men in uniform dozing, leaning and waiting, squatting on the ground with their rifles across their knees and their heads hanging down. Waiting formed a very large part of military life. However, on this occasion the soldiers were not the only ones, as a crowd of about a hundred local people had now gathered and they too sat good-naturedly on the road and pavement, peering in through the Factory gates and even making the odd remark to the soldiers guarding the vehicles in the street. The crowd seemed to know all about the reason for the search and to be quite unworried by any possible consequences. They seemed glad of the spectacle, and the sun improved everyone's humour.

Soon some press arrived but they were not allowed in through the gates. They leaned against the wall, smoked and talked with Charles and Van Horne, who had arrived with Anthony's party although he was supposed to be manning the phone in battalion HQ. After a while Charles noticed that Moira Conn of the *Sunday Truth* was also there, talking earnestly to some of the local people. She looked more attractive than he remembered, with a three-quarter-length dark green skirt and a cream blouse that made the most of her bosom. She had also done something to her hair, which seemed fuller and more wavy. She carried the same large bag and talked and smoked in the same aggressive manner. Van Horne was watching her surreptitiously and, Charles felt, watching him.

Edward flapped around inside the yard like a newly-decapitated chicken but no one took any notice and the whole scene developed an easy-going village fete atmosphere as welcome as it was novel.

After a while there was a stir and commotion by a manhole in one corner of the yard. A group of soldiers that included

Anthony and Nigel was examining something while Edward circled them warily from a distance of ten yards or so. Charles went over and found that a hoard of beer and spirits had been discovered. Anthony was fondling a bottle of Black Bush and commenting on the history of the distillery. The hole had been hollowed out from the side of the manhole but led nowhere. It was in a part of the yard that had been occupied by the Army only in the past year or so after an adjacent house had been gutted by fire. Most likely it had been a hide for one of the many illegal drinking clubs – shebeens – in the area. After the announcement by the search teams that all known tunnels were clean, there was nothing more needed to contribute to the carnival atmosphere of the afternoon, though Edward still worried that there might be other, deeper tunnels packed with explosive. Charles told the press at the gate what had happened. Some suggested that the drink had been the object of the search all along and began to drift away. There were still half a dozen or so left – including Moira Conn, who had given no sign of recognising Charles – when Anthony wandered over. 'Gentlemen – and lady – awfully sorry, Ma'am,' he said. 'Many apologies for bringing you all this way for nothing but a few crates of beer and some liver-warmer. You must get very fed up with this sort of wild goose chase. Feel the least we can do is offer you a share of the spoils. Would you care to join us for a drink?'

This was not an invitation to be refused by members of the press without compromise to professional pride and integrity. There was a general movement in through the gates. Only Moira Conn hung back. Anthony, with exaggerated gallantry, offered her his arm. 'Madam, will you be corrupted?'

Charles waited for the rebuff but instead, with a quick smile of quite unexpected charm, she took Anthony's arm. 'And what makes you think you're the man to do it, Major?'

Anthony grinned, smoothed his moustache and patted her hand. 'Wishful thinking, m'dear, at my age. I can't corrupt anyone any more. No one takes me seriously.'

'I find that hard to believe.'

Anthony's eyes twinkled. 'Ah, but would you dare allow me the chance to prove myself wrong?' Laughing, they walked past Charles into the yard and followed the happy gaggle of press into the Factory. Charles managed to catch Moira Conn's eye for about half a second but there was not the faintest flicker of recognition. It seemed that she simply didn't remember him.

Looking like a bizarre wedding party going into church the little group climbed the stairs leading up to the Army floors of the factory, watched by the envious soldiers in the yard. Van Horne was nowhere to be seen.

Charles was about to follow them into the building when he was summoned back by shouts from the sentry at the gate. There seemed to be some sort of trouble, almost a scuffle, going on outside. When he got there he found that one of the guards had pinioned Beazely against the wall, his forearm across Beazely's throat. 'Caught this one trying to get in. Says he knows you, sir.'

'It's all right. I do know him.'

Beazely was released. He adjusted his spectacles and collar with almost ritualistic movements, as though it were a way of introducing himself. He seemed to expect to be manhandled. 'Great, Charlie. Heard about the search. Great stuff. Got a taxi straight down. Thought you might have rung me, though. Everyone else has been and gone, I understand. Apart from the ones having the social briefing.'

'Well, that's Anthony's doing, not mine.'

'All the same, fruit, you might have told me.' Beazely stepped in through the gates with the air of one who had accepted a pressing invitation and was determined to make up for being late.

'I thought you were going to kill yourself the other night,' Charles remarked as they walked across the yard.

Beazely shook his head. 'Didn't feel up to it, old man. Bit down in the dumps that night, to be perfectly honest. Sought consolation in the bottle. You know how it is. Probably the effects of the explosion at your place. I felt personally involved. Delayed shock, I expect. I'm still frightened, though. Still have my fears. It's different for you buggers in uniform, of course.

It's your job. Anyway, where's all this hooch come from? Enough to drown us all twice over I hear.'

They were climbing the stairs and had nearly reached the ops room, from which came the unmistakable sounds of a party, when Beazely laid his hand on Charles's arm and stopped him. 'I say, old man.'

'What?'

Beazely looked serious, as though about to divulge something very personal. 'Hope you don't mind me tagging along like this.'

Charles was so taken aback that he produced the stock reply without thinking. 'Of course not. Very pleased to have you.'

'Don't want to get in your way, you see. Good of you to put up with me, I know. And you and Van Horne do a good job for me. Don't want you to think I'm not grateful.'

Charles was no better than most of his countrymen at responding to serious and direct conversation. He mumbled a few 'quite all rights' and 'think nothing of its', concluding with an 'all in the day's work'.

'Just thought I'd better say it now, you know, before we –' he nodded towards the ops room.

'Before we what?'

'Go in. I mean – parties and all that – always trouble – just wanted to get things straight.'

That said, Beazely led the way into the party. The ops room was crammed with soldiers and journalists, all talking and drinking as though their lives depended on it. They drank indiscriminately from glasses, cups, mugs, bottles, water-bottles and cans. Cigarette smoke hung like battle smoke just above head level. The radio mush went on in the background, unnoticed. Seated at the radio was Moira Conn, with Anthony and the CSM on either side, apparently instructing her. She had a glass in one hand and held ear-phones to her head with the other. She was laughing at something the CSM was saying. A little to one side stood Van Horne, drinking from his mess-tin and not speaking. Charles turned to offer Beazely a drink but he had disappeared. A few moments later he glimpsed him over the other side of the room, a bottle of whisky in one hand and the inevitable cigarette in the other. He and Edward were talking rapidly at each other. Edward also held a bottle and his fear and anxiety seemed to disappear with the liquid. There was also a glimpse of Chatsworth moving with quiet purpose through the crowd, but then Charles found himself confronted by Henry Sandy who, like everyone else, had a drink in his hand and seemed to have had a fair bit already.

'Who's the bird?' asked Henry. Charles told him. 'She looks ready for anything. Seems to be going great guns with old Anthony, though. Never understand women. Never try though. That's the important thing. Chatsworth claims to have had her already.'

'He's lying. He's never met her before.'

'Correction. He did say as good as, now I think of it. Says he's fixed it for later. Don't know what he's doing now. Keeps buggering off. Why haven't you got a drink?'

'I don't want one. I'd rather have a cup of tea. I don't feel like drinking.'

'I know what you mean. I didn't really but sometimes there's no choice. You can forget the tea. Last I saw of the kettle Sergeant Wheeler was pouring beer into it. There's a plan to get Nigel Beale paralytic. Seems a waste of good drink to me. He'll be no better drunk than sober. May as well bash him on the head with a bottle. It might come to that, of course. Apparently he tried to get Anthony to leave the booze where it was so that we could nab the owner if he ever comes back to get it. Anthony told him to go and feed the horses. Come on, have a drink. It'll do you good. You should relax.'

Charles did not feel the need to relax so much as to sleep. He felt almost sick with tiredness. An overwhelming lassitude spread throughout him as he looked at the others. He eventually allowed Henry to put a cup of something in his hand. That at least would stop people from pestering him to drink. A feeling of impending disaster contributed to his tiredness. He left the ops room and walked along to the partition where he slept.

Though the noise would hardly be any less there he felt that it wouldn't matter so long as he could put up his feet and close his eyes.

To his annoyance, Chatsworth was there. Chatsworth was not sleeping. He stood stripped to the waist before the small cracked shaving mirror which hung on a nail, applying black boot polish to his hands, arms, neck and face. 'Camouflage,' he said curtly.

'What for?'

'Operational.'

'What operation?'

'Need to know.' That phrase, so well used by the CO and Nigel Beale, now had the effect of stilling all curiosity in Charles. He got on to his hands and knees and crawled into his bunk. As he closed his eyes he saw Chatsworth pull out a Gurkha's kukri from his kitbag and begin to blacken the blade. Very soon the noise of the party merged with dreams of kettles, explosions, kukris and Moira Conn. He did not know how long he had been asleep when Chatsworth's eager blackened face broke rudely through his dreams, though it had little more of normality about it than they. Chatsworth was shaking him. 'Where's Van Horne?'

'What?'

'Where is he? Can I trust him? Come on, Thoroughgood, wake up. I need help.' Chatsworth crouched on all fours beside the bunk and had squeezed his head in so that his black nose almost touched Charles's. Beads of sweat had broken through the polish and he was panting slightly. He had on his camouflage jacket. 'What about that journalist mate of yours, Beezey or whatever his name is? Is he any good? Can I trust him? I need two.' Charles was not able to pull his thoughts together. He tried to sit up and struck his head on Chatsworth's bunk. Chatsworth withdrew his own head just in time and carried on talking in an urgent whisper. 'I must have two, one for the vehicle. Go and get them and tell them to meet me by the four-tonner farthest from the gate. We must get back before they all start moving again.'

'What? Who?'

'For Christ's sake, Thoroughgood. One would never have thought you were a serving officer.' Chatsworth sat back on his heels and looked nervously at the sacking over the doorway. Charles had never seen him so excited. 'I've got half of it out and if they see it now we'll never see any of it again.' He stood up. 'Sod it, I'll find them both myself. Hope they're not too pissed. Everyone else is, and you're no better.'

He went and Charles remained on the bunk. It seemed easier to stay where he was and there seemed little point in going anywhere else. He slept again. When he awoke, shivering, he could hear that the party was still going. He crawled out of bed, stood, straightened his clothes, checked that his pistol was still in his pocket, pushed his hair into some sort of shape with his fingers and went back towards the ops room. The noise and the smoke and the smell of drink surged down the corridor like a continuous wave. He was prevented from getting in by a group of figures carrying something out. They had their backs to him and moved with difficulty, all giving each other instructions. He stood back and watched as Henry Sandy and others emerged with an insensible and trouserless Nigel Beale.

'Give us a hand, Charles,' said Henry. 'We're going to bury him.'

No one noticed that Charles did nothing and they made their way towards the stairs. The ops room was now unrecognisable as such. People sat amidst the rubble of bottles and cans on the floor. A group in the corner was endlessly singing 'Bread of Heaven'. In the middle of the room Sergeant Wheeler was trying to do a handstand on a chair, surrounded by advisers and supported by Moira Conn, who held one of his legs by the thigh whilst the other leg waved dangerously about. Van Horne and Beazely were not to be seen. As Charles left the room Sergeant Wheeler and his chair collapsed on to the floor, taking Moira Conn with them. She sprawled, legs apart and with her blouse undone, laughing helplessly. There was a great cheer and then she disappeared beneath a surge of willing helpers.

Charles walked down the corridor to the stairs down which

Nigel Beale had just been carried, or possibly dropped. The air there was clear and refreshing. He paused at the top, hearing someone running up. Presently a small plump soldier came into view, strenuously taking three steps at a time, the hand holding his rifle pumping in time to his steps. There was relief on his serious pale face when he saw Charles. 'Sir – couldn't get through on the ops room phone, sir – Castle Street OP reports one of our lorries being stoned outside the monastery by a lot of kids. Monastery OP rang through with the same report. Don't seem to be no one doing anything about it.' As he recovered his breath he became aware of the party noise and his eyes strayed in that direction.

'Are you sure it's one of our lorries?'

'Yes, sir. One of our four-tonners.'

Charles thought uneasily of Chatsworth's remarks. He could hear people in the corridor and feared that revellers might break out. He told the soldier to go back to the OP and said that he would sort something out. The soldier left and Charles went back into the corridor where he met Anthony and Edward. Edward, very red and very drunk, was holding on to Anthony and seemed to be trying to make some sort of incoherent confession. Anthony, none too steady himself, was holding Edward with one hand and had Moira Conn's shoulder-bag slung over one shoulder. Charles explained to him what had happened.

Anthony's face looked troubled. He leaned forward, propping Edward against the wall. 'What's that, old boy? Lorry-load of stones?' Charles explained again. 'One of ours? Didn't know we had any out.'

'Neither did I.'

'Better investigate.'

'Yes.'

Edward almost fell. They both caught him. 'Company sergeant major says bombs in bog,' he said.

'Just between you and me,' said Anthony, confidentially, 'don't think he's much use, poor fellow. Better leave him here.'

They propped Edward against the wall but he slid slowly to the floor. 'Can't even pee now,' he murmured.

'All right where he is,' said Anthony slowly. 'Not much use but no harm.' He hitched Moira Conn's bag further on to his shoulder and swayed unsteadily for a moment, looking very thoughtful. He put his hand on Charles's arm. 'Lead on, Macduff.'

It looked as though Anthony might be more of a hindrance than a help in dealing with whatever had to be dealt with. 'Why don't you stay here, Anthony? I'll come back and tell you all about it.'

'Duty.'

'But are you sure you're going to be all right when we get outside?'

Anthony gave a little smile. 'Who can tell? Which of us ever knows that? I rely on you if it all goes wrong, Charles. Lead on.'

They had nearly reached the bottom of the stairs when Anthony stopped. 'Berets,' he said. 'Can't go out without berets. Bad for the regiment.' He ignored Charles's protestations about the need for hurry. 'Very few things urgent in this life but dress very important all times. Beret most important of all.' He turned and mounted the stairs with careful deliberation, one at a time. 'Get one for you too. Don't worry. Stay where you are till I get back.' He returned with two berets which, when they were put on, turned out to be so large that they rested on the tops of their ears. Anthony's almost reached the bridge of his nose. 'Wrong ones. Some chaps very large heads. Not like you and me. No matter. Principle that counts.' He again hitched Moira Conn's bag on to his shoulder. 'Lead on.'

They took two men from the guard and went out through the main gate. Anthony had been reluctant to take any at all and would certainly not consider taking more. 'Four must-get-beers like ourselves are a match for any number of villains,' he announced without lowering his voice as they stepped into the street. The night was cool and, not surprisingly, it was raining again. Charles still did not feel properly awake. It was as though he were taking part in a dream sequence in which anything was possible and nothing was questioned.

The lorry was where the soldier had said it was, within sight of the OP outside the main entrance to the monastery. It was slewed across the road, blocking it completely. Its front wheels were up on the pavement and its bumper was flush against the wall of a house. It looked as though it had hit the house and loosened some of the brickwork. The upstairs windows of the house were crowded with shouting people. Behind the lorry the monastery gates hung open at a peculiar angle. The top hinge of one of them had come away and the other was splintered. Further down the street there was the usual crowd of children throwing the usual stones, and one of the lorry's windows was broken because the metal guard had not been pulled up.

'What d'you make of this?' asked Anthony.

'Nothing.'

'Me neither.' They all four stood staring at it for some seconds. 'Could be a bomb, of course.'

'Could be.'

'Better find out.' When the children saw the soldiers they were stimulated to put more effort into their stone-throwing, but they fell back and gave up when one of the soldiers raised a rubber-bullet gun to his shoulder. They then stood in a huddle on a corner and watched, more curious than aggressive. Anthony marched up to the cab and opened the door. A body subsided on top of him, slowly enough for him to try at first to prop it up in the cab and then gradually to bend beneath its weight until he had crumpled in slow-motion to the ground and was sitting in a small puddle with the top half of the body in his lap. Its legs were still propped up against the lorry and Anthony was still wearing his oversize beret. He looked up at Charles. 'I say.'

Charles came closer, having stood back while all this had happened. 'I know that man.'

'Do you know him?'

'He's a journalist called Beazely.'

'Is he, by God? So he is. Seen him before. He looks drunk, poor chap. Blood on his head too. Shows you can't be too careful.' Beazely started to struggle and shout. They got him to his feet and propped him up against the side of the lorry. The blood came from a small cut on his forehead. 'DTs,' said Anthony. 'Seen it before with other chaps. Never with a civvy though. First time with a civvy, would you believe. I say, I've got a very wet arse. Hope I haven't disgraced myself, have I?'

'You sat in a puddle.'

'Did I? When?'

'Just now. That one there.'

'You might have said something, old boy. Little laissez-faire, if you don't mind my saying so. Not very helpful.'

Beazely clung to them both, apparently trying to say

something. He kept repeating one word. 'Sounds like arses,' said Anthony. 'Perhaps he's got a wet one too. Ask him.'

'I think it's glasses. He's probably lost them.' They searched in the cab and found Beazely's spectacles on the floor, with one lens broken. Putting them on had the effect of making him slightly less drunk and, if not coherent, at least again capable of a sort of speech. 'Told him, told him,' he was saying. 'Told him couldn't drive lorry. Couldn't stop it. Lucky house in the way. Otherwise gone on.'

'Told who what?' asked Charles. 'What did he want you to do?'

'Move the stuff. Take it away. All the boxes. Your mate Chatsworth. Said you said I was to help him and Van Horne. Too pissed anyway. Can't drive lorries. Then this stone hit me. Everything went black. Story here somewhere. Someone else'll have to. Charlie write it. Tell me in the morning.'

Charles had no wish for Beazely to go on in this vein. Fortunately, they were stopped by one of the soldiers who had had the initiative to look in the back of the lorry. 'It's stacked with weapons in there,' he said. 'Crates and crates of 'em.'

In the back there were some twenty to thirty crates. One had been prised open and showed four Armalites, black and deadly-looking. Anthony turned to Beazely. 'These all yours, old fellow?'

Beazely shook his head. 'Chatsworth.'

Anthony turned to Charles. 'Isn't there a chap in the regiment –?'

'Yes, Anthony, it's the same one.'

'Thought there was. Where is he now, I wonder?'

Beazely half raised his hand in the direction of the monastery. 'There somewhere. Running. Last saw him.'

With some effort they got Beazely back into the cab and left one of the soldiers to guard the lorry while the other ran back to the Factory to get reinforcements from the standby platoon. Charles had an idea that the standby platoon for the night was Chatsworth's. It took them some time to convince Beazely that he was safe to remain where he was and by the time they set off into the monastery it was clear that events had had a sobering effect upon Anthony. He adjusted his beret as best as he could and left Beazely clutching Moira Conn's bag. 'Delicate situation,' he said to Charles. 'Best just you and me.'

The monastery itself was a high and imposing building, visible in the wet darkness only as a more solid block of dark. Between it and its surrounding wall was a gravel drive, a car park, grass and flower beds. Monks were rarely seen anyway, and on this night there was not even a light in the building. They were inside the gates and making for the main entrance when Charles saw a figure dart in front of a parked car ahead of them. He pulled Anthony's sleeve and whispered, 'There's someone hiding over there.'

'What's that, old boy?' Anthony had not lowered his voice. Charles whispered again and Anthony became suitably conspiratorial. 'One of them, d'you think? Looking for his guns? Better not draw our own on sacred soil, not without provocation. Looks bad afterwards. Anyway, one always feels a bit awkward about this sort of thing, don't you think? I mean guns and all that. End up feeling like some dreadful gangster. Let's try and flush him out.'

They did not have to go far because the figure came running towards them, making for the gate. 'Don't challenge,' whispered Anthony. 'Grab him first and introduce ourselves afterwards.' A few seconds later Anthony flung himself upon the advancing figure with surprising zest, tackling high. Charles, recalling what he'd always understood to be good rugby practice, tackled low. There was a short, confused struggle. The man was on his back but still fighting. There was a lot of grunting from someone. Charles held both the man's feet to his chest but one got free and caught him painfully in the mouth. He grabbed the flailing boot again and held on as tightly as he could. The other was quite inert. After a while he became aware of Anthony's voice saying, 'Let go, Thoroughgood, damn you! Let go!'

Charles let go of Anthony's boot, which was the one that had done the kicking, and found to his relief that the other belonged to the prisoner, who had given up the struggle. Then he noticed that it, too, was an Army boot and that it, too, had above it a pair of Army trousers. Then he recognised Van Horne. They all three got up and dusted themselves down in an embarrassed silence. 'Thought you were one of them,' said Anthony after a while.

'Thought you were one of the monks, sir,' said Van Horne. He was trembling and looked very pale. He seemed entirely bereft of his normal composure.

'What are you doing here?' said Charles. He was aware of sounding annoyed, and was not at all displeased by that. His lip hurt and there was a taste of blood in his mouth.

Van Horne swallowed. 'Helping Lieutenant Chatsworth, sir. Under orders, sir. He found a tunnel leading from one of our tunnels into the monastery and he found arms in the monastery which he said he knew were there all along but he didn't know how to get them. I helped him get them out by bringing them up through the monastery. We were then to bring them back here and say we found them in some tunnel. I was under orders, sir: he told me, I couldn't do anything else.'

'What were you doing when we caught you?' asked Charles.

'I was getting out of it, sir. I was escaping. I was on my way back to tell you. We loaded the arms into the four-tonner but

Beazely panicked or something and didn't wait for us and drove off and crashed it and all the monks swarmed out.'

Van Horne was so uncharacteristically abject that Charles felt embarrassed for him. 'Where's Chatsworth now?' he asked, more gently.

'Captured by monks, sir.' There was a silence. 'I got away but they got him.'

Charles looked from Van Horne to Anthony, and back to Van Horne, but neither seemed about to laugh.

'That's a pretty poor show,' said Anthony.

'I was under orders, sir. I had to do what he told me.'

'Not you. Mr Chatsworth. Does the regiment no good at all, this sort of thing. Monks. Can't recall a precedent.' It was clear that Anthony was deeply moved. He picked up his beret and shook it. 'Well, we'd better see what we can do about rescuing him, hadn't we? Go back to the Factory, Van Horne, and cope with any press interest. Just say that there's a military operation under way and you can't comment until it's over. Charles, come with me. It helps to have two when negotiating.' This was the new, decisive and sober Anthony. Charles followed him, dabbing at his lip with his handkerchief.

If the monks were surprised at seeing two grubby officers with over-size berets, one with a bloody mouth, they did not show it. They were politely uncommunicative and kept the visitors waiting in the hall until the arrival of Father O'Rourke, who was in charge. Father O'Rourke was a wizened, wise-looking little man with bright blue eyes that were never still. The CO had met and clashed with him, and had told him openly that he did not trust him. He now gave the impression of one who, following the capture of Chatsworth, could be surprised by nothing but whose capacity for indignation and outrage was undiminished. He said calmly that he was very angry at the military invasion of his monastery and that he was sure that the consequences of the action would be serious and widespread.

Anthony now showed himself to be politic in a way that should have counted for more in the Army than it ever did. He expressed deep regret at the hot-headed and unauthorised action of an over-enthusiastic young officer, an 'unfortunate young man' in whom he had detected signs of stress only that day, and who would now be the subject of an enquiry. He then added that the only good thing to have come of the episode was that the 'monastery dump' had been found before it could be used by the Provisional IRA to kill people. Father O'Rourke, in denying that the monastery had had any knowledge of the arms, again stressed his sense of outrage and his conviction that the resulting publicity would be very bad for the perpetrators, and not the less so because they admitted to employing mentally unstable officers. Anthony accepted without hesitation that Father O'Rourke knew nothing of what his own monastery harboured in its vaults and speculated that if the monastery vaults were linked, however tenuously, to the Factory tunnels then the arms must almost certainly have come in from the outside. He hoped fervently that the resulting publicity would take account of this and would not implicate the monastery in any way with the storing of arms for the Provisional IRA, though he was, to be honest, more than a little pessimistic as to whether all sections of the community in Northern Ireland would see it like this. He further hoped that the Holy Mother Church would not be embarrassed by the publicity. Father O'Rourke shook his head and said that it was bound to be a bad business for everyone. Anthony said that at least the arms were out of the monastery now, almost as though they had never been in. Father O'Rourke sincerely wished they had not – if he had known about them and had known where to find Anthony he would certainly have told him. Anthony ventured to suggest that they had even been elsewhere. He was sure that it could so easily look as though they had been found in a tunnel beneath the Factory, which would solve everyone's problems, though in order to substantiate this story the 'unfortunate young man's' evidence could be crucial. Father O'Rourke wondered whether the unfortunate young man could be relied upon. Anthony was quite certain that he could. Father O'Rourke wondered whether it would be possible to do something about the monastery's damaged gates. Anthony was quite certain that it would. Father O'Rourke thought it would be best if Anthony spoke to the young man in the privacy of the Factory, and added that he would be glad to be able to cast an eye over the copy of the press statement before it was issued.

And so agreement was reached. Charles was half hoping they would be taken down to retrieve Chatsworth from a cell deep in the earth but he was brought to Father O'Rourke's study by two large and grizzled monks. He looked ragged and dirty and a little smaller than usual. His face and hands were still partially blackened and his trousers were torn. He forced an uncertain grin on seeing Anthony and Charles, which became a dying grimace as Anthony said sharply to him, 'Where's your beret?'

'Back in the Factory,' said Chatsworth.

'I'll speak to you about that later.'

The three of them left the monastery after courteous farewells between Anthony and Father O'Rourke. Charles noticed that Chatsworth was limping slightly. 'Were the monks very rough with you?' he asked.

'Yes, very,' said Chatsworth seriously. 'And they used bad language too. And they pinched my kukri.'

'Before you had a chance to use it or after?'

'Before, unfortunately. Otherwise I might have got away. I shall put in a complaint.'

'You'll do nothing at all,' said Anthony. 'Being captured by monks brings disgrace upon the regiment. You'll do nothing to advertise it.'

'But we got the arms, didn't we?'

'Only through the timely intervention of Thoroughgood and myself. It's lucky for you that we both happened to be present and sober.'

Chatsworth hobbled and skipped a little to keep up. 'What's going to happen to me, then? I was rather hoping for a medal.'

'Quite the contrary. I haven't decided yet, but you may lose your name.'

Chatsworth was silent. To lose one's name and to be referred to by everyone by one's number was a punishment normally given only to Sandhurst cadets and recruits under training. Chatsworth looked worried beneath the polish. Shooting would at least have been honourable.

The party was over when they got back to the Factory. The drink had run out and so the press had departed, though leaving one or two of their number as corpses on the ops room floor. There were a few Army casualties – ghostly survivors, it seemed, of some long-lost battle. Edward wandered about starkly staring, like one who had been too long in the wilderness, and was ignored by everyone. The body of Nigel Beale was said to be on view in the manhole in which the drink had been discovered. Half of Chatsworth's platoon was missing, allegedly with Moira Conn. Beazely, remarkably sober considering his previous state though still not firing on all cylinders, as he put it, clutched her shoulder-bag. 'Probably being rogered by the lot of them,' he said. 'She goes in for that now and again. It was the staff of the Europa last time. Good background stuff to this story but they won't print stuff about other journalists. Have you ever noticed that? Dirt on everyone else but never journalists. S'pose we're all clean-living. Any chance of some black coffee?'

The kettle was found and coffee was made for several. It was drunk from the same various containers as had served for the party. Charles told Beazely what had happened in the monastery. 'This'll make the story of the year,' said Beazely. 'I'll leave out the drink, of course. We can make Chatsworth a national hero if you like.'

'No,' said Charles, 'I'll do this story.'

Beazely waved his hand. 'Don't worry, sport, don't worry. I can handle this one myself. For once in my life I was the man on the spot. Anyway, it's a big story. Needs a professional.'

Charles was tired enough not to be worried by niceties, whch had never really seemed appropriate with Beazely anyway. 'It's our story. We'll handle it. I'll write your report.'

'Now come on, Charlie, that's not how we do business, you and me. Fair's fair, all by agreement, you know –'

'D'you want to live?' Beazely stopped speaking. 'Because if

you do you'll do it my way. It's Chatsworth, you see. He's mad. You've seen that for yourself. Well, he's convinced you betrayed him to the monks. No argument can shift him. You know what he's like. And he's got a knife. All he wants is anonymity, a chance to do good in secret. If you do this story and blow it up all over the place he'll kill you. We can't hold him back for ever. He's an unguided missile. I'll do a story which does you credit and doesn't mention him. How about that?'

Ultimately any appeal to Beazely's sense of self-preservation could be guaranteed to work. He argued but in the end the thought of being stalked for the rest of his life by a vengeful and murderous Chatsworth was more powerful than his pride. He was already convinced of Chatsworth's madness and had been threatened by him once that evening when he had at first refused to drive the lorry. Chatsworth had tapped the kukri in its sheath and remarked that he never drew it without drawing blood.

Charles had to write three accounts of the incident that night. Van Horne had disappeared and, anyway, it would have been unwise to get him to help. One account was for the Brigade Commander, ghost-written on behalf of Anthony, which stated that the arms had been discovered in a tunnel connected with the Factory tunnels and which left vague the actual point where they had been found while implying that it was somewhere under the road. He then did a press statement which elaborated on this by saying that the Army had been moving the arms secretly after dark in order to avoid provoking trouble in the area of the monastery on a Sunday. The ploy had gone wrong when the driver of the lorry had been struck by a stone and had crashed his lorry outside the monastery gates. For Beazely he wrote a more dramatic account, beginning, 'For seven hours I sweated in a rat-infested, booby-trapped IRA tunnel helping soldiers remove crates of deadly Armalites from under the noses of the terrorists. I was part of a specialist "digger" unit . . .'

The story was in time for the late morning editions. Beazely was content, the rest of the press happy, Anthony very pleased. He lit a cigar and drank black coffee. 'Good night's work, old boy. We can pat ourselves on the back, you and I. Spot of shut-eye now, I think. Advise the same for you.'

Charles returned to the sleeping area and stepped carefully over the blissfully unconscious Moore. What he saw next was Chatsworth squatting like a despondent Job amidst the ruins of the bunk. It was utterly smashed. Bits of cardboard and wood lay scattered all over the floor. Kit belonging to both of them was strewn everywhere. Only the sheet of corrugated iron was intact. 'What happened?' asked Charles.

Chatsworth looked up slowly, like a man rudely recalled from contemplation of eternal mysteries. 'Don't you know?'

'No.'

'That bird, the journalist. Moira.'

'Did she do all this?'

'She wasn't alone.'

Charles recalled the rumour of Chatsworth's assignation with her. 'What have you done to her?'

'Me? Nothing. It was what she did with half my platoon. She was supposed to meet me here but I was still with those bloody monks.' He looked again at the devastation surrounding him. They spoke in undertones to avoid waking Moore. 'It took me nearly a week to build. I'll never be able to get the materials for another. I had to pinch them all as it was. And now she's gone off in Henry Sandy's ambulance.'

'Is she badly hurt?'

'She's gone with Henry.'

'Oh.' Charles surveyed the mess. The prospect of sleep was receding rapidly. He knew he would get some somewhere at some time but at that moment he couldn't imagine where or when.

Chatsworth looked at him thoughtfully. 'D'you know something, Thoroughgood?'

'What?'

'You bring me bad luck. You're a blight on my career. You come out on patrol with me and I get shot. You move into the Factory and pinch half my bunk and then you bring into the building the woman who destroys it during an orgy with half my own platoon, instead of with me as she was supposed to do. I go out and through my own initiative I discover just about the biggest arms haul ever found in Belfast and not only do I get no credit for it but it's actually a black mark against me because the two people you recommend to help me panic and cock it up just at the vital moment. All the way along the line it's you, Thoroughgood. Every time I have anything to do with you it goes wrong. The rest of my life is a great success.'

Chatsworth spoke flatly, without bitterness or anger. There was silence for a few seconds. 'I'm only surprised you haven't yet found a way of giving me the pox,' he said morosely.

Charles forced a tired smile that was meant to be suggestive. 'I may yet,' he said and Chatsworth, for the first time in their acquaintance, looked just a little alarmed.

13

The arms find was indeed a big story. It received full local and national coverage. Everyone naturally assumed it to have been the object of the search operation the previous afternoon, which was itself said to have been the climax of a brilliant Army undercover operation. Everyone was pleased, though the Brigade Commander was a little irritated at first that such an event should have taken place entirely without his knowledge. Edward, though in a somewhat confused and indecisive state the next day, soon adopted an authoritative and knowledgeable air tempered by a becoming modesty about his own role in the business. Only Nigel Beale was unhappy, not just because he had come to in a manhole – where, so far as he was concerned, he had been left to die – but also because he suffered total amnesia regarding the events of the previous day and was unable to find anyone who could tell him what his part had been.

The CO, when he returned two days later, was pleased and jealous. Many of the congratulations were directed to him personally and he had been forced to accept them graciously despite his obvious uneasiness at the thought that the battalion could not only survive in his absence but actually flourish. 'Glad to see you haven't all been idle while I was away. Never any excuse for idleness,' he said, and added, 'No excuse for sloppiness now, though. They'll want to get their own back. Must keep on the alert. Hard targets at all times.'

With the CO back and with the worsening situation in Belfast – four soldiers and two policemen killed in three days – Charles spent all his waking hours in battalion HQ, returning to the Factory only for brief and irregular periods of sleep. He and Chatsworth now slept side by side on the floor. As he became more tired he felt more remote from everything he did. He functioned without participating and responded without initiating. He lost all sense of control over his life and did not experience any sense of loss.

Many in the Army complained of having to fight with their hands tied behind their backs, as they saw it. They knew the terrorists and their leaders but were not allowed to kill them, nor to interrogate them properly. If arms or explosives were found they were not allowed to booby-trap the dump. There was a general recognition, though, that internment was not the answer since it was not seen to be just and it created a deep well of sympathy for the internees. Discussions about what should be done were repeated so often that a kind of conversational shorthand developed whereby attitudes and views could be conveyed simply by an introductory remark and no more, the rest being known already. Charles did not join in and his silence was taken for agreement. He sensed that this actually made him more popular, especially with the CO. In fact, he did not himself know whether his passivity was due to not caring or because he didn't know what to think.

The routine was broken when, eight days before the battalion was due to leave and at about five in the afternoon, a foot patrol in the new estate came under fire from a single sniper. No one was hit but Private Williams, a red-haired Welshman who was tail-end-charlie to the patrol, risked his life to pick up a little girl who was standing near them and run with her to cover. There were four high-velocity shots from the direction of a block of flats but it was not possible to tell whether they came from within them or not. Whilst a follow-up search was being organised Private Williams discovered from the little girl where she lived and took her to her house, which was nearby. When he returned her to her mother, the woman spat in his face and said she would rather have seen the girl dead than saved by the Army. With a soldier's sense of justice and chivalry, Private Williams pushed past her into the kitchen and beat up her husband before returning to his patrol. The family later complained and Private Williams had to be withdrawn for investigation and possible charging by the military police or

RUC. When the CO was told he slammed down the ops room telephone so hard that the plastic case shattered and sent splinters flying about the room, leaving the guts of the machine exposed but surprisingly still working. He ordered his Rover Group and shouted at everyone in sight. Once again, Charles and Nigel Beale were the last to clamber into the Land-Rover as it lurched through the gates, treading on each other in their haste. It was not far but it was dark by the time they had reached the flats where the follow-up search for empty cases or weapons had been made, with no result. The CO said nothing until, as they were drawing up, a few token stones were thrown by a group of children on some waste ground. 'What chance do those poor children have?' he said to everyone near. 'Some of their parents are not worth the bullets we ought to be expending on them.'

They got out and stood around. There was still a platoon there that had been about to pull out when the CO arrived. Now everyone hung about, not knowing why they were waiting. There was no purpose in being there. Nothing more was happening, and the gunman was probably out of the area. Private Williams was already back at his company location where the CO would see him and try to get him off, though the legal process had already started. It seemed they were there simply because the CO was so angry with the girl's parents. 'Which is their house?' he asked. He was shown it and made as if to go and knock on the door, but turned back. 'I dare not,' he whispered to Charles, who happened to be closest, 'I simply dare not. I could not answer for my actions. Private Williams was very restrained compared with how I would be if I had to talk to those ungrateful monsters. How anyone could feel like that about their own children I just do not understand. It was the same with that wretched little boy and the pipe bomb. They've got no human feelings at all, these people. They're just brutalised until they're worse than animals and then they set about brutalising everything else around them, starting with their own children.'

They left the house and walked along the road away from the others. They came to an alley which led to the flats. 'I'm sure he was up there,' the CO said, 'and probably still is. He could be in any one of those flats and have a good field of fire and several quick escape-routes. That's where I'd go if I was him.' He led the way into the alley. He just seemed to want to walk and talk and appeared to have forgotten about the others. Charles walked beside him, assuming he would turn back at any moment. It was a long, wide alley, with the high wall of the flats on one side and the backs of houses on the other. Because of the lights from the windows it was not completely dark, and at the end they could see parked cars illuminated by the lights from other houses. It was the time when most of the local people were eating their evening meal and it was very quiet.

441

Charles was trying to read some of the graffiti on the walls, and had just found one neat line which read, 'Is there life before death?' when the CO grabbed him and pushed him against the wall, holding him there. 'Draw your gun,' he whispered urgently. 'There's someone ahead of us.' With some misgivings, thinking it was most likely a dog or some innocent person, Charles eased his Browning from the holster. It was already cocked but with the hammer forward and the safety-catch on. He heard the CO click back the hammer on his own gun and so did the same. He was still convinced it was unnecessary, but he could feel his heart thumping fast all the same. 'Bend double and move over to the far wall,' the CO whispered. 'We'll advance together. Don't get behind me. I think there's more than one of them and they came out of an entrance on the right. We'll follow them to the end. Don't shoot unless I say.'

Charles crouched so that he would not be silhouetted against the lights behind, and crossed to the other wall in three strides. He waited for the CO to move forward and then moved parallel with him, still half crouching. He peered into the darkness ahead and made out two, possibly three shapes bobbing along. They were moving quite fast and he and the CO had almost to run to keep up. For the first time he began to believe that something might really be happening.

As they neared the end of the alley it got lighter. There were definitely three figures, one of them quite small, and they were jogging. Their footsteps could be heard on the cinder. At the end the alley opened on to another bit of waste ground, beyond which were the parked cars. The three figures were quite near the end and were clearly visible at about twenty-five yards ahead when the CO signalled to Charles to stop. The CO was holding his pistol in one hand and was pointing ahead, still crouching. Charles, who favoured instinctive shooting, pressed his shoulder against the wall and held the gun in both hands, slightly low, ready to bring it up. 'Stop!' shouted the CO. 'Stop where you are or we'll shoot!'

The small figure darted to one side. One of the others vanished but the middle one turned, holding something in his hands. For a moment Charles wondered whether he was justified in opening fire but then there was a flash and a very loud bang. At the same time he heard the CO shout, 'Fire, for God's sake!' The Browning thumped five times in Charles's hands in rapid succession and left him with ringing ears, almost concussed by such noise in a confined space. He saw the figure fall and was then aware that the CO was running up the alley ahead of him, shoving the magazine back into his pistol, which had evidently jammed. Charles ran with him, and as they approached the end of the alley the small figure jumped out from the side. He was empty-handed and looked young. Charles stopped and pointed the pistol, shouting, 'Don't move!'

The youngster stopped, staring wide-eyed at Charles, and for half a second they stared at each other, unmoving. Then there was a flash and two more deafening bangs in Charles's left ear. One of the empty cases from the CO's gun hit him a hot, stinging blow on the cheek. The boy crumpled into a heap on the ground. Across the waste ground Charles saw the third figure jump into an already-moving car, which swerved round the corner and was gone.

The CO walked slowly to the boy's body and Charles lowered his pistol. He eased the safety-catch on with his thumb but kept the gun pointing at the other body. The CO bent to look at the boy, who lay on his side, then stood and looked at Charles. His pistol was in one hand, hanging loosely by his side. He stared at Charles with his mouth half open and his eyes suddenly listless. He looked an old man, and vulnerable. Charles stared back and for some seconds they held each other's gaze, without speaking and without strain. The spell was broken by the sound of running soldiers behind them and they both moved into the light so that they could be clearly seen. But by then Charles felt he had entered an unspoken conspiracy.

The man he had shot lay on his back, quite still. He could see neither wound nor blood. He was in his twenties, had curly dark hair and wore jeans and a bomber jacket. His arms were spread out as though in a stage death and his mouth and eyes were open, facing directly upwards. An Armalite rifle lay beside him, its butt resting on his thigh. The boy lay a couple of yards farther on, hunched as though in sleep, with his head resting on one outstretched arm. He was aged about fourteen or fifteen and had dirty fair hair and freckles. His legs were crossed and he was wearing white plimsolls.

Nigel Beale was among the first to arrive and suddenly the CO was himself again. 'Charles got that one,' he said, pointing at the man. 'And just as well too or we wouldn't either of us be here. I got this little bugger as he turned on us with a pistol. Trouble is, the third one got away over there, taking it with him. I would have had him but my pistol jammed and Charles was unsighted.'

It was unforced and matter-of-fact, with all the CO's natural directness of tone and expression. He neither hesitated nor avoided Charles's eye. Charles did not even have to play a role. Normality was made whole again.

Units throughout Belfast were alerted to search for the getaway car but it was not found until the following morning, abandoned in the New Lodge Road. The bodies had to be taken away and identified, relatives informed. Charles and the CO made statements to the police. Charles recounted how he had shot his man and then, without awkwardness and without even the feeling of deceit, said that he had lost sight of the boy after he had darted aside and had only heard the CO shoot. He had not seen the third man run away but had seen him get into the car. It was not possible to say whether he had been carrying a gun. It turned out later that his man had been hit plumb in the heart by a single bullet, probably the first as the other four had all gone very wide. The boy had been hit by both the CO's bullets, one in the top of the thigh and the other fatal one in the groin, where it had ricocheted off his pelvis and lodged in the bottom of his heart. Ironically, if he had been hit by a high-velocity weapon it would have gone clean through him and he would probably have lived.

'One out of five is bloody good shooting with a pistol at that range in that light and under those conditions,' said Nigel Beale. 'Didn't know you had it in you, Charles. Not sure I could've done it, to be absolutely honest with you. I'd've stood more chance if I'd thrown the thing at him.'

Charles felt so detached that only with difficulty could he even interest himself in what was being said. It amused him a little to think that Chatsworth would be speechless with jealousy, but as for anything else, any feeling that it was in any way significant to have killed a man, there was nothing. It was not even exciting, since at the time it had happened too quickly and afterwards it seemed like someone else's history.

Back in the Mess there were drinks and everyone was in high good humour. The CO got slightly drunk and waved his glass around when talking so that it kept spilling. He took

Charles to one side, resting his hand on his shoulder and occasionally punching him in the stomach when he wanted to emphasise something, as was his habit when he was happy. 'That was good work you did this evening. You saved us both and you nailed that sniper. You might feel a bit shaken up at having killed a man but don't let it get on top of you. It had to be done. It was you or him. It's the same with me and that boy. I didn't want to take a young life but he'd have had us both if I hadn't. A boy or even a baby with a gun is as bad as a man. The first time I did it was in Cyprus, and even though he was an older man and a hardened villain I felt sick for days afterwards. But it's not your fault, you must tell yourself. You're there and you've got to cope, that's all. Trying to duck out of the situation would be moral cowardice and you might land someone else in it. Besides, life must go on. You're not facing up to being human if you don't recognise that. So don't let it worry you, eh?'

'No sir.'

'Good man. You'll get over it. But for God's sake do something about your appalling shooting. One out of five at that range is a disgrace. You must go on the range every day when we get back.' He swayed and steadied himself against Charles. 'I forgot, you're leaving us, aren't you? Pity that.' He emptied his glass and stood saying nothing for a few moments. Charles looked in vain for some mute acknowledgment of what had passed between them after the shooting of the boy. The CO seemed a tired man, simple and sincere. 'Perhaps you'll decide to come back. We can't afford to lose young men like you. You'll find you've left something of yourself in this unhappy place and, God knows, these poor wretched people desperately need any influence for the good, any help anyone can give them. I don't need to tell you that.' His dark eyes looked thoughtful but not vulnerable, not particularly personal. 'I think the experience has done you good, too. That's important. I wish you the best of luck in whatever you decide to do. Don't hesitate to get in touch if ever I can help.' He took another pull at his glass, realised it was empty and walked away.

There had been no sign of the lie in anything about him. It had been effortless and natural. Charles had watched carefully for signals but there had been none, no sign of a secret understanding, no flaw in the absolute conviction with which the CO spoke. Either it was a superb act or the conviction was real. If he had been accustomed to doubting himself, Charles might have questioned his own recollection of what had happened.

There was, of course, no danger of Charles feeling sick with remorse, or guilt or anything else. He ceased to feel. Things happened and he took them piecemeal, without any attempt to connect. It was like having some undramatic but possibly dangerous disability or disease that caused no suffering and aroused only limited curiosity in the victim. Even the prospect of returning to Belfast for an inquest was uninteresting. The report of the incident which he and Van Horne wrote for Beazely caused the CO to congratulate him for having handled the press angle so well. 'They got it right this time,' said the CO. 'They struck the right balance. Truthful, not too sensational, straightforward and no thrills. That's good reporting. To the point and accurate.'

The arrangement with Beazely continued to work well. In fact, it was even slicker than before. It was only very near the end of the battalion's tour that it went wrong. Violence was increasing throughout Belfast and shootings and bombings were losing their news value unless there was some special twist. Even Beazely had to leave his hotel sometimes and once or twice Van Horne had to phone through the story to Beazely's paper, posing as Beazely's stringer. Two days before they were due to pull out, when the command structure of the incoming infantry regiment was already in place, there was a big bomb in a city centre post office, not far from Beazely's hotel. There had been no warning and an unknown number of civilians was killed, with many horribly maimed. Charles was with the CO and the Rover Group about half a mile away when it went off and felt the sudden lowering of pressure followed by the heavy solar-plexus thump of a big bomb. 'That was a bloody big 'un,' someone remarked superfluously, simply because someone had to say something. The

CO insisted on driving down to the scene, although it was out of the battalion area. It was a smouldering, gruesome sight, and he walked among the ruins, stepping over the fire hoses, his face taut and pained. A pile of intestines was draped obscenely across a wall. He glanced briefly at Charles and turned away.

As it was late afternoon the story was in plenty of time for the morning papers. Charles wrote it and Van Horne phoned it through, as they could not find Beazely. It was later that evening, in conversation with one of the RUC men, that Charles learned that Beazely was one of the dead. He hurried back into the good end of the office, where he and Tony Watch now sat, and called Van Horne.

'That's it, then,' said Van Horne, when he had been told. 'We've had it. They publish his story on one page and his obituary on the next. Who do they say wrote it – a medium?' There was, uniquely, a trace of emotion in his voice. 'He owes us quite a bit of money still and we can hardly ask for it, can we, without being found out?'

Charles thought. Even now he could not feel very worried. He was convinced it would work out. 'We'll tell them,' he said.

'Tell them what?'

'Everything. I'll tell them.'

'What about me?'

'You'll be all right, don't worry.' He rang the sub-editor, a man called Jack Smiles, of whom Beazely had often complained. Pausing only to make sure that no one could overhear him, Charles told Smiles the whole story. In fact, it was very simple and there was not much to tell. There was a long silence when he had finished.

Eventually Jack Smiles spoke. He sounded like a gravel-voiced TV crook. 'Who else knows about this?'

'No one.'

'Positive?'

'Yes.'

'Right. Make sure they don't, I'll be on the first plane in the morning. I can come to your place, can I? Good. Meantime, I'll make a few alterations to the story and put it out under "Our Special Correspondent" which means anyone, even you, right? And we'll get an interview with the boy's parents and do an obituary. The Beazely story will be as big as the bomb one – service in Vietnam and all that. We've been needing a new slant on Northern Ireland for some weeks now. This'll give it a shot in the arm. See you tomorrow.'

Jack Smiles arrived when he said he would, having taken a taxi from the airport. He was a short, thick-set, businesslike man with a shiny new raincoat. 'Somewhere we can talk quietly? Good. Tragic business, this. Brings it home to you when members of the press start getting killed. Terrible. Tragic. Whole place gives me the creeps already. You see the story and the obituary, did you? Sensational. Went down very well. Surprised none of the other papers got it. They'll all have to re-run it tomorrow, with obituaries. Sounds callous but it's not. We'll all miss him.'

They sat down in the empty Mess at battalion HQ. It was after breakfast and the CO was at the Brigade briefing. 'Beazely hardly ever left his hotel,' said Charles. 'It was very bad luck. Just one of those things, I suppose. He was probably going to get a stamp.'

'Whisky, more like. He must've drunk them dry in the hotel. But tell me straight – you and this corporal have been doing his stuff for the last two months, have you?'

'Yes.'

'All of it?'

'Most of it.'

'No wonder it's been so much better, the idle bastard. And the cut he was giving you was peanuts compared with what we were throwing at him, God rest his soul. When d'you leave the Army?'

'Four days from now.'

'There's a job waiting. We'll send you back here – not for long, just for continuity till we get someone else. Then we'll have you back in London. How's that grab you?'

'No thanks.'

'Why not? Money not good enough? We'll raise it. I can't

believe you've got a better offer, and you've got talent for the work. You got something else in mind, perhaps?'

'No, nothing. I'm not thinking about anything until I've left the Army.'

'I see, one of them. What about this corporal of yours? It was a fifty-fifty effort, wasn't it?'

Van Horne was summoned and asked if he wanted a job. He glanced quickly at Charles, as though to check that everything was on the level, and looked more openly delighted than Charles had ever seen him. ''Course I want a job. But I need money to buy myself out.'

'How much?'

'Two hundred and fifty.'

'Cheque or cash?'

'Better make it cash.'

'Come and see me in London.' They shook hands and Jack Smiles caught the lunchtime plane home. For the rest of the day Van Horne positively and wholesomely grinned.

During the last hectic period of the tour Charles meant to find out about the arrangements for the funeral of whatever was left of Beazely, but he never quite got round to it. He had the uneasy feeling that the manner of Beazely's death, and his employer's reaction to it, was as comic as his life – if either could be called comic. In retrospect, Beazely's existence had never seemed very plausible, and it was not easy to believe that his death was a serious matter. All that remained of him, besides the memory, was just enough money in Charles's sock for him to buy himself out of the Army.

England is indeed a green and pleasant land. Salisbury Plain was particularly warm and beautiful, the air soft and almost inexpressibly gentle. Salisbury Plain, because the CO had decided they would exercise their option as a para-trained unit to parachute back. For some reason not even regular parachute battalions parachuted back from Northern Ireland, and the thing was done amidst a great publicity fanfare. Parachuting was always glamorous, although statistically not very dangerous, certainly not very skilful and in the last resort not even a very effective way of getting to the battle. Despite his dislike for the press the CO had developed a taste for publicity and he ordered all the stops to be pulled out. The arms find and the shooting had placed the battalion firmly in the public eye, and he wanted to keep it there. Possibly he saw it as an aid to promotion.

They took off from Aldergrove, packed side by side into the Hercules transports, each man netted in to stop him being sent sprawling over those near him. This always seemed an unnecessary precaution, as they were packed so tightly that it was very difficult to move in any direction. They sat shoulder to shoulder, each row so close to each other that their helmets sometimes touched during turbulence, and so close to the men opposite that their legs were entwined. Their kit filled the floor space so that the RAF despatchers, who were constantly checking the myriad wires and straps that ran the length of the aircraft, had continually to climb over them, treading on knees, hands and even shoulders. Most men were apprehensive before parachuting and sometimes this showed itself in boisterousness and devil-may-care nonchalance, but this time the soldiers were subdued and thoughtful. They were tired, and relieved to be going, and most wanted simply to get back in one piece.

Each Hercules sat at the end of the runway revving its four engines until the whole plane shook alarmingly and the wings actually flapped. Then it lurched suddenly forward with an acceleration that could be felt in the pit of the stomach. It was very soon airborne, climbing and turning steeply. It was almost impossible to see out, and the roar of the engines soon settled to a steady pitch that precluded all but shouted conversation. Charles yawned, not because he was relaxed but because that was how nervousness affected him. It made him look calm, he knew, but all the time there was a great emptiness in his stomach.

They crossed the Irish Sea in tactical formation and at near sea-level, climbing suddenly when they reached the coast of England. The aircraft was unlit inside, giving it the appearance of a grotesque charnel house, packed with objects and life-like bodies. In the gloom opposite Charles could see Henry Sandy's deathly pallor. Henry hated jumping and sometimes his cheeks seemed to be tinged with green. Their eyes met but Henry showed not even a flicker of recognition.

With three minutes to go they were got to their feet. Each man hooked himself up and checked his neighbour. Their kit was strapped to their legs and the parachute harnesses bit into their shoulders and thighs. They tightened their helmet straps beneath their jaws until it was difficult to open their mouths. The aircraft juddered on to a new course for its final approach, nearly sending them all tumbling over. The despatchers scrambled hastily up and down, squeezing between the bodies or shoving them aside, deftly checking hooks, harnesses and straps. The two rear doors were slid open and the wind shrieked in, competing furiously with the noise of the engines. There were shouted commands and the aircraft bumped and juddered again. The men were pale and concentrated, clinging to their straps to keep their balance. No one had wanted to parachute but everyone wanted to go now, to get out of the doors and be free of the plane. The red light came on and, seconds later, the green. The first few men, helped by shouts and hefty slaps from the despatchers, were suddenly gone. Everyone stumbled along the fuselage with the trained rhythmic stamp, trying to keep balance and place, anxious to go, anxious not to think about it, trying to be like machines.

Just before he went Charles glimpsed Chatsworth and ahead of him, Nigel Beale, in a rare unity of silent concentration. Anthony Hamilton-Smith had already gone, and so had Henry. Suddenly he was himself at the open door with the trailing edge of the wing before him and the wind buffeting his face. Without time for pause or thought he was in the slipstream, whipped along for a second with his boots above his head, a delicious moment of complete helplessness. Next came the sharp curve downwards and the exhilarating sense of uninhibited acceleration until brought up hard by the shock of the main canopy deploying. Then the conditioned look up to check it and the blissful sight of a full canopy blossomed against the blue, then all the drills for kit, distance, speed, and then steering away from everyone else and looking for space. Your friends are your enemies in the air.

All around, the sky was filled with gently falling parachutes. The aircraft were already a great distance off. It was very quiet. There was a warm, playful breeze, not enough to cause problems. The Plain stretched to the horizon in undulating greens, browns and yellows. Below him and off to the right Charles could see the CO, drifting by himself, quite still in his harness, his arms raised to his front lift webs like a toy parachutist. For a few seconds the entire battalion was in the air. Charles could see the press, the television cameras and the ambulance on the edge of the dropping zone. He looked idly down, feeling immensely distant and thinking of nothing at all. He was recalled to himself by the sudden uprush, the green rush, they call it, that comes a second before impact.

ABOUT THE AUTHOR

Alan Judd is the author of eleven novels and two biographies. He previously served as a soldier in the British army and as a diplomat in the Foreign Office. Judd is a Fellow of the Royal Society of Literature and has won numerous awards including the *Guardian* Fiction Prize and the Heinemann Award. He currently writes for the *Spectator* and the *Daily Telegraph*. He has also been a historical advisor for the hit Netflix series, *The Crown*.

Don't miss Alan Judd's brilliantly plotted, pulse-racing
new novel featuring Charles Thoroughgood

ACCIDENTAL AGENT

CHARLES THOROUGHGOOD #6

Brexit looms and Charles Thoroughgood, Chief of MI6, is
forbidden for political reasons from spying on the EU. But
when an EU official volunteers the EU's negotiating bottom
lines to one of his officers, Charles has to report it.

Whitehall is eager for more, but as the case develops,
Charles realises that all may not be quite what it appears.
At the same time, he finds he has a family connection with
a possible terrorist whom MI5 want checked out. In both
cases, Charles is forced to become his own agent, seeking
what he really does not want to find.

Authoritative and packed with in-depth knowledge,
Accidental Agent **is a gripping new spy thriller**
from a master of the genre.

Read on for an exclusive extract . . .

SIMON &
SCHUSTER

The iron gates opened and one of the barriers was raised for Charles's ancient Bristol without his having to slow down more than enough to wave at the guards. They should have stopped and searched the car, of course, but they took pride in recognising the Bristol from a distance and he connived in their rule-breaking. Guarding anything was boring, relieved only by small pleasures. In his operational days he had broken rules and taken chances, albeit calculated, but as chief the opportunities were so limited as to make the occasional flouting, no matter how trivial, refreshing. It made him feel younger, which in turn made him feel it really was time to go.

The building codenamed Hyde Park had begun life as the nineteenth-century Palladian centrepiece of a country estate but successive incarnations as a school, a wartime military hospital, a mental asylum, a secret communications outpost during another war, a country club and a short-lived conversion to a semi-rural business centre had all but obliterated its architectural virtues. It was now converted into modern office suites with a communications centre in the cellars and an invisible array of oddly shaped aerials hidden in the attic. The gracious pillared entrance was cluttered by bulletproof glass and revolving doors. Locals assumed it was part of the nearby BBC monitoring service establishment at Caversham.

The car park, set for security reasons some distance from the house, was unusually full. At the far end were a coach, two army lorries and three police vehicles with people milling around them. But Charles took no notice as he docked the Bristol and hurried up the steps to the lawn that fronted the house. At the security doors he swiped in with his pass and took the lift to the third floor. His office was at the front of the building overlooking the main entrance and the pebbled drive to the distant gates. It was the only private office in the building, the rest being open-plan with meeting areas and glassed smaller offices for temporary use. Normally there would have been only a skeleton staff, plus the odd training course, but for that weekend it was fully manned with virtually every screen live and every desk occupied. Notwithstanding which, the atmosphere was relaxed and chatty. The level of chatter subsided like the trough of a wave as he passed each row of desks, but people smiled and looked up expectantly.

After checking his screen and not finding Gareth's promised summary, he told Jenny, his secretary, that he would be down with Gareth and set off for the first floor, using the stairs this time. There, he found Gareth's desk was occupied not by Gareth but by Sonia, head of assessments.

'Don't worry, I'm not trying to take over operations,' she said. 'Just leaving Gareth a note.'

'Makes a change to see anyone doing anything with pen and paper.'

'Quicker than screens but no one realises it.'

He and Sonia went back a long way. She was about five years younger than him and had started out as a secretary, in the days when secretaries were plentiful. Through working together as she rose through the ranks he had learned to trust her judgement and discretion; later she had been instrumental in securing his reinstatement in the Office after expulsion and arrest. He was responsible for her recent promotion to a senior position. Although publicly respectful of his status, familiarity meant she was not awed and could be trusted to speak her mind, which was one of the reasons he had pressured the reluctant HR director into promoting her.

'You'll probably find him in the control room,' she said. 'He was ringing them every two minutes to check on something.'

'Has he told you anything of his trip?'

'No but I've seen a summary in draft.'

'He hasn't sent it to me yet.'

'He hasn't sent it to anyone but he left it on his screen when he shouldn't have. So of course I closed it for him.' She smiled. 'After reading.'

'Seems very good, from what he told me.'

'So it seems.' She ceased smiling. 'We should talk about it.'

They looked at each other for a moment. Charles nodded.

The control room was on the first floor, off the balcony overlooking the entrance hall. It had about a dozen screens monitoring entrances and vulnerable points of the building, all switching angles every few seconds. The security staff, who were not uniformed, followed them in silence, occasionally intervening to change angle or revert to a previous shot. A telephone rang and was answered in a hushed tone. The silence, Charles suspected, was partly because Gareth Horley was standing just inside the door, his hands in the pockets of his jeans, looking on. He usually wore jeans on his Brussels trips, along with slim brown shoes from Tricker's of Jermyn Street – a fact he had twice mentioned to Charles – a white T-shirt and an expensive brown leather jacket. With his tanned regular features emphasising the blue of his eyes and his dark hair edged with grey, he looked every inch a confident, successful man of middle age travelling for a mixture of business and pleasure, which was the impression intended. He smiled as Charles approached and made way for him.

'Good trip, then?' said Charles.

'Fantastic trip. He told me their bottom line. Agreed at the EU Commission meeting on Thursday. Naturally, they're not going to reveal it to us in the negotiations but they would settle for it if they can't get us to up our public offer to theirs.'

'Sure it's the real thing?'

'Everything else he's said has checked out.'

They spoke in lowered voices. Charles patted Gareth on the shoulder. 'Well done.'

'It's so sensitive, this, more than anything else he's told us. We've got to be very careful with distribution. Number Ten might not want even the negotiating team to know in case by their manner or what they say or don't say they give it away. Remember that Ames and Hansen business.'

Aldrich Ames was a CIA officer who had spied for the Russians. In conducting the damage assessment for MI6, Charles had long sessions with the FBI team doing the same for the Americans. The nature of their questions, their keen interest in some areas and their unaccountable lack of it in others had led him to conclude that they believed they had another spy, but didn't want to admit to it and didn't yet know who or where. The spy turned out to be Hansen, an FBI officer as damaging as Ames. 'Let me see it before you talk to the Foreign Office.'

'I'll finish it off later this afternoon. Just thought I ought to show my face here as I'm in.'

'No sign yet?'

'Any time now, should be.' As Gareth spoke one of the screen-watchers called the supervisor over. She said something to the others, who switched their monitors to one of the rear approaches to the building, a gravelled track that led to high locked gates on the far side of the park bordering a public lane and a wood. Two men were climbing the gates. Charles and Gareth moved farther into the room to get a better view of the screens.

Then came the sound of smashing glass, followed by a shout from the security guard by the cubicles in the entrance hall and then two shots in rapid succession, very loud. Everyone in the control room turned away from the screens to look. The security guard was spreadeagled on the floor and a man wearing a grey suit and carrying a pistol was pressing buttons on the entrance control desk. Another man wearing a raincoat and carrying a sledgehammer ran towards the screened-off office where visitors' passes were issued, raising his hammer. The woman behind the screen tried to get off her chair but slipped beneath the counter onto the floor a second before the man swung his sledgehammer with both hands at the glass door to the side of her office, smashing it. Some control room staff got up from their desks, others sat staring. The supervisor ran to her own desk and pressed the alarm, a harsh jangling that rang throughout the building. Outside, two Land Rovers accelerated abreast of each other from the car park towards the broad steps leading up to the entrance. They slowed as they reached the steps but continued up them, jolting and bouncing, then accelerated again across the terrace and into the entrance. A number of black-clad, hooded men carrying sub-machine guns jumped out of each and ran in through the glass cubicles, which were all now open.

Charles and Gareth flattened themselves against the wall as the control room staff disintegrated in panic. The supervisor shouted into the microphone on her desk, 'There is an incident in the building. Stay where you are! All staff stay where you are!' Before she had finished one of her team, a man, shouted into another microphone, 'Building under attack! Intruders in the building! Evacuate the building! Evacuate now!' Several of the staff ran out of the control room onto the balcony, where they stopped as if suddenly frozen as the intruders split into two groups and ran up the curving stairs on either side. A couple of the control room staff stayed at their desks looking to the supervisor, who was shouting 'They must stay where they are!' at the man with the other microphone, who, oblivious to her, was shouting into it again, 'Do not use the lifts! Lifts not working! Evacuate! Evacuate!' There were more shots.

'We'd better get out of the way, leave them to it,' said Charles. He and Gareth slipped out into the corridor away from the balcony. The first office on the left was unlocked and empty. From the window they could look across to the two Land Rovers parked outside the entrance, their doors open but no one visible.

Gareth locked the door. 'Presumably you're a prime target, if they recognise you.'

'Just as well I'm not in my office.'

'Would they know which it is?'

'Probably not.'

The alarm stopped clanging, though in the silence that followed seemed to go on ringing. There was what sounded like heavy breathing in the microphone. A woman's voice said, 'Intruders . . . intruders . . . intruders on first floor east wing. Staff in east wing must . . . all other staff must evacuate by staircase number one west.' The alarm resumed, then stopped again. A man's voice said, 'Response team due in three minutes repeat three minutes. Remain in your offices and lock your doors. Repeat remain—' His voice became strangulated and the microphone made a noise as if it had been banged against something.